Also by Alyson McLayne

THE SONS OF GREGOR MACLEOD
Highland Promise
Highland Conquest
Highland Betrayal
Highland Captive
Highland Thief

HIGHLAND THIEF

ALYSON McLAYNE

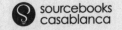
sourcebooks
casablanca

Published by Sourcebooks Casablanca, an imprint of Sourcebooks
P.O. Box 4410, Naperville, Illinois 60567–4410
(630) 961-3900
sourcebooks.com

Printed and bound in Canada.
MBP 10 9 8 7 6 5 4 3 2 1

To my family. I love you all beyond imagining. You fill every day with hugs and laughter...and tickle missiles.

One

MacKinnon Castle, Scotland, 1453

ISOBEL HAD LONG SINCE GIVEN UP TRYING TO FORCE KERR OUT of her dreams.

The one she was having now was a favorite of hers, mostly because it was dark and she couldn't see his face. She knew it was him, of course—his big hands gliding over her skin, his mouth nuzzling the crook of her neck, his leg pressed tightly between her thighs. Without those aggravating eyes teasing her, provoking her, she could wallow in sensation…and pretend that the lover in her dreams didn't, in real life, frustrate the shite out of her.

When a knock sounded on her bedchamber door, she squeezed her arms around his neck, trying to hold him in place—to hold the dream in place.

She wasn't ready to let him go yet…at least, not here.

The knock sounded again, more insistent this time, dragging her up from the depths of sleep, and she slowly opened her eyes and gazed around her dimly lit bedchamber. The fire in the hearth had burned down, and the air had the cool, crisp bite of an early summer morning, making her shiver despite the quilts piled on top of her.

Light seeped through the crack in the shutters, and she turned her face into the pillow with a groan. She'd been up late working on her trap for her brother, Gavin, and she wanted nothing more than to roll over and go back to sleep—preferably returning to her dream.

She may still be an unmarried lass of twenty-three, but she knew where the dream was headed…and she wanted to finish it.

The steward's voice drifted through the heavy wooden door. "Lady MacKinnon, you asked me to notify you as soon as I heard from the lairds. They're on their way back. The message came in just after dawn... My lady?"

She turned her head, eyes opening again, and this time she pushed herself upright. Gathering her hair behind her neck, she then pulled the swathe over her shoulder so the tangled strands hung down the front of her linen shift to her waist.

"I'm coming, Master Carmichael. Hold on." She said the last with a yawn as she stretched toward the silk canopy over her bed.

The cool air hit her bare skin, and she quickly wrapped the loose plaid from the bottom of her bed around her shoulders before padding across the wool rug to the door.

She opened it wide enough to stick her head through. The stooped, elderly steward, who'd been with her family for as long as she could remember, peered back at her, his sparse white hair standing up in tufts around his head, his expression, as always, disapproving. She fought the urge to push the door wide, toss her plaid to the ground, and run down the hallway in her shift, singing a ribald song she'd heard the warriors sing.

Or better yet, run naked.

The man had never quite approved of her, even as a wee lass, and the last few years, the tension had increased between the two of them as Isobel had taken on more responsibility at the castle while Gavin had searched for his son.

The problem was, she never did what Master Carmichael thought a woman should do.

Not that Isobel cared; she was just ornery enough to enjoy the steward's disapproval. If she thought it would do some good, and if Master Carmichael weren't so old, she would set one of her traps for him.

The man wore propriety like a shield, and Isobel was a cannon-ball of inappropriateness flung straight at his head.

He wanted her married to another laird of her brother's choosing and kept occupied with children and the needs of her family. Which was a noble calling, and something her new sister-in-law, Deirdre, did perfectly.

But Isobel was not married, did not have children, and enjoyed devising elaborate plots and traps to put deserving people in their place. She was judge and jury for bad behavior, and when it wasn't a crime that warranted her brother's intervention, or when the offender was her brother, beloved or not, she took it upon herself to call the person out.

Publicly.

Nobody wanted to get on her bad side—except maybe Kerr MacAlister. Aye, that particular laird liked figuring out her schemes and unraveling her traps before they were sprung. She'd long since given up trying to teach him a lesson—and if anyone deserved a comeuppance, it was him.

She stretched out her hand to the steward, palm up.

The man stilled, and the tiny muscles around his eyes tightened. "My lady?" he asked, as if confused about what she wanted when she knew he was not.

She barely repressed a sigh. "The message, Master Carmichael."

"'Tis waiting for the laird in the laird's solar."

"But 'tis not for the laird. It's for me *from* the laird."

"Aye, my lady." He nodded as he said it, as if in agreement with her, but he did not move toward the solar to retrieve the message. "It didnae have your name on it."

This time she did sigh. And rolled her eyes. "Doona worry, Master Carmichael. I shall use *my* key to get into the laird's solar. I need to look through the rest of my brother's papers, anyway. Pray to God I doona mix up any of your neat, important piles."

As his face began to flush and his mouth pinch, she closed the door and snickered quietly. That would teach him.

I truly am a wicked woman to enjoy riling an old man.

She turned back to her room and crossed to the window, so she could open the shutters and let in more light before retracing her steps and adding several logs to the smoldering fire. It began to flame, and she sighed as the blessed heat wafted over her.

The water on her washstand would be freezing, but she couldn't wait for the maids to bring up hot water from the kitchen. She had too much to do. Gavin and his foster family, including Kerr, would arrive sometime today, and she still had to prepare for their stay. More importantly, she hadn't finished the trap she'd planned for her brother.

He'd treated his wife, Deirdre, with little respect when he first met her last spring, dragging her about like an ox rather than a person with rights of her own, and he deserved—nay, he need-ed—to be censured for it, despite his and Deirdre's happy outcome.

Of course, Isobel didn't intend to hurt Gavin—not much, anyway.

Kerr, on the other hand, she'd be quite happy to drag through a prickle bush or two. *Bloody contrary man.*

He liked it when she tried to best him—which completely missed the point.

The only power she held in their relationship was that Kerr wanted to marry her—not that he'd actually asked her yet—and Isobel, thanks to a dying wish from her mother, planned to say no.

Her choice of husband was entirely up to her.

Feeling rejuvenated by that thought, she tossed her plaid and shift on the bed and moved toward her washstand. She made quick work of her morning ablutions, then dressed in a sturdy ari-said that suited her morning tasks.

After brushing out her hair, she pushed the bright swathe behind her shoulders, grabbed her plans and her key to the laird's solar, and headed out the door into a wide passageway lit by candles.

At the end of the hall, she easily unlocked the door to her

brother's solar. Part of her had expected Master Carmichael to have jammed the lock, and a soft spurt of laughter burst from her lips.

She retrieved a candle from the sconce in the wall and stepped inside.

After crossing to the shutters, she opened them to let in the morning light, and then lit the pre-laid fire in the hearth, careful not to smear any ash on her clothes.

The nearby desk was filled with neat piles of organized parchments, as she'd expected, and the quills lay in a straight line. Even the excess sand had been swept away.

She strode toward it and laid down the diagram of her latest trap, pushing back the piles to make room.

Sinking into her brother's chair, she took a moment to go over her plan again with fresh eyes. The problem with trying to catch her brother or one of his foster brothers off guard was that they'd been trained to spot any anomaly—whether it was people who were out of place or changes in their environment.

Luckily, her brother had been distracted with his bride and newly found son, Ewan, and Isobel felt she had a good chance of tricking him this time. But something about the plan was bothering her…something she'd missed.

The sound of lightly running feet caught her attention, and Isobel looked up in time to see her sister-in-law, also twenty-three, hurry through the door. Hope and excitement shone from her beautiful face, but when she saw Isobel at the desk, the light faded.

"Oh," Deirdre said, her disappointment palpable. "I thought maybe you were Gavin. Not that I'm unhappy to see you, of course."

Isobel laughed. "Aye, you are. But 'tis understandable. You're as daft as a duck in love with my brother."

Deirdre plopped down on the chair in front of the desk, facing Isobel, her hands resting on her belly. "I am not daft. Well, maybe a little." She sighed. "I thought they'd be back by now. It's been seven weeks."

"They will be. Soon. I received word earlier." She found the message on top of one of Master Carmichael's piles and held it out to Deirdre. "Here."

Deirdre leaned forward eagerly and pulled the letter from her hand.

Isobel turned her gaze back to her plan and walked her fingers across the paper to guess the number of paces between the edge of the glade and the pit of manure she'd filled up a few days ago.

That's when it struck her. Even if she could distract Gavin long enough so he didn't notice the pit before he stepped into it, how could she stop him from smelling it?

"How'd you get in here?"

The question distracted Isobel, and she looked up to find her sister-in-law's gaze upon her.

Deirdre continued, "I asked Master Carmichael to let me in a few weeks ago, but he was most reluctant. He didn't actually say no, but he also never let me in. And he gave me such a look that I ne'er asked again."

Isobel grinned and held up her key. "He canna keep me out— no matter how hard he tries."

Deirdre's eyes widened. "Did Gavin give you that?"

"Nay." She slipped the key back within the folds of her arisaid. "I took his and had a copy made. How else could I know what was going on in the clan and with his foster brothers? He doesn't tell me everything."

Deirdre's mouth opened in surprise. "So you break in?"

"Nay, that's what I would do if I didn't have a key. I simply unlock the door and step inside. Until he changes the locks, there's naught he can do about it—and he knows it."

Deirdre shook her head. "I'll be sure to tell him you said that as soon as he's back."

"Tell Master Carmichael, too, and watch his face turn purple. 'Tis most amusing."

"Oh, Isobel. That's terrible," Deirdre laughed, shaking her head at the same time. "'Tis a wonder he's still alive." Her amusement made her gray eyes dance.

When she dropped her palm back to her stomach and rubbed softly, Isobel's brow creased. That was the second time her sister-in-law had rubbed or patted her belly. She scrutinized Deirdre's face. She was as lovely as ever with her lush features and long, dark hair—almost as dark as Kerr's hair, which wasn't surprising as they shared a great-grandmother—but her eyes were shadowed and her fair skin peaked.

"Are you feeling well?" she asked.

"Aye. A little tired, 'tis all."

"And the sickness has subsided?"

"For the most part."

The plaid Deirdre had pleated around her middle hid her pregnancy well—not that there was much to see. Based on her last menses, the healer guessed the wee bairn inside her was barely three months old.

When she'd first found out, Deirdre hadn't told anyone, as Gavin had already left with their allies to finish the fight with the MacIntyres and the MacColls, and she'd wanted her husband to be the first to know. Followed by Ewan, of course, Gavin's son from his first marriage, whom Deirdre had raised as her own son after Ewan had been abducted.

But Isobel had figured it out.

It frightened her to think of losing Deirdre to childbirth like so many women before her. If that were to happen, she feared for her brother.

To lose her now would shatter him—would shatter them all. Deirdre hadn't just rescued Ewan after he'd disappeared three years ago, she hadn't just brought Gavin back to them from the dark place that had consumed him, she'd saved all the MacKinnons, Gavin's foster brothers, and Gregor MacLeod as well. When the MacIntyres and MacColls had first attacked, it was Deirdre who'd crumbled the half-built cathedral down on top of them—killing them all.

Except one man, of course—the dark-haired mastermind behind all the attacks on the foster brothers and Gregor MacLeod in the last few years.

Verily, Deirdre was an angel sent to save them, and Gavin loved her beyond reason. So did Isobel.

Not that Deirdre needed to know that.

"Enjoy the fresh air and sunlight while you can," she said, her lips tilting into a wicked grin. "My brother will take one look at you—your breasts even bigger than before, although God knows how that's possible—and you will be on your back staring at the ceiling for days."

Deirdre sniffed—a dismissive, disdainful sound. "Shows how little you know, Sister. 'Tis not always the ceiling I'll be facing. Gavin and I are more imaginative than that."

Isobel burst into laughter. Aye, her beloved friend had a wee bit of the devil inside her too. "Well, take advantage while you still can. Before long, you willna be able to move. You married into a family of giants, not to mention you have Kerr's blood running through your veins. He's part monster. That wee lad you're carrying will be half your size by the time he comes out."

"Nay, I'm going to have a wee lass, as sweet and patient and kind-spoken as you."

Isobel put on a beatific smile. "I am sweet, aren't I? And I do say the nicest things." Never mind that she had a plan laid out before her to lure her brother into a pit of manure.

Deirdre snorted, but then she sighed and placed her hands over her belly again. "You're fortunate to be so tall, Isobel. Your body will easily accommodate a growing bairn. 'Tis how it was with my sisters. I'm afraid I will look like Farmer Busby's prize sow before long."

"You should be so lucky. Ophelia is a dear. I love that pig."

Deirdre's gaze turned speculative as she looked at her. "Your body will change too, when you have bairns. And not only your belly. You may not mind growing rounder at all."

A familiar pang of envy squeezed Isobel's chest—her very flat chest. "I doona think I'll e'er be pregnant. I willna marry Kerr, and he runs off any other man who might be interested in me. I'll have to make do with being an indulgent aunt to Ewan and the rest of yours and Gavin's horde."

Deirdre frowned. "I'll speak to Gavin about that when he returns. And to Kerr as well. It was my intention to do so before, but with Gavin being injured, I forgot. I canna believe Kerr means to cause you distress. You've had an understanding of sorts between the two of you for a long time. 'Tis possible he thinks it's only a matter of time before you marry. If your heart is truly set against him, Gavin must make it clear that he isna to interfere— even if it means he's no longer welcome here for a while."

Isobel dropped her eyes, her lips clamped together to hold in the protest that had risen in her breast. It filled her throat until she couldn't breathe around it.

Gah, I'm an addlepated woman! Kerr MacAlister is not the man for me.

"Doona worry yourself," she said, trying to lighten her voice. "If your cousin e'er works up the courage to ask me, I'll make it verra clear to him that I havenae any intention of marrying him. But for now, there is none other who has caught my eye, and it saves me having to turn down suitors who only want me for this." She circled her finger around her face. "They think they're getting the Beauty of the Highlands, when in actual fact they're getting…" She had to think about how to describe herself. Her real self.

Deirdre raised a brow. "The Devil of the Highlands?"

A puff of laughter blew out. "Aye, maybe. I was going to say the Best Plotter or Trap-Setter of the Highlands, but Devil sounds better."

"Is that what you do? Set traps for people who deserve it? I haven't been here long, but that's what I've heard the castle-folk say."

"I suppose so, but it's not always an elaborate trap. As long as I let them know in some way that their behavior has been noted and found wanting."

Deirdre looked doubtful. "So…a public shaming of sorts?"

"Perhaps." She leaned toward Deirdre. "Doona you see? It balances the scales. Restores power to the person who has been maltreated and maintains the equilibrium of the clan. If 'tis a serious crime like theft or murder, I leave that to Gavin. But in this case," she indicated the parchment spread over the desk in front of her, "the offender *was* Gavin. He treated you terribly and has to pay for it."

Deirdre's eyes grew round as she looked—upside down—at the plan Isobel had devised.

"But…I've forgiven him. What if he gets hurt?"

"The only thing that will be hurt is his dignity. And maybe his shoes. And believe me, he'll feel better afterward. And you will too. I am declaring, on behalf of the clan, that I saw what he did to you and I've condemned it. You'll both thank me for it later."

Deirdre shook her head. "Isobel MacKinnon, you've lost your mind."

"Nay, I havenae. It facilitates healing within the clan. You'll see."

She narrowed her eyes. "Gavin reuniting me with Ewan and marrying me facilitates healing. Every time he tells me he loves me facilitates healing." She rose and turned the parchment around so she could look at it more closely, then stabbed her finger on the pit. "Manure does not facilitate healing!"

Isobel shrugged. "I think it does. Besides, I've already declared that Gavin is on my list. The clan is waiting."

"Let them wait!"

"Nay."

She could almost see Deirdre's brilliant, mathematical mind analyzing and discarding the different options. "Well, then...I'm going to tell him."

Isobel had to bite her lip to hide her amusement. "Nay, you won't. You're an angel, and I've asked you not to."

"You did not."

"Deirdre, please doona tell Gavin about my plans—in any way. Even if he tries to trick you."

"If he's tricking me, I willna know that he's tricking me, will I?"

"Aye, you will. You're a smart woman."

She glared at Isobel. "Well, what about Kerr?"

"What about him?"

"Have you set up a trap for him?"

"Nay."

"Why not? If anyone deserves your ire, it's him. He deliberately provokes you."

Isobel's lips tightened, and she turned the parchment back to face her. "I've tried. Numerous times. He always sees through it. 'Tis verra annoying—much like him. Kerr MacAlister enjoys being on my bad side."

"When was the last time you tried?"

"Over a year ago."

"Over a year ago!"

Isobel looked up at the stone ceiling and around the room. "Is there an echo in here?"

Deirdre huffed and turned the parchment back toward her. She leaned on the desk, eyes intent on the plan. "You obviously haven't tried hard enough. It seems to me you should punish Kerr before you punish Gavin. How will the clan feel if you let Kerr get away with being annoying? You must redress things, Isobel."

"Now who's lost their mind? The clan doesn't care about Kerr.

That was for me. Kerr's punishment now is in me *not* punishing him."

Deirdre scoffed. "You just need a good enough distraction. How are you planning to distract Gavin?"

"I'm not. The man's been walking around with his head in the clouds since he met you. He'll not notice anything amiss until it's too late." Deirdre blushed prettily and smiled. Isobel rolled her eyes. "For the love of God, that's not a good thing."

Her sister-in-law grumbled and then sat back down in her chair. "All you need to do is make Kerr think you're planning to pull the wool over Gavin's eyes, when the trap is actually for him."

Isobel stilled and her heart began to race. A budding excitement heated her skin. "I could ask for his help."

"Is that something you would normally do?"

"Nay."

"Then *doona* do that this time either. Doona do anything out of the ordinary, or he'll suspect you're up to something."

"But how will I get him out there?"

"Out where?"

"To the forest where I've set the trap."

"He'll look for you. He always does."

Isobel sat back in her chair, tapping her fingers on the desk as her mind sorted through the possibilities. *It might work!* She could distract Kerr with a second trap. Maybe a bag of prickles in the tree or a bucket of honey. Meanwhile, she would draw him toward the pit.

She whooped excitedly. "Deirdre, you're a genius!" She picked up a quill and began jotting down the ideas that tumbled through her head.

"Does that mean Gavin's off the hook?" Deirdre asked.

"For now. I canna believe I ne'er thought of this before. Kerr will be looking up at the tree instead of down toward the pit. It's sure to work!"

She jumped up and was organizing her various parchments when a high-pitched screech filled the air.

"Mama!" Ewan yelled as he ran into the solar. He stopped and eyed Deirdre almost accusingly. "I was looking for you. You weren't in your bedchamber."

Deirdre opened her arms, and the lad crawled onto her lap. He was an exact replica of Gavin, with his blond hair and blue-green eyes.

And Isobel's eyes too. Aye, the MacKinnon line still had the bearing and coloring of their Norse ancestors. Maybe Deirdre would change all that with their next bairn.

"She was conspiring with me in here, Ewan," Isobel said, stepping around the desk to scoop up her nephew. "We were planning to bring down a monster. Can you imagine? Your mother, a monster-slayer!"

His eyes widened, looking like two brightly colored fairy ponds. "A monster! Can I come? I'll need my bow and Horsey." He referred to his pony, of course, and squirmed down. "Doona leave yet. I'll be right back."

Isobel laughed as he ran from the room as quickly as he came in. "Well, that's your day planned," she said to Deirdre.

"Aye, thank you for that."

"You can send him with me if you like—to my open pit of horse manure. I'm sure he'll be much help. Although I canna guarantee he willna fall in."

"Sounds like a wonderful adventure," Deirdre said dryly. "Maybe next time."

Isobel gave her friend a quick hug before gathering up her papers and then hurrying from the room. She crossed to the circular stairwell on the other side of the passageway and headed down. Near the bottom, the stairs opened up to the great hall where servers and kitchen staff hurriedly cleared dirty trenchers and platters of food from long tables in the middle of the room. Soon they would be neatly stacked, along with the benches, against the wall in the opposite corner—until the next meal.

A second stairwell was located at the opposite end of the cavernous room. In between, a fire burned in a grand hearth that heated the hall and the rest of the castle.

Candles burned along the walls and in two large, circular chandeliers that hung from the ceiling on chains. Light also streamed in from outside through a ring of murder holes high up along the exterior wall. The small windows were accessed by an interior balcony used by archers to defend the castle in times of need.

"Master Carmichael!" she called as she stepped off the last stair and hurried toward a breakfast table set up for the laird's family in front of a smaller hearth. A flowered wall-hanging hung above the mantel and several chairs with embroidered seats and foot stools had been pushed back against the wall to make room for the table.

Fresh rushes crunched underfoot as she weaved her way around the busy castle-folk. At the table, she spooned oats into a bowl and poured milk over top, not even sitting down to eat. She had too much to do to ready her trap in time for Kerr's arrival— and to prepare for the men coming.

"My lady," Master Carmichael said from behind her, and she jumped.

How did he always manage to sneak up on her? "Is everything ready for my brother and the other lairds?"

"Aye. We've been preparing for days."

Isobel was a head taller than him, and still he managed to look down his nose at her—or at least give the impression of it. He must have practiced that look just for her. She couldn't imagine he would ever use it on her brother.

Judgmental ablach.

What was he upset about now? That she hadn't waited for the others to eat? Or that she was eating while standing, scooping the oats into her mouth? Something she'd seen the men do hundreds of times.

Well, she'd give him something else to be upset about.

"If there's naught else to do, then please tell the stable hands I need more manure."

Master Carmichael turned an astonishing shade of purple.

Two

Laird Kerr MacAlister squeezed his stallion's reins and bit his tongue to stop himself from yelling at the men on horses and on foot around him to pick up the pace. *A pack of bloody turtles!*

'Twas a possibility he might grind his teeth to nothing by the time he and his foster family arrived at Gavin's castle later on this afternoon. War was a long and bloody business, and he'd been chafing to return to Isobel ever since the battles at Clan MacIntyre and Clan MacColl had ended.

Fortunately, they'd overcome Castle MacIntyre without too much trouble because so many MacIntyre warriors had been killed during the botched attack against Gavin's clan earlier in the year. And when Kerr and his allies—six strong lairds and fifteen hundred men—arrived at the MacColl castle, the clan pleaded mercy before the first arrow had loosed. The only death had been the execution of Laird Boyd MacColl—Deirdre's brother—and not because he was their enemy, but because he was the worst kind of degenerate who preyed on defenseless girls.

He'd been hanged by his brother-in-law, who was now laird, before they'd even arrived. His clan did not mourn his passing.

Kerr's only consolation was that Gavin was anxious to get back to Deirdre, and *he* didn't hide his frustration one bit. Nay, his foster brother had groused about their slow progress almost the entire time, which, of course, had made his other foster brothers, Darach, Lachlan, and Callum—all lairds of their own clans—go even slower. Or maybe it only seemed that way because Kerr itched to race back to Isobel's side.

Winter would be upon them soon, and unless something changed, he would be back with Clan MacAlister in his castle while Isobel stayed at hers. It would be five months before he would see her again. Five months of her possibly meeting someone else and maybe even falling in love.

It was a risk he took every time he left her alone, but he knew Isobel wasn't ready for him yet—or maybe *he* wasn't ready for her.

A year and a half ago he would have laughed at that idea, but after seeing the way his brothers had had to grow and change to be the men their wives deserved, he'd begun to doubt himself.

What could he offer Isobel MacKinnon—the Beauty of the Highlands, the bright star at the center of her clan, the most captivating woman he'd ever known—that she didn't have already?

Surely she could find a better man than him—a better family to marry into. His father had been a monster. His uncles had been monsters. And their blood pumped through his veins.

Abuse of all kinds had been an everyday occurrence within Kerr's clan. His own mother had been denied happiness, liberty, and eventually her life by her husband.

She'd been murdered as payback for Kerr daring to thrive in his foster father's home. No one had stopped Madadh MacAlister from gutting his wife, or even condemned him for it. No one had been strong enough or brave enough.

Except a son who'd come home to find his mother dead on the floor of the great hall and left for the dogs to chew.

He'd been barely seventeen when he killed his father, and several of his uncles and cousins too—a feat everyone had thought impossible.

Kerr had been the one expected to die that day.

Then had come the job of digging out the rest of the rot in his clan.

Maybe it would be best if Isobel did fall for someone else.

He reined in his black beast of a stallion, Diabhla, and stopped abruptly beside a grove of Scots pine. The early morning sun cast long shadows on the ground as men continued to march by.

Nay, losing Isobel wasn't an option. He knew, as surely as his foster brothers had known with their wives, that she was meant to be his. But what kind of a family would he be asking her to join?

He rubbed his hand over his jaw, digging his fingers into his skin.

"Are you well, lad?" a voice asked beside him.

He looked up to see Gregor MacLeod sitting astride his horse, staring at him with concern. Lines etched his cheeks and around his eyes, and slashes of gray marked his ginger-colored hair and beard. Even so, he still looked as strong as an ox and as clear-eyed as any of Kerr's foster brothers.

This was his real father. A man who had taken him into his home and under his wing at ten years old, even though Kerr's devil of a sire had tried to murder him and everyone he held dear.

Gregor had trained Kerr to kill his father before the lad had even known a woman. Not to end a rival, but because he knew Madadh MacAlister would one day turn on his son.

And he had.

"Aye. I'm as well as can be expected, having to travel with a bunch of nattering old fools," Kerr said.

"Usually you're right there in the thick of it, nattering back at us—the loudest one of all. Doona think you can pull the wool over my eyes."

Kerr shrugged and then rubbed his hand over his jaw again. He scratched down hard in his frustration, and Gregor frowned.

Shite. Nothing got past the old badger.

"You wouldnae be thinking about Isobel, would you?" Gregor asked.

He sighed. "Maybe."

"And are you thinking about how you should have married her by now? That winter will be upon us soon and you've let one more year slip by?"

He clenched his jaw and stared hard at the top of Diabhla's head. Was it wrong to want to punch his beloved foster father in the face? "'Tis possible I may be thinking that, aye."

"Well, doona. She's not ready. And neither are you."

He jerked his head up to meet Gregor's gaze. "What do you mean by that?" he asked. Never mind he'd been thinking it himself.

"The two of you like your wee dance. The back and forth, the annoyances and retaliations. The verbal sparring. You're both still trying to win. Marriage isna about that—although that interaction with your spouse can be rousing. Kellie and I argued regularly, and we often ended up in our bedchamber afterward."

Gregor grinned at Kerr, but it was tinged with an underlying sadness that was always there when he talked about his wife.

Kellie MacLeod. The woman who had inspired Gregor to be a better man and bring peace to the Highlands—and who had died in childbirth before she could see all the good her husband had done.

Gregor had never stopped loving her.

"What are you two reprobates gossiping about?" Laird Darach MacKenzie asked as he steered his horse to the side and joined them. His men marched on behind him. He'd been the first to fall for his wife, Caitlin, and they were expecting their first child soon. Kerr couldn't wait to see Darach besieged by daughters—all as lovely and prone to trouble as Caitlin. She had turned Darach's ordered world upside down last year, and now he wouldn't have it any other way.

Kerr sighed and rolled his eyes. "Nothing!" he said.

"Isobel!" Gregor said at the same time.

"What about Isobel?" Darach asked. "Are you finally going to quit dancing around and decide to marry her?"

"I havenae been dancing," Kerr protested. "But when I do dance, you'll know it. I'm dazzling."

Laird Lachlan MacKay, possibly Kerr's most annoying foster

brother, appeared from behind a tree on his brute of a stallion. "Aye, you do dazzle when you dance. Watching you is like staring into the noonday sun on the hottest summer day. It burns your eyes, and you have to look away. But still you canna get the blinding image out of your mind."

"What are you doing, lurking back there like a giant rat?" Kerr asked, as Darach and Gregor chuckled. Lachlan had fallen for his wife, Amber, next, and watching him spin in circles trying to pin her down had been payback for all the pranks he'd pulled on his foster brothers over the years.

"I'm surprising you. See?" He pointed to Kerr's face. "You're surprised!"

"'Tis not surprise on my face you're looking at. 'Tis irritation, and a wish to be anywhere but here with you scoundrels." He glowered at them, as darkly and menacingly as he could.

"He's mooning over Isobel," Darach told Lachlan.

"Nay. I'm contemplating murder and how to get away with it. Three murders to be exact."

"Make that five," Gregor said and pointed to Callum and Gavin, the last two foster brothers, who were weaving toward them through the marching men.

Kerr groaned. He'd never hear the end of it now. But maybe he could rile up Gavin and set him on the others to break up this impromptu meeting—with him at the center. "Gavin!" he yelled. "Your new bride is waiting at home, wondering where you are, while these lazy sons-of-donkeys are sitting by, idly chatting. They're a bunch of uncaring bastards."

Gavin looked at him before scrutinizing the faces of Gregor and the other men. "You better have a damned good reason for stopping. Is this about Kerr and Isobel? He wouldnae be trying to throw you to the wolves, otherwise."

"I was doing no such thing!" Kerr protested, his voice rising in false innocence. They didn't believe him. They never did.

"Aye, you were. You're as subtle as a rampaging boar," Callum said as he and Gavin reined in beside the others. Callum was their mother hen—if a mother hen could kill you in the blink of an eye and know what the enemy was thinking before they did. His wife, Maggie—a warrior woman who was the best shot in the Highlands—was with bairn too, and she'd taken to climbing out of windows, no matter how high, to get away from his coddling.

The five of them faced Kerr in a semicircle, like members of the Inquisition. "Is this where I confess to being a witch and you all drag me to a wood pile and burn me at the stake?" he asked.

"Doona jest about that," Lachlan said with a shudder. "I still have nightmares about that happening to Amber."

Amber was a healer and had encouraged the rumors that she was a witch in order to stay safe from her previous laird, whom Lachlan had killed.

Kerr grimaced. "Sorry, Brother. I forgot about Amber's deception. I should ne'er have made light of such cruelty."

"We're not interrogating you, Son," Gregor said. "We only want what's best for you. And Isobel."

"Isobel will decide what's best for her—who's best for her," Gavin said. "My mother made sure of that before she died. But even if she hadn't insisted that Isobel be allowed to choose her own husband, I wouldnae have it any other way. Nor would you," he said, pointing at Kerr.

Kerr shrugged and tried to look unperturbed, even though he growled inside. His brothers forgot that on most days, he only pretended to be a civilized man. He was more a dark, wild Celt at heart than a Scot.

Aye, he supported Isobel choosing her husband. *As long as she chooses me.*

He sighed and rubbed his hand over the back of his neck, trying to put into words the doubt and turmoil that raged in his heart. How could he tell his beloved foster brothers and father that he wasn't the man they thought he was?

Even knowing the foul blood that ran through his veins, he couldn't imagine letting Isobel go. "I doona know how to... That is to say... I doona think..."

"That's not news to us, Brother. We all know you doona think," Lachlan said, his voice matter-of-fact but his eyes glinting with amusement.

In less than a heartbeat, Kerr retrieved a rock that he kept tucked in the folds of his plaid—for moments like this—and flicked it at Lachlan's head. His foster brother ducked just in time with a whoop of laughter.

But when he straightened, Callum, Darach, and Gavin all pinged him with pebbles—thrown just hard enough to sting, making Kerr smile.

"Settle down," his foster father commanded. His tone took Kerr back to his youth, usually when Gregor caught the boys rough-housing and in danger of breaking something or setting the castle on fire. Kerr often wondered if Gregor had had any idea what he was getting himself into when he decided to foster five rambunctious lads.

"How did you manage it?" Kerr asked.

Gregor's brow creased in confusion. "Manage what?"

"The five of us. 'Tis not like you handed us over to someone for training and ne'er saw us again. You were right there with us in the thick of it."

"Aye, I've wondered that myself," Darach said. "Especially now I'm about to have my own bairn. I canna fathom what I'll do when there's five of them."

Gavin laughed. "And knowing Caitlin, they'll all be girls—as sweet and kind as her with a faithful hound on their heels named Trouble."

Darach shook his head, looking a wee bit fearful. "Nay, our first bairn will be a lad who'll grow big and strong and keep his sisters safe and out of mischief. Besides, I've forbidden Caitlin to have girls." He said the last with a smile.

"Send them to Maggie," Callum said. "She'll teach them to wield a dagger."

"Or Amber," Lachlan added. "All women should know how to defend themselves." He pointed at Kerr. "Starting with Isobel, if she's going to take on you as a husband. You'll smother her with your first kiss."

Kerr knew his brother jested, but he couldn't help thinking of his mother. Would she have survived his father if she'd known how to protect herself? Probably not. Where would she have gone? Kerr hadn't met his mother's family, but he didn't remember her ever talking about them. Like his cousin Deirdre, she'd been married off and never thought of again.

He frowned at Lachlan. "And *you* doona jest about *that*, Brother. Have you forgotten my mother's fate?"

Lachlan's smile turned down. "Och, I'm sorry. Forgive me, Kerr. I spoke without thinking."

"As did I." Kerr leaned forward over his horse and reached out his arm. Lachlan also leaned forward, and they clasped hands to elbows.

"'Tis a good thing you doubt yourself," Gregor said. "It shows you want the best for Isobel. You're a good man, despite who your father was. You would ne'er allow anything to harm her—even yourself." He leaned back and appraised Kerr with knowing eyes. "If you're beginning to question what sort of husband you'd be and if you'd be able to make Isobel happy, maybe you are ready for marriage."

"Is that what this is about?" Gavin asked. "You doona think you're good enough for my sister? Is that why you're still waiting?"

"I'm still waiting because I havenae had the opportunity. We've been attacked four times in the last year and a half, gone to war twice, and before all that, Ewan was taken. Not to mention trying to unravel the conspiracy against us. 'Tis not written in the stars, yet, to woo my reluctant bride."

"Aye, it's been a difficult few years," Gregor said. "And we still doona know who's leading the conspiracy against us."

Kerr scowled along with several of his foster brothers. "I canna help but think my clan will be attacked next."

"Maybe. Maybe not." Callum shifted on his horse, tapping his fingers against his leg, something he did when he was thinking. "I doubt Fraser kidnapping Caitlin was part of the master plan, else we would have met with a heavier force against us at Fraser's castle. Same with Lachlan's attack on Machar Murray and the MacPherson clan. We took both those clans out of play before our enemy could set them against us. And we took out Maggie's cousin too—and therefore her clan—when we came to her rescue, although she's adamant she didn't need my help."

The men laughed. "Knowing Maggie, she could have survived and thrived without you," Gavin said.

"Survived, aye, but not thrived. My warrior wife loves me despite my nagging her to stay off her feet and put her daggers down. I'm sure she's been climbing out of windows to amuse herself since I've been gone."

"And what of your clan?" Lachlan asked Callum. "It seems you scuttled the plan against them too."

Callum nodded. "We surprised the enemy by coming o'er the mountains. It would have been much worse had we travelled the low road where they waited."

"Which doesn't mean their armies willna strike again—at any one of us. We must stay vigilant," Gregor said quietly.

"Aye," they all agreed.

"When your fathers attacked me so many years ago, they only did so because Kerr's father had bribed, threatened, or curried favor with them," Gregor continued. "He was a master at manipulating people and events—the same as the leader of this conspiracy. Kidnapping Gavin's son to control him sounds like something Madadh MacAlister would have done."

"Are you saying my father has come back from the dead?" Kerr asked. "I wouldnae doubt he would be well-favored by his demon masters."

"I'm saying 'tis worth noting the similarities."

"Your uncle maybe?" Gavin asked. "He's the only one left alive. Or any cousins? Other than my wife, of course."

They all chuckled softly. When the moment passed, Kerr considered the possibility. "Nay, I doona think my uncle has it in him. He was broken by my father as a lad. He's still broken. He just wants to be left alone with his art. I have well-placed spies within my uncle's home in Edinburgh, and I've heard naught from them about suspicious behavior."

"What of your father's bastards?" Lachlan asked Kerr. "Are there any others besides Andy and Aulay?"

"Possibly. My father had no qualms about forcing himself on women. But even if there are others, where are they getting the men? And the access and legitimacy to influence the other clans? Someone must be backing them, like the Campbells or the MacDonalds."

"Aye," everyone agreed again.

Then Gavin suddenly punched Kerr on the shoulder. "You're naught like your father in any way. I would ne'er let you near Isobel if I didn't think you could make her happy."

Kerr's brow rose as he rubbed his arm. "How can you say that? All we do is fight."

"Aye, that's the point. You fight endlessly, but you ne'er try to change her or think that she should hold her tongue. I doona know many men who would be strong enough to let Isobel be Isobel and not feel diminished by her."

"Or try to control her," Callum added. "She's smart, and she understands people. She'll be an asset to you, if you let her—once she stops creating mischief, that is."

"You doona have to tell me that," Kerr growled, irritated that they thought he didn't know how smart Isobel was. And he *liked* the mischief she created.

"Didn't she try to run you through a prickle bush one time? And dump sour milk on your head?" Darach asked.

He grinned proudly. "And she almost succeeded. Both times!"

"She has my vote," Lachlan said.

Another round of "ayes" filled the air.

"Have you seen how the clan looks to her to right a wrong?" Kerr asked. "It may be too small an offense to warrant their laird's intervention, but they hope it has caught their lady's eye. And 'tis why she'll have a trap waiting for Gavin when we get home. Maybe two in case the first one fails. He may have married my cousin, but he did her wrong at the start."

Gavin's face fell, and a sick look entered his eyes. Not for himself, Kerr knew, but at the reminder that he'd treated his wife poorly when they first met.

Gregor reached out and patted him on the shoulder. "No one likes to get on your sister's bad side. But we'll be there to help you wash up afterward."

"Bah," Kerr grumbled as the others snorted. "Isobel doesn't have a bad side. Or a good side for that matter. She's not a bloody rectangle."

"Technically, a rectangle has four sides," Callum added.

"A line, maybe?" Darach asked.

"Not a line. A plane," Lachlan said.

Gavin shook his head. "My wife, the mathematician, would tell you you're all wrong. My sister isna any of those things. She's a stone wall. On one side is—"

"Shut it, ya wee *ablachs*. Or I'll tell Isobel everything you said, and you'll all be on her bad side—whate'er shape that is!" He steered Diabhla sideways and urged him into a swift canter. He was done ambling along. He whistled sharply to get the men to pick up the pace.

"Move your arses, lads! Half a day's march to the MacKinnon castle and the loveliest lasses in all of Scotland. They'll cheer your arrival and swoon from the sight of sweat-slicked, brawny muscles. Show them you're Highland warriors and not a bunch of sluggish Englishmen!"

The warriors cheered and whistled and did exactly as Kerr asked—hastening to reach Castle MacKinnon and Isobel.

Three

KERR REINED IN DIABHLA AND SEARCHED THE STAIRS THAT led up to the heavy wooden doors of the MacKinnon keep. The noise from the surrounding bailey, filled with returning warriors and excited castle folk yelling out to one another, faded into oblivion. Anticipation rose in his chest—and then crashed like lead to the pit of his stomach when he saw the stairs—the fifth step down to be exact—were empty.

Isobel wasn't here to greet him.

He dropped his gaze and scanned the crowd, seeing faces lit up with pleasure as the conquering heroes were welcomed home, their plaids and linen shirts and shifts untied and loosened due to the late summer heat. But none of those faces belonged to the woman he'd hurried back to see; none of the voices was hers.

His jaw tightened in disappointment. *Where is she?*

"Gavin!" he heard his cousin Deirdre shout out, followed by her son Ewan yelling excitedly, "Da! Da! We're over here."

He peered toward the stables and saw Ewan waving his arms frantically from atop the corral, his blond hair bright in the afternoon sun. Deirdre held tightly to his legs so he wouldn't topple over.

From beside him, atop his horse, his foster brother Gavin yelled back, "Deirdre! Ewan!"

He leapt from the back of his horse and weaved his way through the crowded bailey toward his family. When he was almost upon them, Ewan jumped from the fence and into his arms. Gavin gave him a quick, hard hug, and then shifted him to his hip and wrapped his arm around his wife. He dragged her tight against his body and kissed her upturned face.

"Da's kissing Ma again!" Ewan announced, something he'd done often in the weeks Gavin had lain in his sick bed, recovering from injuries sustained when he and Deirdre thwarted the attack against him and his clan.

Kerr glanced back up to the keep, and this time his breath stilled in his lungs. Isobel had exited the doors and was rushing down the steps to her usual position, her bright red-and-green skirts billowing behind her, and her long blond hair glinting in the sun. She stopped abruptly when she hit her spot and placed one hand on the stone railing, the other on her waist, as if she'd been there the whole time.

What had she been doing?

She pulled back her shoulders in a queen-like fashion that made his stones tighten, and searched the bailey.

Please be looking for me.

When her eyes landed on him seconds later, the air he'd been holding punched up from his lungs in an audible whoosh. Angels in heaven, she was lovely. Still, after all these years, she took his breath away. She was tall and willowy, with fair skin that lightly tanned in the summer and hair so blond it was almost white. Her locks curled gently all the way to her hips and blew around her slender body in the breeze.

He knew the details of her face by heart—perfectly bowed lips, a small yet stubborn chin, high cheekbones, and a wee pert nose. And her eyes, which had inspired so many verses in songs over the last few years, were a bright blue-green surrounded by heavy dark lashes that called to a man like a siren to a sailor.

'Twas no wonder people called her the Beauty of the Highlands.

She held his gaze for a long moment before flicking her eyes away. He waited, and when she glanced back at him seconds later, he urged Diabhla forward. Gavin's horse trailed behind.

Isobel glanced away again, a small, stiff smile curving her lips, as if she tried to pretend she was unaware and unaffected by him, but she glanced back twice more, until finally she pinned him with her gaze and glared.

Aye, not unaware of me at all.

He reached the bottom of the steps and gave her a slow smile. "Isobel," he said.

"Laird MacAlister," she replied. "I see you didn't die."

"Not this time."

"Well, there's always another battle."

A grin broke out on his lips, and he chuckled. She glanced away again, scanning the crowd below her, and he looked her over from top to bottom. She was rosy-cheeked, and the hair at the top of her forehead was slightly wet, as if she'd splashed water on her face. Her long bright locks looked freshly brushed, and the pleats of her arisaid were newly pleated.

So that's why she'd been late. She'd had to wash up.

But she'd missed a spot—aye, the bottom of her skirt was brown with soggy mud. Where had she been? In the forest, most likely, setting a trap.

But for whom?

She was an infant when he first met her, and he'd been fascinated by the wee creature with the bright hair and loud lungs.

I still am.

Yet after all this time, they weren't any closer to being betrothed. Nay, at times he thought they were farther apart than ever. Truth be told, he'd never even kissed her. Although she'd tried to kiss him, when she was fifteen. His memories of that incident were vague—he'd been deep in his cups—but he was pretty sure he'd laughed at her. And then kissed someone else.

Like a donkey's arse.

Squeezing the bridge of his nose between his finger and thumb, he barely repressed a groan. That was not the kind of slight a woman like Isobel would forget—or forgive.

Aye, he was surprised she hadn't tried to spring one of her traps on him lately. He should have walked into the last one. Let her win. But knowing Isobel, she would have realized he'd tricked her, and it would have backfired on him. Besides, he wasn't the kind of man to lie about anything—and she wasn't the kind of woman who would appreciate it if he did.

"Laird MacAlister, may I take your horse?"

Kerr dropped his gaze to the eager young groomsman who stood beside Diabhla, holding onto Gavin's stallion.

"I'll wipe Diabhla down for you and put him in the stable," the lad continued. "And we'll bring your saddlebag to your room."

Kerr swung his leg over his horse and dismounted. "Aye, thank you, lad."

He patted Diabhla on the neck before stepping around the groomsman and up the stairs toward the keep. When he looked at Isobel again, it was to see her cresting the top of the stairs as she hurried to the keep's entrance. Her hair swayed from the movement and curled softly down her back and over her arse.

Heat warmed his belly and spread outward as he imagined that bright swathe of silk trailing over his bare shoulders as she leaned over him, riding him slowly as he lay flat on his back. His hands had ahold of her arse and squeezed gently as he raised and lowered her along his cock—

"By the love of Christ, Kerr, you'll want to take care of that before you follow her upstairs," Lachlan said as he brushed past him.

Kerr came back to himself with a start and looked down to see his plaid tenting obscenely in the front. A slow burn of embarrassment heated his cheeks.

"Aye, you'll take out the dogs' eyes if you're not careful," Darach said, and his foster brothers burst out laughing. Darach's two huge deerhounds, Hati and Skoll, raced ahead of them as Darach mounted the steps.

Kerr was a big man, and that wayward part of him, with a mind of its own, matched his size. He'd had women pursue him over the years for that alone—not that he'd taken them up on it. He hadn't been with a woman since he'd decided on Isobel four years ago.

But it was well past time he made her his wife—for that reason alone, as well as all the others.

Callum stepped past him next and drilled him hard and sharp on the shoulder with his fist. Pain exploded in his arm, and Kerr hollered, clapping his hand over the nerve that Callum had surely hit on purpose.

"Think on the pain, Brother. That'll help," Callum said as the others howled.

"Ye wee shite," Kerr groused through gritted teeth as he kicked out with his foot. But Callum was expecting his retaliation and jumped several steps out of range. Kerr leaned over, trying to breathe through the pain.

"Hit him again on the other arm before Gavin sees him," Gregor added as he moved past. "Although I doona think either he or Deirdre will be joining us for the midday meal."

Lachlan had reached the top of the stairs and faced them. "Nay, but Ewan will be there, especially if Gavin and Deirdre are occupied. And you know how curious the lad is. He'll be full of questions." He cocked his head, and an evil grin creased his face. "On second thought, come on up as you are, Brother."

Between the pain in his arm and the thought of Ewan asking embarrassing questions in front of Isobel—while his brothers made comments to amuse themselves in the background—Kerr's lust waned, and his plaid fell flat.

He straightened with a sigh, still rubbing his arm.

Maybe he could convince Isobel to turn her talents for revenge against his foster brothers. If anybody needed to be taught a lesson, it was the four of them. And Gregor too.

Gavin may not have been part of this particular ribbing, but he'd been right in the thick of it in the past.

The bastards.

Yet another reason for him to marry Isobel. None of them would aggravate him afterward for fear of getting on his wife's bad side.

Not that Kerr considered it a bad side. Or a side at all.

Nay, it was simply Isobel.

The others were crowding through the door to the keep when he started to lumber up the stairs. "You'll regret it. All of you! My sweet Isobel is going to have your hides one day."

———

Isobel heard the door to the keep slam shut behind her and refused to turn around. She continued checking the table that had been set out for the family—foster family and actual family—as she listened to the approaching men. A washstand had been set up against the wall by the small hearth, and Gregor MacLeod and his foster sons headed there first to clean off the day's dirt before they ate.

She strained to identify the laughing voices and heard Lachlan, Darach, Callum, and Gregor, but not the deep-throated growl of Kerr. Was he there? Maybe even sneaking up behind her? He should be inside the keep by now.

God's truth, she only listened so she could prepare a sharp-witted retort in case she needed one—which she always did.

An arm slipped around her waist, and she caught her breath, but it was only Gregor. "Hello, lass," he said and gave her an affectionate hug.

She returned the embrace. "Hello yourself, you old badger. Glad to see you made it back alive." She braced her shoulders and faced the rest of the group, but Kerr was not among them. "And all of you, too," she said to her brother's foster brothers—which sort of made them her foster brothers as well.

Except Kerr. She wouldn't claim that man for anything—neither as a foster brother nor a husband...no matter how often in her dreams she'd claimed him as a lover.

The men swarmed in to greet her before taking their seats around the table. She signaled the servers to bring the trenchers of meat and greens and to fill their cups with ale.

Behind her, the door opened and banged shut, and this time she did whirl around to see who had entered. Immediately, her gaze clashed with Kerr's. He stared at her intently as he crossed the cavernous great room toward her. Those dark brown, almost black hooded eyes pinned her in place like a hawk, making her feel like a trapped little mouse.

Or maybe a mare watching her stallion approach, causing her flanks to quiver and her head to toss in defiance—but wanting his claim nonetheless.

Nay, this man wasn't a stallion, he was a marauding bear.

His thick hair was as dark as his eyes and hung in wind-blown tangles to his shoulders.

She gasped when she saw it, and disappointment tightened her chest. "You cut your hair," she blurted out, and then regretted it. The last thing she wanted him to think was that she cared—or had even noticed.

She bit her lip. *Too late.*

He raised his hand, gripped the shorter strands, and then released them. "Aye. A close call during battle. Gregor had to even it out."

"A small price to pay," Gregor said, as he tore a hunk of bread in half.

"Aye," the others agreed.

The hollow in her stomach turned to ice. How close had the sword or dagger come to his throat to cut off a chunk of his hair?

Usually, it was tied back with a leather thong, emphasizing a face too hard and ruthless-looking to be considered handsome.

Except for his lips. Aye, those lips—full and prone to laughing—hinted at Kerr's softer side...the side that had loved his mother and hers, and adored bairns of all ages.

His nose had been broken several times, but it didn't detract from his face. Nay, it made him look even more roguish, while the thick sweep of lashes around those intent eyes turned them almost pretty.

Not that he was a handsome man—not like Gavin or Darach—but according to every woman who'd ever been within his powerful presence, he was a desirable one.

Every woman but her, that is.

He was the biggest of the foster brothers—in every way, if one believed the rumors. Rumors that were confirmed by the ribald jests Kerr and his brothers had thrown at each other when they thought no one was listening.

But Isobel was *always* listening. Sitting in a wee alcove unobserved while the folks of the village and the castle talked was one of her favorite things to do—that and planning, then executing, one of her traps.

Which she'd been doing all morning and part of the afternoon. And she'd finished just in time.

She could hardly contain her glee that *finally* she would catch Kerr unaware.

She. Would. Win.

And then what?

The strange question came out of nowhere, and her stomach hollowed, leaving her feeling a little empty inside. When Kerr stopped in front of her, he must have seen it in her eyes, for he lifted his hand and brushed his thumb down her cheek. Those hard eyes softened as he gazed at her.

"Isobel, sweetling, what is it?" he asked quietly.

She dropped her chin, appalled at the sudden prick of tears at the back of her eyes and the thickening of her throat.

She shook her head and coughed to clear the obstruction. "'Tis naught. A piece of dandelion fluff that I inhaled earlier. You know how I react to them."

He lowered his hand and stepped back. "Aye. Were you in the forest?"

The question threw her, and she coughed again as she considered her answer. What could she say to make him follow her back to her manure pit later on without giving the game away? "'Tis not your business, Kerr MacAlister."

Perfect.

"Were you setting a trap for Gavin? Or someone else?"

She raised a brow and tried to look down her nose at him in the manner of Master Carmichael. It didn't work. "Whate'er I was doing has naught to do with you, so keep out of it."

"Do you want my help? If it's for Gavin, he'll be hard to catch unaware, and he'll spot the trap ahead of time. Same as I would."

She rolled her eyes. "I could catch you if I tried, but I doona care to."

He winced, and she felt a stab of guilt.

"He's distracted by Deirdre right now," she added, rushing past the uncomfortable emotion. "He's not as sharp as he used to be. Well, not here. I'm sure he was verra sharp on the battlefield."

Kerr planted his hands on his hips, making him look even bigger and a wee bit ferocious. "He'll see it, Isobel."

"Nay. His head will be in the clouds. Especially once Deirdre tells him she's with bairn."

His brows shot up, and a smile cracked his face. Her stomach flipped again, and her toes curled, but this time it wasn't from unease. Nay, it was because with that grin on his face, and the joy radiating from his eyes, Kerr MacAlister was as handsome as any of his foster brothers.

"Gavin's having another bairn?" he asked.

"Aye," she said a little breathlessly, not liking the feeling that was besieging her at all. Kerr MacAlister did not make her toes curl. Only her fists, right before she decided to punch him. "And Gavin isna having the bairn. Deirdre is. A man may be able to stab someone in the guts or take a blow to the head on the battlefield, but not a one of you could go through what a woman goes through on the birthing bed or the nine months leading up to it. Or even the monthly discomfort before that!"

He stared at her for a moment, his eyes wide with astonishment, and then he threw back his head and laughed. "You have the right of it, sweetling. We'd all be reduced to mewling *ablachs*, for sure." Then he swept her into a bear hug and twirled her around.

She'd been hugged by Kerr before—many times—but somehow this felt different. Or maybe she was different.

She'd been worried about him when he went to fight the MacIntyres and the MacColls. Nay, not only him. She'd been worried about all of them. Especially as she'd found out about the conspiracy against them just before they'd left. She'd confronted Gavin about it immediately, and she could see he wasn't pleased that she knew—or that she'd gone through his papers to find out—but she didn't care.

She wasn't pleased he hadn't told her.

If Gavin and the others would confide in her and talk to her about things, she could help. They had to know they could trust her. She'd bring a different perspective to a problem that needed solving. She was good at figuring out intrigue in the clan and knowing what needed to be done. She would be good at figuring out things on a larger scale too.

It took her a moment to realize that Kerr had stopped spinning her around and her feet were back on the ground—and that her arms were still linked around his neck. She inhaled deeply, and the scent of horses and leather, the outdoors, and smoke from the fire filled her nose. And something more than that. Something that was purely Kerr.

Her mouth watered, and she suddenly found herself light-headed. From him twirling her around, no doubt. She unclenched her fists from where she gripped his hair at the back of his neck and trailed them down his chest. The rough-looking locks had been surprisingly soft, and she missed the silken feel of them in her hands.

For the love of God, what's the matter with me? I doona miss any-thing about this…this…behemoth.

Never mind that when her body was against his and her feet were touching the floor, her head had tucked perfectly beneath his chin—which, for a woman as tall as her, had made her sigh. She felt small against him.

His hands slipped around to grasp her hips, and she stepped back as he pressed her away from him. She ended up going farther than either of them had intended, and she let out a little yelp as she almost toppled over. Luckily, Kerr gripped her hard, and she steadied.

The lairds at the table stopped talking and looked over. "Are you well, lass?" Gregor asked, sounding a little uncertain as he looked from Isobel, to Kerr, then back to Isobel—not wanting to step on Kerr's toes, no doubt. Well, she had no such reservations.

"No more than a mishap," she said, as she moved past Kerr to the head of the table, grinding down on his toes with her heel when she walked by.

He grunted but didn't follow her like he might have done before. Instead, he moved stiffly away from her and sat next to Callum, several seats along the bench. He whispered something to his foster brother, who grinned and nailed Kerr on his shoulder with his fist.

Kerr groaned in pain, and the men snickered softly.

"What?" she asked, confused about what was happening.

"'Tis naught, Isobel," Gregor said.

She frowned at him and leaned forward. "But—"

"Isobel told me that Deirdre is with bairn," Kerr interrupted, flashing her a pained smile. He'd wrapped his hand around his arm where Callum had punched him.

The men erupted in celebratory shouts and cheers. "Another grandbairn for me to spoil!" said Gregor, lifting his mug in celebration. "That makes three out of the five of you who've done your duty." He shot a mock glare at Lachlan, who shrugged—the lone holdout of the married lairds.

"If Amber and I decide to have bairns, there's time," he said.

Isobel's eyes widened. She couldn't imagine that Lachlan would abstain from intimacy, and Amber was a renowned healer with knowledge of herbs… Did that mean she knew of a reliable way to stop her husband's seed from taking root? A safe way?

She leaned forward again and pinned him with her gaze. Color slowly crept up his cheeks when he noticed.

"Lachlan MacKay, are you saying—"

"Nay, Isobel," Kerr cut her off, his voice sharp.

She turned her head. He sat on the opposite side of the table from Lachlan near the other end. He no longer looked in pain. Instead, his mouth was compressed into a taut line, and his hand was clenched into a fist.

He's angry! Because I would question Lachlan about Amber's herbs?

She slowly sat back in her chair, her shoulders straightening and her chin lifting high enough to show him her displeasure. He forgot himself, to speak to her in such a manner. *She* was lady of this castle. "Did I hear you were travelling back to your clan tomorrow, Laird MacAlister?"

A muscle jumped steadily in his jaw above his dark, shaggy beard. They stared at each other, neither willing to give an inch. "I willna be leaving so soon, Lady MacKinnon. I would beg a rest at your home, a chance to see my brothers before we go our separate ways for the winter."

"Verily, you've spent the last two months with your brothers," she said, her voice still icy. "Surely that's enough for any man?"

"It's enough for me," Lachlan said, and Gregor jabbed him with his elbow.

She looked at Lachlan again until he slumped back in his chair. Then she passed her gaze over all the men, one by one. Except Kerr—she was afraid if she looked at him again, she wouldn't be able to look away.

They may be her brother's foster family, but they were in her home. She ruled here. No one told her what to do. Her eyes finally fell on Kerr.

No one.

And she opened her mouth to tell him so—

"Grandda Gregor!" Ewan yelled from the bottom of the stairs that led to the upper levels. Everyone looked up to see Ewan barreling toward them, and the tension dissipated. She sighed and let Kerr's transgression go as the moment passed.

"Da said you had a present for me," Ewan hollered.

"He did, did he?" Gregor patted down his léine and plaid. "Hmmm, I think maybe your da was mistak—oh! What's this?"

Gregor pulled a wooden warrior, intricately whittled and smoothed over, from the folds of his plaid. Ewan reached his side, his eyes pleading as his hands stretched upward. "'Tis a Highlander swinging a sword," Gregor said. "Do you think he's battling his enemy?"

"Aye!" Ewan enthused. "A giant or maybe a dragon!"

"Or maybe an Englishman," Darach added.

The men all nodded in agreement, and Isobel snorted. The reviled Englishmen.

"May I have it?" Ewan begged.

"This?" Gregor asked, holding up the warrior. "I didnae think you liked these kinds of toys."

Ewan had a table full of toy warriors in his room, and Gregor knew the lad spent hours setting up battles between them or against a bigger, deadlier foe—much to his mother's chagrin.

"I do!" Ewan said.

Isobel rubbed her hand down his back. "Your grandda will give it to you if you sit down and eat." The lad hesitated, then ran around to an empty spot beside her.

Gregor handed the small carving across to him. "If you're sure you like it…"

Ewan grabbed it with an excited smile and settled back in his seat. "I'll name him Gregor. He's big and strong."

Gregor beamed.

Then Ewan pulled a second toy warrior from his sporran. "But he's not quite as big as Kerr."

"Verra observant, lad!" Kerr grinned as Gregor scoffed loudly.

"But my da is the biggest and strongest of all." Ewan pulled a third warrior from his sporran and proceeded to bash the other two with it.

"What?" Kerr bellowed. "If you knew the number of times I knocked your da flat on his back—"

But Ewan wasn't listening as he used the wee Gavin to pummel the wee Kerr. Then he picked up his newest warrior, Gregor, and the two of them hacked Kerr with their swords.

Isobel was certain if Deirdre were here, she would be horrified.

When the servers came around with the food, she dished greens and meat onto her trencher and then Ewan's. "So, how did the battles go?" she asked between bites. "I know the MacColls surrendered and Boyd MacColl, the wee weasel, was hanged by his sister's husband before you arrived, but what happened earlier at Clan MacIntyre?"

"It was a siege, lass," Gregor said.

"Aye, but what happened? You were there for almost three weeks before you took the castle."

"Mostly we waited until the time was right," Darach added.

"And when was that?" she asked.

"When all our men were in place, and we wouldnae be turned into an army of hedgehogs stuck with arrows," Lachlan said. The men, including Ewan, laughed.

Isobel did not. Instead, she repressed an irritated sigh. "You're not going to tell me, are you?"

"Another time, lass," Kerr said. "Everyone's tired from the long march."

She bit her tongue in frustration. She wanted details, but when she asked, she was made to feel like her questions were an imposition—like always. The lairds would never speak freely in front of her about certain things, as if she were a child in need of protection. She assumed they held back because she was a woman, and it irked her—and made her do things like copy the key to Gavin's solar to keep informed.

Now she wanted to dump them *all* into her manure pit.

Surely she wasn't the only woman who was interested in leadership? From everything the men had said about Callum's wife, Maggie, and Lachlan's wife, Amber, they led as much as the men did. And the men accepted those women for who they were: strong and capable of defending themselves and others.

So why not me?

Was it because she didn't know how to fight or shoot an arrow? If that were so, then it was their fault for not teaching her. Besides, there had been many strong queens and kings in history who weren't fighters yet commanded respect and led their people well.

She could be one of them.

With a disgruntled sigh, Isobel pushed back her trencher, no longer hungry. She summoned a smile for the lairds, albeit a frosty one, her anger and frustration simmering beneath the surface, and rose from her seat. "If you'll excuse me, I have much to do. Enjoy your meal…and your visit to my home."

"Stay with us, Isobel. Eat with us," Kerr said, his eyes filling with concern.

"Aye, lass. We'd like your company," Gregor said.

"Nay, thank you. My duties are calling. I've had enough to eat." She stepped away from the table.

"Can I come with you, Aunt Isobel?" Ewan asked, jumping up to stand on the bench.

Her smile softened, and she stepped toward him to kiss the top of his head. "Not this time, sweets. I'm sure your uncles and grandda want to spend time with you."

"Aye, lad," Lachlan said. "Let's see your da pummel your uncle Kerr again."

Ewan grinned, pulled the toy Kerr from his pocket, lifted him high in the air and dropped him onto the table with a crash.

Isobel bit her tongue—hard. It was time for her to leave.

She'd work on her plan to catch Kerr unaware, and then maybe she'd start with Gregor and set a trap for each of the other foster brothers as well.

She could be an asset to these idiotic men, but they couldn't see past the ends of their swords—neither the steel ones nor the ones made of flesh.

Four

Kerr turned his head to watch Isobel retreat from the great room and down the passageway toward the kitchens. From there, he suspected she'd exit into the bailey and continue setting her trap for Gavin. He longed to go after her, but he knew she needed time to stew, time to regain what he and his brothers had taken from her.

He understood why the men didn't want to talk about the battle. They'd lived through it, and war was never what the poets and bards made it out to be. It was bloody and desperate. Horrific. Until you'd been in battle, seen men being cut down around you, crying and writhing in the dirt, you could never understand it. The sounds of war stayed with you. The smell of it.

When she was no longer in sight, he turned his gaze back to his foster family.

Callum caught his eye. "You'll do yourself no favors, keeping things from her."

A wave of irritation shot through him. "You doona have to tell *me* that. I'm well aware of what Isobel wants, of how she thinks and feels. Besides, I doona need advice from a man whose wife climbs out of windows to escape his nagging." Snorts and chuckles exploded around the table.

When the amusement died down, Darach said, "'Twas not the time or place to talk about death and destruction. We're all tired and in no mood to revisit the battlefield."

"Aye, but it doesn't lessen the denial she felt, the rejection," Kerr said. "She wants to know everything—needs to know."

"Queen Isobel," Gregor said. "She'll rule where'er she

goes—and not by dumping sour milk on people's heads. Are you prepared for that?" he asked Kerr.

"I look forward to it."

The men nodded in approval.

"Verily, she's much too good for you," Lachlan said.

Kerr chuffed out a laugh. "Aye, that's the honest truth. The first you've told in ages."

"'Twas a lesson I had to learn with Maggie," Callum said. "I almost lost her because I told her only what I thought she should know, trying to keep her safe and separate from my clan's troubles, when together we could have solved the problem sooner. 'Tis not for me to decide what is or isna appropriate for her to hear. Or what she can or canna do."

"'Twill be the same with me and Isobel."

"Only once you're married," Gregor cautioned. "You doona know for sure she'll have you, and if she marries someone else, her loyalty will be to her husband and not to you."

Outwardly, Kerr stilled, and he pinned Gregor with a lethal gaze for daring to suggest Isobel might marry someone else. Inside, however, the blood raged through his veins, and his deadly warrior rose, yelling and beating his chest. He wanted to fight the man he considered a father—fight them all.

"Isobel will not marry someone else." Even his voice sounded different. Deeper and harder. Unforgiving.

"Good. Then tell her only that which does not compromise the safety of your allies. The rest can wait until after you've married her…ye wee *ablach*."

Laughter burst out again, and the tension eased. Kerr sighed, and that part of him—his dark Celt—retreated with a growl. He rubbed his palm over the back of his neck, still considering slicing off some of Gregor's whiskers for daring to suggest Isobel wouldn't marry him.

And if she doesn't?

With a grunt, he shoved the thought aside, and then dug into his meal. By the time he finished eating, she wouldn't be so angry—although the feeling might lurk beneath the surface…as it had for years.

Is that why she fights our union? Is there something unresolved between us?

The question stuck with him, and he frowned. "How did you convince Maggie to forgive you?" he asked Callum. "I know about the marksmanship contest between the two of you, but surely there was more to it than that?"

"You mean for not coming back for her when I said I would?" Callum asked.

"Aye."

"Well, to start, I apologized. And I asked for forgiveness. Then it was a matter of time, of rebuilding our bond and earning her trust again. 'Twas good we were on our journey o'er the mountains, so we could spend our days together and work things out." He cocked a brow at Kerr. "Why? Have you done something to Isobel?"

"I doona know, exactly, but…something is between us. Something I've said or done. Or not said or done. I doona know if she's even aware of it."

"She's a complicated woman," Darach said.

"Meant for an uncomplicated man," Lachlan added, and he wasn't teasing this time. Kerr's needs were simple, and his thoughts were direct. Aye, a simple, deadly man.

He looked back in the direction Isobel had disappeared. "A second truth from you today, Brother." Rising from the bench, he stepped over it. "I think 'tis time I figured it out."

"Can I come with you, Uncle Kerr?" Ewan asked.

"Nay, lad. I'm going with your aunt Isobel—where'er it is she's going. On a merry chase, no doubt."

The men laughed and wished him luck as he walked across the

Great Hall, the rushes on the floor crunching beneath his boots. The central area was busier now as more of Gavin's men streamed in for the midday meal, and numerous servers darted around them. Once he reached the opposite end of the cavernous room, he entered the passageway into which he'd seen Isobel disappear.

He bypassed the kitchens and headed for the door to the bailey. After pushing it open, he stepped into a warm September day and waited for his eyes to adjust to the bright light.

His gaze found Isobel immediately, standing near the stables, her back to him, directing some of the groomsmen in their work. They'd attached a covered cart behind a pony whose reins were tied to Isobel's horse's saddle.

She was planning something—a trap for Gavin most likely, and a pang of envy shot through him.

Aye, he wanted Isobel to set a trap for *him*. He wanted her thoughts turned to him like his were turned to her, even if it was to devise some way to cause him discomfort and embarrassment. And to take him down a notch.

The embarrassment would come from being blind to her trap—chagrin that she had beaten him. But also pride that she'd done so. And amusement. And his brothers' and Gregor's amusement too. Those donkeys would like nothing better than to see him doused in honey and running from an ornery bear.

He approached her, keeping his hands loose by his sides when he wanted to slip them around her waist like Gregor had done. And if he could hold her close and swing her around like he had before, even better. Although Callum wasn't here to punch his shoulder, causing him enough pain to overcome his body's natural response to her nearness.

"Where are you off to?" he asked when he reached her side.

She stiffened but did not look at him. "'Tis not your business."

He shrugged and whistled. A groomsman came running. "Prepare Diabhla. I'll be going with Lady Isobel." He didn't say where, as he didn't know yet, but he presumed out into the woods somewhere. He glanced around and saw her guard, standing back as they always did and sworn to secrecy. He nodded at them, and the one in charge, Lyle, with hard eyes and a battle-scarred face, nodded back. He would die before Isobel was harmed.

As would Kerr.

Gavin had chosen the guard well, vetted by Isobel, of course, and whittled down by her to as few men as Gavin would allow. Kerr would have chosen more, especially with the threat of the conspirators against them, but Isobel was a tough negotiator.

Another way she'd be helpful to him and his clan when she married him.

"Suit yourself," she said. "But doona stick your nose in where it doesn't belong. No matter how helpful you think you're being."

"I'm nothing if not helpful, sweetling."

She made a dismissive sound, and he smiled. He stepped closer to the cart but didn't need to look beneath the tarp to know what was under it. He could smell it.

Manure.

His darling Isobel was going all out to teach her brother a lesson. He hoped Gavin was enjoying himself with his wife, because he was in for a big stink of a surprise if Isobel was successful.

"Have you thought about what will happen if Deirdre is with Gavin? Or Ewan?" he asked.

Her nostrils flared as she inhaled sharply. In irritation, no doubt. "They willna be, not that it's any of your business."

"Aye, you said that before."

She moved to her horse after the groom finished tying down the corner of the tarp. Kerr stepped forward to help her up, but she shot him a look, and he backed off. "How can you be sure they willna be with him?"

She huffed in exasperation and rolled her eyes. "I'm not an amateur, Kerr. If I say they willna be there when the trap is sprung, then that's how it will be." In a smooth movement, she put her foot in the stirrup, pulled herself into her saddle, and then urged her horse forward. The smaller horse, more a pony, really, was tugged along behind them, and the cart rolled into motion.

Kerr looked back to see Diabhla being led from the stable. He whistled, and the stallion leapt toward him, leaving the groom with empty hands and a startled look on his face. Kerr sprung onto his back without the horse even slowing, and they soon caught up to Isobel as she approached the portcullis.

Again, she didn't look at him, but this time instead of her body stiffening, her shoulders relaxed.

So she wants me to follow her. Whether that was a good thing or a bad thing, he couldn't decide. Either way, it made him happy, and a grin stretched across his face. "Lead on, my queen. I shall follow you anywhere!"

"I'm not a queen." Her tone was dismissive—or tried to be—but he could hear the hint of excitement beneath her words.

What was she up to?

"Aye, you are. Queen of my heart," he said it with the exuberance of a lovesick fool, and when her cheek twitched like she was trying not to laugh, he almost punched the air in triumph.

She pinned a frown in place, still refusing to look at him, and pursed her lips. "Are you my subject, then?"

"Depends. Do you want to subjugate me?" He dropped his voice an octave as he said *subjugate*, so the word rasped from his chest. The question sounded dark and forbidden...like temptation.

She jerked her head toward him—finally—her eyes wide with disbelief. A flush rose up her cheeks, and he could practically see her mind whirring, wondering what he'd meant exactly, or if she'd misheard him. For all of his and Isobel's verbal sparring over the years, they'd never spoken about carnal things—about how it might be between them.

Maybe he should change that.

She bit her lip, an unconscious gesture, he was sure, and then looked forward again. "Nay, I want to dunk you in that cart full of manure behind me."

He snorted. "I think I'd prefer subjugation."

"I'm sure you would, but we doona always get what we want."

"Ah, sweet Isobel. That's where you're wrong. You may be my queen, but someday soon, I hope, I'll be your king. And I'll subjugate you too."

———

Isobel pressed her lips together before she made some sort of embarrassing sound—a high-pitched squeak or, God forbid, a witless giggle. Her mare tossed her head, reacting to her tightened grip on the reins and the tension in her legs. She tried to inhale slowly, deeply, to calm herself without alerting Kerr to the fact that she was doing so, but it was almost impossible because of the way her heart raced.

He would hear her, see the tiny changes in her body, and know he'd affected her—no matter how much she'd try to pretend otherwise.

What had he meant? *Subjugation.* Was that…some kind of physical intimacy she'd never heard of? Aye, she was still a maid, but she'd been privy to many bawdy conversations amongst the castle folk and the warriors—without their knowledge, of course.

She hadn't imagined Kerr's tone, the look he gave her. Then again, he could have been playing games with her—confusing her on purpose.

She could ask him his meaning, but she didn't want to give him the satisfaction.

Besides, she should be happy. He was doing exactly as she wanted, following her toward the trap she'd set for him, while believing it was a trap for Gavin. Instead, a confusing mix of emotions careened inside her—uncertainty and nervousness, indignation and irritation. All swamped by an overwhelming yearning for...for what?

For him?

Nay, that couldn't be right. His talk of subjugation, and his raspy tone of voice, had simply brought to mind the intimacy of her dream this morning—and how she'd woken up with an ache in her body she hadn't assuaged.

And it wasn't the first dream, either. She had one recurring dream of him holding her down while he—

Nay! Kerr in real life is my nemesis, not king to my queen.

She huffed out a frustrated breath, unable to contain it any longer.

"Just ask me," he said with a hint of laughter.

"Ask you what? Surely, your mind is addled." She glanced at him sideways, then wished that she hadn't, as the sight of him on his horse, so big and brawny beside her, a devilish grin on his face, made her cheeks heat up...again.

"If you wait much longer, your head may burst. 'Tis too much fire to hold in, dearling. Havenae you been to the blacksmiths? Verily, so much heat and pressure will lead to an explosion. What am I to tell poor Gavin and Deirdre?"

She gave him an icy smile and turned away. He wanted to rile her and 'twas hard *not* to give in. Maybe she should start yelling at him. That always made her feel better, in control, especially if he yelled back. Their argumentative back and forth was a dynamic she was used to—one she excelled at—not this talking about sexual deeds she didn't understand...but wanted to.

What did he mean?

"You want to know," he said, almost mimicking her thoughts. "Your curiosity is boundless."

When she bit her tongue instead of answering, he shrugged and looked forward. "Or you can play it safe and skip over all those unsettling feelings that are making your pulse quicken and your mind fluster like a—"

"I am not flustered!"

"Then ask me a question…anything. About the battle, about war in general, about what I supped on last night. Rabbit, by the way, roasted over the fire."

She squeezed her lips together again before she blurted out something else she'd regret. Or worse yet—laughed. She did not want to go back to talking about subjugation—at least not with him. But she did want to know about the battle. And the conspiracy. And about his childhood, and his father, and how Kerr had killed him.

She'd wanted to know those details for years. He was right; she had an insatiable desire to know *everything*.

"Was it good?" she asked.

"My dinner? Aye, it was verra good. Gregor always brings along some of his special spice to put on it. The flavor bursts in your mouth."

The talk of spiced rabbit only reminded her that she hadn't eaten much of her midday meal and she already felt a twinge of hunger. She ignored it and turned her horse away from the castle in the opposite direction of the village.

"You asked earlier about the battle," he said. "We weren't trying to exclude you. But…"

"But what?" she prompted.

"We killed men, Isobel. Young men who had wee sisters who adored them and mothers and fathers praying for their return. Older men with lads and lassies at home and wives who couldnae feed them on their own. Even if you manage a quick kill, their deaths stay with you. As they should. We do what we can afterward to help the innocent victims, but it's ne'er enough."

"I'm sorry. I know that, of course, but…"

"But you want to know about the strategy we used. How we

outsmarted them. Our triumphs, our mistakes. The broad strokes. I'll tell you, but understand that for you, it's an intellectual exercise…for the men who fought—including Gregor and my brothers—it's a horrific reality."

Guilt swamped her. "Forgive me. You doona have to say anything. I shouldnae have asked."

"Nay, I want to. My brothers go home to their wives and perhaps share the details that bother them most. I'll tell you what I can. Maybe it will ease my mind too."

She looked down and squeezed her hands around the reins. Why, if she knew it hurt him to tell the tale, did she want to know? Why couldn't she be more like Deirdre and be happy raising her bairns, loving her husband, and helping her clan?

She was certain Deirdre had never been struck with the burning desire to see justice done over what some may consider small slights within the clan—a scorned woman, a bullied man, a child made to feel like an outcast.

"I feel…incomplete without the knowledge," she said hesitantly, trying to make him understand, to make herself understand. "Like I'm missing pieces of the picture. I doona need all the details, but I do need to know. Even in broad strokes, like you say—the order of events, why you made the decisions you did, how you executed your plan."

Kerr didn't answer immediately, and she found herself holding her breath. When he nodded, she let it out quietly. They were almost at the forest's edge and that would give them another ten minutes to talk before they reached the trap site.

"The MacIntyres knew we were coming, of course," he began. "The village had been abandoned, and everyone was walled up within the castle, which is set up much the same as Castle MacKinnon—no moat, no mound that it was built upon, but tall, strong walls, and set within cleared land so they could see us coming."

"Why did they fight, when their laird was already dead from the attack on us last spring?" she asked.

"He'd left someone in charge of the castle. It was that man's decision."

"Did you parlay with them first? How did you approach the castle without being stuck with arrows, like Lachlan said?"

"We tried to parlay, but they refused. We set up just out of range—surrounded the castle—and waited."

"For what?"

"For our men inside—our spies—to aid us in taking the castle, mostly. But we also hoped that seeing our greater number would weaken their resolve, and they would surrender before lives were lost."

When he didn't elaborate, she raised her brow. His answers so far only made her want to know more.

He continued. "The night before we attacked, some of our men approached the wall by crawling across the open field unseen. They were hidden at the base of the curtain wall when the assault began. Inside, our spies had created a diversion by starting a fire that raged quickly in the tannery. MacIntyre men had to be diverted from manning the walls to put out the fire. Before that, a small group of us had entered through a hidden door into the castle, let in by the steward, who sided with us. Once inside, we waited for the fire to start, and then split our forces. Half of us headed to the portcullis to open the gates for our approaching army, led by Gregor, who charged the wall on horseback. The other half searched for the MacIntyre leaders to take them out."

"And it worked?" she asked, her breath held tight in her throat.

He nodded. "We took the castle in less than an hour and were able to put out the fire with only minimal damage to the other buildings. We started rebuilding the tannery, with the help of the MacIntyre tanner, the next afternoon."

"What group were you with?" she asked.

"I snuck through the passageway and then fought to open the portcullis."

"And Gavin?"

"He killed the man who was leading the MacIntyre defense."

The breath gushed from her lungs on a sharp exhale. Suddenly the battle didn't seem so exciting. This was what Kerr had meant—the intellectual experience of the battle versus the reality of war.

"Did he try to surrender?" she asked.

"Of course not. Gavin would ne'er have killed him if he had. The man was a good fighter, defending his home—doing what he was charged to do. His mistake was in failing to take into account that his people came first. His laird was dead. He was their leader now. He should have negotiated a surrender."

She nodded, still deflated. "Your reputation for fairness and justice should have swayed him."

"That was our hope."

The trail they'd been following narrowed, and Kerr moved closer, his leg brushing hers. A tree branch protruded into her path at eye level, and before she could push it out of her way, he reached across and snapped it off, his massive, muscular body looming over her. He then tossed the offending branch to the ground and sat back in his saddle.

As much as she denied it, a melting sensation invaded her muscles. It was the same feeling she'd felt when he'd swirled her around and her head had tucked up so perfectly beneath his chin.

She'd turned soft then too—and hated herself for it.

Or maybe she hated being perceived as soft—as weak and ineffective. Wasn't it the same thing? *Maybe not.* Deirdre was soft, but she wasn't weak or ineffective.

Gah! It was too much for her to figure out right now. Especially with Kerr riding so close.

Up ahead, a glade appeared, and Isobel brought her attention back to the task at hand. She reined in her mount at the end of the trail and surveyed her handiwork, trying not to let her eyes rest anywhere that might give the trap away. Kerr stopped beside her and also perused the glade.

She held her breath and wondered what he saw.

She'd marked the edges of the pit with a fallen twig on one side and an overturned stump on the other. To her eyes, it looked natural. She'd carefully chosen the spot to dig and then spent a full day shoveling manure into the hole and weaving the long grass, leaves, and twigs to go over top. The moment he stepped on it, Kerr would fall through.

High up in the tree branches on the other side, she'd rigged a second trap that was a decoy. That was the trap she wanted Kerr to see, to focus on. She'd also laid a trip wire near the stump that would release the trap up in the tree and send "manure" raining down on him. Of course, there wasn't really any manure up in the tree, only dirt, so the cloth bag, covered in leaves, had the proper weight to it.

She wanted Kerr to see the trip wire and walk across the glade to investigate it, telling her the entire time that she needed his help, that Gavin would see the trap like he had.

Right up until he stepped into the pit of manure.

A perfect plan...that she now felt reluctant to set in motion. He'd been so open with her, shared the emotional toll of war with her. How could she reward him for it by dumping him in horse shite?

"Dearest, do you intend to sit here all day?" Kerr asked. "Are you so enamored with my presence that you doona want to proceed? 'Tis not often we get to sit so close."

Her cheeks heated, and irritation raced through her, chasing away her hesitation. She threw him a look that would shrivel a weaker man.

Pit of manure it is.

She dismounted, and her guard settled into the trees around

the glade, staying far away from her handiwork. They knew better than to warn one of her targets what they were walking into.

Isobel grasped her mare's reins, led her to a tree in the glade, and tied the horse to a branch. Then she unfastened the pony's lead from the saddle and pulled it toward the stump, the cart following behind. She parked the manure on the safe side of the stump, leaving the pathway over the pit the most logical way to reach her side.

It also camouflaged the smell of the manure she'd already shoveled into the pit yesterday.

She didn't look at Kerr as she crouched to tie the pony's lead to the overturned stump—she didn't dare—but she strained her ears for any sounds of his horse, or his feet, walking across the grass toward her.

Surely he'll tie his stallion beside mine and then cross to my side? And be looking up.

When she heard his mount on the opposite side of the glade, she jerked her head toward it, only to see the horse happily munching on some grass…alone.

Kerr had to be behind her. Either watching her or looking for her traps. *Had he seen them?*

She straightened and glanced up at the decoy in the trees before quickly dropping her gaze—as if she hadn't wanted him to see her doing that. Then she turned around and gasped.

He stood right behind her…so big and tall, his wild hair snarled across his shoulders, his gaze—dark and rapt—on her face.

Her breath caught in her throat, and her heart thrummed in her chest—even more than it had from the excitement of finally getting the better of him. His gaze held hers, and she shivered.

This wasn't the Kerr bent on riling her, or the noisy and boisterous one who was full of mirth and loved playing with the bairns, or the Kerr who scared her sometimes when he sensed danger, and all that energy within him coiled into deadly readiness.

Nay, this Kerr was someone else entirely. He peered at her like he wanted to swallow her whole, his every sense tuned to her—her eyes, her expression, every twitch of her body—and right into her mind.

He raised his hand, gently rubbed his knuckles down her cheek, and then squeezed her chin between his thumb and knuckle. "What are you up to, love?"

She froze in place and had to swallow before answering. "I told you. 'Tis a trap for Gavin."

He continued to stare at her and then slowly glanced up at the trees where she'd looked moments before. His eyes shifted down and she knew he was tracing the trip wire all the way to the stump by her feet.

He released her and squatted on his haunches, studying the glade with his eyes alone and not moving in any direction. Certainly not to the edge of the pit like she'd planned for him to do.

She turned away and fussed with the tarp tied over the cart. When he didn't say anything, she swung back and glowered at him, hands fisted on her hips. He rose to his feet, and she had to tip up her chin to maintain eye contact. "I suppose you're going to say that Gavin will see the trap. That if you can see it, then he'll see it too. But you were looking for it. Gavin will be too intent on Deirdre and Ewan to see anything out of the ordinary."

"Nay. He'll be even more diligent with his wife and son here. But earlier you were adamant that they wouldn't be, which is it, dearling?"

Before she could respond, he took a slow step sideways away from her. Not toward the pit, exactly, but now, at least, he was directly in line with it. The urge to move behind him and shove him into it struck hard, but she knew she had about as much a chance of doing that as she had of moving a mountain. She spun around and strode three steps down the side of the pit away from him—the suspense was killing her, and she couldn't stand still doing nothing.

After a small hesitation, she also stepped sideways so now she was directly across from him—on the other side of the pit.

How can I make him step forward?

She looked up at the decoy and placed her hands on her hips. Then she sighed. Loudly. "So how do I make him not see it, then?"

When he didn't answer, her muscles tightened until she felt pulled taut, like the strings on a lute. After what seemed like forever, she glanced over her shoulder. He stood in the same spot. Watching her.

Nerves tightened her belly and caused a muscle to twitch in her cheek. Thankfully it was the cheek facing away from him or he would have noticed; he stood only three paces behind her.

"Or have you not seen it, after all? Have my trap-making abilities finally outpaced your trap-detecting senses?"

"I've seen it. And I've seen you too."

"Of course you have. I'm right here, Kerr." She smiled at him, softly, enticingly, and then lowered her eyes before turning back.

She strained her ears, waiting to hear a yelp or a grunt. A thud as he stepped toward her into the pit. It wasn't deep, only about three feet, but it was filled halfway with animal dung from the stables—mostly horse manure, but goat, sheep, and cow dung too. He would fall in almost up to his knees, at least.

And he would ne'er forget it. More importantly, neither would she, or his foster family, or either of their clans—the MacAlisters or the MacKinnons.

More time ticked by. She felt like ants were crawling all over her as she waited. *What is he doing?*

She couldn't risk glancing back again. Instead, she reached with one arm behind her neck and slowly pulled her long swathe of hair forward over one shoulder, exposing her nape.

And then she waited.

Five

KERR STARED AT THE BACK OF ISOBEL'S NECK—LONG AND strong, yet also vulnerable and tender-looking. Her hair shone brightly in the sun, and damp tendrils curled around her hairline from their midday ride.

His fingers twitched, wanting to touch the silky tresses, and his mouth watered, wanting to kiss below her ear.

She was Eve to his Adam. Delilah to his Samson.

She was Isobel and he was Kerr, and she would never entice him to her side. Ever.

Unless she wants me there for a reason.

He looked at the ground and saw nothing out of the ordinary— leaves, grass, a few twigs—nothing to indicate anything was amiss. He stepped forward carefully, feeling first with his foot, dipping his toes down…and then he stopped.

There.

He grinned and looked back up at her exposed neck, tempting him closer. Who was he to refuse her? Without another thought, he leapt forward and landed directly behind her—almost on top of her.

Her shriek of alarm pierced his ears as he clamped his arm around her waist and squeezed her against his chest.

So worth it.

"Kerr!" she yelled, her hands clutching his forearms.

Then he lowered his head and pressed his lips to the crook of her neck.

Her skin was warm and soft, and despite the strong smell of manure around them, she smelled sweet like wild roses when he inhaled.

And wasn't that like the dichotomy of Isobel herself? The Beauty of the Highlands was the same woman who made traps filled with animal dung. The Lady of Clan MacKinnon, hostess to great lairds and ladies, also dug through abandoned hedgehog dens to find quills to dump on people's heads.

"What are you doing?" she squealed, her words strained. She rested heavily against him, as if she couldn't hold herself upright.

He brushed his lips along the side of her neck to her ear and nipped the lobe. The air shuddered from her body.

"Exactly as you wanted, am I not?" he asked.

"No, I—"

He nipped her ear higher up. "Truth, Isobel. You lured me across. You wanted me to walk toward you. I succumbed." A hint of amusement laced his voice, and he knew she would hear it, would react to it.

"I did no such thing. You've lost your bloody mind." She regained her strength and pulled his arms away from her middle, then stepped forward and turned to face him. A hectic flush covered her chest and cheeks. Her lips had reddened, and her blue-green eyes glittered at him brightly. They looked like jewels, almost too stunning to be real.

He placed his fingers over the vein that pulsed madly in her neck, fascinated and buoyed by all the signs of her arousal. His heart raced too, and his lips still tingled where he'd touched them to her skin—the first time he'd kissed her anywhere that was remotely sensual.

She glared at him and batted his hand away from her throat. He raised his palms upward in surrender, his grin unhidden now, and lifted his foot as if to take a step backward. "*Och!* I canna go that way, can I?" He stepped forward instead. She refused to give ground when he crowded her, and her skirts brushed against his legs.

"When did you see it?" she demanded, her head tilting back to meet his eyes.

"See what?"

"The second trap," she huffed.

"I didn't. You hid it well. I saw *you*."

"What does that mean?"

"It means I know you, Isobel. I know the sounds of your excitement and the expressions on your face—down to every flicker of your eyes. I know the different ways you hold your shoulders and how your mind works. I know the pace of your walk and what that means about your mood and your intentions."

"Am I so predictable, then?"

"Nay, the opposite! You continually surprise me. You are the most complex, fascinating woman I've e'er met. And you may not want to hear it, but you are mine."

Her eyes narrowed on him, but for a moment, uncertainty had flashed in those blue-green depths. Her body had softened, almost imperceptibly, and she'd arched toward him.

Her jaw, however, remained clenched in anger.

"Did you miss me when I was gone, Isobel? Did you worry about me?"

She dropped her eyes, stared at his chest, and then very softly said, "Aye."

He barely held back a groan.

"But you say I'm yours like you own me, Kerr. I'm not a cow. I'm a woman." Her voice dropped. "I have my own wants, my own needs."

"And I'll meet every one." The blood pounded in his veins, engorging every inch of him.

"You canna. No one can be everything to another."

"I can. To you."

"Not when you annoy me so much."

"You're not annoyed now."

"I am."

"Nay, Isobel. Your body is roused, and your mind is stimulated.

As is mine. You're enjoying yourself even if you're feeling confused and vulnerable."

She stiffened at his words.

He didn't say anything else. Instead, he let her think about everything he'd declared—about the connection between them and his desire for her...his need for her.

She placed her hands on his waist and slowly pushed them up his body until her palms rested against his ribs. His linen shirt felt as light and thin as a cloud between them.

"Then prove it," she said. "Show me why I should be with you."

His eyes jumped to hers, but she'd lowered her lids. His Isobel was brave and strong. Why, if she really wanted what she'd asked for, would she not look at him?

He grasped her waist and took a step backward, sliding one heel over the edge of the pit.

"Are you asking me to kiss you, dearling?"

"Aye," she said, and then closed the distance between them until he felt the swing of her skirt against his legs.

He smiled. "As you wish," and then he slowly lowered his head.

How long would she last? Long enough for them to kiss?

Their first kiss?

She'd softened in his arms, like her resistance was melting, and she leaned into him more heavily...as if she anticipated his touch.

For a moment he let himself believe it, and then her muscles bunched beneath his hands and she shoved hard on his chest, harder than he'd expected. He'd known Isobel was strong, but not quite that strong. Still, he was able to grasp her waist as he tumbled backward, and the triumphant expression on her face turned to horror as she realized she was being pulled into the manure trap with him.

At the last possible second, he bent his knee and shoved off the edge of the pit, propelling them both backward over the trap. He wouldn't know until he landed if he'd gone far enough, and for the first time, he regretted his decision—not because he would land in a little cow dung, that had happened many times before and would again, but because Isobel would land in it too.

He would have hurt her.

When solid ground slammed into his back and her soft body slammed into his, he was filled with relief…and other feelings too. He grunted and squeezed his arms more tightly around her waist, her face tucked against his throat, her breasts pressed against his chest. Small puffs of air warmed his skin as she tried to catch her breath.

God's blood, she was soft against him, so warm, and she smelled so good.

The edge of the pit cut into the backs of his thighs, and he pulled his knees up, his heels on the edge, which forced her legs to straddle his hips. His plaid bunched up between them, his sporran having fallen to the side. From underneath, the open air cooled his privates, so close to hers.

He was as hard as a bloody mountain, and he groaned again as she pushed herself up into a sitting position, her pelvis grinding down on his. Their eyes clashed, and for a moment, lust flared hotly in her gaze. His hands slid down to her hips, and his fingers dug in. Her mouth opened on a wee gasp, and he could see the tip of her tongue behind her teeth, enticing him. She looked undecided, like she was tempted to rock against him.

He was about to lift his hands, to thread them through her hair and pull her down for that kiss she'd requested, when a gruff voice asked from the edge of the clearing, "Lady Isobel, do you need assistance?"

She stiffened, her face flushing a rosy pink as she yelled out, "Nay!"

Brow furrowed, she shoved off his body. When her knee jabbed into that engorged part of him, he groaned—and not in a good way. He breathed through the pain that knifed through his stones and thighs, even into his belly, knowing it was worth every minute as he watched her straighten her clothes, her cheeks still burning, her eyes cast down.

'Twas Lyle who had spoken. Kerr sat up and glared at him. He couldn't tell for sure, but he thought he saw the stony-faced warrior smirk before disappearing back into the forest, leaving Kerr with the illusion, once again, that he was alone with Isobel.

She hurried away from him toward her horse.

"Dearling!" he called out. "Doona forget your manure."

When she made a rude gesture toward him and kept walking, he burst out laughing. "At least take your poor pony. He doesn't deserve to be abandoned."

She untied her mare, and he sat up, grinning. By God, she was magnificent. He loved everything about this woman.

"It's time, Isobel!" he said, his voice deepening and sounding possessive. He didn't want the words to come out commanding, but they did anyway. "We canna keep dancing around like this!"

She stopped, her foot in the stirrup ready to mount, and lifted her gaze to his. "'Tis your own little jig you're dancing, Kerr. I ne'er agreed to accompany you." Then she turned her horse and urged it into a gallop back down the trail.

Six

ISOBEL RODE HER MARE UNDER THE PORTCULLIS AND INTO the bailey with her head held high and her shoulders back, despite the fact that she wanted to pull her plaid over her head and hide.

Her guard had said nothing to her, of course, but she could sense their amusement, and she knew they'd be talking about her later on. Which she wouldn't have minded if she'd been successful.

She gusted out a frustrated breath. How could she have messed up so badly? Kerr hadn't seen the trap—he'd seen *her*. All she'd had to do was ignore him, and he would have eventually tumbled in.

But nay, she'd tried to force the issue, and he'd picked up on her intent—not the trap.

Then there was the fact that he'd kissed her. He'd even bitten her ear! And what had she done? Had she hit him? Or called for her guard? Nay, she'd turned into a weak, blathering fool—not that she remembered a word she'd said.

Remembering would have meant thinking, and as far as she could tell, her brain had turned off.

And her body had taken over. Heat filled her cheeks again. She groaned silently and tilted her chin up higher.

"Isobel!"

Glancing toward the corral beside the stable, she saw Deirdre standing at the fence, waving at her. Behind her, Gavin was in the ring with Ewan, who rode a small, sedate mare.

Isobel hesitated before going over—Deirdre would want details, and she wasn't yet ready to share them. But she couldn't ignore her sister-in-law.

She forced a smile and steered her horse toward the corral. "What are you doing here? I didn't think we'd see you for days," she teased.

"Ewan wanted to show Gavin how he rode his horse. The new tricks he'd learned." She blushed a little and laughed. "He kept knocking on the bedchamber door."

Isobel laughed too, a real laugh, and suddenly she felt a little better. She wasn't the only one who'd been thwarted today.

A groomsman came over when she dismounted. She gave the horse a customary rub on the nose before turning to lean back against the corral beside her friend.

"You told Gavin you're with bairn?" she asked.

"Aye. He's happy, of course, but I can sense a wee bit of worry too."

Isobel looked over her shoulder at her brother—a changed man in the last four months after finding his son and meeting and marrying Deirdre. "Congratulations, Brother! I couldnae be happier for you!"

He walked toward them and gave her a tight hug over the fence. "Me too, Sister. Another bairn for us to cherish."

Behind him, Ewan performed one of his tricks on the horse, and Deirdre's eyes widened with concern. "Gavin!" she squeaked, pointing at their son, who had urged the mare into a trot across the corral.

Gavin raised his brow and strode back toward Ewan. "He knows how to keep his feet in the stirrups, love. Better than some people I know!"

Isobel snorted as Deirdre made a face at her husband's back. He was right. Her sister-in-law was a terrible rider, and for some reason, she couldn't keep her feet in the stirrups…and then she panicked when she couldn't get them back in.

Deirdre stepped closer and dropped her voice. "Now, tell me what happened. I can see from your face that Kerr didnae fall for it."

Isobel huffed, feeling irritated all over again. "My face?"

"Aye. You rode in verra queen-like. Your back straight and chin high. Haughty, even." Deirdre's eyes twinkled, and she pointed at her face. "That expression right there! 'Tis a sure sign that you're displeased about something—usually having to do with Kerr."

Isobel sighed and dropped her forehead onto her arms. "He knew. I was too impatient and tried to get him to step where I wanted him to step. I should have ignored him and done nothing out of the ordinary, exactly as you told me to do. All that work for naught."

"I canna believe I'm encouraging you but…you'll get him next time," Deirdre said, patting her shoulder.

"There willna be a next time. At least, not like that. I need to think of some other way to trick him. One that doesn't involve traps. No more manure or honey."

"Or bees, or prickles, or buckets of ants… Or you could just marry him."

She peered sideways at Deirdre. Her sister-in-law looked amused. And why wouldn't she? Isobel was amusing everyone today. "I think maybe you've missed the point about the manure," she said. "I did not try to dunk Kerr in it because I wanted to marry him. 'Tis quite the opposite. I thought you understood that."

"Aye, so you've said, dearling. And I support your decision, of course, but you have to admit that he's a braw man, and he adores you. The two of you together create sparks like steel against flint. Maybe before you make a decision, you should try kissing him. Or at least try not to fight with him. Give yourself a week or a month where you stop resisting and…allow him in. Who knows what will happen?"

"I can tell you what will happen—my head will burst from the pressure. He said so himself."

She thought back to her conversation with Kerr about *subjugation*, and her gaze sought Deirdre's. "Can I ask you something of a personal nature?"

"Of course. Anything."

Isobel slid closer and dropped her voice. "Does Gavin ever *subjugate* you? Or maybe…you *subjugate* him?"

Deirdre's brow furrowed in confusion. "You mean like…control him? Make him do what I want?"

"Aye, in an intimate way. Bed play. Is this something people do?"

Deirdre's cheeks flushed. "I doona know what other people do, but…well, Gavin's a strong man, and he certainly led our intimacy in the beginning. Sometimes he'll hold me still or…position me," she whispered the last words. "Is that what you mean?"

"I'm not sure. 'Tis something Kerr said. Or rather, how he said it."

Deirdre's eyes widened, and her voice rose. "You've been talking to Kerr about bed play?"

Isobel glanced around quickly, her cheeks heating. "Shhhh." When she saw no one was watching, she leaned toward Deirdre again. "Not really. Just small things to irritate me. He knew I didn't know what it meant."

"*I* doona know what it means. When you finally allow him to *subjugate* you, let me know."

"Allow him to?"

"Aye, although it doesn't sound like you'll have much say in the matter—if you're being subjugated. It could be interesting." Deirdre smiled and winked. Twice.

Isobel felt the urge to poke her friend in the offending eye. The last thing she wanted to think about was interesting bed play with Kerr. She had enough of that in her dreams.

"Mama! Aunt Isobel!" Ewan yelled. They looked up to see Gavin walking across the corral toward them with an excited Ewan in his arms.

"Did you see me?" Ewan asked.

"I did, sweet boy, and you even kept your feet in the stirrups."

Isobel couldn't help the wee jab at Deirdre—not after she'd suggested Isobel let Kerr subjugate her.

"It's nap time, Ewan," Gavin said firmly. He handed his son to Deirdre then climbed over the fence. "Annag will stay with you, while your mother and I have our own nap."

Ewan's face lit up, and he opened his mouth to say something, but Deirdre quickly cut him off. "Nay, you canna sleep with us. Your father was mistaken, we're not napping. We have work to do."

Gavin's eyes closed as he realized his blunder. Isobel bit her lip to stop from laughing.

"What kind of work?" Ewan asked.

"Important work. Mathematical work that you haven't learned yet," Deirdre said.

Isobel snorted. "Aye, your father is using your mother's geometry set to determine the best angle for entry."

Deirdre kicked her in the shin, and Isobel hopped backward, her laugh breaking free. "I didn't say entry to where."

"Entry to where?" Ewan asked.

"To my solar." Gavin lifted his son into his arms again. "Your ma and I will be working in there."

"On the desk, sweetling," Isobel explained. "And your da may be doing all the work. In fact, I think your ma's only there for the ride."

Gavin shot his sister a frown. "Brat," he said, then grasped his wife's hand and led her toward the keep. Ewan stuck out his tongue at her as they retreated, and Isobel returned the gesture, making her nephew giggle.

Deirdre glanced back over her shoulder, a smirk on her face. "Isobel, go get subjugated."

She froze in place, then frantically cast her gaze around the bailey, looking for Kerr, praying he wasn't nearby. When she didn't see him, and no one was eyeing her with shock or, even worse, speculation, she sighed in relief. The last thing she wanted was for Kerr to know she'd been asking her sister-in-law about *that*.

She looked back and saw her brother lean over and kiss the top of his wife's head, their child between them. A wave of longing filled Isobel at the simple show of affection, making her feel the absence of love in her own life all the more keenly.

It surprised her how much.

She glanced back toward the portcullis, her eyes drawn there again as if looking for someone. Then she huffed in denial.

I am not *looking for* him.

But when men on horseback entered the bailey, she couldn't look away. After a moment, she saw Kerr's dark head poking up from behind another warrior. A strange fluttering sensation filled her chest.

God's blood, I am an idiotic woman.

She couldn't help thinking about what Deirdre had said— about letting Kerr kiss her, about letting him *in*, even just for a short while.

Her friend hadn't meant into her body, although that's what Isobel would like, there was no denying that. Aye, she'd more than enjoyed the feeling of him beneath her in the forest, her legs on either side of his hips. And when he'd kissed her neck and bit her ear, she'd had to lean against him for support, her knees turning to mush.

He switched direction, heading toward the stables, and when Isobel saw his face clearly, she let out a shocked gasp... It wasn't Kerr!

This man's face was leaner, finer, and his hair, although the same color and texture as Kerr's, was cut to the base of his neck. Kerr's hair hung down to his shoulders.

When the man drew near, he reined in and dismounted not far from where Isobel stood. Who was he? He was tall like Kerr, and she could see he was strong and knew how to handle his weapon—he'd hefted the claymore one-handed from his saddle and sheathed it across his back without looking—but he wasn't as broad through the shoulders and chest as Kerr. Not many men were, not even Gavin.

He was more like Callum, his body leaner but still muscular, his movements quick and decisive. Still, there was something about him that reminded her of Kerr. Was it the inky darkness of his hair?

She moved a little closer, intrigued, and then froze in place when he met her gaze. And that's where the similarities to Kerr ended.

This man's eyes were a bright blue, and his face, although strong and handsome, didn't hold the power of Kerr's face. She supposed many women would find him attractive, very attractive, but that flutter in her chest when she'd thought he was Kerr had died.

She would have turned away, gone on with her business—a new plan to trick Kerr was already forming in her mind—but the stranger never took his gaze from her...which was unusual. When first meeting her, most men either dropped their eyes in deference or seemed to lose their ability to think and speak.

This man had barely reacted, other than a slight widening of his eyes.

It was...surprising.

The horse nickered and then nudged him, and the stranger rubbed his hand up and down his mount's nose, all while staring at Isobel.

She cocked a brow at him, and suddenly he smiled. Twin dimples creased his cheeks, making him even more handsome. More a rogue.

"You must be Lady Isobel," he said.

"Is it that obvious?"

"To me, it is."

He still hadn't dropped her gaze, and she found herself tilting her head in curiosity. Where would he take this conversation?

Surely he wouldn't flirt with her. She couldn't remember the last time that had happened. She was a laird's daughter, a laird's sister, and born to be a laird's wife, although that was debatable. Men outside of her station, almost all men, it seemed, thought of her as untouchable—because of Kerr and Gavin, but also because of *her*.

Her reputation for justice preceded her. Her power and wealth preceded her. Her physical appearance preceded her—the Beauty of the Highlands. It wasn't that her clan didn't love her—they did, and she certainly loved them—but she had no doubt many people were a wee bit intimidated by her.

Yet this man hadn't looked away. It was almost as if he challenged her. She found herself stepping closer.

And then he ruined it by musing, "As I looked upon thee, I saw a Great Highland Beauty."

Isobel almost rolled her eyes. If this was flirting, she hadn't missed much.

Words flew from her mouth—words that Kerr would have batted back to her. "Nay, sir. I'm sorry to say you're confused. The Great Highland Beauty is the other lass—the red-headed healer from Clan MacKay. Or perhaps you meant the black-haired beauty married to my brother? We doona have a name for her yet, but we're taking suggestions. I'm the Beauty of the Highlands."

His brow crinkled. "I've only heard the song once, and I could have sworn the minstrel said Great Highland Beauty."

"Only once? Oh dear, my popularity must be waning."

He blinked at her. Several times. She barely restrained her smile.

"Perhaps I can write you another one and revive it," he suggested.

"What a lovely idea, but you might name me the Lovely Lass of Loch Linnhe and confuse the matter further."

A muscle twitched in his jaw. Still, he gave her a small bow. "I am but the vessel, my lady. My muse takes me where she wills."

"Are you so easily led, then?"

"By you? Aye."

She bit her lip to stop from laughing. She couldn't tell if he was serious or not. It seemed Kerr had ruined her for conversation with other men.

"Your name, sir? You doona belong to my clan. Are you a MacAlister, perhaps?"

His head snapped back, and his dimples disappeared. "Nay. I'm Branon Campbell of Clan Campbell. Cousin to Laird Campbell."

She raised her brow. "I meant no offense. 'Tis only that you remind me of a MacAlister I know."

"None taken, of course." He smiled again, but this time it didn't meet his eyes. He looked away from her and moved to his saddle bag, which was strapped to his mount's hindquarters. He opened one of them and rummaged inside.

She watched him closely, wondering why he was here. He was a braw, well-spoken man, and it took a certain amount of confidence to speak to her in such a forward, familiar manner.

She stepped to the side of his horse and ran her hand down its warm neck, the fur soft and smooth beneath her fingers. "What brings you to Clan MacKinnon, Branon Campbell?"

"I have some business with your blacksmith."

"He's a fine craftsman. Are you buying weapons from him?"

"Five claymores for Laird Campbell. The MacKinnon black-smith has an attention to detail that our blacksmith does not, although his swords are just as sharp, strong, and well-balanced."

"And as deadly," she said.

"Aye. You doona need a fancy sword to kill a man." His eyes met hers. "Or a woman."

Her hand stilled on his horse. Was that a threat? She sharpened her gaze on him and looked for any telltale signs of anger, but his expression was pleasant, his tone agreeable.

Which was worrying, if indeed he was upset.

What did she know about the Campbells? The obvious, of course—they were a large, strong clan who had warred with many other clans in the past. Their laird, Camran Campbell, was old enough to be Gregor's father, and he was considered a man of great cunning and intelligence, but also a careful man. She'd once heard her father describe him as having the patience of Job.

"Does my brother, Laird MacKinnon, know you're here?" she asked.

"I assume his men reported my arrival. Not much seems to happen in the clan without his knowledge."

"True. You canna get anything past him and his allies."

For some reason, she wanted him to believe the MacKinnons were invincible, but after the near-fatal attack last spring, she knew that to be a fallacy. Every clan could be infiltrated. Every castle could be invaded. Every laird could be struck down.

She thought back on the papers she'd sifted through in her brother's solar. In particular, the parchments she'd studied from Callum's wife, Maggie—cobbled together from when she'd spied on her black-hearted cousin—and the notes that Gavin, Kerr, and the other lairds had added to it.

Nothing about the Campbells had come up in Maggie's report. The lairds had discussed whether that made them more or less suspicious.

She'd always thought it made them more suspicious, but she had a conniving mind.

"Sir!" a voice called from the direction of the stable.

She looked over to see a skinny, pimply-faced groomsman hurrying toward them. Behind him, her guard, Lyle, faded into the shadows of the stable. He must have sent the groom over to break up her conversation with Branon Campbell.

She repressed an irritated sigh. God save her from overprotective men.

"May I help you?" the groom asked Campbell.

"I have business with the blacksmith on the morrow," he replied. "I need to stable my horse."

"Aye, we have room." The lad grasped the reins and shot Isobel a nervous look. Her clan knew she did not like to be handled.

"Eachann," she greeted him.

"My lady," he stammered. Then he grabbed Campbell's shirt sleeve and tugged him toward the stable, the horse trailing behind.

Branon glanced at her over his shoulder and nodded. She nodded back, not bothering with a smile this time.

The man may be tall and braw, and most women probably found him charming and intelligent, but to her, he wasn't tall enough or broad enough. And he definitely wasn't *annoying* enough—and that fact left her both cold and hot at the same time.

Especially when that ever-present *annoying* voice growled at her from behind. "Who was that?" Followed by Kerr's warm, heavy hand landing possessively on her shoulder.

Seven

ISOBEL STIFFENED BENEATH HIS HAND, AND KERR KNEW HE'D made a mistake. But right now, he didn't care.

A dark possessiveness had overtaken him when he'd seen her with that man, and it didn't matter if it was an innocent exchange, he'd been pushed by a primitive instinct to protect and claim his mate.

Marching in long, hard strides across the bailey, he'd arrived just as the man turned and walked into the stables.

Kerr wanted his head…almost as much as he wanted Isobel's heart.

And he couldn't have either…yet.

Slowly, she turned toward him, looking every inch the queen— her eyes narrowed, her back straight, her chin high—and he braced himself for a meteor shower of sharp, cutting words she would surely rain down upon him for his overprotective, possessive behavior.

Instead, she opened her mouth and said, "Mooooo." Like a cow. A really good impression of a cow.

The surprise was enough to bring him back to himself, and his dark side, that he worried was like his father, receded back to where it had come from.

"What was that?" he asked. He furrowed his brow, but he was pretty sure he knew where she was going with this, and he didn't like the uncomfortable feeling that rose within him one bit—guilt, chagrin.

"Mooooo," she said again.

"All right, Isobel. I understand. You doona need to rub it in."

"Mooooo," she repeated.

He sighed in frustration and rubbed his hand across the back of his neck. Trying to figure out what to say—how to get out of this.

"You're making a point. You're a woman, not a cow, and I doona own you, but—"

"Mooooo!"

He planted his hands on his hips and glared at her, but he could see in her eyes she was enjoying herself, and a laugh built up in his chest. Well…if she was his cow, and he was her owner, then she needed branding.

He stepped in close and cupped her cheeks, holding her head lightly in place before leaning in for a kiss.

She jumped back as their mouths touched, and he had a fleeting impression of softness and warmth. "What are you doing?" she exclaimed.

"Sorcery!" he yelled, placing a hand over his heart. "A talking cow!"

She had no trouble sustaining *her* glare. "You doona own me, Kerr MacAlister. I may speak to whomever I please or do whatever I please. Especially in my own home! I am not your wife, your betrothed, or even a member of your family. If I need protection, I have a guard, my brother, my clan. I doona need you."

He winced. "I liked you better when you were a cow. Your soft, sweet mooing didnae hurt my ears so much."

"I'll hurt your ears plenty if you doona get it through your thick primitive skull that I am not yours."

The words hurt, especially as he knew she was right—for now, at least. He tried to look conciliatory as he raised his hand and brushed his palm down the outside of her arm. "But you could be. If you wanted to." He grasped the tips of her fingers between his. "Isobel—"

She let out an exasperated sigh, yanked her hand away, and marched past him toward the keep, her guard moving with her.

They blended into their surroundings and looked like regular castle folk.

He turned to watch her go, so tall and slender in her green and red arisaid, her neat pleats from before a little askew. He reminded himself she'd only been *talking* to that man. Kerr was the one who'd messed up her pleats earlier. And she'd liked it.

He smiled slowly. And she'd liked their *discussion* just then. Aye, he'd seen the way her eyes had lit up in excitement as she mooed at him. Even when she was yelling at him, she'd been excited.

And she'd been more than excited when she'd lain on top of him in the woods earlier, when she'd pushed herself upward and sat with her knees on either side of his hips.

He sighed and rubbed his hand over his chest, the feeling there expanding until it felt like it pushed against his ribcage.

Isobel MacKinnon likes me.

She climbed the stairs, and when she reached the top and pulled open the door to the Great Hall, she finally glanced back at him.

He lifted his hand and waved. "Until later, dearling!"

He could imagine the huffing sound she'd most likely made, and he grinned—until she pointed toward the portcullis and yelled, "Two days!"

Then she turned and entered the keep, letting the door slam shut behind her.

His stomach churned. What exactly had she meant by that? Was she telling him he had to leave in two days?

God's blood! Why didn't I just walk into the pit of manure and make her happy?

A whistle caught his attention, and he spun back toward the stable to see Lyle standing at the doors, signaling for Kerr to come quickly but cautiously. Then he disappeared inside.

Kerr growled and stalked forward. He knew that man Isobel had been talking to was no good. Lyle wouldn't have signaled him without reason.

He paused inside the doors and let his eyes adjust to the dim light. Lyle stood about halfway down the aisle between the stalls. The man who'd been talking to Isobel stood at the door to a stall on the opposite side between them—and he was ready for an attack.

He didn't hold his sword, it was still in the leather sheath on his hip, but Kerr noted the slight widening of his stance, the subtle angling of his body, and how he balanced on his feet to enable sudden movement. He held his hands loosely by his sides, so he was ready to grip his sword and pull it out if either Kerr or Lyle came at him.

The blackheart knew how to fight, and Kerr suspected he would fight dirty. Which suited him just fine.

Kerr leaned against the doorjamb almost lazily, but inside, anger and suspicion raged. More so knowing that this man—this stranger—had been near his Isobel, possibly putting her in danger.

His gaze never left the stranger's face, which remained expressionless. But that revealed as much to Kerr as if he'd looked panicked or fearful. The man was no stranger to conflict and believed in his ability to hold his own against two hardened warriors—especially one of Kerr's size and renowned caliber.

Kerr pulled his knife from his belt, reached for an apple that sat in a bucket on a shelf next to him, and proceeded to peel it.

"Lyle," he said, nodding.

"Laird MacAlister," Lyle replied.

Kerr sliced off a piece of the fruit and put it in his mouth. "Is there a problem?" he asked between chews.

"Could be. I was just asking our visitor why he'd threatened Lady Isobel."

Kerr straightened from the doorjamb, all pretense of being relaxed gone. He eyed the stranger with deadly intent.

"'Tis not true," the man said, his eyes darting from one to the other. "I did no such thing."

But Kerr knew that Lyle was seldom wrong in his analysis of situations, and he had an advantage over most men—he could read lips, and he understood body language better even than Gregor. He'd been born partially deaf and had honed that ability in order to "hear" as best he could.

"Tell me," Kerr said, his voice flat and hard.

"He was intent on our lady, too intent, and when he didnae like how she responded, he said the swords he was here to buy would be able to kill a man…and a woman. His implication was clear—to me and to her."

The stranger's eyes widened with surprise, and his gaze darted to Lyle, the first uncontrolled reaction Kerr had seen from him, telling Kerr that Lyle's interpretation had been correct.

In that instant, Kerr leapt toward the blackheart, grabbing a long, heavy wooden hoe that leaned against the wall, and smashed the handle down on the man's wrist as he tried to pull his sword from the leather sheath.

The man grunted in pain as his sword clattered to the ground. But he didn't cry out as most men would have done, and instead moved to grab Kerr's sword with his other hand, proving he was a highly trained warrior and a dangerous man.

But Kerr was bigger and stronger and even more dangerous, more deadly with the MacAlister rage—his father's rage—burning behind his eyes. He forced the stranger backward into the stall and pinned him against the wall. The horse neighed in alarm, and Lyle smacked its rump to get it out of the way.

"Who are you?" Kerr growled, nose to nose with the stranger. He'd pressed his knife to the blackheart's throat and leaned his body heavily against him so he couldn't move. Lyle stood close beside him, ready to help if needed, but he knew better than to interfere.

Kerr would take care of the man himself for daring to threaten Isobel.

"Branon Campbell," the man finally wheezed, after he stopped struggling.

"He said he's Laird Campbell's cousin," Lyle added.

Kerr eyed the man's face. Something about him looked familiar, but he was certain he'd never seen him before. "I'm acquainted with Laird Campbell, and I know many of his cousins. I doona recognize you."

It was possible the man had lied to impress Isobel. The thought almost made Kerr smile. Campbell could have said he was a king and Isobel wouldn't have been impressed.

"I'm a bastard. My mother was Laird Campbell's cousin. I was raised in a small keep on the edge of the eastern border."

"And now you're close to the laird?"

"Nay, not close, but…I do what he asks of me."

"And what did he ask you to do here?"

"To pick up some swords from the blacksmith. Fancy ones. That's all, I swear." His gaze turned pleading. "Please… Talking to Lady Isobel was a mistake. But I'd heard the songs sung about her, and I was curious. I'm used to…"

"Having your way with women?" Kerr asked through gritted teeth, ready to slice the man's throat.

"Not in that way, I promise! Women like me. They always have. I've…known several highborn ladies."

He was a braw man and probably charming when he wanted to be. All good qualities in a spy. "And yet you threatened Lady Isobel?"

"It wasn't a threat. Not really. I was vexed by her attitude toward me, and I let my annoyance get the better of me. I didnae come here to harm anyone."

The words rang with truth, but it didn't mean the man wasn't here for nefarious reasons. Most likely the swords were his cover.

Could it be that Laird Campbell was the head of the conspiracy against Kerr and his allies? The Campbells had always been on the list of clans who had the power and means to provide the money for it.

Looking into Branon Campbell would be a good place to start their investigation.

"Where were you last spring? My foster brother and laird of this clan, Gavin MacKinnon, was injured during a failed attempt to kill him and his allies. Gavin was fortunate to recover. He canna remember many details of the attack except this...the leader of our enemy had hair as dark as mine."

Branon's eyes widened. "Are you saying that because my hair is dark, I must be this man? If I were, I'd be an idiot to come back here."

"I agree."

Footsteps sounded behind him, and Branon darted his eyes over Kerr's shoulder. A soft whistle told Kerr it was his foster brothers and Gregor, alerted by Lyle's men, no doubt.

Kerr tightened his hold, and Branon brought his gaze back to him...and this time he looked worried.

"I asked you a question," Kerr said.

Branon licked his lips. "I wasn't anywhere near Clan MacKinnon when the attack happened. I was in Edinburgh all winter. I ne'er returned to the Highlands until last month. Several high-ranking people—including members of the clergy—can vouch for me."

Good to know. They could send their own spies to verify the information and find out what this man had been doing in Edinburgh.

'Twas significant that Branon Campbell had so far remained unknown to them. Kerr suspected he might be one of Campbell's most valuable assets. A man that well-trained was trained for a reason.

The question was what to do with him now—interrogate him further and see if they could break him, or set him free and follow him? He would assume he was being followed, of course, but Kerr suspected interrogation would not yield the results they wanted. Worse, they might be given false information and end up farther away from the truth than before.

"Gregor?" he asked, knowing his foster father would understand—they were at a crossroads.

"'Tis your call, lad," Gregor said.

He took a moment to decide, and then chose his words carefully. "Branon Campbell said he's here to collect some swords for Laird Campbell. Bring the blacksmith here to verify his story. Apparently, the laird appreciates his artistry as much as we do. A good artisan is hard to come by."

Artisan was a code word, and someone left the stable immediately to bring back the blacksmith...but also someone else.

Years ago, Gregor had woven a web of spies throughout the other clans that Kerr and his foster brothers had since added to. They'd also sent an artist into the clans to draw people's faces— the laird's family, important warriors and advisors, possible spies. The artist, Alec, could see a person one time and create his or her exact likeness.

Before they let Branon Campbell go, his face would be recorded, and then they'd distribute the drawing to their web of informants. Branon's days of living in the shadows were over.

"Is this the kind of peace and protection the great Gregor MacLeod and his sons bring to the Highlands?" Branon asked indignantly. "I meant Lady Isobel no harm. Maybe I flirted a wee bit, but certainly not enough to bring death and destruction to all our clans. Laird Campbell will not take kindly to me being abused."

So, he'd decided to try and bluff his way out of his predicament. Kerr would play along. Maybe that would alleviate the man's suspicions when he was finally released.

"We only protect the innocent...and punish the offenders. I willna hesitate to beat—and kill—any man who threatens what is mine to protect."

"No one is killing anyone," Gregor said, sounding a little irritated.

"Aye. You need to be certain," Darach said. "I canna afford another war at this time. I wouldnae have Caitlin worried unnecessarily with our wee bairn arriving so soon."

"Same. Maggie needs me at home. I doona want to leave again, if 'tis only a misunderstanding. We know how you feel about Isobel, Kerr. Is it possible you overreacted?" Callum asked.

"Nay. Lyle confirmed it." He would play the stubborn accuser who was won over by his brothers' and Gregor's reason.

"Lyle's made mistakes in the past," Lachlan said.

"Not this time. I saw it in the blackheart's eyes."

"'Tis not unusual, surely, for men to be interested in Lady Isobel," Branon reasoned. "Do you attack and interrogate all of them? Threaten to kill them? And the guard was nowhere near us when I spoke to your lady. No matter what tricks he used, he surely couldnae have discerned my words."

Footsteps sounded behind him as more people entered the stable. "Kerr," Gavin said, moving to the front to stand beside him. His blond hair was mussed, and his plaid looked like it had been hastily thrown on. If the situation weren't so serious, Kerr would have grinned at Gavin's bad fortune—finally he was back with his wife, but duty and family kept interrupting their reunion. "The blacksmith is here. Let Branon Campbell go so we can ask him our questions."

Kerr met Branon's eyes. The man was too highly skilled to give anything more away, but that didn't matter; the interrogation was a ruse intended to give Alec time to study the blackheart.

Kerr released him. "Come forward, Bruce," he said as he turned his head to look for the blacksmith. In the back, shrouded in shadows, he spotted Alec, avidly taking in every detail of Branon Campbell's face.

Bruce stepped up beside Kerr. "Aye, laird?"

"Do you recognize this man? He says his name is Branon Campbell and he's here to buy swords from you."

"I've ne'er seen him before, but I *am* expecting a man by that name. He's to buy five of my swords for his laird—the fancy ones. Has he done something wrong?"

"Aye, he threatened Lady Isobel."

"I did no such thing!"

But Bruce knew better than to doubt Kerr, and he scowled at Branon. "The blackheart! He'll have no swords from me."

"I believe your telling is true, Kerr..." Gavin said, holding up his hand as Callum and Darach protested, "...but I willna risk war at this time. We've been besieged from all sides. Clan MacKinnon, all of our clans, needs time to rest and regroup. I'm sure Isobel would understand."

He walked forward and stared into Campbell's eyes. "If my family have no more questions for you, you may go—immediately and without your swords—but doona return to my land. Ever. Else you'll lose your head."

Gavin turned and left the stable. Then a whistle sounded outside. The message to the warriors was clear—be vigilant.

Word would spread. They had an enemy in their midst.

Kerr stepped back and let Branon Campbell walk away.

Eight

KERR TOOK THE STAIRS TWO AT A TIME UP TOWARD THE highest turret in Castle MacKinnon. The lairds had regrouped in Gavin's solar after the interrogation, and they'd all agreed that Branon Campbell was most likely a spy, putting Laird Campbell at the top of the list for who led the conspiracy against them—or at least provided the men and the gold for it.

Gavin remained adamant that the man who'd led the attack against him last spring, the tall one with the long black hair, was the leader. If Laird Campbell was involved, and it made sense that he was, the other man was still the driving force behind the attacks.

But Gavin had also said that Branon Campbell seemed... familiar. Kerr had had the same feeling, and his gut was telling him Branon was more than just a pawn or a soldier.

They'd released him only after Alec had finished his first few drawings and their trackers had been set in place. He had no doubt they would lose Branon at one point, but now that they knew his face, they would find him again.

He paused on the landing at the top of the stairs and placed his candle next to another lit one in a wall sconce—a clear indication that someone, most likely Isobel, was outside. This was a favorite spot of hers when she wanted to be alone.

Perhaps he shouldn't disturb her. He hesitated and looked back down the stairs. If she hadn't ordered him out of her home in two days' time, he would be able to continue their courtship at a slower pace. But even with the progress he'd made with her today—touching her intimately for the first time—he didn't think he could convince her to marry him so soon.

Every moment had to count.

He reached into his sporran for a leather tie and secured his hair at the back of his neck. He knew from experience that the wind blew harder up here than down below, no matter what time of day or year. When he was done, he braced his hand on the heavy wooden door, pushed it open, and stepped outside into the cool, gusty breeze.

The turret was only about four paces square, and in the distance, Kerr could see the half-built cathedral, the village, and the forest beyond. The loch snaked down one side of the village.

Isobel sat on the stone floor with her plaid covering her head, her back against the castle wall, and her legs stretched out in front of her toward the battlements.

She did not look up at him when he came out.

He eased the door closed so the wind wouldn't bang it shut, and then slid down the wall perpendicular to her.

The battlements blocked some of the wind from blowing down this low, but it was still cool, and the occasional gust caught his plaid and tried to rip it from his body. Kerr did as she did and tucked the material around his knees and over his head.

He stretched out his legs so their feet almost touched. When she pulled her heels up toward her arse and tucked her skirts in around her knees, his gut tightened.

She would not make this easy for him.

"I remember you coming up here often when you were younger, especially after your father died," he said.

Her fingers, which had been restlessly plucking at her plaid, stilled. "Aye. 'Tis a good place to grieve. No one can hear you if you cry out your heart to the wind."

He nodded. "'Tis what Gavin did when Ewan went missing."

Sadness transformed her face, despite the fact that her nephew had been recovered and Deirdre had been brought into their lives because of it.

"I'm sure this spot felt like his only refuge," she said. "He still had to be laird, he still had to be strong for his allies. He couldnae fall apart, no matter how much he might have wanted to."

"You stayed strong too, Isobel. We managed—all of us—to help Gavin through it as much as we could. We worked together."

"We did."

"You and I made a good team."

Her fingers tapped against her leg—once, and then twice more. She looked at him. "You know what else I do up here?"

He paused, knowing that she was setting him up for something—something he wouldn't like. "What?"

"I think. And I plan. Some of my best traps have been imagined up here."

"Is that what you were doing? Planning another trap...for me?"

She turned her face forward again and pulled her hood farther over her head. "Perhaps. But two days isna much time to execute it."

Two days. It hung in the air between them like an executioner's blade.

"Isobel—"

"Nay, Kerr. I willna change my mind, and 'tis beneath you to beg."

Now *he* tapped his fingers on his leg. If she would not relent and let him stay until fall, how could he possibly convince her? He did not want to spend another winter alone in his castle.

"If I'm to go home so soon, then we doona have much time."

"Time for what?" she asked.

"Time to talk about *us*."

"There is no *us*."

"Aye, there is. There has been for years." He said it quietly, yet with steel in his tone. "We just havenae been saying it with words."

Her brow furrowed. "Your brains are addled if you think me dumping you in manure is the same as me professing our togetherness."

It was a lie. He heard it in her voice and saw it in the way she shoved a stray lock of hair that had blown across her face back under her hood.

"Be brave, Isobel. Take a chance."

"I willna be with someone who annoys me."

"I only annoy you because you want something else from me. Something you're afraid to ask for or to receive. You doona have to be strong with me all the time—like the castle's curtain wall. I'm not an invader. Let me in, and I will fight *with* you, *beside* you."

In a heartbeat, he shifted his body next to hers. She glanced at him, startled, and panic crossed her face.

At me being so close? Or at the conversation we're having?

Or her response to it?

He trailed his knuckles down her cheek. "If there's something between us, something I've done in the past that's hurt you, tell me so I can make it right."

Something flashed in her eyes. Pain of some kind.

"What is it, love? Isobel…let me in."

For half a moment, he thought she would relent; he could see she wanted to, but then she pulled her head away and scooted sideways—still within reach, but their bodies no longer touched.

She cleared her throat and then said, "Two days, Kerr."

He ground his teeth together. What could he say to get through to her? They needed time together to dig out what was wedged between them, to relearn how to behave with each other. She had to know that he was her safe place.

"If I am to go home in two days' time, Isobel, then you shall be coming with me—that is what we need to plan for." There. He'd said it. Truth…even though she wouldn't want to hear it.

Her brow rose. "I'm not going anywhere with you. Besides, I have other plans."

"What kind of plans?"

She shrugged.

"Tell me, Isobel!" His voice had deepened, and he knew he wasn't doing himself any favors.

"My plans doona include you, Kerr. They are not your concern."

"Are you going somewhere?" he rasped.

She looked at him, her lips pressed tightly together.

"For God's sake, Izzy, answer me!"

"I havenae decided yet, but it looks better and better by the second that yes, I am going somewhere. Is that what you wanted to hear?"

"Nay! I want to hear again that you missed me when I was gone. That you worried about me—like you admitted to before. That you were happy to see me arrive back safe and sound. That when I kissed your neck today, your knees grew weak and shivers ran up your spine. That when we spar, or you try to trick me and dump me in a pile of dung, you feel more alive than at any other time during your day. That when you see my hands, or my body, or my lips, you think about them touching your hands, and your body, and your lips.

"That when you see me, *really* see me, Isobel, that you know I *really* see you too."

Her cheeks had flushed a bright pink, and her mouth had parted on a little "oh." The vein in her neck beat quickly, matching the quick pace of his own heart.

He took a breath, tried to calm himself before he said…

"Isobel, I want you to marry me!"

———

Emotion swamped Isobel—turbulent, choppy waves of ecstasy and anger, disbelief and frustration, desire and denial—all underscored by a great need and confusion. She experienced so much all at once that she didn't feel like she could contain it within the confines of her body.

She wanted to burst into tears. She wanted to laugh and whoop. She wanted to run away screaming. She wanted to hurl herself into his arms.

To shout *"Nay!"* To sob *"Aye!"*

Isobel wanted to melt into his skin so no space existed between their bodies, so she was a part of him and nothing existed but *them*. But she also wanted to hit him. Hard. To shove him backward against the wall and…and what? Crawl up his big, braw body? Or smack him in that beloved face?

Nay, not beloved—smirking face!

She squeezed her eyes shut and shook her head. Being with him scared her to death. Kerr would take her over. Not only would she lose herself, she'd be left with no ability to think for herself.

"You canna force me to go anywhere," she rasped, ignoring what he'd asked her. How his words had made her feel.

She finally looked at him. He'd raised his brow, his eyes intent on her. A muscle twitched in his jaw above his scraggly black beard that he'd probably hacked at with a knife and no more. Rarely had she seen him clean-shaven. The last time had been at Gavin's wedding. She'd wanted to rub her fingers over his skin then, feel the tiny prick of the whiskers growing back in. Now, after two months of him sleeping around campfires and bathing in streams, she wanted to scrape her fingers through the coarse hair, grab hold of it, and tug.

He rubbed his hand over his nape and sighed. "Then doona make me leave the day after tomorrow. Isobel, I asked you a question."

She shoved herself up from the stone floor, and he rose to face her, his big body swamping hers in every way—taller, broader, thicker, harder. And blocking her from the door.

Fear at her own weakness drove her, and she stumbled backward until she hit the battlements behind her. He followed, his arms raised to steady her.

She wanted to swat his hands away, but at the same time she wanted him to pull her safely into his arms and tuck her beneath his chin.

Like he had before.

Turning around, she leaned on the merlons that topped the stone wall and tried to remember every reason why she didn't want to be with Kerr. All the things he'd done or hadn't done, said or hadn't said that had turned her against him—and she had a list of them, starting when she was fifteen.

And she vividly remembered each one.

All the words they'd exchanged were etched into her memory. Every time he'd touched her was burned into her skin—especially after today.

He stepped up beside her, not touching her, and they stared outward. The wind tugged at her hair and clothes, whistled in her ears, and she felt battered and buffeted both inside and out.

She closed her eyes and tried to focus. Took a deep breath in… and exhaled.

Doona get distracted, Isobel.

When she opened her eyes again, she felt calmer. Back in control. Kerr had asked her to marry him. Why had that surprised her? They both knew what his expectations were for them.

But there was no *them*. No *us*.

And she didn't have to say yes.

Besides, she had another goal. Another plan she'd already put into motion. One that had formed in her mind as she'd ridden back to the castle from her failed trap site and crystallized when Kerr had treated her as if she were a cow and Branon Campbell was set on reaving her from his territory.

Kerr intimidated any man who might look at her with appreciation in his eyes.

Well, if he was willing to chase after real suitors, he could chase after imaginary ones too.

She raised her chin and pulled back her shoulders, most likely looking haughty and queenly, exactly as Deirdre had said. "Do you want to know how I knew Branon Campbell was either addle-pated or up to no good?" she asked.

That muscle jumped again in his cheek. "How?"

"He tried to entice me. A subtle tease and seduction. No sane man would do that, knowing what you would do to him."

He frowned. "You make it sound like—"

"Nay," she interrupted. "I doona make it *sound* like anything. I am stating fact. You have made claims on me that I do not accept. You have threatened people who might want to get close to me. You have forced me to act in a stealthy manner, to hide my behavior and my true feelings from my friends and family…in case you hurt someone I care about."

He spun toward her. "I havenae hurt anyone!"

"You haven't had to. Yet."

"God's blood, Isobel. Branon Campbell could be a spy, a thief, an assassin. I was protecting you, and I willna stop doing that. Ever. And what do you mean you hide your true feelings? What aren't you telling me?"

The wind tugged her plaid from her hair, and her long locks tangled angrily around her shoulders. "'Tis not your business, Kerr. We are not married, nor are we *betrothed*." Her voice trembled a wee bit as she said it, and she took a quick breath before continuing.

"For future reference, I want you to know that I have ne'er spoken to Branon Campbell before today, so doona make assumptions that aren't true about him, or me, in the next few days. Doona make assumptions about any man in my acquaintance that aren't true."

His brow pulled down over his eyes, and she felt like a mouse being observed by a hungry hawk. He seemed to grow bigger, harder, darker all at once. Yet he also stilled in a way that she found so disconcerting, so deadly. She understood that he changed when he sensed a threat, especially to those he loved—or in this case, an unknown threat to *them*—but it never made it any easier.

"What kind of assumptions do you think I'll make, Isobel?" His voice was low, the words clipped. "And why?"

She'd set up her trap, more of a trick this time, and now she had to carry it through—without any buckets of ants, pits of manure, or bags of hedgehog quills to give her away.

Still, she had a moment's hesitation. *How big is the price to fool Kerr like this?*

"You might assume that I have been with someone. A man. That I have feelings for him. And that I plan to leave with him."

"Who?" he ground out, those hawk-like eyes narrowed on her and his jaw clenched.

"Perhaps no one," she said. "Perhaps I havenae decided yet. Perhaps I ne'er will."

He moved closer, and her heartbeat accelerated—fear and excitement dancing in her blood.

"Tell me, Isobel. Now."

"Or what?" she asked.

He ran his hand up her arm and under her hood to cup the back of her neck. "Perhaps *I* havenae decided yet," he said.

The last time she'd experienced Kerr's dark, deadly stillness, so different from his usual personality, was when Gavin had lied to them so he could separate Deirdre from Ewan—in order take her back to her former husband and break Ewan's bond to her.

Thankfully, her brother had changed his mind and returned home with Deirdre, a changed man.

And Kerr had come back to himself.

But not this time. Not yet.

Anger rode hard on the heels of her fear, and she poked her finger into his chest to emphasize her words. "Your implied threats and possessiveness are not loving, or exciting, Kerr. They're controlling and manipulative. And I willna stand for it. Ever. I am free to do as I like, to choose whomever I like.

"And I doona choose you!" Isobel lifted her skirts and darted away from him to the door. He reached it at the same time she did and simply laid his palm against the wood to stop her from opening it.

She wrenched on the handle several times before glaring up at him. The wind had torn back his hood, and strands of inky hair whipped around his face. The color of his eyes had intensified, turning them darker than she'd ever seen, and all that power that emanated from him was centered on her.

She didn't know whether to quake in her boots or glory in his undivided attention. It was like being showered with primal potency.

"Let me go, Kerr."

"I will ne'er let you go, Isobel."

"Did you not hear a word I just said?"

"I heard everything you said. I always do. And I know when you're lying. You've been mixing lies with truth e'er since I came back this afternoon."

She stretched up as high as she could and tried to look down her nose at him, even though he towered over her. God's blood, the man was a giant!

"Then hear this truth. I'm going to open the door now, and you are going to let me pass. You canna hold me against my will. You are not a monster, even though you act like it sometimes."

"Are you sure about that, sweetling? I feel verra much a monster right now. You've banished me from your home, and you've implied there's someone else you have feelings for—and that you may be going away soon. What am I to think, Isobel?"

"You can think whate'er you like. You're a free man and I'm a free woman."

"Nay, we are tied to each other. Mayhap not through words or ceremonies but through something deeper. You are meant for me, Isobel MacKinnon, as I am meant for you."

"Perhaps, but I still get to *choose*, Kerr. And I havenae chosen you."

"Yet. You haven't chosen me *yet*."

He stepped back and removed his hand from the door. She yanked it open, her hood falling off and her hair catching in the wind. But when she tried to step inside, he wrapped his arm around her middle and pulled her back against his body.

He cocooned her—an oasis from the cool, blustery wind. When his lips touched her ear, she shivered. "Doona do something you'll regret because you want to defy me, love. We aren't enemies. You and I doona spark against one another to make ash, we create flame."

Nine

KERR WATCHED ISOBEL DISAPPEAR DOWN THE CIRCULAR stairwell, her candle in her hand, the bright curls that had escaped her plaid hanging in disarray past her waist.

His jaws were clamped so tightly together, he didn't know if he could ever open them again. Surely his teeth had fused together. He held onto his control with the smallest thread—any more pressure would snap it in two.

She'd been wrong when she'd said he wasn't a monster. He'd come from a family of monsters, and their blood coursed through his veins. Right now he felt like tearing into living flesh and bone. In particular the man with whom she was, or perhaps wasn't, running away with.

He heard her footsteps fade, and then waited another minute, counting down from sixty in his head. When he finally reached zero, he stepped through the open door and into the darkened stairwell. He didn't bother with a candle, even though darkness enclosed him. He liked the darkness. He chose it.

His feet barely skimmed the stairs as he ran downward, his hand on the wall helping him balance, his mind counting once more with every step. When he reached the level where Gavin and Deirdre's bedchamber was located, he stepped out into the lit passageway and strode to Gavin's door, not caring one whit whether he was disturbing him and Deirdre or not.

He pounded hard on the wood—three quick knocks, a pause, and then two slow, so Gavin knew it was him and to hurry.

Still, it seemed to take forever.

He was about to knock again, when he heard the bar slide back.

The door yanked open and Gavin stood there in his thigh-length shirt and nothing else, his hair mussed and a glower on his face. He blocked Kerr's view into the room and most likely had a sword in his hand on the other side of the door to be safe.

No one had the luxury of being careless anymore—even in their own castle.

"This had better be good," Gavin gritted through his teeth.

"'Tis about Isobel. Meet me in your solar." Kerr turned on his heel and continued down the passageway. Behind him, the door hinges squeaked. He assumed Gavin had stepped into the hall.

"God's blood, I'm a little busy right now!" his foster brother yelled.

"I doona care," Kerr yelled back.

He continued to march toward the end of the passageway while Gavin cursed behind him before the bedchamber door thudded shut. Kerr expected his brother was dressing and kissing his wife goodbye.

He felt ornery enough to hope he'd caught Gavin at the worst possible moment.

When he reached the laird's solar, Kerr fished out his key, unlocked the door, and stepped into the room. The wooden shutters were already open, letting in the daylight. He crossed to the hearth, crouched in front of it, and layered the tinder with the kindling. After grabbing the fire striker and flint from the mantel, he set the wood aflame. He was adding more logs to it when Gavin stormed in.

"I'm here. What is it?" his foster brother asked as he strode across the wool rug toward his desk.

"Isobel has ordered me to leave Clan MacKinnon in two days. She said that she may be leaving as well...with another man."

Gavin spun toward him. "What?"

Kerr rose, his hands curling into fists at his sides. "She implied that she's been hiding her true feelings from us for some time."

Gavin snorted. "That doesn't sound like my sister. Who is this man?"

"I doona know."

"Is he a MacKinnon? Where did she meet him and when?"

"I doona know that either."

"Well, what do you know?"

Kerr sucked in a deep, tense breath and tried to release his anger and fear, his worry that he'd lost Isobel for good, but it didn't work. "Not much." He let out a dark growl. "God's blood, I am not prone to words right now. 'Tis my fists that want to do the talking, and according to Isobel, that's part of the problem."

Gavin sat down heavily behind the desk, facing him. "She's right, Kerr. You canna threaten every man who shows an interest in her."

"And when exactly have I done that? O'er the winter when I'm not here? O'er the spring and summer when I've been away fighting battles with my allies? Besides, if a suitor willna stand up to a threatening stance or glare from me, then they're not good enough for *my* Isobel. Would you have let someone bigger than you or stronger than you keep you from Deirdre? Nay, you would have died to get to her."

Gavin shoved his fingers through his hair and released a pent-up breath. "It doesn't matter what you think or what I think. It only matters what Isobel thinks, and if she wants to be with a man who willna lay down his life for her, then that is her mistake to make."

Kerr made a disparaging sound in the back of his throat. "You doona believe that any more than I do. You would step in."

Gavin grunted. "Probably. But Deirdre's been impressing upon me that Isobel can make her own choices—as my mother wanted. How would you feel if the situation were reversed?"

"Pretty damned good." But he knew that wasn't true.

How would I feel? Trapped. Controlled. Like my mother.

A wave of doubt hit him, crushing him from the inside until he could barely breathe.

His father had been a monster. His uncles and cousins had been monsters. They'd beaten down his entire clan for generations.

And I'm one of them.

Shame slithered through his belly, and he swallowed back the bile that rose in his throat. With heavy strides, he crossed to the chair in front of the desk and slumped into it. "Maybe 'tis for the best. My blood is bad."

Gavin made an exasperated sound. "Christ Almighty, doona start that again. You are not your father, Kerr. You doona rape or torture or kill people for your own pleasure. You kill to protect people, which is why you killed your father. And you didn't stab him from behind. Nay, you waited until he attacked you—still just a lad. A big one, aye, but not the brute you are today. And now look at the health and prosperity of your clan. You're a good man, with good blood. Your mother's blood."

Pain welled inside of Kerr at the mention of his mother—her soft, sweet voice and gentle hands, her kind words and loving heart—and he leaned his head heavily in his hands. "If only he'd left her alive long enough so I could protect her too."

He heard Gavin's chair scrape back, and then his foster brother leaned across the desk and laid his hand gently upon Kerr's head. "Aye, Brother," he said softly. They stayed like that for a moment before Kerr lifted his head. Gavin pulled his hand away and sat back. "Now, tell me exactly what my sister said so we can figure out what to do. If we push her too hard, she'll run to this other man to spite us—and that canna happen with our enemies in our midst."

Kerr scraped his nails through his beard as he thought back on their conversation. "She was vague at best. She said she had plans that didn't include me and that she may, or may not, be leaving soon—with someone else. She insinuated she's been seeing this man in secret, and that I forced her to hide their…courtship."

Gavin snorted. "And you believed her? Isobel could no more keep something like this quiet than Ewan could."

"She might if she thought I would kill the man."

"Would you?"

Kerr sighed. "Not if she truly loved him and he loved her…but if I thought he was using her or had hurt her in some way—aye, in a heartbeat."

"As would I," Gavin said. "Or at least banish him from my land on threat of death."

"We canna let her run off, it isna safe. We have to do something."

"Are you sure she isna tricking you? If it's a secret, and if she's worried you'll hurt this man, then why would she tell you about him?"

Kerr's shoulders sagged. "Because I asked her to marry me."

Gavin's head jerked up. "You did?"

"Aye."

"Well, what did she say?"

Kerr sat back in his chair. "She said naught at first. I could see she was conflicted and confused. And defiant, of course. But 'twas good to put into words what's between us. She needed to hear them, and I needed to say them."

"Aye, 'tis good to be direct. Hopefully, she'll come around."

Kerr's brow raised. "Did you not hear a word I said? She isna planning to come around, she's planning to elope with someone we've ne'er met."

"I heard you, but…"

"But what?" he asked, exasperated by Gavin's hesitancy.

"If she has truly chosen someone other than you, if she truly loves that person, then we have to accept it."

"Bah! She doesn't love him—whoever he is."

"I agree. I suspect my sister is up to one of her tricks again. Doona give up on her, Kerr."

"I'm not going to, but she's told me to vacate your home in two days. If I canna convince her to marry me by then, I'll not see her again until spring. 'Tis too long, Gavin. We need time together, so

I can court her and break through her walls. I doona want to be alone this winter, and I canna woo her from a distance."

"I'll speak to her. You can stay here for as long as you like."

He shook his head regretfully. "Nay, you canna override her on this. It will not work in my favor." Kerr squeezed the bridge of his nose. "I need more time."

"What are you thinking?"

He shrugged. "Maybe you shouldn't know."

Gavin shot him a hard look, and Kerr raised his hand to waylay any protests, then continued. "If she is planning to run off as a way to get back at me—at us—then I need to act quickly. I've lost too much time already. And there's something wedged between us—not a man, something else. I need to unearth it and that willna be easy. Isobel will resist." He raised his eyes to Gavin's. "We need time alone."

Gavin's face turned dark. "You will not take advantage of her, Kerr. You will be married, with her consent, before you bed her, or I will have your head."

"I wouldnae do that, and you know it. I will ne'er be with your sister in that way until she is my wife." He shot Gavin his own dark look. "Not like you had planned to be with my cousin before you married her."

Guilt etched Gavin's face, and he slumped back in his chair. "Aye, you have a point. But the situation between Deirdre and me was different."

Kerr grunted, unwilling to concede the point. "That doesn't change the fact that you have no moral high ground on which to stand. 'Tis fortunate *I* still have mine."

Gavin muttered something under his breath that sounded suspiciously like "*ablach.*"

They sat in silence, each lost to their thoughts, and then Gavin asked, "Do you want me to speak to her?"

"Aye, and Deirdre too. We need as much information as we can get. But doona come across too strong. She'll only dig her heels in. And doona tell her she has to let me stay. 'Tis her home, not mine. If I am truly unwelcome, I willna remain."

———————

The knock on her bedchamber door startled Isobel. She jumped up from her desk and quickly shoved her papers under the pillows on her bed.

Deirdre's voice came through the door. "Isobel, are you in there?"

She crossed the wool rug that covered the stone floor and opened the door.

Her sister-in-law stood in the hallway with her hair mussed and her cheeks flushed.

It looked like Gavin had been pulled away unexpectedly—by Kerr, no doubt.

Things were already going to plan.

"What's going on?" Deirdre asked.

Isobel tugged her inside, cast a quick glance into the empty passageway, and then closed and re-barred the door. When she turned around, Deirdre had crossed the room and was perusing the blank parchments on her desk.

"What do you mean what's going on?" Isobel asked as she joined her friend.

"Kerr pounded on our door a few minutes ago and dragged Gavin away. It must have been important or Gavin would ne'er have left—certainly not at that moment."

Isobel smirked. "Why? What were you doing?"

"Geometry," Deirdre said, and they both laughed. "What have you done now?"

"What makes you think I've done anything?"

Deirdre shot her a look, and Isobel sighed. "Fine. I have done something. But I canna tell you what it is."

"Why not?"

"'Tis a secret."

Deirdre's face fell. "Doona you trust me?"

"Of course I do! But if your husband, who is also your laird, demands you tell him where I am, and impresses upon you that I might be in danger, then you would be hard-pressed not to tell. If you doona know, you willna be caught in the middle."

Deirdre's eyes widened. "Where are you going, and what danger? Och, love, what have you gotten yourself into?"

Guilt swamped Isobel. She'd been pondering how best to trick Kerr, and she knew that the best way to do it would be to include Deirdre—to use her trustworthiness and her good nature to make Isobel's lie seem real.

Yet how could she do that to her beloved sister-in-law and friend? She sighed. *I canna.*

She led Deirdre to the side of the bed and sat on the edge of the mattress with her. "'Tis naught to worry you, Deirdre. Just another one of my tricks. And I willna be in danger, I promise. 'Tis something I've done many times in the past."

"I'm already worried. Isobel, we were recently attacked, and Gavin was almost killed. Ewan was taken for almost two years. Our enemies will not hesitate to take you too if they catch you."

"No one's going to catch me. Gavin has his best men guarding me." Technically she hadn't lied. She just didn't elaborate that if all went according to plan, Lyle and the rest of her guard wouldn't be there.

"Then tell me what you're planning."

"Nay. It will be a surprise to everyone. Including you. Besides, Kerr will be able to read your every emotion. He'll sniff out the trick, if I'm not vigilant."

"Can you at least tell me what the trick is, if not how you're going to execute it?"

Isobel wavered. If Kerr had told Gavin what Isobel had told

him, then it was only a matter of time before Deirdre found out. Best if her friend heard it from her first. But she'd have to choose her words carefully.

"In the next day or two, Kerr may worry that…I've run off and married someone else." She said the last quickly, wanting to get it over with. Saying it out loud made it seem worse, somehow.

A look of horror grew on Deirdre's face. "That's awful! You canna do that."

A ball of guilt grew in Isobel's stomach. She jerked to her feet, trying to squash it down. "And dumping him in a pit of manure was all right?"

"Nay, but…at least he was expecting you might do something like that. This is different."

"Why?"

"Isobel, it will tear him apart. He'll go berserk when he finds out. Have you thought of that? He could hurt someone."

"He already knows, and I made sure he understood it wasn't anyone from around here."

"Then who does he think it is?"

"It doesn't matter who he thinks it is. He just has to catch me eloping and discover I'm alone. That's the trick—there ne'er was another man. I will have won!"

She said the last triumphantly, and Deirdre gave her a quizzical look. "Won what?"

An unsettled feeling filled her belly. She didn't know how to explain to Deirdre the dynamic between her and Kerr. "I will have beaten him at this…whate'er it is that's between us."

"So the two of you are at war?"

"I ne'er said that."

"A contest?"

She huffed out an exasperated breath. "The man is annoying, and he baits me. He figured out my trap earlier today. I wager he willna figure out this trick."

"So 'tis a mental challenge."

"You could say that."

"And by making him believe your trick, you've proven that you're smarter than him."

"Nay! 'Tis not about being smarter. 'Tis about…winning this round." She didn't know how else to say it.

Thankfully, Deirdre's face cleared. "Ah, I see. You're outwitting one another. And then what?"

"What do you mean?"

"Well, if you win this round, you'll be even with him. He won one, you won one. Will you then marry him and put your contest aside? You could build a wonderful life together—have bairns, help your clans, grow old with each other. Be friends rather than enemies."

Her jaw tightened. "Kerr isna my enemy. He's my…my… adversary. And I didn't say I would marry him."

"So, what, then? Is the purpose of the ruse to push him away? What if he ne'er comes back to you, Isobel? What if he lets you go?"

She pressed her lips together, a strange feeling in her chest— like it was being squeezed from the inside out. The urge to yell at her friend intensified. "Where are all these questions coming from? 'Tis a wee game we're playing, naught more."

"So it's fun to fight with Kerr?"

"Doona put words in my mouth, Deirdre."

"I'm sorry. I'm just trying to understand."

"Well, you doona, obviously. 'Tis something between me and Kerr that I canna explain. *He* will understand." She spoke harshly, her chin raised and her words clipped—her tone of voice one she'd never used on her friend.

Quiet descended upon them, suffocating them. Deirdre's fingers trembled on her lap before she curled them into her palm. She dropped her eyes, like she used to when they first met.

Regret and sorrow filled Isobel. She quickly sat down, wrapped her arms around Deirdre, and squeezed her tight. "I'm sorry, love. Forgive me."

Deirdre hugged her back. "Nay, I'm the one who's sorry. I shouldnae have questioned you in such a way. You're right. 'Tis between you and Kerr. I just hope it will lead to what you truly want, and not what you think you want."

Isobel's brow furrowed. *Isna that the same thing?* She shook her head to clear the unsettling thought and sat back.

"Does Gavin know it's a trick?" Deirdre asked.

"Probably."

"But Kerr will believe it."

"Maybe... Yes, I believe he will."

"He has more to lose than Gavin," Deirdre said softly. "He'll lose you." Their eyes met, and Isobel's heart stuttered. "Things may turn out differently than you think, Isobel. You ne'er know what the future will bring. Look at me and your brother. Married. Parents to Ewan. Another bairn on the way. Five months ago, I ne'er imagined that was even possible. There may be someone else in your path...in Kerr's path too. Someone new without the years of strife between you. Someone...easy."

If Deirdre's words had meant to soothe her, they were having the opposite effect. Anxiety had curdled her stomach, and Isobel rose from the bed.

She paced to her desk and sat down. "Aye, you may be right." She said it with a lightness she didn't feel.

Smoothing the blank piece of parchment, she then picked up her quill and dipped it into the ink. She liked to name her plans, but she hadn't been able to come up with a good title for this one yet. The last trap had been called the Manure Maneuver. She'd been quite pleased with that one, not that the great name had done any good. The best she'd been able to come up with for this one was the Suitor Surprise or the Suitor Swindle—and they were both shite.

Suppressing a sigh, she left a space at the top, refusing to believe her lack of a good title might be a bad omen. Then she began scribbling on the parchment.

"What are you writing?" Deirdre asked, crossing to stand behind her so she could see the parchment.

"A list of things to do. The first step is done. I've dropped hints about my upcoming elopement, and Kerr has told Gavin about it. I'll cross it off as soon as I've written it."

Deirdre snorted as Isobel finished the sentence and then crossed it off with a hard stroke before starting a new line. "Next, I need to write a letter for Gavin that Kerr will find." She re-dipped her quill as she thought about it. "I'll leave it on Gavin's desk in his solar. Or maybe have someone slip it under the door. Kerr has his own key. He'll see it."

"You think he'll open Gavin's correspondence?"

"Well, if he doesn't, he'll go find Gavin to open it. By that time, I'll be gone."

"Gone? Isobel, you said you would be safe!"

"I will be, but Kerr needs to come after me and know where to find me. I'll leave clues for him to follow. Doona worry, Deirdre. He'll find me. He always does."

She raised the quill and ran the soft end of it back and forth over her chin. "Maybe I should speak to Father Lundie."

"About what?"

"About anything, really. Kerr seeing us together is more important than the actual conversation."

Deirdre shook her head. "Poor Father Lundie. He's too dear a man to be used for your nefarious purposes." She walked to the washstand by the window and poured herself a cup of water from the jug that sat beside the basin. "Oh, I forgot! He willna be here. He's leaving for Clan MacAlister on the morrow. He received word earlier from the priest there."

Isobel crinkled her brow. "Well, that speeds things up. Now it will have to be tonight. Ah well, 'tis better this way. Kerr willna have time to process everything, and he'll be more inclined to act from emotion rather than reason. 'Twill work in my favor."

A knock sounded at the door, and then Gavin called out, "Isobel, it's me."

"Shall I answer it?" Deirdre asked.

Isobel nodded, and then turned over the parchment on her desk.

She rose, smoothing her palms over her dress and straightening her shoulders. It felt like putting on armor, and she thought back to what Deirdre had said...

Am I at war with Kerr?

Deirdre pulled the bar across and opened the door.

Gavin stepped inside and kissed his wife on the lips, lingering for a moment. "What are you doing here, love? Are you helping my sister plan and plot?" Deirdre immediately looked guilty, even though she'd been doing nothing of the sort.

Isobel strode toward them. "'Tis not your concern what I'm doing, Brother."

"It is when I hear you're planning to elope with a stranger."

Gavin met Isobel's gaze over Deirdre's head. The speculative look in his eye—almost as if he knew something she didn't, understood something she didn't—had her raising her chin defensively.

"He isna a stranger to me, Brother, and 'tis my choice whom I marry. Mother made certain of that on her deathbed."

"Then tell me who it is so I can get to know my new brother-in-law."

"Nay. I'll not have him subject to your scrutiny."

Deirdre's eyes popped open. "Isobel, you said you weren't really—"

"Hush, love," Gavin interrupted her. "Let my sister have her games. She'll need something to comfort her in the long, lonely nights ahead."

He gently nudged his wife toward the door. Isobel stepped aside as he opened it. He kissed her cheek before whispering into her ear, "It willna work, Sister. You'll be left out in the cold. Alone."

A chill rose within her, and she shivered. He wasn't talking about her plan tonight.

Was she pushing Kerr too far? Too hard?

Gavin wrapped his arm around Deirdre's shoulders, and she wrapped hers around his waist, and then they walked together along the passageway to their bedchamber, their steps in sync, their bodies and hearts woven together.

Isobel's gut tightened, and her chest clenched. She lifted her chin a fraction higher. "Doona underestimate me, Brother. He'll come!"

Ten

KERR SAT ON THE BENCH AT A TABLE IN THE GREAT HALL, tapping his fingers on the wood. The sound of the pipes playing a feisty reel filled the air, but his fingers were not tapping in time to the music. Nay, they were tapping in time to his growing worry and frustration.

Where is she?

The tables had been pushed back, and Gavin's clan, and warriors from the other clans, filled the large room—dancing, laughing, eating, and drinking. It was a celebration of their victory—a *cèilidh*. A celebration of life in the Highlands despite the struggles for power that took so many innocent lives—even with the protection of lairds like Gregor MacLeod and his foster sons.

Kerr sat back far enough so he could see all four entrances to the Great Hall—the main entrance, the side entrance that led out past the kitchen, the sets of stairs on opposite ends of the hall that bracketed the great hearth and led up to the living quarters of the laird's family. Isobel had disappeared into her bedchamber hours ago and hadn't come down yet for the celebration.

He was about to drag Deirdre away from Gavin and send her up to bring Isobel to the feast, when a bright swathe of white-blond hair caught his attention. He whipped his head around to see her standing on the first step of the staircase closest to him, glancing around the room. She had a smile on her face as if she were simply enjoying the dancers and the music, but her eyes landed intently on each face.

She's looking for someone. For me? Nay, her gaze never strayed toward his despite how close he was.

She must have seen him when she first came down—before he'd seen her—and now she avoided his eyes. He was about to go to her when she stepped off the stair and walked purposefully into the crowd.

Her chin was raised in that haughty way he loved—the one that made him want to kiss her until all that attitude and queenliness melted away.

He noticed a folded piece of parchment in her hand that she tucked into a deep fold of her arisaid as she passed in front of him. A letter? Or maybe a list? Isobel loved making lists.

She disappeared into the crowd, and he rose from the bench to keep an eye on her. She should be easy to see with her height and bright hair, especially since he towered over almost everyone, but she was gone.

He strode quickly around the table and moved into the throng of revelers. The people stepped back to make way for him, drunken smiles etched on many of their faces. Finally, he spotted her sitting at a table on the far side of the room, deep in conversation with Father Lundie—the priest who had married all of his foster brothers and whom he hoped one day would marry him and Isobel.

The father had a befuddled look on his face, and then his brow rose in surprise at whatever Isobel had said to him. She lifted her hand from the table to pat his arm in reassurance, and Kerr noticed the parchment she'd put in her pocket moments ago now sitting on the table where her hand had been.

She glanced up when he approached and quickly covered the parchment again, drawing it closer toward her.

She leaned forward and whispered into the priest's ear, causing his cheeks to redden. Kerr stopped directly in front of them, his eyes jumping from one to the other.

"Father Lundie. Isobel," he said in greeting.

The priest smiled up at him. "Laird MacAlister, please join us!"

Isobel's brow furrowed before she dropped her gaze and angled her head downward—which meant she didn't want him to read her expression.

Because she's hiding something?

He sat on the bench across from them and pushed his foot forward until it bumped into hers. She flicked her gaze upward, and he saw annoyance there but also excitement.

Aye, she was up to no good, and his blood surged in anticipation.

"Lady Isobel was just asking me about handfasting," the priest said. "'Tis considered a binding ceremony before God, of course, but you must know that the two of you doona need—"

"Father Lundie!" Isobel said sharply.

He swung his gaze toward her, looking befuddled again, and hesitated. "My lady…'tis only that I'm leaving on the morrow for Castle MacAlister to see Father Grant…'tis early enough in the season that you could travel there for a wedding…or I could come back and perform the ceremony here, of course…I'm sure I willna be long." He stumbled as Isobel's frown deepened with every word. "I only meant that you doona need to resort to handfasting…"

Kerr also frowned, growing still on the outside, while inside, that dark part of him raged. *Why is Isobel talking to the priest about handfasting?*

She quickly tucked the parchment into her arisaid, stood up from the bench, and then darted into the crowd again. Kerr rose as well and stared after her, but as quickly as before, she disappeared.

He fought the urge to bellow her name. Instead, he stepped onto the bench for a better look. He should be able to spot her from here.

A bright flash—there!

She was talking to her guard, Lyle, at the base of the second set of stairs that led up to the keep's private quarters. She'd pulled up her plaid like a hood so her hair was covered, but she'd turned back to look at him and he'd seen the bright flash of long blond tresses hanging down the front of her body.

Their eyes met over the boisterous crowd, and this time he did bellow. "Isobel!"

People looked up at him, raised their drinks, and laughed, but the clans were too intent on enjoying themselves to pay him much attention.

But she'd heard him. Aye. And she proceeded to ignore him.

With a raised brow and a tilt of her chin, she turned back to a stony-faced Lyle, who listened to her with his arms crossed over his chest, his gaze shifting between the two of them. She pulled out the parchment from her arisaid and pressed it into his hand. He nodded—once—and then tucked the letter into his sporran, before Isobel lifted her skirts and took the stairs upward, two at a time.

What was in the parchment?

Kerr stepped off the bench and marched toward Lyle, his eyes boring into him. People darted out of his way. Some of the braver men and women smacked him on the back as if encouraging him on his journey.

Lyle's expression never changed, and his gaze never wavered.

Kerr stopped in front of him, and neither man spoke. Finally, Kerr said, "What's she up to now?"

Lyle shrugged, and Kerr knew that unless Isobel was in danger, Lyle would give nothing away. He would never break his lady's trust.

Kerr dropped his eyes to the man's sporran and the letter hidden inside. "Give me the parchment and I'll take care of it." Lyle would never hand it over, but maybe he would throw something Kerr's way—like who it was addressed to.

"Nay," the guard said simply.

"Why not? You canna leave your post yet. I promise to deliver the letter for you."

"I am to hand deliver it, as soon as it's convenient."

"To whom?"

Lyle's lips stayed closed. Kerr threw his hands in the air in frustration. "God's blood, man! Give me something. We both know the person Isobel needs protection from the most is herself. She's planning something, and you'd better hope she doesn't get hurt while she's doing it or you willna see the light of day!"

Lyle never even twitched. Finally, he said, "'Tis her brother who will protect her. I'll do as *he* asks."

Kerr scowled at him. That was true, of course, but also utter shite. Lyle would take matters into his own hands if Isobel were in danger. He wanted to protect her almost as much as Kerr did, as much as Gavin did.

Then it dawned on him, and he searched Lyle's face again. If he could hear the warrior's thoughts behind that impassive expression, he was certain they'd be filled with the verbal equivalent of eye-rolling and foot tapping.

Aye, Lyle had given him a message, but Kerr had been too hot to pick up on it right away.

He spun back to the crowd, intent on finding his foster brother—doing exactly as Lyle had told him to do. Again, the crowd parted as he made his way through it.

The last place he'd seen Gavin was in Deirdre's arms, dancing a feisty reel, but they weren't on the dance floor anymore. He stood on the bench again for a better look, and after scanning the crowded dance floor, he finally saw Gavin leading his wife toward the other set of stairs on the opposite end of the hall from where Lyle stood guard. They were going to disappear upstairs.

Hell no!

It gave Kerr a perverse sense of satisfaction to whistle a sharp, piercing note that stopped his foster brother in his tracks. Gavin looked back over his shoulder with a frustrated frown and immediately saw Kerr standing on the bench. Deirdre passed him and kept going, tugging on her husband's hand, but Gavin pulled her into his body for a hug and spoke into her ear. She nodded, and then proceeded by herself past the other guard stationed at the foot of the stairs and disappeared up the stairwell.

When Gavin caught his eye again, Kerr jerked his head toward Lyle. Gavin nodded, and with one last, longing gaze toward the empty stairwell into which Deirdre had disappeared, he reversed his steps.

From his perch on the bench, Kerr saw his other foster brothers and Gregor also heading in the same direction. They'd all heard the whistle and seen Kerr signal Gavin.

He pushed through the rest of the crowd, a little rough this time in his impatience. Gregor and Lachlan already stood beside Lyle, waiting. Callum and Darach arrived next, and then finally Gavin.

Lyle didn't look the least bit intimidated by being surrounded by six imposing lairds. Especially Gavin, who had a scowl on his face.

Gavin's eyes drilled into Kerr. "This had better be good. I have plans with my wife."

His brothers snorted. Over the years, they'd taken great pleasure in foiling each other's romantic interludes. That hadn't stopped when they'd married.

"Deirdre looked done in after all that dancing," Lachlan said, his eyes laughing. "I'd be worried if I were you."

"Aye, she needs as much *sleep* as she can get at such a delicate time," Darach added.

Callum patted his arm. "Treat her gently, Brother. Let her rest. Deep down, I know Maggie appreciates all my coddling." He grinned as everyone scoffed.

Kerr's impatience rose. "God's blood, everyone stop talking! Pretend your lives depend on it…because, believe me, they do!" he threatened.

Silence reigned for a moment before Darach, Lachlan, and Callum burst out laughing. Gregor placed a calming hand on

Kerr's arm, but he could see the amusement in his foster father's eyes too.

"For the love of God, Kerr, why am I here?" Gavin grated, his hands fisted on his hips.

Kerr pointed at Lyle, who didn't even flinch. In fact, he suspected the bastard was enjoying himself. "He has a letter from Isobel and he willna let me see it."

"It's for you?" Gavin asked with a confused frown.

"Nay, it's for you!" He switched his attention to Lyle. "Give it to him now!"

Lyle didn't move, other than to shift his gaze to his laird.

"Lyle?" Gavin asked with an exasperated sigh.

"Lady Isobel gave me a parchment, and she asked me to give it to you…and only you." He dug his hand into his sporran and took out the folded piece of paper that had Gavin's name written across it in Isobel's distinctive handwriting. Lyle handed it to his laird.

"How long ago did she give it to you?" Gavin asked.

"Nay more than a few minutes. Laird MacAlister was dogging her heels. He signaled you almost immediately."

"What does it say?" Kerr asked, even though Gavin hadn't opened it yet. He crowded behind his foster brother for a better look, resisting the urge—barely—to snatch it from him. His gut was hammering at him that something was about to go very wrong.

"Not here," Gregor said. "Take it up to Gavin's solar. We'll look at it there."

"'Tis probably another of Isobel's traps. And Kerr is stepping right into it," Lachlan said.

Kerr gnashed his teeth together, and then he grabbed the parchment and raced up the stairs. Gavin cursed loudly and chased after him, but Kerr didn't care. If he had to wait one more minute to know what Isobel was up to, he was going to start breaking things.

Could she really leave me and elope with another?

The thought left him feeling cold and scared, but also hot and furious at the same time. Panic beat within his chest like a trapped animal.

The other lairds followed behind them. Their boots scuffed on the stone steps and echoed loudly in the circular stairwell.

When Kerr reached the top, he marched down the shadowy hallway, lit by candles in wall sconces every few feet. His eyes darted to Isobel's door as he strode past, but he resisted knocking. He needed to see what was in the letter first.

At the end of the hallway, he stopped in front of Gavin's solar and looked back at his foster brother, barely able to contain himself. Gavin scowled at him and snatched back the letter before he fished out his key from his sporran and swung the door open.

He walked to his desk and sat down. Kerr stood directly in front of him.

"Take a bloody seat, you donkey," Gavin said.

Kerr didn't want to, but he forced himself onto one of the chairs. Behind him, he heard the clang of the poker and another log being added to the fire. Sparks crackled, and the room brightened.

Gregor placed a lit candle on Gavin's desk as Gavin finally broke the seal on Isobel's letter. He opened it as the other men settled in around them, some standing, some sitting in additional chairs.

When Gavin's jaw tightened and a muscle jumped in his cheek, Kerr sprang up from his chair. "God's blood, what does it say?"

———————

Isobel sprinted past the kitchens and toward the keep's side exit near the stables, praying she'd been successful in avoiding her guards. She didn't have much time. Kerr would be right behind her once he'd read her letter and searched her room.

She'd exchanged the soft, fine clothes and slippers she'd been wearing at the *cèilidh* for rugged boots she'd be able to run in, and a sturdy wool arisaid in grays and browns that would blend into the night. Then she'd tied back her bright hair and grabbed her bag from under the bed.

The clues she wanted Kerr to find in her bedchamber had been planted earlier in the day—her mostly empty wardrobe, her desk cleared of all her parchment save one piece of paper that had fallen beside the bed with a partial list penned onto it—including items such as extra blankets in case one fell into the loch—and she'd hidden a pewter love token under her pillow that her father had bought her at a spring market when she was a lass. She'd fallen in love with the pretty flowering heart back then, and he'd happily indulged her.

She didn't think Gavin would recognize it, since he'd been living with Gregor and his foster brothers by then, and she hoped Kerr at least would believe it was from another man.

Pushing through the heavy wooden door at the end of the hallway, she stepped out of the keep and into the dark bailey. When she could see well enough to make her way, she hustled along the perimeter, passing several lovers clinched together. A frisson of envy jolted through her every time she came across a whispering, panting pair, and she couldn't stop the images from earlier in the day flooding her mind—Kerr holding her from behind as he nuzzled her neck, her body lying on his with her legs spread across his hips, her head tucked beneath his chin as he swung her in a circle.

She didn't stop at the stable for a horse. Instead, she wasted no time heading toward the portcullis on foot. She planned to walk through the gates with a smile on her face like she owned the place.

Her brother may be laird here, and Deirdre his new lady, but she was the old laird's daughter, and she'd been taking care of everyone since her mother had died. No one would stop her.

She lifted her chin and repeated those words to herself as she made her way around the bailey.

It was still early enough that a few people streamed into the castle, but no one, other than her, was heading out. She decided that if the guards tried to stop her, she'd bluff her way through with a smile on her face.

As she approached the gates, a large group entered from outside, talking and laughing. One of the guards stopped to talk to them. A second guard eyed her closely as she walked around them on her way out.

"My lady," he called out when he recognized her, sounding startled.

She waved and kept going. "Good evening, Kenneth. I willna be long!"

"Where's your guard?" The young warrior followed her, his brow furrowed with concern.

She laughed and pointed into the inky darkness ahead of her. "Didn't you see them? Ah, well, 'tis not your fault. Lyle could sneak through a room full of hounds without alerting them. Keep a sharp eye out for the men behind me, though. Doona let them sneak by too!"

Kenneth slowed and looked back toward his abandoned post.

Isobel squeezed his arm. "'Tis all right, lad."

He nodded and hurried back. "Thank you, my lady. They willna get past me this time."

A niggle of guilt flared in her breast. She had no doubt he would catch hell from Gavin and Kerr for letting her continue without a chaperone, but when she thought about Kerr's face when she sprang her trick—and the chagrined expression he was sure to be wearing—she decided it was worth it.

So what if she was outside of the castle walls on her own for a short while? All the village folk came and went by themselves. All the maids and cooks in the castle walked around freely on their own. Those women didn't have a guard.

Still, she glanced around a little uneasily as the night swallowed her up. Deirdre's words circled in her head: *Our enemies will not hesitate to take you too if they catch you.*

A shiver ran up her spine. She straightened her shoulders and walked faster.

She had a long way to go if she intended to beat Kerr to the loch. Hooking her leather bag firmly over her shoulders, she lifted her skirts and sprinted along the path.

Few people could run as fast she could with her long legs and quick stride, and even less people could run as long as she could without having to stop. Tonight, she needed both speed and distance.

When she reached the halfway point to the village, she slowed and came to a stop near a lone Scots pine. In the distance, the half-built cathedral loomed faintly against the moonlit sky.

Where is he? She caught her breath and peered into the darkness.

A whicker sounded softly, and then a voice whispered, "My lady."

She let out a startled squeak and clapped her hand over her mouth.

"I didn't mean to scare you," a lad said, his voice cracking mid-sentence and dropping an octave. He stepped out from the shadows of the tree, pulling a horse by its reins.

"Alick?" she asked.

"Aye."

She heaved a sigh of relief and squeezed the young man's arm. "Did you have any trouble?"

"Nay. Everyone assumed I was coming up for the *cèilidh*."

"And you are." She took the reins from the lad. "Go enjoy yourself. I saw Flora inside, dancing up a storm. No doubt she misses you." Isobel moved to the side of the horse, stepped up into the stirrup, and swung her leg over the saddle.

Alick remained where he was, looking up at her. "Are you certain you want to do this, my lady? I'll come down to the loch with you. Make sure you're all right."

"Doona worry, lad. My brother and the other lairds will be right behind me. Naught will happen. Have fun tonight…and thank you!"

She pressed her heels into the horse and clicked her tongue behind her teeth. Alick stepped back as her mount surged forward. A gleeful, perhaps even wicked laugh escaped her as she guided the horse onto a less travelled path that led down toward the loch. The rocky beach was her favorite place for a picnic, and a good spot to anchor a boat.

Not that she intended to go far on the damn thing. Rowing over the loch was the last way she wanted to travel, and Kerr knew it. But her home was almost entirely surrounded by water. If she were truly eloping, she'd have little choice.

Tonight, however, was just for show. Thank the saints she didn't intend to push off from shore—at least not far. She'd never learned how to swim, no matter how much she'd practiced. She was too skinny to keep her head and body above water easily, and eventually she'd sink like a bag of bones—which sometimes she thought she was.

A day at the beach never involved a leisurely swim for her. More like wild thrashing in the water as she tried to stop herself from drowning.

When she arrived at the edge of the sand, a horn blared in the distance, the note long and haunting. She whipped her head around and peered into the darkness as if the man she'd run from could cross the land between them in one giant stride and emerge out of the night like a Celtic warrior of old—sword in hand, massive chest and shoulders blocking out the moonlight, and an intent stare on his face reserved for her only.

An excited shiver raced up her spine.

Kerr was coming for her.

Kerr stormed across the bailey, Isobel's letter crushed in his fist. Torches lit up the darkness. Revelers who'd spilled out from the *cèilidh* quickly stepped back when they saw him coming.

His face felt etched into a permanent scowl.

After reading Isobel's letter and finding her room empty, his brothers and Gregor had tried to convince him that Isobel was setting him up. Gavin was near certain of it and thought he should leave Isobel to stew in her own mess, but Kerr refused to listen.

He couldn't take the chance they might be wrong.

Hopefully, she *was* tricking him—lying about the other man in order to best Kerr in some way. If that were true, it meant she *wanted* to be caught, *wanted* him to chase her.

But does she still want me?

Or was this Isobel's way of proving to him that he'd never be more than the foil to one of her tricks?

An icy fear crystallized in his veins, and the air punched up from his lungs in a sudden *whoosh*. She'd been slipping away from him for years, and he'd just let her drift like a skiff floating away on the loch as he'd helped his brothers secure their clans and their futures...their families.

But now it was his turn. He had to make Isobel listen to him, to *hear* him. And he needed somewhere private to do that—without her brother or her guard getting in the way, without Deirdre or this other man claiming her attention.

But first he had to find her.

As he approached the stable, he whistled sharply. A groomsman came running with Diabhla saddled and ready to go. Someone must have given the order already.

When a grim-faced Lyle followed behind Diabhla with the rest of Isobel's guard, Kerr cursed under his breath.

He didn't have a plan yet, but he knew whatever it was, Lyle wouldn't like it. Gavin either, although Gavin would understand—and trust him—even if he kicked Kerr in the arse when he saw him again.

Aye, *that* was a certainty.

It wasn't the first time she'd evaded her guard, and Kerr knew it wouldn't be the last, but this time felt more urgent. And not only to him—he could see a pinch of worry at the corners of Lyle's eyes.

"'Tis worse than we thought," Lyle said. "I received word that Branon Campbell escaped his guard before he crossed the border. He could be anywhere."

"God's blood! We knew we would lose him, but not this soon. What happened?"

Lyle shrugged and mounted his horse. "She's about fifteen minutes ahead of us. She didn't take a horse from the stable, but she did ask earlier if she needed a special bridle to take a horse across the loch. So…we could assume she has a horse—provided by someone else—and she plans to cross with it to the mainland."

Kerr mounted Diabhla and urged the stallion toward the portcullis. Lyle fell in beside him. "Or we could assume that she's set a false trail and isna going anywhere near the water. 'Twas obvious you'd ask the groomsman about her horse."

It suited him to nudge Lyle in a different direction. If she was with another man and they were making a run for the border, as her letter suggested, Lyle would find her before she left MacKinnon land. But if this was an elaborate ruse set up for him, he wanted to be alone when he found her.

Lyle fisted his hand around the reins. "I agree. She's a clever woman. Maybe too clever this time."

The observation irritated Kerr. Isobel wasn't too much or too little of anything—she was just Isobel. Smart, caring, amusing, devious—and he wanted the whole of her, not just parts of her. Aye, she had her faults, but so did he.

He inhaled deeply before speaking to calm his temper. Even so, his words came out clipped. "We'll cover more ground if we split up. She may talk her way past the sentries at the ports and the borders, the same as she did with the guards at the gate. You should go there."

"And where will you go?" Lyle asked as they passed unhindered under the portcullis and onto the open road, picking up speed.

"I doona know yet. I need to be alone to hear what my gut is telling me."

Lyle frowned. "If she's with someone else—"

"She's not!" Kerr reined in and spun toward Lyle, who did the same. The others gathered around them on their horses. "She's waiting. For me."

There. He'd said it. And to his relief, he realized he believed it.

"You don't know that. She may not choose you."

"Aye. But she's not choosing anyone else either."

"You canna stop her, Laird MacAlister."

"I doona have to. She'll stop herself."

"For her sake, I hope that's true." Then Lyle whistled sharply and veered off with his men, shouting instructions to them as he went.

Kerr heaved a frustrated sigh and squeezed the back of his neck. He'd been terse with Lyle and regretted it. Not that the man would care; he was too focused on doing his job to be put off by Kerr's rudeness.

He turned Diabhla back to the path and urged the stallion into a trot. They knew from the guard at the gate that Isobel had come this way on foot.

Unprotected.

The thought sent a chill up his spine. He leaned forward and Diabhla picked up his pace. His enemy, and that of his allies, was still out there, still plotting against them. The conspirators would love to get their hands on the beloved sister of Laird MacKinnon and future wife of Laird MacAlister.

Where would Isobel go? He knew how strong and fast she was, and he suspected she'd broken into a run as soon as she was out of sight of the castle. But was she still on foot? Or had someone given her a horse?

A lone tree loomed ahead of him, a common place for people to meet, and Kerr slowed. He peered at the ground, looking for signs in the dirt that she'd been there, but the light from the moon shone too weakly for him to make out fresh prints. He could light a torch, but he shouldn't need to—not when Isobel had planted clues for him to follow.

He looked up at the tree again, and then turned to a faint path that led away from the main road toward the loch and a small, rocky beach. They'd taken Ewan there for a picnic the day Gavin had snuck off with Deirdre, intent on returning her to Lewis MacIntyre. Fortunately, Gavin had brought her home again that night.

Was that where Isobel had gone?

He closed his eyes, tried to quiet his doubt and fear so he could hear what his heart, his body, was telling him. There, deep in his gut.

An urge to ride forward.

He pressed his heels to Diabhla's flanks, and the stallion broke into a swift canter.

The anticipation of what he would find at the beach beat at his imagination, and he quickly tempered it—he couldn't be distracted by his own hopes or fears.

He would deal with what he found when he found it—and if an opportunity to get closer to Isobel presented itself to him, he would take it.

After what seemed like an eternity, the trail ended at the top of a bluff, and he heard a horse nicker nearby. Drawing his sword silently, he guided Diabhla off the trail and dismounted.

Loosely tied to a branch on a scraggly tree, a mare stood with her ears pricked forward. She'd turned her head to watch Kerr and Diabhla approach. When he rubbed his hand up her nose and whispered soothingly in her ear, she leaned into his palm and huffed out a breath.

Did the horse belong to Isobel or to someone else? He dropped Diabhla's lead and softly commanded him to stay put, before approaching the edge of the bluff, crawling on his belly the last few feet.

He squinted, trying to make out the shapes in the dark. Someone was crouched by the water where a small fishing boat with oars had been pulled onto the sand. The figure rose, and he almost whooped triumphantly.

It appeared to be a woman—a tall woman—although it was difficult to get a sense of perspective from up here. Her hood was pulled over her head, so he couldn't be certain, but deep down he knew it was her.

She moved like Isobel. She held herself like Isobel. She had the shape of Isobel.

And she seemed to be alone.

He waited a few more minutes, watching her, trying to get a sense of her plan as she paced beside the boat. She looked often toward the bluff and the bottom of the trail that led to the beach, like she was waiting for someone.

For him? Or her mysterious lover?

She crouched down again and fiddled with something on the beach. Then she rose and shoved the vessel into the water while she remained on shore.

What's she doing?

The boat glided out about fifteen feet and then stopped. She tugged on something next to a large rock—maybe the rope—like she was testing it.

Aye, that was it exactly. The last thing she wanted was the boat to get away, especially with her on it. Isobel was fearless about everything except being on the water.

She must be planning to board the boat and then let it float out to sea like she was escaping. But without actually drifting away.

That was the trick. She wanted to make him think she was eloping when she wasn't.

He sighed and scrubbed his hand through his beard. His fingers scraped through soft, trim strands instead of the thick scraggly mess he was expecting. He'd forgotten he'd asked one of the maids to thin and shape his beard before the *cèilidh*, as well as fix the uneven way Gregor had hacked off his hair after they'd taken the MacIntyre castle. The heavy mane was barely long enough now to tie back with a leather thong.

Which he would do if he was going into battle—and this *was* battle.

My toughest and most important one yet.

He reached into his sporran, pulled out a tie, and secured his hair at the back of his neck. Then he returned to the horses and set Isobel's mount free with a slap on the rump. The mare ran back in the direction of the castle. Someone would find her tomorrow.

A plan was forming in his mind—one that would upset numerous people. But if it brought him closer to Isobel, it was worth it. Act now and apologize later had seen him through many complicated situations in his life.

This was one of them.

He ran his hand over Diabhla's flank and found the waterproof leather pouches over the horse's rump. After untethering them, he hung them around his neck. The rain wouldn't soak through the leather, but a full dip in the loch would not keep the water out, and the essential goods he always carried would end up drenched.

Grasping the reins, Kerr led the stallion away from the main trail Isobel expected him to ride down and toward the head of a steeper trail he knew emerged onto the beach closer to the boat. If she was watching the other bluff, it would also put him behind her.

He might be able to surprise her, and she wouldn't have as much time to make her escape.

Not that he didn't want her to. Aye, that would play right into his hands.

At the trail's head, he dropped the reins and whispered for Diabhla to halt. He didn't want the horse to lose his footing and run him down, even though he was more likely to take a tumble in the dark. Over the years, Diabhla had proved that his senses were sharper than Kerr's at night.

He waited until Isobel turned away from him and paced in the opposite direction along the shore. Her steps on the loose rocks echoed loudly in the quiet of the night, making his ire rise all over again.

She was alone, unprotected, when their enemies could be anywhere—*anyone*. And they were deadly.

He maneuvered down the steep decline—knees bent, crouched over, hands grabbing rocks and shrubs to stop him falling. He reached the bottom as she turned around and saw him. She stopped in her tracks with a loud gasp as he straightened to his full height.

"Isobel," he said evenly, so she would know it was him and wouldn't be frightened.

She let out a squeak—a sound she would surely deny were he to remind her of it later—before lifting her skirts and dashing toward the boat. The exertion caused her hood to fall back and the bright strands of her hair to loosen behind her. Her long, quick gait ate up the distance.

He could have beaten her there, but that wasn't his intent. Nay, he wanted her on that boat.

Striding toward her, he let out a sharp whistle for Diabhla. The stallion whickered in response before following Kerr down the trail, his hooves thumping on the dirt path and loosing rocks that slid noisily to the bottom. When he reached the beach, his iron shoes clipped rhythmically along the stony shore toward Kerr.

Isobel shoved hard on the boat to push it into the loch, and then she scrambled on board, her skirts and leather shoes getting soaked in the process. Fierce triumph shone on her face in the moonlight as the skiff glided away from him.

His heart expanded proudly, and a grin tilted up the corners of his mouth. That was *his* lass. She hadn't trained in weapons, like Callum's wife, Maggie, or self-defense, like Lachlan's wife, Amber, yet she was still out here, executing her plan—successfully!

She'd had to escape the castle, get him here alone while sending the others in another direction, and trick him into thinking she was eloping.

"Well done, love," he shouted as she used an oar to shove the boat out farther, causing the rope to stretch taut between them. Diabhla huffed in his ear behind him, almost as if he laughed at the two of them.

"You canna stop me, Kerr MacAlister," she said, standing to face him, her voice filled with glee. "I love another."

"I doona intend to stop you. I intend to join you."

"What?"

Without missing a step, he reached behind his shoulder, pulled his big sword from the sheath that was strapped across his back, and in one swing, cut through the rope that anchored the little boat to shore.

"Kerr, nay!" she yelled. He felt a moment's guilt upon hearing the fear and panic in her voice as the boat floated untethered upon the water. Then he hardened his heart. He had to do this. For both their sakes.

He stepped into the loch as he re-sheathed his sword, the icy cold soaking through his leathers and freezing his skin beneath his wool socks. The air had cooled, and the chill wasn't pleasant— the days may still retain the warmth of summer, but at night, fall approached like a charging boar.

Reaching behind him again, he grasped Diabhla's lead and slid his hand to the end before tugging on it. The stallion followed without protest, his hooves splashing into the water.

"What are you doing?" Isobel yelled as she tried to control the boat with the oar—and failed miserably.

In his other hand, he grasped the rope floating nearby that had anchored the skiff to shore. He quickly knotted it to Diabhla's lead and then let go. He stepped toward her, the water rising icily along his legs with every stride. "I canna have you leaving with another, Isobel—whether your intent to do so is true or not."

"You canna stop me. You doona own me, Laird MacAlister!"

"Maybe not, but you sure as shite own me."

He grasped his pack from around his neck and tossed it toward the boat. It landed at Isobel's feet, and she jumped in surprise, her arms flailing as the boat rocked. She tumbled backward and landed on her arse on the wooden bench behind her with a yelp.

He pushed off with his feet and made it to the boat in a few long strokes, fear that she would fall in or toss his pack into the water fueling his speed.

"Hold on," he said, as he grasped the side and then hauled himself upward.

She screeched again, curses filling the air this time as his weight caused the boat to almost tip over—or at least it felt that way. He pulled himself over the edge, and then grasped her arm as the keel straightened, so she didn't fly off the other side and into the water. They had a long night ahead of them. He did not want her soaked too.

Instead, she fell against his chest, causing him to tumble backward against the stern. He squeezed his arm tightly around her waist to steady both of them, and her breath puffed like hot, wet kisses against his neck...and despite the freezing swim he'd taken in the loch, his body stirred as warmth spread through him like wildfire.

He grunted in response, and she raised her face to his—so stunning in the moonlight—her eyes filled with anger and fear, but also with excitement. And something else...desire.

He raised his other hand and stroked back the bright stands of hair that had fallen across her cheek. "Good plan, love. It's worked out beautifully."

Then he cupped the back of her head, lowered his mouth, and for the first time ever, pressed his lips to hers.

Eleven

THE BLOOD IN ISOBEL'S VEINS POUNDED THROUGH HER BODY and whooshed past her ears like a rising gale, blocking out all sound. She could barely think, barely breathe, as Kerr, his lips cool from his swim yet still so soft, kissed her.

He kissed her!

Not tentatively, nay, there was no doubt he'd taken control, yet he didn't shove his way in. Instead, he enticed her, seduced her with gentle, firm pressure that ebbed and flowed like waves, his tongue sliding—barely there—against the seam of her lips. A whisper of sensation exploded into an inferno and cascaded through her body.

She gasped as heat and lust roared within her, causing her lips to part and her body to shudder. She cleaved to him, closer, tighter, her hands squeezing the sodden material of his linen shirt. She wanted to sink into the massive chest and abdomen beneath her, to sink onto the hard ridge at his pelvis.

Aye, exactly like in her dreams. She wanted to be *impaled* by him.

In every fantasy, every nighttime reverie she'd had about Kerr, even when she'd been too young to fully understand them, he had slowly taken her over.

Taken her.

His big hands guiding her, driving her to release. That other big part of him, the cock she'd heard others whisper about when they'd thought no one was listening, the one that was a constant source of ribbing, and possibly envy, between him and his foster brothers, pushing unerringly inside her body.

God in heaven, she ached to be joined to him now.

He groaned as she moved against him, and the vibration rumbled along her skin, setting the tips of her breasts and that heated, heaviness between her legs on fire. She moved again—undulating like an animal in heat—and he squeezed her waist, keeping her tightly in place against him. The other hand fisted in her hair, holding her still, as his tongue thrust into her mouth. He filled the sensitive cavern, rubbing like silk against her tongue and along the roof of her mouth. She thrust back—with her tongue and with that other greedy part of her—her knees opening to ride up alongside his hips.

His mouth tore from hers with a groan, and his head tipped back as she jerked against him again, unable to stop herself—not that she wanted to. Nay, she felt a surge of power, even though she'd completely lost control. And the expression on his familiar face was contorted into one she'd never seen before—a grimace of pained desire.

And she reveled in it.

"God's blood, Isobel!" His voice throbbed with need. "I knew it would be like this between us. A bloody firestorm. But we need to…we have to…"

She felt his resistance building and clung tighter to him. He was denying her, battling with himself to slow things down. Yet even as he said the words, his hand at her waist slid downward along her spine and increased the pressure between them until his palm clamped like a vise around her backside, pushing their hips together as he thrust upward—and all the layers of wool between them suddenly seemed like the flimsiest of silk.

He wasn't gentle this time. His mouth captured hers, and she was ready, open and waiting for him. She snaked her arms upward to squeeze around his neck and drive her fingers into that silky hair, pushing free the leather that secured it. Gratitude that it hadn't been cut so short that she couldn't fist it like he did hers saturated every inch of her, and she gave thanks that the sword that had butchered the locks in battle hadn't swung a few inches closer to the veins in his neck.

She crushed him in her embrace, fear that he'd almost died riding alongside her desire.

When she yanked her mouth free, gasping for air, he dropped his head and kissed down her throat. "Sweet Jesus. If Gavin were to see us now…" He found the pulse at the base of her neck and laved it with his tongue until she shivered. "We should go back, Izzy. We need a priest."

"A priest?" she asked hoarsely. An alarm started ringing in the back of her head, but she was so drenched in feelings and emotions that she struggled to make sense of it.

This is Kerr. We doona talk about priests.

"Aye. Father Lundie is still there. He can marry us tonight."

It took all her willpower, every stubborn inch of her character to slowly push herself upward from his chest. She clenched her teeth and ignored the way their bodies aligned at this new position, the way his hand released her hair and dropped down to grip her hips, his fingers digging into the curve of her arse. She ignored the rumble in his chest and the way his lips parted on a groan. Mostly, she ignored the need to rock against that hardened part of him between her legs—against *Kerr*.

Instead, she forced herself to sit still and the muscles in her face to screw up into a frown. "Are you mad, Kerr MacAlister?" she asked breathlessly, thwarting her attempt to sound queenly and commanding. "I won't marry you—ever! Didnae you receive my letter? I love anoth—"

"Christ Almighty, Izzy!" he roared. "Doona say those words. Especially after the way you just kissed me. Although calling that a kiss is like calling a Valkyrie a sweet lass."

Her scowl deepened, and this time she didn't have to force her face into any expression. Aye, the anger rose within her, replacing the lust that had besieged her so wildly moments ago.

She reached for it now, embraced it in her arms like a woman welcoming home her lover.

Nay, not a lover—a sister welcoming home her berserker brother.

She poked her fingertip into his chest, emphasizing each word. "I will love whoe'er I like—and it willna be you. Row me back immediately. I was waiting for someone."

He captured her finger in his hand, his eyes on her face as he raised the tip to his lips. Kissed it. "I know who you were waiting for."

Her breath caught at the soft, warm pressure, the wet flick of his tongue on the sensitive skin. She tried to yank her hand away, but he held tight, continuing to stare up at her. And then he bit down, and she shuddered.

Her anger dissipated in the blink of an eye, and she was once again consumed by fire.

"Aye, Izzy. I'll row you ashore." He sat up and brought their bodies together—pelvis to pelvis, breast to chest. "You'll be on land with me in no time."

A strange tone underlaid his words, and she frowned. What was he up to? He sounded determined, almost as if he was about to do something she wouldn't like.

But she didn't have time to decipher his mood as he grasped her waist and lifted her off him and onto the seat behind her. A small grunt escaped his lips, and she understood the feeling. She felt it too—a protest at their separation. She bit her lip to stop her own groan from escaping.

Aye, the loss of his heat and hardness was like being shoved out from under warm quilts on a cold winter day—while in the throes of the most enticing dream.

He swiveled her hips, turning her to face away from him. She lifted her legs, one at a time, over the bench when they caught, and then she untangled her skirts, raised her head…and froze.

Blackness surrounded them, and the only sound she heard was

that of water lapping against the boat's hull and a horse huffing somewhere nearby.

"Kerr," she croaked, as fear rose like a fist in her belly and grabbed on, suffocating her from the inside.

His arms wrapped around her waist from behind and squeezed. "Breathe, dearling," he murmured, his lips warm against her ear. "We willna be on the loch for long."

"It's so dark. I can barely make out the shore." She heard the panic in her voice and knew she could do nothing to stop it.

"Aye, love. We drifted out, and a cloud has covered the moon. It will soon pass. I can steer the boat in with the oars, and Diabhla will help pull us across."

"Diabhla? Why is he pulling us?"

Kerr glanced toward the sounds of the horse swimming somewhere to his left. Isobel followed his gaze but could see nothing of the stallion against the dark water surrounding them.

She closed her eyes, tried to calm her racing heart, but even sitting in the boat, she felt the inexorable pull of the black, cold depths beneath them.

"He isna yet," Kerr said, "but he'll be at the end of the lead soon. I didn't want to leave him behind."

"Behind where?"

"On the beach. He might have followed us, and 'tis too dangerous at night for him to swim untethered in the loch."

He grasped her waist and tried to push her onto the seat across from them, but she let out a frightened squeak and clamped her hands around his wrists. "Nay, I'll fall in!"

"I'll not let that happen, and if it e'er did, I would pull you out."

"But what if I sink under and you canna find me?"

Gentle fingers grasped her chin and turned her head to the side. As she peered at him, the cloud that covered the moon drifted away, and she could make out the familiar lines of his face and shape of his head. She used her imagination to fill in the dark, devouring eyes that never failed to incite some kind of emotion in her. Usually annoyance or excitement at getting the best of him. Or lust.

Right now, the steadiness of his gaze calmed her. He would keep her safe.

Then the boat lurched to the side, the end pulling around, and she let out a high-pitched squeak.

"What was that?" she yelped, her previous certitude forgotten.

"Diabhla. He's at the end of his lead." His hands released her, and with nothing to hold onto, her arms flailed. He rose behind her, and the boat rocked, but instead of pushing her across to the opposite bench like she expected him to, he nudged her forward until she perched on the edge of her seat. Then he squeezed onto the bench behind her, his long legs enveloping her on either side.

She grasped his bare thighs—his plaid having ridden up—to steady herself. The smoothness of his skin startled her for a moment, and she flexed her hands over the hardened muscles, her fingertips tracing tiny circles through the smattering of soft hair on top.

He leaned against her back, bending her forward, and grasped the handles of both oars. She straightened when he leaned back, more than a little annoyed.

God's blood! The man is as big and heavy as a bear!

"Doona think about the water, Isobel. Close your eyes and think about us. You forgot your fear when you were kissing me." She could hear the smile in his voice, the self-satisfied amusement, and it irked her. Heat rose up her cheeks, and she tried to pretend it was anger, but she knew it was more than that. She was embarrassed. And more than a little excited again at the intimacy of their position. The rigid shape of his cock pressed against her backside, and she wanted to tilt her hips against it.

She stared hard at the other bench, willing herself to move toward it before she made a fool of herself—again—but her eyes kept slipping sideways to the unending black water that surrounded them. She inhaled deeply, slowly, and tried to release her fear, to command her legs to work.

She failed.

He laid his chin on her head as he dipped one of the oars into the water in small repetitive circles and the boat turned. "Doona worry, lass. We'll be there in no time."

When he'd set them in the other direction, he reached forward again and pulled hard on the oars so the boat slid backward with a great surge.

She raised her eyes, startled, and her gaze landed on the opposite shore that now lay ahead of them, causing her mouth to drop open in confusion. This shoreline was much closer than the one she'd been staring at before—and they were travelling *away* from it.

She screwed up her brow, her mind reeling, as she attempted to get her bearings. Maybe Diabhla had gotten turned around and Kerr was trying to lead him back in.

But then the aggravating man pulled the oars again, his muscles bulging against her arms, and the boat travelled farther *into* the loch…and away from the beach she stared at.

Something caught her attention—movement—and she looked up to the top of the bluff. For a moment, she thought she saw a man, but then a cloud darkened the moon again.

She squinted her eyes. *Did I imagine that?*

When the cloud cleared, they were too far away for her to make out anything.

Anxiety churned her guts. "Why are we going this way?" she asked, twisting to look behind her, but his massive chest and arms blocked her view.

"We're crossing the loch," he said, continuing to row. "I'm taking you to the other side."

Shock coursed through her. "Nay!" She pointed ahead of her at the receding shoreline. "Take me there, Kerr!"

But instead of answering her, he kept rowing, picking up speed until the wind ruffled her hair.

"Go forward," she yelled. "We could drown. The boat's not big enough, and the loch is too wide to cross!"

Without pausing, he dropped his head into the crook of her neck and inhaled deeply. She shivered, her breath catching in her throat at the feel of his lips on her skin.

Then he bit her. "This is my favorite spot, my favorite smell, in all the world," he murmured. "I would know your scent, the feel of you against my mouth anywhere."

And for a moment, she melted. Her eyes drifted shut, her spine softened against him, and her mind fogged over. The surge of the boat rocked rhythmically beneath them, and she unthinkingly tilted her head to the side to give him greater access.

He wasted no time and laved her skin hotly with his tongue. "If my hands were free, Izzy, I would touch you all over." His voice had roughened. "I'd stroke up the insides of your thighs and over your belly and breasts. I would squeeze just hard enough to make you moan and your woman's mound weep." His legs widened on either side of hers, and when her own thighs loosened, she imagined his hands on her body doing exactly as he'd described.

Nay! She *knew* what he was doing.

Sitting up, she gave her head a shake, and then blinked to dispel the lethargy and heat from her body that his shocking words had produced.

Not so shocking, considering what we just did.

She had to clear her throat before speaking. "Stop it. You're trying to distract me."

"Is it working?"

"Is it working on you?" she countered.

He huffed out a laugh and then nudged forward with his hips. "Does it feel like it's working?"

The hard ridge that pressed behind her from the tip of her

tailbone to her waist felt like a deadly weapon. She wanted to push back against it—to sheathe the steely sword.

She'd spent years denying this pull between them, and now that she'd loosed it, she couldn't reel it back in.

"Do you want me to keep going?" he asked. "Tell you where I want to put my lips and tongue? It's all true, whether it's meant to distract you or not." He nipped at her, and she jumped. When he sucked on the bite, she barely stopped herself from groaning. "Should I tell you how I want to nibble over your arse and up your spine? Then turn you over and bite the undersides of your—"

She elbowed him hard in the gut, and he grunted—and not from desire this time.

"God's blood. Your elbows are sharp as daggers! Did Gavin teach you how to do that?"

"I taught myself how to do that. I'm not helpless, Kerr. Take me back or I'll scream. Sound travels across water. Someone is sure to hear me, and Gavin will have your hide for this—after Gregor strings you up by your toes and Darach's hounds feast on your belly."

He snorted in amusement but kept rowing; the land receded alarmingly quickly. Obviously, he didn't care that he was about to become the dogs' dinner.

"Bloodthirsty wench. What will Lachlan and Callum do? Will they defend me?"

"Nay. Lachlan will stand by and give advice on how to do it better."

He nipped the curve of her ear, and her mind went blank.

"And what will the brilliant mind of my last foster brother come up with?" he asked.

She tried to make her voice strong, but every moment he had his tongue and lips on her ear, her limbs grew heavier and she found it harder to concentrate. "Callum will tell the others not to kill you so he can devise a different, more horrible way to punish you."

He bit the lobe this time, and then straightened. "You have the right of it, love. They're as bloodthirsty as you are. But we're half-way across. If we turn around now, we'll be on the water longer."

She could feel his heart pounding strong and fast in his chest, powering the incredible strength he put into every stroke of the oars.

"Besides, I'll have a difficult time rotating Diabhla," he continued. "I'll have to jump in and pull him around physically. 'Twill be hard for him. Hopefully he willna kick me in the crown and knock me right to the bottom. I wouldnae be able to save you then. Or myself."

Her hands clenched his thighs, and this time she dug her nails in. "I can still scream so they know where I am." She inhaled deeply, filling her lungs to yell so loudly his ears would ring for days.

"And let the monster know we're here too," he added, before she bellowed for help.

She hesitated, and her breath gusted past her teeth. "What?"

"Aye, we'd never see the beast coming for us in the dark. I wonder if it would take Diabhla first. Or maybe tip o'er the boat and gobble us all up at once."

Her stomach tightened at his words. She turned her head to look at him, but it was too dark to read the truth in his eyes. Did he jest? "Loch Ness is a far way from here."

"True, but I've heard of sightings as far away as Eire. And stories abound about other such monsters on the mainland. Maybe we haven't seen this one because it hunts only at night."

A sense of inevitability filled her as she turned back to watch the land fade quickly away. He had her well and truly trapped. And she'd helped him do it—*she* was the one who'd devised the plan to get on a boat and float out on the water; *she* was the one who'd plotted so Kerr alone would know where to find her. She couldn't fight him for fear of rocking the boat, and she couldn't swim away.

And talking hadn't helped.

But maybe she hadn't said the right things? The great Laird

MacAlister wasn't one to be ordered around. Maybe she needed to tempt him—to bribe him. Surely if she offered the right incentive, he'd return her home.

But what does he want?

Me.

Aye, that was obvious from the bulge pressing into her back. And the need in his voice when he'd touched her.

Kerr MacAlister wants me. Needs me.

She tried to tamp down her own excitement at the thought, but it washed through her like a tidal wave. She forced herself to breathe deeply, to calm herself.

She wouldn't have to take things too far. Surely he would turn the boat around at the first hint of her offer.

Gentling her hands, she let her fingers drift to the insides of his thighs. The tips circled over his skin, slowly, barely there, before she changed the pressure and scraped with her nails.

For the first time since he'd started rowing, Kerr's rhythm faltered, and she felt his chest expand against her back before the air shuddered from his lungs.

"Izzy, what are you doing?"

"What do you mean?" she asked coyly.

He huffed out a laugh, then groaned as she scraped her nails farther along his thigh. "Is this how you intend to take your revenge? Because if it is, I may steal you away more often."

"Doona think of it as revenge, Laird MacAlister, but rather as a promise."

"A promise?"

"Aye. An exchange of sorts. If you take me back to MacKinnon land, I'll indulge you…like this." She trailed her hands over the tops of his legs to the outside and then stretched back along his thighs. When she reached the muscled curve of his bare arse, she dug in her nails before lessening the pressure and drawing them forward again.

He grunted in response, dropped the oars, and wrapped his arms around her middle, holding her tightly in place. He nipped the crook of her neck, hard enough that she knew he was aroused, but also angry. "So, you'll touch me intimately in order to get what you want. There is a name for women, for men, too, who trade in such acts. Usually, the women have no choice in the matter. They need to eat, or their children need to eat. My brothers and I try to help them whene'er we can. Gregor taught us this—we help the most vulnerable among us. 'Tis not so with you, Lady MacKinnon."

"You have abducted me, Laird MacAlister. I *am* vulnerable. All women are vulnerable. And my nobility doesn't protect me. Women of rank have less choice than many women of common birth. We may not starve, but we are traded at the whims of our fathers, our kings, sometimes even our husbands—abused by them, owned by them. You should understand this more than most."

His breath froze. She waited, holding her breath too. Finally, he said quietly, "You bring my mother into this, Izzy. Some would say that's not a fair fight." He turned her chin toward him, the tips of his fingers feeling like brands against her skin, and stared into her eyes. "I would ne'er abuse you, and you know that. But I'm fighting for something of great importance here. I'm fighting for us. And I willna be bought with your physical affection, although you can certainly keep trying."

He reached for the oars, forcing her to bend forward again, and then continued their journey. She missed his arms around her, and she closed her eyes to fight against the feeling, to contain it, but it felt too big for her skin.

When she opened them, she peered into the dark night. She could barely make out the shore in front of her now and surmised they must be close to landing on the opposite side. She couldn't believe how far they'd come in such a short time.

Had she run out of options, then? Was she to be his prisoner on the mainland? She should try again. Perhaps she needed to be more explicit.

"Not many men would turn down what I'm offering. I could not risk a bairn, of course, but surely there are acts other than tupping that you—"

"Isobel," he said tightly, sounding grim rather than enticed.

Embarrassment flooded through her, but her anger soon followed. "What? 'Tis all right for you to say such things to me, but I canna say them to you?" She slung her words at him—like burning coals from a trebuchet. She wanted them to stick to him, burn down into his skin and set him on fire. "You can think of such things, dream of them, but I canna do the same? Think of what you'll be missing, Laird MacAlister—my hands on you, stroking you. My mouth on you." She hesitated before saying the last, hoping she had the right of it. "Sucking on you."

She'd heard the act described a few times, but she had a hard time imagining it.

Apparently, she'd understood correctly for he exploded, "God's blood, Isobel! Have you done these things already? To other men?"

Her eyes widened, and she jumped when he dropped the oars with a loud thunk. His hands grasped her waist again and this time he lifted and turned her. She shrieked as the boat rocked, and she ended up facing him with her knees perched on the bench. She clutched his shoulders to balance herself.

"Answer me!" he demanded.

"Will you take me back if I do?"

"Nay! 'Tis obvious to me, now, more than ever, that we have lost our way. Isobel, we are meant to be together."

"Then why did my mother demand, on her deathbed, that Gavin give me the choice of whom to marry? Why did she refuse him the right to pass me over to you?"

"Because she loved you. And you *should* have that right. All women should."

"Yet you're taking it away from me."

"Nay, I'm not. We need time together. I'll row you back to Clan MacKinnon if you agree to come with me to Clan MacAlister so we can spend time together, so we can rebuild the trust between us that has somehow been broken. Stay with me over the winter, and if I havenae changed your mind by then, I'll take you back and ne'er bother you again." He threaded his fingers through her hair and rested their foreheads together. "Please, Izzy. Come with me."

The intensity and sincerity in his voice struck a chord in her heart, and she felt a "yes" rising in her chest. She wanted to please him. She wanted to cleave to him, to tilt her head the smallest amount and touch her lips to his, but then she heard a strange crunching sound, breaking the spell he'd cast over her, and the boat slowed and came to a halt.

Lifting her gaze over his shoulder, she saw that they'd landed on a pebbled shore. A splash caught her attention, and this time when she looked, she could see Diabhla rising from the water, outlined against the sky by the moonlight.

Relief shot through her to be back on land, even if it wasn't her clan's land, and nothing could stop her from getting off that boat.

She turned her gaze back to Kerr, felt his fingers tighten in her hair as the boat gently swayed against the beach. The urge to smile, to laugh, bubbled up in her throat, and she realized that for all their fighting and the nerve-wracking trip across the loch, she was enjoying herself.

Aye, she was sparring with Kerr, pitting her wits against his, and while he may have won their last two battles, no way would he win this one.

She grasped his wrists and pulled them down so he no longer held her head, and then straightened. The anticipation hung between them as she let him wait—let him wonder—before finally pursing her lips in a queenly manner. "'Tis too late, Kerr MacAlister. We have already arrived."

Twelve

KERR GRASPED THE END OF DIABHLA'S LEAD IN ONE HAND, HIS sword in the other, and heaved a frustrated sigh as he trailed behind Isobel through the woods. He couldn't see her anymore—he'd deliberately fallen back out of sight in a failed attempt to bring her to heel—but he could still hear her as she cursed and stomped through the underbrush like an angry boar.

Occasionally, she shouted a barbed insult at him which usually involved more cursing and a fair amount of name-calling. He would have felt guilty about putting her in this situation except he could tell by the tone of her voice and the feistiness of her insults that deep down she was relishing their adventure. Only his Isobel would consider a morning of wandering aimlessly through the forest, besieged by mud, sharp twigs, and insects, in another laird's territory—after she'd been kidnapped—a fine way to spend the day.

Although she would never tell him that. Quite the opposite.

Aye, if she were truly unhappy, she would be poking his chest in furious condemnation and yelling at him. The difference was subtle, and maybe other people wouldn't see it, but to him it was obvious.

She was enjoying their game—except Kerr wasn't playing.

Last night, she'd stayed with him after he'd found them shelter and built a fire to keep them warm. He'd wanted to hold her as they slept, sharing their body warmth and his spare plaid while their others dried near the fire, but she'd kept her distance—and he'd insisted she keep his plaid.

But when he'd woken briefly, as light began to creep over the horizon, he discovered she'd moved a little closer and had stretched out the plaid in the night to cover them both, giving him hope for their future. The second time he'd awoken, he'd been fully covered and she'd been pinning her now-dry arisaid in place—and then refused to wait for him as he strode out to a point to get his bearings. He was pretty sure a hunting cabin he'd been to as a young man was only a few hours' ride away. He would have liked to take her there, but she refused to follow him in the direction he wanted to go.

Instead, she'd turned the opposite way. When the trail she'd been following petered out, she forged her own path through the woods—without any kind of sword or dagger to clear the way.

He'd tried to reason with her, to cajole her into cooperating, but she wouldn't be swayed. He'd even tried to intimidate her with a pointed glare and growl in his voice that would have frozen the most seasoned warrior in his tracks. But not Isobel...nay, she just kept walking away from him with no purpose in mind other than to do the opposite of whatever he wanted.

And part of him rejoiced at that. Aye, he'd worried that the bond between them had been broken over the years, but he could see now that Isobel trusted him completely with her well-being. She was not afraid to stand up to him or disregard his wishes, and it was obvious she had no fear that he would abandon her, no matter how much she pushed him away. Even when she couldn't see or hear him trailing behind her through the woods, she still believed he was there...that he would never leave her. Otherwise, what was the point of all the insults?

"God save us!" she exclaimed from the other side of the bramble bush he'd been walking quietly beside. "'Tis your changeling I'm looking at, Laird MacAlister. A knotted, wicked-looking stump that could be your brother—with your wooden heart too."

He squinted at the bramble bush between them, but he couldn't see her...or his stumpy likeness. A clever retort sat on the tip of his tongue, but he would not reveal himself to her until she called out for him.

If he did, his only option would be to follow docilely behind her or lift her up in front of him on Diabhla and ride away. But that was a last resort. To do so was far more of a betrayal than stealing away with her on the loch.

She'd put herself on the boat, even when she couldn't swim. She'd trapped herself. Forcing her to ride away with him would be using his strength against her.

Besides, he'd gotten what he wanted—time alone with Isobel away from her castle and clan. He would wait her out. She'd need him soon enough. Her stubbornness was no match for her being tired, cold, and hungry.

"Did you hear me, Kerr? I said—"

She stopped talking in midsentence, and the hair on the back of his neck rose. He listened intently, his sword ready to hack through the bushes in one slice to get to her.

Her steps had also stopped, but he could hear nothing else alarming. Was she toying with him, seeing if he would reveal himself? Or was someone else there? Or something?

To hell with his plan. He dropped Diabhla's lead and brought his great claymore down on the brambles in front of him, just as Isobel screamed—a real scream. He leapt through the gap, the prickles scratching at his plaid, but he didn't see her.

There! The bottom of her skirts, almost camouflaged by the underbrush, poked out from behind the trunk of a large Scots pine. He raced to her in several strides, faster than he'd ever run before. The dead leaves and twigs scattered under his feet. More of her became visible as he drew near. Her plaid was open, the hood hanging down her back and her hair loosely braided over one shoulder. Her hand covered her mouth while the other gripped the tree beside her.

Grasping her arm, he pulled her behind him and scanned the

small clearing in front of them for danger—his sword raised and his weight balanced perfectly on his feet. A man about Kerr's age sat in front of a small fire, eating his meal of what looked like roasted rabbit. A huge battle axe—as big as Kerr had ever seen—rested beside him against a fallen log.

He was as dark as a MacAlister but for his eyes, which even from this distance Kerr could see were a bright blue. And even though he was sitting down, the man was obviously larger than him, which was surprising because Kerr had outgrown the biggest man he'd ever met—Gregor—by the time he was sixteen years old.

A veritable giant, the stranger looked as unconcerned to see a hardened and skilled warrior raise his sword to him as he might if a cook in the MacKinnon kitchens had swung a carrot with deadly purpose.

"Kerr," Isobel squeaked from behind his shoulder. "The wolf!"

The gigantic man glanced behind the log to where a patch of sunlight shone through the trees. Kerr followed his gaze, and his eyes widened at seeing the tip of a gray tail poking out from behind one end of the log and the tops of two soft-looking white ears poking out from the other end. A wolf, indeed. And a large one, if the length from tip to tail was any indication.

"She sleeps," the man said, reaching behind the log to pat what apparently was a monster wolf. "She brought me one rabbit and ate the remaining five. She's mad at me."

The man spoke with an unusual accent, which sounded like it had a Norse influence. A sell-sword, perhaps? His clothing was not typical of a Scot—he wore leather braies and a fur vest, with golden arm bands around massive biceps. Light glinted off a gold pendant that rested in the hollow of his throat.

His dark hair hung to his waist, braided at the sides and tied back—neat and clean without the tangles or mats common for a lone male traveler. His clothing was neat and clean too, with signs of repair rather than thread worn and ripped.

Kerr lowered his sword to waist-level and scanned the glen.

When he saw no sign of other men, or worse, other wolves, he returned his gaze to the stranger, who now gnawed on a bone.

The man dropped his hand to his leg and grunted in frustration. "She gave me the skinniest one, too, greedy female." He tossed the small bone over the log and a soft growl emerged from behind it, the ears twitching.

Isobel pressed closer to Kerr's back, her hands clenching his waist and her body shuddering. It felt good to have her leaning on him—both physically and emotionally—and for a moment, he considered what he could say or do to make her press even closer. The man grinned at Kerr, revealing straight, well-cared-for teeth, and Kerr was suddenly reminded of his foster brothers— especially when the stranger lifted a brow and tossed another bone at the wolf, who growled again and then yawned. She emitted a funny little squeak at the end of the yawn, and sat up on her elbows to stare at them over the log.

A chill ran down Kerr's spine when he saw the she-wolf, yet at the same time he couldn't help admiring her beauty, even with blood still crusted on her white muzzle. The light-gray markings around her blue eyes were perfectly symmetrical, and her ears looked soft enough to touch. Her head, however, was so large that Kerr worried about the size of her body. If she attacked, would he be able to stop her?

Behind him Diabhla let out an agitated huff. Kerr was glad to have the big stallion at his back, but at the same time, he worried about him. Would the wolf try to take him down?

"A magnificent creature," the other man said, referring to Diabhla. "He is safe. You are all safe. We do not hunt humans or working animals."

When the wolf flopped back down out of sight, Kerr slowly lowered his weapon. "Where are you from, outlander? I canna place your accent, although it has certain peculiarities of Norse travelers I have met."

"My mother was born in that place, but I was raised farther south on the mainland. I travelled to Orkney several years ago, and I've slowly been making my way south to Cambria. I like the legends I've heard about that land—of kings, wizards, and magical swords."

Isobel relaxed her grip on his waist, and he knew she was listening, her curiosity piqued. He hadn't known she was so frightened of wolves, but he suspected that she had seen the animal before it lay down—and it was indeed a giant.

"And how did you meet your travelling companion? Did you raise her as a pup?" He'd heard of a few other men, loners mostly, who had taken in wolf pups and lived with them like they were dogs. "Is she your pet?"

The traveler barked out a laugh. The sound boomed across the glen, and Kerr actually felt it vibrate through his body.

"Já, she's my pet. She comes when I call her and chases her tail when I command it!" He patted the wolf behind the log again—loud whacks with the flat of his hand. "Sit up, puppy! Roll over, puppy!"

"Not so rough! You'll hurt her," Isobel commanded, sounding like herself again. Kerr doubted she was right; the wolf had several layers of thick fur over bone and muscle. Still, he couldn't help smiling at the tone of her voice as she spoke to this giant, dangerous-looking Norseman.

The wolf sat up again, a blur of movement, and clenched the man's hand in her jaws. Just as quickly, the man grabbed her head behind her ears with his other hand and they tussled for a moment before the man leaned over and kissed the wolf's forehead. His fingers dug into the side of her neck and kneaded deeply. The wolf released the man's hand, closed her eyes with a groan and leaned into his fingers.

After one final scratch, the man let go and straightened in his seat. The wolf shook her head and rested her chin on the log, this time watching them with ice-blue eyes.

The man stood, rising about a half foot taller than Kerr, and bowed his head in greeting. "I am Eirik Kron. Come, sit with us." He waved them toward the fire, and then tossed the remains of the rabbit from the spit to the wolf. She caught the carcass in her mouth and crunched down. "We have guests, *Siv*, and little to feed them. Bring back more rabbits, and don't eat them all this time."

The she-wolf's name was *Siv*? It sounded familiar to him—like he'd read it during his youth at Gregor's keep. Master MacBean, their tutor, had made him and his foster brothers study Norse mythology as well as other tales and legends. He was certain Siv was someone's wife. Or Sif, maybe.

"What a bonnie name," Isobel said, stepping out from behind him. She hesitated for a moment before walking toward the giant man and his pet wolf. Kerr switched his weapon to his other hand, so his sword arm was on the opposite side of Isobel, and then stayed half a step ahead of her.

"'Twas Thor's wife's name, correct?" Isobel asked.

"*Já.*" A pleased smile crossed Eirik's face. He stepped toward the edge of the glen, and with one hand, he lifted a huge log from the brush, dragged it to the fire as if it weighed no more than a spindly branch, and laid it down for them to sit upon. "You've read the stories, then?" he asked, brushing off the dirt and removing any twigs that stuck up from the bark. "Siv is a common name for females among my people."

"Aye," Isobel said excitedly. "I read the *Poetic Edda* over and over when I was younger—it is a much cherished addition to our library. My ancestors are Norse. 'Tis said my grandfather, many generations back, crossed the sea and conquered this land. The story goes that his wife, Hilde, was a Shield Maiden who fought by his side. They named their first daughter Siv."

"Are you a Shield Maiden too, then?" Eirik asked her, without a hint of surprise in his voice.

Isobel slowed, and Kerr was surprised to see a faint blush steal over her skin. "Nay, I have ne'er been in battle. Sword fighting is not a skill my family taught me." But then her eyes lit up and a smile formed perfect dimples in her cheeks. "But I can set traps for deserving people, which takes much planning and physical labor. They ne'er see it coming." She stole a sideways glance at him, and Kerr quirked a brow. He didn't need to remind her that *he* had seen it coming—on several occasions. She shrugged and turned her attention back to Eirik. "My clan come to me if they feel they or someone else have been wronged—a slight of a personal nature that is too small an offense for my brother's attention. I set things right, balance the scales, so to speak. I doona hurt anyone. Only their dignity."

Eirik nodded. "It is an important role to play within the community. Otherwise, resentments fester and boil over."

The wolf, finished now with the rabbit carcass Eirik had tossed to her, lifted her haunches in the air and stretched out her back. When she rose to her full height, Isobel froze. Kerr stepped fully in front of her again, his weapon at the ready as the blood pounded in his veins.

God's blood! The creature is almost double the size of a normal wolf. How can I protect Isobel if they both attack at once?

Eirik noted their concern and whistled. Siv jumped in the air and bounded toward the brush behind her, disappearing within it. "And bring plump ones this time!" he yelled after her.

When he glanced back at them, he smiled and lifted a placating hand. "She would never hurt you. Nor would I. You are safe here with us. She wants to feed you, not eat you."

"How can you be certain?" Isobel asked, her voice cracking as she poked her head out again from behind Kerr. "She's an animal. A wild animal."

"She's not an animal to me, Lady MacKinnon. She's my beloved companion."

Lady MacKinnon?

Every muscle in Kerr's body loosed and hardened at the same time, ready to protect Isobel at all cost. He searched the glen again for any threats he may have missed. Had he led her into a trap?

"How do you know the lady's name?" he asked, his voice low and deadly. He would kill the man first and then take out the wolf when it came to protect him.

Eirik sat down, grinning, and rummaged through his pack. He brought out some bread, broke it into pieces, and then stretched his arms out to them. A peace offering. "You are a big man, Laird MacAlister, and yet you walk as quietly as a mouse through the woods. But I am even bigger and quieter. And I was listening. Your lady is quite inventive."

Isobel turned a brighter shade of red this time, her eyes widening. Most likely, she was thinking over every insult she'd thrown at Kerr today, making Eirik laugh again.

The man liked to laugh.

"We saw you land last night," he said, when he'd caught his breath. "And then we watched you for much of today to make sure the lady was safe." He nodded at Kerr. "'Tis apparent *she's* not the one in trouble."

Isobel started giggling, and soon she moved out from behind him and took the final steps toward the fire, Kerr hot on her heels. After taking the bread from Eirik, she sat on the seat he'd made for them.

"Thank you. I'm starving," she said, and then winked. "Kerr preferred to walk aimlessly through the woods today rather than feed me."

More laughter, then the man grabbed the blade of his axe, which was leaning against the log beside him, and held the handle out to Kerr. "Take it," he said. "I would ease your mind about my intentions. But if we're attacked, you'll have to save me too, and I warn you that I will squeal like a lad upon seeing his first Valkyrie."

Isobel snorted. Kerr could tell she was looking at him, and he wondered if she remembered how he'd compared their first kiss to a Valkyrie. He wanted to look at her, to peer into her face, but he didn't dare take his gaze from Eirik. Not yet, anyway.

"Throw it to me, instead," he said. If the man had ulterior motives, he could pull Kerr off balance when he grasped the handle.

Eirik nodded and tossed the axe to Kerr effortlessly. He grabbed it out of the air without taking his eyes off the other man. The huge, heavy weapon felt good in his hand, perfectly balanced. He would have liked to examine it, but that could wait. It was likely the man had other weapons hidden on his body—the same as Kerr did.

He laid the axe down and then sat beside Isobel on the log, his sword across his knees and still in his grip.

When Eirik threw him a hunk of bread, he caught it easily with his other hand and devoured it. All he'd had since waking was an apple taken from a tree when he was trailing behind Isobel. He lowered his guard a little as he ate, knowing that if the wolf approached from behind, Diabhla would warn him. And if Eirik attacked from the front, Kerr would be ready.

The stranger lifted a leather flask to his lips and swallowed before passing it to Isobel. Kerr tensed, but she received it without incident and took a drink.

"Is it mead?" she asked as she blotted the excess from her lips with her plaid.

"*Já*, honey mead. My grandmother's recipe."

"It's good. Different than I've tasted before." She took another swig and then passed it to Kerr.

He looked directly at Eirik as he drank, and then lobbed the flask back to him with a grateful nod. "'Tis verra good. My foster father, Gregor MacLeod, has a love of mead. I'll endeavor to describe it to him. Mayhap one day you'll meet him and he can taste it himself."

"It would be an honor. I've heard much about Laird MacLeod and his five foster sons. The people I've met speak of your alliance with hope in their voices. They say you are men of principle and justice."

"Aye, it is our intent to bring peace to the Highlands, but 'tis not always easy."

Isobel made a scoffing sound in the back of her throat. "'Twas not peace you were bringing to our clans last ni—"

"Isobel," he warned. It was one thing to speak of their conflict amongst their family, but not with strangers—even friendly ones.

Eirik glanced from Kerr to Isobel and back again. "The mead is strong. Even a small amount can loosen your tongue."

Kerr nodded, but he suspected Isobel was overly excited— giddy almost—and had forgotten herself. She'd seldom travelled from MacKinnon land...and certainly not since Ewan had been taken from them several years ago. It must feel like a newfound freedom—once she'd gotten over the fear of drowning in the loch.

Aye, she wasn't lady here. She had no guards, no rules, no responsibilities. Only her own inner compass to keep her in check—and he'd seen how well that had gone over this morning.

He sometimes thought she had a far ways to go before she grew into the lady he knew she could be. But other times he would see the way she cared for her people, or how, as Eirik said, the clan responded positively when she "caught" someone in one of her traps, and he knew she was born to lead by his side.

Lady MacAlister.

Eirik leaned forward, resting his elbows on his knees. The gold pendant around his neck swung away from the hollow at the base of his throat, and Kerr was close enough to see that it was an intricately carved Viking longship. The sail was billowed, and a dragon's head adorned the prow.

"Oh, how magnificent," Isobel said, her rapt gaze on the pendant.

Eirik cupped the pendant in his hand. "Thank you. It has been in my family for generations. It is said Odin himself gave it to the first *Fyrstr* of the *Varda*, my namesake."

"*Fyrstr* of the *Varda*?" Isobel asked.

Eirik paused, his gaze fixed somewhere in the distance as if remembering. "In my native language it means…leader of the family…or clan. The *Fyrstr* was usually a warrior, like one of the great Scottish lairds, and the *Varda* was like Laird MacAlister and his allies, watching and protecting good people while fighting against evil."

"Is there a female equivalent of the *Fyrstr*?" Isobel asked.

"*Já*, she is called the *Fyrsta*, and she's often a warrior too." Then he sighed and released the pendant. "But those days are *nei* more. The *Varda* was scattered to the winds hundreds of years ago. It has only been me and Siv for more moons than I can count."

Isobel reached out her hand to the big man. Kerr tensed, but he did not demand she keep her distance. He felt the great sadness in their Norse companion and knew there was much more to the story than he was telling. What had happened to his people?

After a moment, Eirik lifted his hand too, and Isobel squeezed it. "You and Siv are welcome anytime at my keep."

"Our keep," Kerr corrected, "at Clan MacAlister. And as Isobel said, her brother's keep too, once he's met you."

Isobel gave him such a look, her eyes wide with disbelief and her mouth pursed in an offended moue at his presumptuousness, that Eirik's laughter boomed once more through the glen.

His entire body shook with it, and it was so loud Kerr could barely hear himself think. Fortunately, he also couldn't hear Isobel scolding him—saving him from her sharp tongue and drowning out any additional refusals from her to marry him.

When Eirik toppled backward over the log, his legs as big as tree trunks and pointing straight up into the air, Kerr burst into laughter too. Isobel maintained her scowl for as long as she could, before finally shaking her head and joining in.

Their eyes met, and she was so lovely, so filled with joy, that he took his gaze from Eirik—for a second—and lost himself in her.

It was a moment cut from time. Perfect in its beauty and clarity, and he felt so much love for the woman sitting next to him, it seemed like his chest might burst from the pressure.

Then the huge wolf, Siv, appeared at her side, dwarfing her, with a mouth full of torn carcasses and her teeth dripping with blood. Siv turned her head and stared directly at him, the ice-blue of her eyes chilling.

Kerr stilled—other than to grip the hilt of his sword and wrap his other hand around Isobel's arm, ready to pull her from harm. His laughter died abruptly, and when Isobel saw his expression, hers did too. She whipped her head around and let out a startled squeak.

He waited, not wanting to spook the animal or drive its instinct to attack.

Then the wolf dropped five plump dead rabbits at Isobel's feet, threw back her head, and howled.

Thirteen

KERR STRETCHED HIS LEGS OUT ON THE GROUND IN FRONT OF him as he studied Eirik's battle axe, his back against the log he'd been sitting on earlier. It was a beast of a weapon, with double-sided blades, an extra-long wooden haft wrapped in leather and then reinforced with langets, and an edge so sharp he'd cut his skin just by resting his thumb upon it. And it was heavy, heavier than any other axe he'd hefted. Few men could wield such a weapon, and he suspected if Eirik ever used it against him, he'd slice Kerr in two and send him straight across Bifröst and into Valhalla.

"Do not touch the blade," Eirik said from where he stretched out on the other side of the fire, his head resting comfortably against the fallen tree, his eyes closed. They'd eaten their fill of roasted rabbit, greens, and barley that Eirik had thrown in a pot and cooked over the fire, before finishing with apples and cheese. Eirik, like Gregor, carried his own container of spices with which to season the meat.

It had been delicious.

"Too late," Kerr said. "If Isobel asks, I'll say you threw the weapon at me and I caught it in my bare hands—with only the smallest of scratches."

Eirik grinned, his eyes still closed. "A worthy warrior for such a fine lady."

"Now you say that…when she's not here," Kerr chastised—much to Eirik's amusement.

He looked toward the woods where Isobel had taken an adoring Siv to wash her muzzle a few minutes ago. The two females had become fast friends when Siv had laid her head on Isobel's lap after presenting the rabbits to her, and then fallen asleep as Isobel had stroked her ears, twirling her fingers through the thick, soft fur, a look of wonder on her face.

He felt strangely at ease with the outlander, strange because he hadn't known Eirik long, and lowering his guard could put Isobel at risk, especially with a dangerous predator in their midst. But Kerr had had no indication—either by their actions or his own intuition—that the huge man or the wolf meant them harm.

Nay, it was the opposite. He felt with a certitude, deep down in his bones, that they were safe.

Still, that didn't mean someone else couldn't do them harm. And Isobel and Siv were well and truly out of sight. He couldn't even hear Isobel anymore, talking to the wolf as they walked away, her hand resting on the animal's flank.

"Doona worry, Laird MacAlister," Eirik said. "No harm will come to your woman. Siv would alert me if someone else approached. And if we were taken by surprise, she would protect Isobel with her life." He opened his eyes and looked straight at Kerr. "Trust me."

"I do." He looked back down at the huge axe and shook his head. "I doona understand it, but I do."

Eirik grinned. "It is because of Siv. Everyone is enamored with her."

Kerr snorted. "Aye, the giant wolf with the giant bloody fangs put me right at ease."

The big man barked out a laugh. "But she brought back all those plump rabbits—filled your belly. She'll return Isobel safe and sound so you can play more games with your beloved."

Kerr grunted, and then hefted the axe in his hand and swung it down in an arc—right to left, left to right, over his head—as if he were fighting someone. He dropped his arm back down, the muscles strained from maneuvering the heavy weapon so quickly. "I doona want to play games anymore. I want to call Isobel my own."

Eirik nodded. "You were right to bring her here. She leans toward you, seeks you out, but she pushes you away at the same time. Something needs to shift between the two of you."

"I hope her brother sees it that way. I could lose her and my closest friend…and cause a rift within our alliance for stealing her away—even if she did set it in motion."

"Marry her, and I am sure Laird MacKinnon will forgive you—if he believes she is happy."

"I'm trying, but she makes it difficult."

"*Nei*, she is already halfway there."

Kerr lowered the axe and raised his brows. "Truly?"

"*Já*. But what do I know about women? I bungled everything with my *vif*. It is only by Odin's grace she agreed to be mine."

Kerr's eyes widened. "You're married?"

"*Já*."

"But you're…you're…"

"A lone wolf?" The big man burst into laughter again at his jest. When it died down, he said, "I will see her soon. She is with a friend now."

"She's travelling with you?"

"*Já*. You do not think I would look this good without a *vif*, do you?"

Kerr grinned. "Nay, I doona suppose you would." He dropped his gaze back down to the weapon in his lap and traced his fingers over the intricate gold inlay along the blade—in the shape of Norse runes, wolves, the sun, and the moon. "It's beautiful," he said.

"Thank you. It was my father's blade, and my grandfather's before that."

"Have you had to use it much?"

He nodded. "There is much evil in this world. I do as you and your brothers do—try to bring peace where I can. Sometimes that peace comes with a swing of my blade."

Kerr studied the other man. "What happened to your people? Did you lead them? Or your father?"

"Not in recent years, *nei*, but before we left our homeland, my ancestors did. Over time, my people have scattered, searching for a new home, but I am happy as long as I have Siv by my side…and my *vif*, of course."

Kerr snorted. "Of course." He heard a bark in the distance and the familiar sound of Isobel's laughter. It made him smile; Eirik, too. "How are you getting around?" Kerr asked. "I doona see any horses. Are you travelling on foot?"

"We have a longship—small enough that I can handle it myself. I built it when we first crossed the sea to Orkney. It is hidden in a cove north of here."

Kerr leaned forward. "Eirik, you can make your home with us. If you want to settle, I would be happy to have you at Clan MacAlister. Or at the homes of any of my brothers and our foster father, Gregor MacLeod. I would vouch for you. Isobel would too."

Eirik sat up and stretched his arm out to Kerr. The men clasped arms over the fire in the way of warriors and brothers. "Thank you. It is an honor you have bestowed upon us. I will speak to my *vif* about a short stay, but I doona think our home is in the Highlands, as much as I like it here."

Kerr nodded, squeezed Eirik's arm, and sat back. He could hear Siv and Isobel approaching through the brush. He glanced over his shoulder to make sure Diabhla stayed calm, and was amazed to see him standing at ease, munching on some grass on the other side of the glen—the same as when Siv first brought back the rabbits. The stallion wasn't bothered by the giant predator at all. Maybe the beast smelled domesticated to the horse, like one of Darach's hounds.

"Laird MacAlis—"

"Please, call me Kerr," he interrupted. He wasn't much for formality—none of the brothers were.

Eirik nodded. "What are your plans? If you want some time

alone with Lady Isobel, there is an abandoned cabin a half day's ride from here. I stayed there with Siv for a few nights when we first arrived. We followed the creek inland from the beach. The bed is in decent condition, and we left firewood and kindling in the basket by the hearth."

"Sounds ideal," Kerr said, returning his gaze to watch for Isobel and Siv at the edge of the glen. "I stayed in a hunting cabin out this way when I was younger. It could be the same place—inland from a long promontory. The creek widens and churns over the rocks a few miles farther east."

"*Já.* That sounds like it."

"I wanted to head there at first light, but Isobel had other ideas. I canna say I blame her. I rowed her across the loch against her will. Although she's enjoying herself now."

Eirik smirked. "You would not believe the things I did to impress my *vif.* None of them worked. But I was persistent, and finally she came away with me."

Isobel appeared with Siv at the edge of the woods, and the unlikely friends headed toward them. She looked happy and carefree. Not plotting anything, for once.

"Maybe someday I'll meet her," Kerr said, "and hear *her* side of the story."

Eirik hooted in delight. "I think she would tell a different tale from my own remembrances."

"No doubt."

"Ah, well. She loves me now."

Kerr couldn't help grinning. "I'm sure she does."

"You are welcome to stay with us for a few days, but if it were me, I would want to be alone with my beloved. She will not bond with you in the same way if we are together, *já?*"

"Agreed. I'll do my best to convince her to ride to the cabin. We'll stay a few days, a week at most. Any longer and Gavin will have my head, whether I've won over his sister or not."

"Stay a few days where?" Isobel asked, close enough to hear part of their conversation.

"A cabin—not far from here," Eirik said. "Your warrior laird knows where it is. The forest can be dangerous, especially at night. I have Siv's sharp ears and nose to protect me."

"And sharp teeth," Kerr added.

Isobel's face fell. "Canna you stay with us?" she asked Eirik.

"*Nei*, we must keep heading west, but we will try to come back before the week is out."

Kerr wondered who Isobel would miss more—the outlander or his pet wolf. Or if she wanted to keep them around so she wouldn't have to be alone with him. That hurt, but for the first time, he considered that she might be nervous. He peered at her closely and thought he detected a small tremble in her cheek.

My Isobel, worried to be alone with me.

He scrubbed his hand over his face, dragging his nails through the short growth of beard that darkened his cheeks. Then he met her eyes, resigned. "Sweetling, if you want to go back, I will take you. Eirik is right, the forest can be dangerous. An unexpected fall can kill you, or a wild animal could attack. Let alone who we might run into in the woods. I would protect you, of course, but still you could be at risk."

After laying it all out like that, seeing the dangers that could befall them, an urge rose to get her back on the boat and return her to the safety of Gavin's keep.

Eirik nodded. "We have come across several groups of men recently on our travels. Mostly we stayed clear of them. Some looked like hunters, but others had the hardened look of warriors."

The hair on the back of Kerr's neck rose. "How many?"

"Two groups. Four in one, five in the other. But they were north of here and travelling east, using the back roads and game trails to move around. Same as you."

Kerr made a harrumphing sound in the back of his throat as

he pictured the trail Isobel had chosen this morning coming to an end—and then her pushing forward through the dense brush despite his objections. She colored slightly under his perusal, as if she knew what he was thinking, and then raised her chin in that haughty way that made him want to kiss her until she forgot herself—like she had last night on the boat.

Aye, that's what he had to keep remembering when they were back at her keep—not that he'd failed to get much time alone with her, but that she'd clamored to get closer to him, her mouth hot and hungry, her hands squeezing his flesh. And he would remind her of it every chance he got.

"Nay, I doona want to go back yet." She laid her hand on his arm. "You brought me here, and now I'm not leaving. Not yet, anyway. We'll go to this cabin you mentioned. The one you wanted to take me to this morning. We'll be safe there. We can bar the door at night against any brigands or wild animals."

His eyes shifted to Eirik, who gave a brief, barely discernible nod. Kerr schooled his features, so she wouldn't see the conflicted emotions running through him. On one hand he wanted to whoop victoriously, but on the other he wanted to bundle her onto that boat and row her back across the loch where she would be guarded by hundreds of loyal warriors.

It also eased his conscience to know that he'd offered to take her back and she'd refused. His only choice now would be to force her onto that boat and back to Gavin, and that could cause irreparable damage to their relationship. Surely Gavin would be more inclined to forgive him, knowing he'd tried to convince Isobel to return.

Gavin knew how stubborn his sister could be.

When Kerr failed to answer, she narrowed her eyes. "I should have been more clear, Laird MacAlister. When I said I doona *want* to go back, what I meant was I *willna* go back." Then she released Kerr's arm and turned to Siv. Wrapping her palm against the side of the wolf's face, she scratched behind her ear. Siv closed her eyes and let out a wolfy groan. "Until we meet again, my sweet friend," Isobel said. And then she leaned down and squeezed her arms around her neck. "Be a good girl for me and mind your master."

Eirik snorted once more in amusement, and when he caught Kerr's eye, he winked.

Fortunately for both of them, Isobel hadn't noticed.

———————

Isobel sat in front of Kerr on his huge stallion, her eyes closed, trying to ease the excitement in her body—her mind, too, if she was being honest—with regular, controlled breaths. Breathe in two, three, four…breathe out two, three, four…breathe in two, three, four…

But the horse swayed beneath her, the saddle pressed hard between her legs, and Kerr held her tightly against him, smelling so…manly—like horses and smoke from the fire and leather.

There was no other word for it…she ached for him…and no amount of counting was going to take that away.

They'd been riding for over an hour now, and every second had turned into some kind of prolonged torture—worse than when they'd been on the boat, which didn't make sense because he'd been talking to her during their trip over the loch, saying lusty things and nibbling her neck.

But since they'd left Eirik and Siv in the clearing, Kerr hadn't uttered one word to her—and still the feelings surged through her body.

She'd kept quiet too, afraid that if she opened her mouth to speak, a wanton moan would escape, or worse, she would tell him to slide his hand—the one he'd wrapped firmly around her hip—down between her spread legs. She wanted him to cup her mound and hold his palm tightly against it. To somehow absorb the ache.

Her controlled breaths caught in her throat.

Angels in heaven, why am I thinking about that?

Because you've never stopped *thinking about it.*

Aye, ever since Kerr had helped her onto Diabhla, and then swung his leg up behind her, encircling her waist with his arm and pulling her snugly against him, she'd been a bundle of nerves and excitement, of heat and tingling awareness.

They'd said goodbye to Eirik and Siv, and Isobel had felt a keen disappointment to be leaving them, but she'd also felt burgeoning anticipation about being alone with Kerr for the next few days, doing God knows what at the cabin.

Certainly not *that.*

She wasn't married to him, and she didn't *want* to marry him… did she? And if she did let him do *that*, he'd have her standing before Gavin and Father Lundie in a heartbeat, tying her to him for life.

"Isobel."

She jumped, inhaling sharply as Kerr said her name—his voice low and growly like an ornery bear.

"Mmmm hmmm?" she murmured, not trusting herself to form words yet.

"You stopped breathing."

Stopped breathing?

She forced herself to laugh, but it came out sounding like a goat in distress. "Of course I didnae stop breathing. I'm not dead."

"Then what was that weird sound you just made? That definitely sounded like something dying."

She frowned and pursed her lips, tried to return to her regular, rhythmic breathing in an attempt to calm herself—breathe in two, three, four…breathe out two, three, four… But she could barely get the numbers counted in her head before she was desperate for air again.

Her heart was pounding fast enough and strong enough to feel it in her body.

"How do you know I'd stopped breathing?" she asked almost accusingly.

"Because I felt your breaths against my chest—long and deep. Your ribcage expanded and contracted against me. It was... soothing."

"Soothing?" She'd been struggling their entire ride to stay calm, to quash her lusty thoughts and carnal desires, while he'd been feeling soothed by her?

"Aye." He said it a little hesitantly, as if trying to figure out her mood and why she sounded angry.

"Well, I'm glad one of us could feel so at ease!" She crossed her arms over her chest and glared straight ahead, her body as stiff as the saddle beneath her.

He sighed and lifted one of his hands out of sight behind her. She guessed he was rubbing his face or squeezing the back of his neck. Something he did when he was frustrated or uncertain. Maybe both.

Good. It pleased her she wasn't the only one feeling out of sorts.

"We'll be there soon," he said, his tone placating. "It will be dark in a few hours. We willna have to do anything other than cook our meal and rest. You must be exhausted after our late night and early morning."

She *was* exhausted—from more than lack of sleep.

She'd been fighting this desire for Kerr, always trying to stay one step ahead of him, to be strong and invulnerable to him for so long. Maybe she should do as Deirdre had suggested and let him in. Stop fighting and see what happened.

She closed her eyes, and a wave of tiredness overtook her— along with a tightening of her throat and the welling of tears behind her lids. What was wrong with her?

She wanted to turn in Kerr's embrace, to wrap herself around him, and weep.

And that, as she'd heard Kerr say, scared the shite out of her.

Kerr pulled her even closer against him, his chin resting on top of her head, and she allowed her spine to soften. She counted in her head again, but this time she counted to ten, and then twenty, and then thirty. And when those emotions rose—uncertainty, the need to run or push him away—she allowed them to move through her body, to not shove them down or act on them...but rather to experience them, to sit with the uncomfortable feelings and sensations they caused within her until they wore themselves out and dissipated on their own.

She inhaled deeply several times, and her agitation faded. A heaviness slowly invaded her limbs, and she leaned against him, feeling safe and secure. When something wet trickled into the corner of her mouth and she tasted salt, she couldn't even raise her hand to wipe the tear from her face. She felt exposed, vulnerable, but unable—or maybe unwilling—to do anything about it.

Her last thought as she drifted into sleep was that she wished it was dark so Kerr wouldn't see that she'd been crying.

Fourteen

"I THINK SIV WAS TRYING TO TEACH ME HOW TO FISH," ISOBEL said as she stood behind Kerr in the middle of the cottage. He crouched in front of the hearth, laying the kindling for their fire. She felt useless standing there but she had no idea what to do. The cabin was small but neat and tidy, with a bed, a few chairs, and a table. It didn't need cleaning, and if it did…well…she'd never cleaned a day in her life. Where would she start? With water and a rag, she supposed, but she'd have to find water first. "I tried to catch the ones she chased toward me, but they slipped right through my fingers. I couldnae keep ahold of them."

"'Tis hard to catch fish with your bare hands. You need bait and hooks. Or nets." He finished piling up the wood he'd brought in from the lean-to outside, and then reached into his pack.

"I wager I could fashion a trap," she said as she stepped closer. If she had to start the fire herself one day, she'd better watch. Someone in her household had always laid the wood for her, and if she'd had to light it, she'd used a candle.

He pulled out flint and a striker, and then glanced at her over his shoulder. "Why a trap?"

"I like traps. Something like they use to catch the spiny lobsters and crabs."

His brow furrowed before he turned back to the hearth, like she'd said something idiotic. And maybe she had. But coming here—being away from her routine and her safe, predictable life, even though she could dig holes and fill them with manure or climb trees and attach bags filled with honey to a trip wire—made her realize how incompetent she really was.

No matter how good she was with traps, she'd never caught a meal before, and she certainly had no idea how to prepare that meal if she did catch it. She couldn't even light the fire on which to cook it.

"'Tis much easier to fish for them rather than trap them," he said, and then used the striker on the flint and struck a spark into the kindling. It caught on the second try, and the wood burned. He leaned in and blew on it, coaxing it to life.

Isobel crouched beside him and blew on it too, excited to help. The flame almost went out.

"Gently," he said, and cupped his hand around the tiny flicker, nursing it higher again with soft, even breaths. When the fire caught, he shifted the wood into a better position and sat back on his heels. "I can teach you how to make a rod and bait the hook. And if we can find enough rope, I can show you how to weave a net."

Something inside of her unfurled. "You would do that?"

His eyes lifted to hers. "Of course. Why would you even ask?"

She shrugged, afraid that if she spoke her voice would tremble.

He rose and reached for her hand, pulling her up close beside him. "There's a creek nearby. We can go out first thing in the morning and catch our breakfast." He grinned at her. "I'll even show you how to gut and scale our bounty."

She grinned back. "I'm looking forward to it. I'm not afraid to get my hands dirty. I shoveled two loads of manure into a pit for you to fall into."

He chuffed in amusement, and then leaned down and gave her a quick kiss. "Next time I promise to step right in. Your hard work shouldnae go to waste."

Her lips tingled where he'd kissed her, and she had a hard time catching her breath. "If you teach me how to fish, there willna be a next time."

"Ah, sweetling, you say that now…"

"You're right. You're bound to do something to annoy me. I'd be remiss not to set things straight."

He grinned again. "Always."

When he turned back to his pack, pulled out his extra plaid and tossed it on the bed, a strange fluttering filled her stomach. She pressed her hand to her middle and darted her gaze back to him, but his back was to her as he headed to the door.

"Where are you going?"

"To skin that last rabbit before it's dark. I'll make you some of my famous stew. I have some turnips and onion, and I picked wild garlic yesterday during our trek through the woods."

The door banged shut behind him, blocking the light that had streamed in, and she realized it had grown darker in the cabin. She turned to the fire. It burned brightly, crackling in a comforting way. Picking up an iron poker that leaned against the hearth, she nudged one of the logs, wanting to feel useful. Sparks flew up, making her think of the sparks created when Kerr had struck the steel rod against the flint that had lit the kindling.

She laid down the poker and grabbed the flint and striker Kerr had left on the mantel. The striker felt heavy in her hand, and the part she gripped was too big for her. Way too big, seeing as it was made for Kerr's giant paw. Still, she struck it against the flint. Nothing happened. She kept trying, determined to create a spark, to prove she could do something of value besides dig traps for people who'd broken the social covenant of the clan.

When it finally lit, she whooped excitedly. The tiny spark floated to the wood floor, and she quickly stamped it out. She tried several more times until she started to get the hang of it.

"Are you trying to light the cabin on fire?" Kerr asked from the doorway, making her jump.

"Nay. I'm practicing."

"Good," he said, and then stepped inside. He moved toward the fire, a piece of leather stretched between his hands that carried chopped-up pieces of raw meat. When he reached the table, he laid it down and grabbed a large pot from a shelf. After checking to see that it was clean, he dumped the meat inside, retrieved his spices from his pack, and shook the mixture over the food before stirring it with a big wooden spoon.

A hook already hung above the fire, and he looped the pot's handle over it, then adjusted the height with a chain.

"Can I help?" she asked.

He passed her a medium-sized clay bowl. "Aye. There's a rain barrel to the right of the door. Bring in some water so we can wash the vegetables."

She took the bowl from him, glad to have something to do, and made her way outside. The sun had almost set, and the gloaming was upon them. Taking a moment, she looked up at the sky and admired the pink-and-orange clouds. When a whicker sounded to her right, she peered over to see Diabhla standing not far away, blending into the shadows of the cabin. He was not restrained in any way.

She walked over and rubbed her hand up and down his broad nose, the short black hair under her palm silky soft. "Hello, beauty," she crooned. "You look as much a bandit o'er here in the shadows as your laird, just as imposing and dangerous-looking." He snorted into her hair, blowing dirt into the strands. She grimaced and brushed it out. "And just as annoying too."

Then she sighed and kissed the top of his muzzle. "But still kissable."

The rain barrel stood at the corner of the cabin, and she walked over to it. As she lifted the lid and dipped the bowl in, she wondered if there was enough water in there for her to have a bath later on. She shivered as she imagined herself naked in the tub with Kerr right outside.

Or what would happen if he came barging in.

"Concentrate on the task at hand, Isobel," she chastised herself, and then headed back inside.

Kerr stood at the table, peeling turnips with his dagger. The sight stopped her short and she almost burst into laughter. He looked up at her and smiled, causing her heart to do a wee flip.

"What?" he asked. "Did you ne'er expect to see me preparing vegetables?"

"Um… I suppose I didn't." She moved forward and placed the bowl of water on the table beside him.

He pointed to the three peeled turnips sitting in a pile. "You can rinse those, and then give the meat a stir."

She did as he asked, her fingers cooling in the water as she sneaked sideways glances at him. "What else do you know how to do besides cook?"

"Lots of things," he said, waggling his eyebrows at her. "I'd be happy to show you some of them later on."

He was trying to make her laugh. It was working. "Can you cook anything besides stew?"

"Porridge, of course, and oat cakes. Nothing fancy. Soups and stew are easy, and they taste delicious. I also do as Eirik did today and throw greens into a pot with some barley. You can learn too, if you want, Izzy."

"Does Gavin know how to cook?"

"Aye. Gregor made sure all of us knew how to survive in the woods. We learned to forage for food and to identify which plants were edible and which were poisonous. Otherwise, we could throw the wrong kind of mushrooms into our soup and die. If all we knew how to do was hunt, we'd get sick of our meals before long—as well as get sick. People who only eat meat doona fare well o'er the long run."

She finished with the turnips and stepped to the hearth to stir the chunks of rabbit in the pot. It confounded her to think that Gavin and Kerr knew how to cook—they all did. What else had they been taught that she'd missed out on besides fighting and weaponry?

Her mother had tried to teach her needlepoint, but it had bored Isobel to tears and she'd never had any real talent for it. Her mother had created some beautiful pieces that Isobel now cherished.

"Can you sew?" she asked as he brought the turnips over and began cutting them up and dropping them into the pot.

"Aye. 'Tis verra inconvenient to be on a mountain and have a tear in your plaid or a hole in your shirt and not know how to repair it. Many a time I've darned socks while sitting in front of the campfire. We all have."

"And what about things like herbs for medicine? Do you know how to use those too?"

"In a rudimentary way, aye, but not like Lachlan's wife Amber. She's the finest healer I've e'er met."

He said it with such respect, almost reverence, that Isobel felt a stab of jealousy. What greater skill was there than saving people's lives and helping to bring new lives into the world? And she'd heard all about how skilled Callum's wife Maggie was with her bow and dagger. She'd saved Callum and his people several times. The way she'd heard Gavin's men tell the tale, Maggie was a modern-day Valkyrie.

Kerr reached for the wild garlic and onions lying on the table and swished them in the water before slicing them over the pot like he'd done with the turnips.

He glanced over at her, and then back down. "What's that look on your face mean?" he asked as the pungent vegetables fell over the meat.

She shot him a startled glance. "I doona have a look."

"Aye, you did. Your mouth was pursed almost as if you were angry, yet your eyes revealed a vulnerability you usually doona show. And you're gripping the spoon as if you want to strangle it."

She dropped the spoon with a clatter into the pot—she probably would have ruined the food anyway—and stepped back. Her chin lifted automatically, trying to look down her nose at him even though he was a head taller. When she realized what she was doing, she dropped her chin and sighed, mad at herself.

"There it is again," he said, his keen gaze on her face. He finished up with the vegetables, put his dagger on the mantel, and pulled on the chain to raise the pot higher over the fire. After wiping his hands, he turned to her and laced his fingers with hers. "What is it, Izzy? As much as I try, I canna always read your mind."

She huffed, somewhere between amusement and exasperation. "But you can sometimes?"

"Better than anyone."

She pressed her lips together, knowing how it would sound if she grumbled about her limited education. She'd been the cherished daughter of a laird and was now the sister of a powerful laird. She'd had tutors who'd taught her to read, and they'd discussed history, literature, and commerce with her—far more than what most women, common or noble, were taught.

And she'd been afforded the freedom to choose her own husband and spend her days as she pleased, which usually meant mingling with her clan and listening to their successes and failures, their laughter and complaints—and then acting accordingly, so every small injustice was investigated and put right.

No one had told her to do that. One day she just did. And then the next, and the next.

But right here, right now, she had nothing to contribute, no useful skills. It made her life so far seem…silly.

"I just…I wish that I could be someone about whom people spoke with esteem, like you did when you mentioned Amber. Or how I've heard Finn and Artair speak about Callum's wife, Maggie. They couldnae stop talking about her skill with the bow and dagger and how she fought the men that came after them." She curled her fingers into fists and punched him lightly to demonstrate.

Kerr raised his brow, one corner of his mouth tipping up as he caught her hands again. "Maggie didnae fight with her fists, Izzy. She flung her daggers and shot her arrows—better than anyone I've seen. She was brave, aye, but she never engaged in hand-to-hand combat with enemy warriors. They would have broken her in two." His brow furrowed and then cleared. "Maybe you're thinking of Amber. She had some tricks up her sleeve. She knocked me down the day we met and twisted my stones." He laughed as he said it, his eyes shining with amusement but also admiration. "Of course, Lachlan towered o'er us in seconds, glaring at me and threatening to stick a sword in me if I hurt her. Otherwise, I would have dislodged her immediately, twisted stones or not."

Astonishment rippled through her, and her jaw dropped. "The healer is also a fighter?"

"Not a fighter in the way you're thinking, but she knew how to defend herself, how best to escape if she was attacked. 'Twas a difficult and dangerous time for her before Lachlan arrived, yet she still tended to her people—like you do."

"Me? I doona heal anyone, and God knows someone is always on my heels to make sure I'm safe." She rolled her eyes as she said it, even though she knew she was being ungrateful. But some days she longed to be able to wander through the woods alone or shop in the markets without one of her guards coming after her.

"God willing, someone *will* always be with you. Your brother protects you and Deirdre the same way the rest of my foster brothers protect their wives. The same way Gregor protected us when we were young. 'Tis no shame in that, Isobel." He cupped his hand around her cheek and caught her gaze so she couldn't look away. "And you do heal. You heal the fabric of your clan. You spot injustice, see what needs to be done, and do it. You are their lady. Queen Isobel. You lead them as much as Gavin does—or your father did before him. Every person in your clan knows they have equal value in your eyes."

He leaned down and pressed a soft, lingering kiss to her lips. "That is your talent."

"So you're saying I have a skill for…strategy? For understanding people and clan politics, and then…fixing things?"

"That's part of it, aye. You know what needs to be done to bring people together, to make things right."

Her mind whirled as validation saturated every inch of her. She'd thought Kerr and the other lairds were dismissive of her accomplishments and considered them to be nothing more than pranks—amusing tricks she pulled with little value to the clan.

"Does Gavin feel this way?" she asked.

"Most of the time. Certainly he does when he sees the good it does."

She scrunched up her brow, trying to understand. "Then why do you shut me out? If I'm such a valuable resource, why do you and Gavin and the others ne'er include me in your discussions? This conspiracy against us…I may see something that the rest of you have missed. Or know something you don't."

"No one doubts your abilities…"

"Then what? Is it because I'm a woman? Do you not trust me? Do *they* not trust me?"

Kerr lifted his hand and squeezed the back of his neck. "'Tis not *you* they mistrust." Then he turned back to the hearth, lowered the pot over the fire and gave it a stir.

Isobel stared at his back, so broad and powerful, the muscles flexing and contracting under his thin, linen léine as he put down the spoon and crouched beside his saddlebag, looking for something.

"Kerr," she said, her hands fisted at her sides, her jaw tight. "What does that mean?"

He rose with a full leather flask in his hands, pulled the wooden stopper, and took a drink. She watched as his Adam's apple bobbed in his throat. When he finished, he held it out to her. "'Tis ale."

She shook her head, and he slowly tipped some ale into the pot and stirred the mixture.

"Kerr," she pressed him.

"What it means is that you may marry someone who is not an ally to Gavin and the rest of us. You will be loyal to him, not to us. If he is a laird, you will be lady of his clan, not mine or Gavin's. You will have his best interests and your children's best interests at heart." He took another swig of the ale, and then stoppered it and put it on the mantel. "As it should be."

Her breath caught in her throat, and a chill rolled over her. "What are you saying? That I would betray you? All of you?"

Kerr continued to stir the stew, not looking at her. The silence stretched between them. "You wouldnae want to, but it could happen," he said finally. "If you loved him, you would want to please him. If he was a conniving man, he could trick you or wear you down. If he was an evil man, he would leave you with little choice. What if he threatened to harm you or your children? Or anyone else?"

"Gavin would ne'er let me marry someone like that."

He snorted in disbelief. "When you want something badly enough, Izzy, you doona give up until you get it. And your mother made sure Gavin doesn't have a say when it comes to that."

She continued to stare at him, her chest constricted, her skin feeling hot and tight. "Well, *I* would ne'er marry someone like that!"

"Then what if you marry a good man, but one who isna as strong as you? What if someone else convinces him to get information from you? Maybe they offer him money, and he thinks it will impress you. He loves you, you love him, he's a good father…"

"For heaven's sake, you're being absurd! I would ne'er marry a man like that either."

He spun to her, his eyes hooded, a muscle twitching in his clenched jaw. "Then what kind of man would you marry? Because you've already said you wouldnae marry someone like me."

Heat and ice invaded her body at the same time. "And do you

wonder why? The fact that we are here, alone in this cabin, proves it. No other man but you would have dared take me against my will."

"And no other woman but you would have set up a trap in the middle of the night, by herself, and on the bloody loch when you canna even swim. And I've known too many men who have taken women against their will. Most of whom I've killed because of it—including my own father. The difference between me and those men is I have your best interests at heart!"

"Nay, you have *your* best interests at heart." She poked her finger hard in his chest when she said it.

He caught the offending digit and pressed it flat against his body. His heart pounded beneath her palm. "When do you ever feel more alive, Isobel, than when you're with me?"

The question startled her, and her eyes widened under the directness of his gaze. She pulled her hand away. "I feel verra much alive when I'm lying in my own bed under my own covers by myself—safe."

"You'd feel more alive if you were in your own bed under your own covers but *with me*." He stepped back and released her hand. "But keep lying to yourself, sweetling. The more you protest, the harder you'll fall when the time comes."

She gasped, infuriated, and an angry denial formed in her head, but it got tangled on her tongue and she sputtered like an idiot.

He turned away from her and quickly stirred the stew. "There's some barley in my bag. Toss a small handful in and let it cook for a while, stirring occasionally. If it gets too thick, add some more ale or water." He pulled on the chain again so the pot rose a few inches above the fire.

"You're leaving?" she asked, her anger evaporating.

She knew Kerr wouldn't leave her to fend for herself, but a gulf had widened between them with every sharp jab of their tongues, especially when they'd talked about her marrying someone else. Now, she wanted to grab onto his shirt and yank him back to her.

He handed her the spoon. She clutched it like a shield.

"I'll be outside. Bar the door if you feel you must. Maybe you'll feel *safer* with me sleeping out there."

Then he grabbed his dagger from the mantel and strode to the door. It banged shut behind him, sounding like a ball of iron flung from a trebuchet and into a castle wall.

A fatal shot.

She instinctively wrapped her arms around her middle to cover the wound. Still, it spread until her chest constricted and her throat ached.

She'd been fighting with Kerr her whole life, so why was he affecting her this way now?

Nay, not her whole life…she'd adored him when she was younger, had been half in love with him at fifteen. She'd only been fighting with him since…since that night. Since she'd felt such a sense of rejection and betrayal that she'd frozen on the inside— except for the humiliation. Aye, she'd felt that emotion burning like a red-hot coal in her belly.

But then she'd stopped crying, put on her queenly smile, and boxed up her heart.

She'd been a younger version of herself—still a lass, but well on her way to being the Beauty of the Highlands, the woman they all talked about, the girl who held a special place in Kerr MacAlister's heart—except he'd chosen someone else.

She sighed and pressed her thumb and fingers over her eyes.

Maybe it was time to let that painful memory go…if she could dig that deep.

―――――――

Kerr sat on the sturdy branch of the Scots pine, his back against the trunk, his feet tucked up, and his plaid blending into the foliage. No one would see him if they came near the cabin.

Below him, Diabhla grazed in the moonlit field.

He had his dagger out in case someone did approach, and he'd been idly carving a stick in his hands as his mind played over the recent exchange with Isobel—the different twists and turns it had taken, the different emotions she'd displayed—and the way his dark side had emerged at the end, agitated over the talk of Isobel marrying someone else.

He'd had to leave before he scared her, before the cruelty of his father's blood undid all the progress he'd made between them the last few days...although progress sounded like wishful thinking right about now.

She was such a complicated woman—fierce, brave, and keenly intelligent, as well as kind and generous, with a wit that kept him on his toes. On the surface, she often appeared proud and haughty—and she was; she truly owned her place in the world as Lady MacKinnon—but below that shield of privilege, she had a softer side—a vulnerable side.

But vulnerable to what? To whom?

Surely she knew that she owned him?

It surprised him that she envied Amber and Maggie... Or maybe she envied their purpose and their free rein to use their skills. She'd been born to lead but she wasn't allowed to—she'd been excluded from the inner circle of his alliance with his foster brothers and Gregor.

He could understand how that would infuriate her. Hurt her.

Well, if stubborn Isobel MacKinnon would ever marry him, become Lady MacAlister, she could rule equally by his side.

Alas, his Izzy knew how to hold a grudge, and she was angry at him for something.

He heard the door squeak and looked up to see her step out of the cabin and onto the porch. She carried something in her hands, but even with the moon out, it was too dim to see what it was. A bowl of stew, perhaps?

She glanced around the porch, as if looking for him, and then peered into the moonlit glen surrounding the cabin. Her gaze drifted to the lean-to on the opposite side of the clearing before she spotted Diabhla. Kerr unfolded from his plaid and dropped his leg off the branch, swinging it to catch her attention.

When she saw him, he waited for her to say something. If he spoke, his voice would surely come out a growl—his anger still simmered below the surface.

Besides, if he did speak first, what would he say? Apologize for leaving or for wanting her to marry him? Nay, he wasn't sorry for either of those things. While he had many regrets in his life, asking Isobel to be his wife wasn't one of them. He didn't want her to have any doubt about his intentions.

Finally, she placed the bowl on the railing and reentered the cabin. Apparently, she didn't know what to say to him either.

A spoon poked up over the rim of the bowl she'd left, and it pleased him that she'd brought him some food. The stew was an olive branch.

He watched the woods for a few minutes, methodically checking for movement or the glint of steel as Gregor had taught him to do, and when he was convinced no one was out there, he jumped down and strode to the porch. Picking up the bowl, he sat beside the rain barrel, which afforded him more cover. After rewrapping himself in his plaid and laying his sword across his lap, he tried the stew.

It was good.

He must have eventually dozed off because when he opened his eyes, alerted by sounds within the cabin, the moon was behind the building and darkness stretched across the ground. The door creaked open a moment later and Isobel stepped out. She was backlit from the fire burning in the hearth—her hair mussed and her clothing rumpled as if she'd been asleep.

She peered toward the tree he'd sat in earlier, lines forming across her brow. Her eyes looked soft and drowsy.

Vulnerable.

"Isobel," he said quietly.

She gasped and spun toward him, her hand rising to her chest. "Oh, you startled me."

"I'm sorry. It wasn't my intent."

"I know…" She opened her mouth as if to continue, but then she closed it again.

"What is it?" he asked.

"Come inside," she blurted out.

"Why?"

"Because I…I…come inside. Please. I canna sleep. I want—I need—you in there with me."

He closed his eyes, savoring her words. Then rose without saying anything. After sheathing his sword, he picked up his empty bowl from the top of the rain barrel and followed her into the cabin. Barring the door behind him, he then crossed to the table and laid down his sword.

She took nervous steps to the bed and sat gingerly on the edge. Then she pushed backward to the far side against the wall.

There was room for him to join her, but instead he dunked his bowl in the wash water, pulled out the chair, and sat down.

"Kerr!" she protested.

He raised his brow and saw that same hint of vulnerability in her eyes he'd seen earlier…as well as her mouth forming into a stubborn moue.

"What?"

"I want you to sleep beside me." She pointed to the side of the bed nearest to him.

He sighed and rubbed his hand across his face. "Are you sure that's a good idea, Isobel? We discussed this earlier—you didnae seem to want me near your bed."

"Well, you canna sleep there." She pointed toward his chair. "You'll end up falling asleep the next time you need to protect me."

He snorted. "I would ne'er sleep if you were in danger." But she had a point. If he was drowsy during the day, he wouldn't be as sharp as he needed to be. He drummed his fingers on the table—once—and then pushed back his chair and stepped to the side of the bed.

When he hesitated, she took his hand. "Doona you want to sleep beside me?" She'd jutted her chin up in what he now knew was a defensive gesture, and he could see the uncertainty in her eyes.

"Of course I do." He squeezed her fingers as he said it. "'Tis only…we're getting into dangerous territory."

"Nay, we're not. We'll sleep, naught more. I trust you in this, Laird MacAlister."

He rubbed his jaw, undecided, and then reached behind him for his sword and leaned it up against the bed.

She handed him the plaid she'd been using earlier and then fluffed the pillow, moving it to a more central position.

"The stew was good," she said, attempting to ease the tension.

"Aye. You did a great job."

"I was nervous. I thought I was stirring it too much."

"It was perfect."

She laid back on the bed with a pleased smile. Her hair spread out on the pillow like a bright halo, and his breath stopped. He squeezed his eyes shut…

She trusts me not to take advantage. That means keeping my hands to myself.

He would do this if it killed him.

He laid down beside her, but he was too big and his entire side pressed against hers. He glanced over, hoping she had more room, but she was squeezed tight between him and the wall.

"I'm too big," he said, sitting up. "I'll sleep on the floor beside you."

She sat up too, and he could feel the softness of her breasts against his arm. "Nay, it's too hard down there. We'll sleep on our sides."

He almost groaned at her words. Aye, he was definitely *too hard down there*.

She laid back down, shifting onto her side toward him, and then tugged at the crook of his elbow. He resisted, his palm squeezing his nape. It would be a challenge being so close to her, but it would also weave them more tightly together. And hopefully build her desire for him. He'd already set it aflame when they'd kissed in the boat. Maybe he could set the embers burning, waiting for him to kiss her once more.

He turned away from her and laid down. He was still too big, and her body curved tightly against his back and arse. Her breath puffed warmly on his neck, setting his skin on fire.

Hell, he was already on fire—every part of him aching, even his teeth. He turned his face into the pillow, not knowing whether he would laugh like a madman or howl like a cat in heat.

Her hands rested between his shoulder blades, and her fingers moved restlessly against his shirt. Then she slowly glided her palm up and over his side until it rested across his chest.

"Is that all right?" she asked. "'Tis a little more comfortable."

He had to swallow before answering. Still, he sounded gruff. "Aye. 'Tis good." He raised his hand and clasped hers, weaving their fingers together, and then pressed her palm over his heart.

She sighed quietly, and her body softened against him, causing warmth to spread through his chest. At this moment, with him, she was happy. He bent his head and kissed her knuckles.

For now, that was all he needed.

Fifteen

"YOU'VE GOT ONE!" KERR YELLED AS ISOBEL YANKED ON HER fishing rod and pulled a wriggling fish, caught on the end of her line, out of the water. She swung it toward them with a whoop, and the fish landed with a *splat* at her feet.

Its speckled body, a dull brown on top with a yellow underbelly, flopped on the creek bank as it gasped for air. She took a quick step back, her hand clamped over her mouth as her enthusiasm waned.

The hook was still caught in the poor creature's mouth, and she couldn't help thinking about how much it must hurt.

She'd been so excited this morning when Kerr had woken her to go fishing. It was a beautiful day, and the walk to reach the creek had been invigorating. Once there, she'd impatiently watched and listened as Kerr had shown her how to make a fishing rod.

Finding a worm to bait the hook hadn't been a problem—she liked digging in the earth and getting dirty, especially when she made one of her traps—but when it came time to push the hook through the worm, she found herself squeamish. The worm had fallen off three times before she succeeded.

Still, that hadn't prepared her for this...this...horror she felt watching the poor fish suffocating to death at her feet.

Without thinking, she kicked the wretched thing back into the creek.

"Why did you do that?" Kerr asked, grabbing her rod from her. He lifted it and pulled the fish out of the water again. But this time it wriggled loose and fell back into the creek with a splash.

Kerr lowered the rod and shot her a dark look. Guilt swirled through her belly, making her squirm.

"Are you hungry, Isobel?" he asked, his brow pulling low over his eyes.

"Aye."

"Do you want fish for breakfast?"

She lifted her thumb to her mouth and chewed on her nail, thinking about it. "Is there any stew left?"

"Nay."

"Do you have oats? Maybe we could have oat cakes?"

"Aye, or maybe we could have trout. Have you ever had brown trout freshly caught and pan-fried over the fire with a touch of salt?"

She shook her head.

"I didnae think so. Otherwise, you would ne'er have kicked that fish back into the water." He handed her the fishing rod. "If you want to eat, find another worm."

She wrinkled up her nose, and when he turned back to the creek and cast his own line into the water, she barely resisted making a face at him like she was twelve years old.

Why did I think fishing would be fun?

She sighed and moved to the pile of dirt they'd already dug up to look for a second worm. Behind her, Kerr grumbled, "That was a big one, too."

"What was I supposed to do…let it suffer?" She pushed her hands into the soil and sifted her fingers through it.

"You could have whacked it on the head. What do you think happens to all the animals that grace your table?"

She didn't answer. When she found another worm, she stabbed it onto the hook without looking and ended up poking her finger.

"Ow!"

"What happened?" He glanced over at her.

"Nothing." She rose and recast her line, feeling that same sense of excitement rising again when it plopped into the water. Apparently, she liked catching fish and eating them, just not killing them.

She had thought to ask Kerr to teach her how to hunt too, but if her reluctance to kill a fish was any indication, she doubted she could shoot a deer.

"What other things did you learn to do when you were out in the woods?" she asked.

He shot her a quizzical look. "You mean like hunting?"

"Nay, like…foraging for food or treating an injury. What kinds of things did Gregor teach you?" A familiar mix of wistfulness and resentment sparked in her belly at her question, and she tamped the feeling down.

When she'd been growing up, every year after harvest, Gavin and the other foster brothers had gone to Gregor's to learn exciting things, useful things, while she'd been expected to stay home and master needlepoint.

The unfairness of that still hurt.

When her mother had died, she'd sworn to never pick up another needle again. Now she learned that darning socks was one of the skills the lads had had to learn. Well, she'd sooner pick up a needle to darn a sock than to decorate a pillow.

"Is there something you want to tell me, Izzy? Are you planning to run away again?"

"Of course not. 'Tis just…there are so many things I doona know. So many things my father and brother failed to teach me. Things my mother didn't know…like how to make a fire or cook fish."

"You've ne'er laid a fire before? Even with the amount of time you spent in the woods?"

She shook her head, feeling useless again, the same as she had the night before. "The fires at the castles were always pre-laid, and I only had to light them with a candle. I know you use kindling on the bottom to start it, but…is there a trick to it?"

"Sometimes, depending on the wood." He glanced over at her with an encouraging smile. "At least you know how to use a flint and striker, now."

Somehow that made her feel worse, and she dropped her chin so he wouldn't see the shame in her eyes. "I suppose."

"How about after this, you build the fire and cook the fish for us…if we catch any," Kerr said.

"Are you certain? What if I burn it?"

"I'll keep watch. Then afterward, we can walk through the woods and I can show you some other things you should know. Maybe find some berries or apples to eat too."

"I saw a nest on the way here. I can climb up and look for eggs."

"Aye, but only if it's safe. It's not worth the trouble of falling and breaking a leg."

She sniffed dismissively. "I've had many tough climbs in the woods to lay traps for people. Believe me, it was well worth the danger."

"You also had your guard with you who could step in if you fell. 'Tis not the same when you're deep in the woods. Injury is a big concern in the Highlands."

She felt chastised, and her resentment rose again. "I know that."

"Do you? Because it took me a long time to learn that when I was a lad."

"Well, maybe if someone had taught me when I was a lass I would know it by now too."

She dropped her eyes to hide her anger. She hadn't been afforded the same training as the men because she was a woman. She hadn't been afforded a lot of things because she was a woman, and the exclusion still hurt.

Finally, she glanced up and found him watching her.

"Just ask, Isobel," he said.

"Ask for what?"

"For me to teach you. When you were a lass, you used to beg me and Gavin to take you with us to Gregor's. I couldnae do it then, but I can teach you whate'er you want to know now." He reached out and squeezed her chin gently. "Let go of the resentment, dearling, and ask."

He turned back to the creek, pulled up his line, and then cast it again in another spot. After a moment, Isobel did the same.

He'd said something similar when they were at her trap site—*she could ask him anything*. Her mind filled with questions and she wanted to blurt them out, but at the same time she didn't want to seem too eager…as if that would lessen her somehow.

She rolled her eyes at her own idiocy. Maybe she needed to delve into her own head before she delved into Kerr's head.

She scrunched up her brow and decided to start with an easy question. "What else is a big concern in the Highlands, besides injury?"

"Getting lost," he said without pause. "It's easy to lose your bearings and end up going in circles for weeks or longer. That's a much bigger worry than other dangers like wolves or wild boars or coming across brigands."

She snorted. "Aye, Siv was terrifying as she lay sleeping in my lap."

A bemused expression crossed his face. "I have ne'er seen a wolf as big or as friendly as her. But doona be fooled if you see another one. Climb the nearest tree as fast as you can. Callum's wife, Maggie, was lucky to survive when she encountered a pack of wolves on her own. And I've seen a boar rip through a hunting dog and almost take off a man's leg. They're smart and unpredictable. Unfortunately, brigands can be even worse—especially toward a woman."

She swallowed and was about to respond when her rod pulled hard in her hands and the line tugged downward. "I've got another one," she yelled excitedly. "Kerr, I've got one!"

"Pull it up gently," he said, but she'd already yanked on the rod.

The fish, also a brown trout, came flying toward her. When its tail flapped right next to her face, she squealed and dropped the rod. The trout hit the ground at her feet, the same as the other one, and flopped around, gasping for breath. Horror and pity seeped through her again.

"Doona even think about kicking this one in." Kerr quickly put his rod aside and scooped up the wriggling fish. Pressing firmly on the corners of its jaw, he opened its mouth and freed the hook from inside.

He gripped the tail, but then he hesitated and looked up at her. "Do you want to turn around?"

"You're going to kill it?" she cried.

"Of course I am. We canna eat it alive."

"Do it quickly, then."

He crouched down and lifted the fish into the air. But instead of killing it, the trout slipped out of his hands and flew over his head. It landed, flopping on the ground behind him.

Isobel didn't think. Instead, she darted toward it, but Kerr twisted around and grabbed it first, only to have it slide out of his hands. He fell forward as she stepped past him and grasped the fish to throw it back into the creek. But the poor thing was like a greased pig and landed on the edge of the embankment.

Kerr reached for it, but she threw herself over top of him, knee in his spine, to get there first.

He grunted and rolled onto his back, holding her by the waist. Neither one of them could quite reach the fish without dislodging the other.

But Isobel had done enough to save the poor thing, and it flopped over the edge on its own, landing with a splash in the water.

Silence reigned, and then she burst out laughing.

"You think that's funny, do you?" Kerr grumbled. But she knew he wasn't angry. She'd heard him use that tone of voice many times when he pretended to be mad at wee Ewan. 'Twas a favorite game they played.

"I should throw you into the creek like that bloody fish," he continued.

She laughed harder, her elbows digging into his chest as she struggled to get free. He smiled up at her. His hands still clenched her waist, and their bodies were pressed together. Her hair had fallen forward, enclosing them in their own private grotto.

Slowly, her laughter dissipated, and her eyes drifted down to his mouth. They hadn't kissed—really kissed—since they'd been on the boat, and it became clear by the way his body had hardened beneath hers that he was thinking similar thoughts. She bit her lip and raised her eyes back up, but he was staring at *her* mouth now.

"Kerr."

"Aye," he answered hoarsely.

"You said I could ask you anything."

He slowly looked up…held her gaze. "Aye, Isobel."

She let the moment draw out, let the tension in the air build between them. Then she leaned down so her mouth was inches from his. "What's a lass got to do to get some breakfast around here?"

He sat up with a loud, indignant roar, and she burst out laughing again.

———————

Kerr banned Isobel from the creek after that and sent her to find firewood so he could catch their breakfast in peace. She went off happily, Diabhla wandering along behind her, and foraged for berries along the way.

She would save those for later to go with the oats.

By the time she returned with a basketful of wood and a handful of berries, he'd caught another plump brown trout.

"Just in time for you to gut the fish," he announced with a wicked grin. He laid the dead fish on a log and handed her a knife.

"You think I canna do it?" she asked indignantly.

"Do *you* think you can do it?" he asked with a raised brow.

She knew it was a challenge, and she made a derogatory sound in the back of her throat before taking the knife from him and picking up the fish. She had a moment of regret as she admired the finned animal's beautiful coloring—the yellow scales on its belly almost golden in the sunlight, and the brown speckles on top looking almost red in certain places—but then her stomach growled and she turned her attention back to what Kerr was telling her.

The knife was a bit unwieldy because it was made for Kerr's bigger hand, but she finished without any real problems. Cutting into the dead fish didn't bother her nearly as much as seeing the poor thing suffocate.

He nodded approvingly at her work, and a spark of pride burst in her chest.

"Now what?" she asked eagerly.

"Rinse it, and then you can start the fire. And doona get any fish guts on your clothes. They will stink, and you havenae any others to wear."

"Now you tell me," she grumbled.

"'Tis common sense, Isobel."

She rolled her eyes when she turned her back on him and returned to the creek. Finding a shallow spot, she crouched down on a rock and rinsed the fish. When she was done, she checked for any guts on her clothes...and sighed. They were filthy—even more so than when she'd wrestled with Kerr on the embankment earlier.

The memory made her smile, but then she got a whiff of her plaid and wrinkled her nose. It stank of horses, fish, and the musty smell of dirt. And her hair! She could only imagine how tangled it must be. This morning she'd been so excited to go fishing that she'd rushed through her ablutions and then barely brushed her messy blond strands before loosely braiding them.

Her hair now hung around her face, and she *tsked* when she spotted a dead leaf in it. After pulling it out, she picked up the fish and headed back to where Kerr stood beside a shallow pit surrounded with rocks.

"Is that for the fire?" she asked curiously.

"Aye. You doona want to light the grass aflame. The dirt and rocks stop the flames from spreading to the forest."

She carefully laid down the fish and moved toward him. He squatted on his haunches and inspected the pile of dead branches and twigs she'd collected earlier. "This is good for the kindling. We'll lay the bigger pieces on top to sustain the flames. The wood is dry, and as you can see," he broke a branch in half, "it snaps easily. That's how you can tell if it's dry enough."

"But?" she asked.

"But we still need an inner layer of tinder—bark, dried leaves, dead grass. Material that will easily catch fire."

"All right." She rose and headed to a downed tree on the edge of the clearing and pulled off some pieces of bark that were dried out and curling upward. She brought them back to the fire pit and then gathered up whatever dried leaves and grass she could find.

"Is that enough?" she asked when her arms were full.

"Nay. Double that amount. You'd be surprised how fast you go through it. And the last thing you want when you're nursing a flame is to run out and have to go back for more."

She gathered up additional tinder and piled it within the fire pit. Next, she picked up some twigs. "Do I lay the smallest pieces on first?"

"Some people do. I've always mixed the kindling with the bigger sticks and built them up around the tinder like this..." He turned his hands sideways and crossed one of them over the other at right angles to demonstrate. "And then I cross-hatch them over the top and pile more tinder on the roof. The layering leaves enough space between the wood so the air can flow through and feed the flames."

She pursed her lips, picked up twigs and branches, and tried to erect walls around the tinder how he'd described. When a branch was too long, she broke it into pieces with a grunt. Kerr picked up another branch to help her, but she pinned him in place with her stare. He slowly lowered the branch and backed away from her with his arms raised and eyes wide.

When she sighed in frustration a moment later, he raised one brow. On her nod, he reached out and straightened her wood a little. "Think of it as building a very windy cabin around the tinder. At the front is an open door, preferably facing the wind, where you can strike the spark inside. That way, the wind can blow the flames into the wood around it."

When she finally finished, she excitedly took the striker and flint from him. Several sparks failed to reach the tinder. One landed on her skirt and singed a wee hole. Another time, she knocked the striker into her little cabin and had to rebuild that section. But she finally got the hang of it, and when a spark landed on the dried leaves and began to burn, she let out an excited squeal.

"You've done it, lass!" Kerr exclaimed. "Now blow on it gently, the same as I showed you last night."

She tucked her hair behind her ears and leaned down to the wee door, using soft puffs of air to fan the flames. When she could see the bigger pieces burning on their own, she sat back with a satisfied sigh and a happy smile on her face.

Behind her, Kerr squeezed her shoulder.

She raised her hand and laid it over his. "What do I do now?"

"You cook us our breakfast."

"'Tis a good thing we didn't make oatcakes," Isobel said, laying the small plate that Kerr had packed for them at her feet. Wee bones from the fish lined the edge. Kerr had shown her how to de-bone it after cooking, but some of them had remained behind.

"Why? Doona you like them?" he asked from across the fire.

"I love them. But I doona know how I would have managed to flip them and fry the fish at the same time. I was afraid I would burn everything as it was, and all I had to do was stir the oats. 'Twas verra stressful."

"It gets easier with practice. But if you're worried about something burning, you can always take it off the fire for a minute. 'Tis what I do sometimes."

"I didn't think of that."

She picked up her bowl of oats and berries from the log beside her and stirred it before taking a spoonful.

"Mmmm. This is good too. Why does everything taste so much better? The fish was the best I've e'er tasted."

"I told you," Kerr said around a mouthful of oats. "Wait until we catch a duck and roast it o'er the fire. The meat is so succulent, it melts in your mouth."

"Can we do that tonight?" she asked.

"Possibly. But you may be tired by then and not want to cook. The rest of the day will be busy."

"Doing what?"

"Everything."

"We canna do everything. Surely you can narrow it down."

He grinned. "You'd be surprised. You said that you wanted to know all that Gregor taught me. Well, there's a lot to learn in the woods."

"Can you teach me how to wash my clothes? They smell awful," she said, wrinkling her nose.

He froze, and his eyes darted to hers. "Your chemise too?"

She felt the heat rise along her cheeks as she followed his train of thought. She wouldn't have any dry clothes to wear if she washed her long linen undershirt as well. "Nay, I doona suppose so." But then she blurted out, "Although it would be nice to have it clean too."

He blew out a puff of air and scraped his nails through his beard. "Aye, then. We'll do it later. You can wear my shirt. It will cover most of you."

"But then what will you wear?" she asked. Her heart was beating so fast and loud, she was sure he would see the vein pounding in her neck.

He raised a wicked eyebrow, and despite her embarrassment, excitement darted around her body like a hummingbird in a flowering tree.

She dropped her eyes and shoveled in the last few bites of oatmeal—best to have her mouth full, else she'd ask him to wash her clothes right now.

When she finished eating, she picked up her plate and walked around the fire toward him. "I'll take your dishes to the creek and rinse them."

And dunk myself in the water too, before I burst into flame.

She reached for his empty dishes, but instead, he grasped her hand and laced their fingers together.

"Thank you for breakfast, Izzy. 'Twas a feast for a king." Then he pressed his lips to the back of her hand.

"Um…thank you for teaching me," she said, sounding strangled.

He smiled, looking a little smug, and then kissed her fingers, leaving them hot and tingling. "When you come back, bring a bucket of water so we can douse the flames. We canna leave them burning unattended."

He handed her his dishes, and she fled.

Sixteen

"YOU PROMISE NOT TO LOOK?" ISOBEL ASKED HIM.

Kerr squeezed his thumb and forefinger over his eyes and tried to picture Gavin's face glaring at him. Or better yet, Gavin's *and* Gregor's faces glaring at him. They stood in front of him in the woods, frowning down at him as he sat with his back against a tree—*not* peeking at Isobel.

"Of course I willna look," he said over his bare shoulder toward the creek below. He'd stripped off his shirt earlier and given it to her to change into after her dip in the cool water.

"Because my shift will get wet washing my arisaid, and it willna hide anything."

He clenched his jaw to contain the demented laugh that rose in his throat. "I'm well aware of that, Izzy."

When the water splashed behind him, he puffed out a heavy breath and tried to distract himself from the scene he imagined taking place—her thin linen chemise soaked and clinging to her body as she washed her arisaid, the bar of soap he'd given her clenched in her hand, her hair rolled up and tied back in that mysterious way women had of securing it…although soft, silky strands had already started to escape the knot and tumble down the sides of her face.

He bit back a groan.

Or maybe she'd chosen to bathe first and was using the soap on herself, running her hands across her skin, pushing the lather over all those places he wanted to lick and kiss, her breasts lifting, her waist twisting and bending.

He was rock-hard thinking about it—hell, he'd been rock-hard all day—and that part of him with a mind of its own was jutting upward obscenely against the soft wool of his plaid, thick and long and desperate for the soft clutch of Isobel's body.

This time he did groan. Loudly.

"What was that?" she yelled from behind him.

"'Tis naught," he said and wrapped his hand over his plaid and around his cock, desperate to relieve the ache. It wouldn't take much; he hadn't touched another woman since he'd decided he wanted to marry Isobel.

For four long years, his hand had been his only intimate companion.

He'd tried to woo her during that time, but war, Ewan's disappearance, and that *thing* between them, whatever it was, had gotten in the way. If she still rejected him after their time together here, he didn't know what he would do.

"Kerr!"

"Aye?" he ground out.

"How will I know when it's done?"

His mind was so clouded with need, he couldn't discern her meaning. "When what's done?"

"My arisaid. How will I know when it's clean?"

"I doona know, Izzy. Just guess. Make sure you've squeezed soap through all of the material and then rinse it well."

"All right."

More splashing, and he gripped his fist harder around his cock before letting go and forcing his hands away. Nay, he couldn't disrespect her in that way. He rose quickly and looked for something he could do—anything—to distract himself. He would find Diabhla and repack his supply bag. He was about to whistle for the stallion, when Isobel let out a high-pitched screech, and he spun toward her, his warrior rising in an instant as his mind honed in on how to keep her safe.

"Isobel!" he yelled, drawing his sword and leaping down the

embankment. His eyes darted around as he ran along the rocky shore toward her, but he couldn't see any attackers.

She clutched her soaked arisaid in front of her. "Turn around!" she screamed and took several steps backward, the water rising above her knees. "And doona step on your shirt or I'll have to wash that too, and then what will I wear?"

He slowed and glanced down. The shirt he had given her lay at his feet. Still dry, but definitely in need of cleaning after the day they'd had traipsing through the woods. He almost picked it up and threw it at her to teach her a lesson. She obviously wasn't under attack or in any kind of trouble.

He sheathed his sword and stared at her, hands on his hips and his brow furrowed. After several deep, hard breaths, he loosened his jaw enough to speak.

"You screamed," he said, trying not to notice the exposed curve of her hip on one side and the length of her thigh on the other.

"You turned around," she said accusingly.

"I didn't turn around until *after* you screamed."

"Well, you stood up, and I thought you were going to turn around."

"Why would I do that? I gave you my word. Does my promise mean nothing to you?"

"Nay." She chewed her lip guiltily. "I just…my nerves overwhelmed me."

He huffed out a frustrated breath and rolled his eyes heavenward—partly asking the Almighty for patience but also to avoid looking at Isobel directly. He was a powerful, determined laird. He could trust himself to keep his eyes up.

But did *she* truly not trust *him*?

There was an easy way to find out… And if Isobel agreed to do as he asked, it would tell him so much about the future of their relationship.

He dropped his gaze back down and looked her directly in the eyes. "Have you rinsed out your dress?"

"Aye."

"Then toss it to me so you can have your bath while I squeeze out the water."

Her jaw gaped. "I canna do that. Have you lost your mind?"

"Nay." He held out his hand to her. "Your dress, Isobel."

He could see in her face the moment she decided to do as he asked. Her chin lifted slightly, those rosebud-red lips pursed almost in defiance, and her shoulders pulled back. He almost punched the air in triumph. Isobel wanted him to see her like this—practically naked—otherwise she would never consider it.

No one tells Isobel MacKinnon—soon to be MacAlister—what to do.

She balled up her wet dress and lobbed it straight at his chest.

He took his gaze from hers for only a second as he caught the dress. When he looked back, he tried to do the right thing—to anchor himself on her eyes and not look down—but she'd spun away from him and was stepping deeper into the water.

And without her gaze to lock onto, he faltered.

His eyes dropped from the bright halo of her hair piled on top of her head, slid down the length of her back, her waist tucked in at the bottom, and came to rest on the rounded globes of her backside—high and tight and curved like an apple he wanted to bite.

His knees weakened.

The wet chemise clung to her skin, dipped into the cleft of her arse, and molded over the tops of her legs, bringing to mind all the fantasies he'd had over the years about wrapping them around him.

He took an involuntary step toward her, like a predator scenting its prey, only to have her dive beneath the water. Her head appeared a moment later, her hair down and slicked back. He watched avidly as she worked her fingers through the strands and lifted her chemise over her head.

She caught his gaze as she reached for the soap on a nearby rock, and then turned away from him and rose out of the creek up to her waist to wash her linen shift. Her hair, darkened and sleek from the water, hung down her naked back. "I thought you were going to squeeze out my dress?" she asked.

"I am."

"Liar. You're watching me."

He shook out the sodden material and wrung it with his hands. Water poured out onto the rocks at his feet. "There."

She glanced over her shoulder. "You're still watching."

"You ne'er asked me to turn around."

When her only response was the sound of water splashing as she spun back and rinsed out her chemise, he couldn't help the exultant smile that creased his face. She dipped under again up to her shoulders, and then faced him. He quickly schooled his features.

"Here," she said, and flung her chemise at him.

He caught it easily.

She dunked under again and appeared farther out into the creek, with the soap still in her hand. He couldn't see beneath the water, but he assumed she was washing herself. He clenched his jaw as his imagination went wild—especially when her eyes landed on him…roaming his bare chest and stomach. And lower.

There was no hiding his body's response beneath his plaid, and he decided he didn't want to. He liked having her eyes on him. Hopefully, her interest in his body was as keen as his interest was in hers.

They were both vulnerable here, and he wanted her to know how much he desired her.

For good measure, he flexed a little harder as he squeezed out her chemise, bulging his arms and shoulders, popping out his chest, and clenching his stomach. 'Twas a lucky happenstance he'd given her his shirt to put on.

"Is it cold in there?" he asked as she lathered up the soap and rubbed it into her hair.

If he saw her naked, he would even things up by showing her his body as well—preferably before he took his own dip in the cool water to rinse off the day's dirt and sweat.

Isobel was curious—about everything. He was certain she would be curious about *that* part of him as well.

He would show her his *full* potential.

She dunked under the water to rinse her hair, and he laid her clothes flat on the rocks to dry. When he straightened, she'd swum closer.

"Are you coming out now?" he asked.

"Maybe. Turn around."

He shook his head, and then released his sword, his sporran, and loosened his plaid. Her eyes widened with surprise, but also with excitement as his plaid dipped low.

"You need to dry off," he said. He grasped the edge of the rectangular-shaped material and stretched it out in front of him, as naked now as she was. "Come, Isobel. I canna take much more of you frolicking in the water."

"I'm not frolicking."

He shrugged and let the silence stretch between them. The pressure mounted for her to do as he'd asked.

Finally, she spoke. "Lift the plaid higher so you canna see me. And this time, no peeking."

"Are you sure?" he asked, one eyebrow quirking.

Her throat bobbed as she swallowed. "I'm sure."

He raised the plaid until he could no longer see her face. The bottom edge hit the tops of his knees, and he wondered if she was hoping it would go higher.

Then he heard splashing, and when she rose from the water and started walking toward him, her face came into view. He adjusted the plaid as she moved closer, so as not to expose her body. He would not break her trust in this.

But he would watch her. When she saw his eyes on her face she hesitated, and panic flitted there briefly.

"I canna see anything, Isobel. Keep coming."

She rushed the last few steps. Before she could grab the plaid, he wrapped his arms around her shoulders, covering her all the way down to her knees, and pulled her tight into his embrace.

She fit perfectly against him, tucked beneath his chin.

"I'm getting your plaid wet," she protested, sounding breathless.

He smiled against her hair. "I doona mind. It will be wet after I bathe too."

He wanted to kiss her. Nay, he wanted to do a hell of a lot more than that. Her pelvis rocked against him, maybe unconsciously, but he knew what it was even if she didn't—an invitation.

His stones jerked in response, tight and hard against the base of his cock, swelling so taut, he gritted his teeth against the ache. Without thinking, he slid his palm down her spine and over her arse to grip the back of her thigh before he stopped himself.

"Izzy?" he ground out, more a grunt than an actual word.

"Aye," she croaked.

"Should I take that swim now?"

Seconds passed that seemed like hours. Time seemed to stop between them. Finally, she said, "Aye."

He let out a frustrated breath, and then closed his eyes, trying to find some calm in the middle of the storm. When he opened them, he released her leg and cupped her jaw with both hands. He stared at her…and then lowered his head and kissed her. Hard.

Letting go was a test of his resolve, especially when she rose up on her tiptoes and pushed against his lips.

He pulled away abruptly, his heart pounding. He could see she wanted more, and when she dropped her eyes to his mouth, he quickly stepped past her and strode to the water. One hand gripped his cock and stones to relieve the ache. He didn't look back, but he knew without a doubt that her gaze traced his back-side like his had traced hers.

"Dry off, Isobel," he said over his shoulder. "I may be a while. I wouldnae want you to get a chill while I cool off."

———————

"You want to do what?" Kerr asked as he wheeled toward Isobel, his eyebrows raised so high he wondered if they would ever come down. Around them, the birds chirped loudly to one another, and he could almost imagine they were as perturbed as he was.

Although he didn't know why he was surprised. He'd known it was coming.

She took another step along the trail, the leaves crunching beneath her shoes, before seeing he'd stopped and turning to face him. Diabhla stopped as well and swung his head around to watch them.

"You said you would teach me everything Gregor taught you," she said. "Well, a lot of your time spent with him was learning sword play and other forms of combat."

"I have ne'er *played* with a sword in my life. Nor have my brothers. We learned how to use weapons to kill other men with weapons. Is that what you want, Isobel?"

"If that's what it comes to, aye." She took a step toward him, and he almost grabbed her by the folds of his shirt—looking so damn provocative on her, despite how big it was—and dragged her all the way in for a kiss. Except his arms were full of her wet plaid and chemise, and he feared if he started kissing her, he would not be able to stop—and neither would she.

Lord help him. How was he going to get through the night?

"I want to know how all the different weapons work, and how to defend myself if I need to—like Maggie and Amber. And I want to know about war and strategy and the best ways to take a castle or defend it."

"You want to lead."

She stilled, and her eyes darted to his. "And why not? Because I'm a woman?"

He sighed. He'd always known it would come to this. "Nay, because you doona have a castle to defend or a clan to lead. Gavin does…and now Deirdre along with him." She gasped, and he could see the hurt in her eyes, but he pushed on. "And when Gavin dies, then Ewan will have a castle. You are not the heir, Isobel."

"I know that."

"Do you? Because unless you plan to get rid of your loved ones, you need to find another castle to defend, another clan to lead." He stepped closer. "My castle, Izzy. My clan. Say the word, love, and we can be married." He shifted her wet clothes to one arm and grasped her hand. "We can do it right now. Handfast one another right here. And then we can have a church ceremony with Father Lundie and our families when we return."

He moved even closer, and her gaze rose to his.

He dropped his voice seductively. "Think of everything I could teach you about bed play. We could have a wedding night tonight. You like to learn new things. I have no doubt you'd become an expert at it in no time…and you wouldnae have to worry about sleeping in my dirty shirt."

Her cheeks flushed and her fingers tightened on his, but after a moment she took a step back. Then another, as if she still didn't trust herself standing so close. When she released his hand and turned around to continue along the path back to the cabin, he suppressed a sigh and caught up.

He'd made progress with her the last few days. Great progress. She just needed time to come to a proper conclusion—one that ended with them in their marriage bed…and leading his clan together.

"What if Eirik had turned out to be a bad man?" she continued, as if he hadn't just asked her to marry him…again. "I wouldnae have been able to fight him off."

He snorted. "You're not the only one. Eirik is like Gregor—a force of nature—but even bigger."

"Well, you can beat Gregor. I'm sure you could beat Eirik too. You would think of something."

Warmth exploded in his chest as pleasure coursed through his veins. 'Twas the greatest boon, knowing that she thought him capable of such feats; that boded well for her assessment of him as a husband.

"I would protect you to the death, sweetling. If Eirik did get the better of me, it wouldnae be an easy fight. Besides, I think Siv would turn on Eirik if he e'er put a foot wrong with you."

She smiled. "My great defender. Maybe I'll keep an eye out for an abandoned wolf pup like her and raise it as my own."

"I doona think there are any other wolves like her."

She made a sound of agreement in the back of her throat, and they continued, walking in silence back to the cabin. He could see she was tired, and he considered asking if she wanted to ride Diabhla. But he liked having her next to him.

The sun was low in the sky, and the air had begun to cool. In her arms she carried a basket of greens, fruit, and herbs they'd foraged for in the woods earlier. He'd shown her where to look for them, which plants were edible and which ones were not. And he'd made a special point of testing her over and over again on the plants that would kill you if you made a mistake and put them in your stew.

In addition, they'd made a crude bow and arrow that she'd practiced with, but when it came time to use it on a rabbit they spotted, she'd put the bow down. Instead, she'd started investigating ways to build a trap. He could have shown her how, but in this she didn't want—or need—his help. Of course, he doubted she'd be able to kill the rabbit once she caught it.

"Are you tired, love?" he asked when she sighed.

"Aye. 'Tis a pleasant kind of tired, though. Tramping through the woods always leaves me feeling this way—happy and content—yet feeling like once I stop, I willna rise again until morning. And my head is full of everything you've taught me today." She reached across and slipped her hand into his, linking their fingers. "Thank you."

His heart swelled in his chest. "You're welcome."

She grinned up at him. "And tomorrow, after our lesson, I'll be even more tired, I'm sure."

"You have no idea. You will hurt in places you ne'er even knew you could hurt. At the end of the day, you'll be glad to slip into the cold stream…although you may not be able to get out again."

She looked at him sideways, and he had to repress a grin. Maybe if he pushed her hard enough, she wouldn't want to keep training. God knows Gregor had pushed him and his brothers beyond their limit countless times. He suspected that once Isobel had a basic understanding of things, she would delegate tasks that were better handled by other people—like sword fighting.

'Twas part of being a good leader.

"Maybe we shouldn't start with sword play, then," she said, sounding a little leery. "You can teach me some of what Amber knows—how to defend myself if I'm attacked."

"I can do that. But remember that most of what Amber knows depends on her aggressor being surprised. The techniques I'll teach you aren't to be used to fight a bigger opponent. You doona have the strength or knowledge for that. They're to give you time to run away."

"Run away?"

"Aye. Take Eirik for example. If he had come after you, there's naught you could have done to save yourself. He's too strong and too skilled. He could easily contain you with one hand. But if you did something he didn't expect and broke his hold on you— maybe imparted a little pain, like when Amber twisted my stones, or if you were to bash in his nose with the back of your head— then you might have time to get away."

Her eyes lit up. "The first one…that sounds like a great move! I want to know how to do that."

"Of course you do," he said with a sigh. "But if you want to learn the technique as an excuse to fondle my privates, you doona have to go to so much trouble. You may fondle them at will—after you handfast me."

"Kerr!" she reprimanded—but he thought he detected a hint of laughter beneath the rebuke. Excitement too.

"What? You doona want to fondle them? Or you doona want to handfast me?"

She shot him an exasperated look, and then pulled her hand free, making him regret his joke. He almost grabbed her hand back and apologized, but another part of him wanted to see where this conversation would lead.

She ran her fingers through her drying hair, lifting it away from her face and behind her shoulder. It was an unconscious movement, but from his experience, when women tried to spark his interest, they often played with their hair.

It encouraged him to see Isobel do the same.

"I doona know yet what I want," she said quietly, keeping her eyes straight ahead.

Which means she might *want me.*

Hope burst like a bubble in his heart and he almost danced a wee jig. Although he was pretty sure if he did, his chances with Isobel would diminish. It would be best if she didn't see him dance like that until *after* they were married.

Ahead of them, the trail dwindled to an end. He slowed, placing a hand on Isobel's arm and whistling softly to Diabhla. The stallion stopped without making a sound. Isobel glanced up at him inquiringly, and he put a finger to his lips. He crept forward through the trees, still hidden, and settled in to watch the cabin and surrounding glen to make sure no one had arrived while they were gone.

Isobel crawled up beside him. "What's wrong?" she whispered.

"Nothing that I know of. But we need to be certain."

She settled on the forest floor beside him, and he tried not to be distracted by her fresh scent and the way her hair shone in the dying rays of the sun. Or the way her legs were exposed above her knees when his shirt rode up on her.

He returned his attention to the glen, looking for any sign of disturbance at the cabin or the lean-to, scanning for any movement or a glint of steel. He listened, too, sensing for disturbances in the forest, including sounds that should be there but weren't.

When he was certain it was safe, he said, "We can go." He helped Isobel up and whistled for Diabhla.

Approaching the cabin felt almost like coming home, and he imagined he was a farmer, not a laird, and Isobel was his wife, not another clan's lady. Reaching out, he took her hand, palm to palm.

She squeezed back, and the only thing that could have made the moment any better was if she had a baby balanced on her hip and he held the hand of another child. And maybe a third child riding Diabhla.

He hoped what he saw in his mind's eye was a vision of their future.

When they reached the cabin, he hesitated for a second before he laid her wet clothes on the railing, took the basket from her hands and put it down, and then opened the door wide. She raised her brow at him.

He took both of her hands in his. "Can I carry you over the threshold, lass?"

Understanding bloomed in her eyes, and her cheeks reddened.

She knew what he was asking—would she handfast him, right here, right now. Say the words and then allow him to carry her into the cabin, over the threshold, and to their marriage bed.

She dropped her gaze from his and peered into the cabin. Her eyes landed on the mattress covered in Kerr's extra plaid. Slowly, she returned her gaze to him. "You didnae listen before. I said I wasn't certain yet."

"All right... When will you be certain?"

She sighed and met his eyes. "I doona know, Kerr. Maybe tomorrow. Maybe never." Releasing his hands, she picked up the basket she'd been carrying and entered the cabin on her own.

He scraped his fingers through his beard in frustration. It had been worth asking her again—if for no other reason than to keep his intentions in the forefront of her mind.

Still, the rejection hurt, and he knew deep down that he shouldn't have pushed.

"Kerr."

He glanced over and saw Isobel standing at the door, hands on her hips. She didn't look mad, exactly, but definitely determined. "Aye?" he answered warily.

"Other than the days Ewan was found and Gavin and Deirdre were married, this has been the best day of my life. Please, doona ruin it by pressing me for something I'm not yet ready to give." Then she spun around and went back into the cabin, softly closing the door behind her.

He grinned, and then danced that little jig. When he finished, he said loudly so she could hear, "And tomorrow will be even better. I'll knock you into the dirt with the flat of my sword more times that you can count. Your wish is my command, Lady MacKinnon!"

Seventeen

ISOBEL WAS LOST IN ONE OF THOSE SECRET DREAMS ABOUT Kerr that seemed so real, the heat of his body pressed to the length of hers was scorching. The scent of him—musky, male, and enticing—drifted up her nose and across her senses like nectar to a honeybee.

She burrowed in deeper…her arms pulling that big, muscled body closer, her legs opening to him, so he pressed hard against her center. Her cheek rested on a firm chest covered with a sprinkling of hair, and she nuzzled into it.

He shifted closer, angling his shoulder, and she found the tiny nub of his nipple.

Greedily, she sucked on it.

Kerr's low groan filled her ears, and the vibration that rumbled through his warm chest and into her body woke her. Slowly, she opened her eyes and found herself staring at the notch in his throat…and she realized she wasn't dreaming this time.

Heart racing, she raised her head, expecting to see his dark gaze upon her filled with wicked amusement, but his eyes were still closed in sleep. Even so, his breaths had quickened, and his cock lay hard against the front of her hip.

God's blood…he was huge down there too.

His bare thigh had somehow become wedged between hers—and need crashed through her body. She clenched her jaw, trying to contain it, but it raged uncontrollably.

Unable to help herself, she rocked her pelvis against the bulging muscles in his leg. Heat and heaviness spread in her loins, and then arced like lighting through her belly to the tips of her breasts and lips, making her gasp.

Dropping her eyes, she quietly panted as she stared at the expanse of his chest—so big, so tanned. She wanted to rub her cheek along his skin like a cat, her teeth grazing—nipping occasionally—her throat filled with the sound of purring.

Even in sleep, his pectorals bowed outward with a little valley down the center, and she wanted her breasts pressed there with nothing in between them; she wanted that coarse hair to tease her own hardened nubs.

Without stopping to think, she found the tie of his shirt, which she was wearing, and pulled it loose, so the too-big neckline fell off her shoulders and exposed her small, sensitive breasts.

The lightest of touches from her own fingers made her breath catch... She couldn't imagine the pleasure from Kerr's fingers drifting over them, from his mouth sucking on them.

And she wanted to know. Desperately.

She rocked against him again, her whole body undulating, and he responded, the beast at her hip growing even bigger, harder. His arm wrapped around her back and pulled her closer, and the sensitive tips of her breasts brushed through the hair on his chest. She cried out, sharp and needy, and he woke immediately—she felt it in the sudden stillness of his body, heard it in the changed rhythm of his breathing.

Impatiently, she stroked her hands up and over his shoulders, cupped the back of his neck, and pulled his mouth down to hers.

Their lips touched, and he let out a growl that sent shivers down her spine and to the tips of her nose and toes. She rubbed against him as he filled her mouth, their tongues tangling and sucking. He teased the sensitive cavern in a carnal dance—in and out, rubbing and licking, teeth grinding and nibbling.

When he pulled back for air, she was too filled with fire to stop. She trailed hot, wet kisses down his throat and laved her tongue into the dips of his clavicle—completely lost to the sensuality of the moment.

His breath shuddered from his lungs. He cupped her head and tilted up her chin. "Isobel?" he asked roughly, his eyes heavy-lidded and dark with arousal. A flush tinged his cheeks, and his mouth was swollen.

She answered by nipping his bottom lip before drawing it into her mouth and sucking on it.

His hands fisted in her hair as he thrust his pelvis forward, his cock pushing upward on the inside of her hip. Holding her tight and at his mercy, he angled his head and delved back inside her mouth, taking over, commanding her until all she could do was open up to him and accept all that carnal power.

Surrender to it.

She writhed against him as he kissed her like a man possessed—wanting more, wanting everything—and she whimpered with need and physical pleasure.

Her leg wrapped around his hip, and her heel pressed into his muscled backside, trying to get closer, to rub all her soft dips and curves against his brawny strength.

Releasing her hair, he slid one hand down her body to palm her exposed breast.

She groaned at the contact, her head falling back and eyes closing. Arching her spine, she pressed the hard, sensitive nub at the center tightly against his palm. The rough calluses drove her mad.

"God's blood, Isobel. You're awake, aye?" His voice was gruff, demanding.

A brief laugh puffed up from her lungs. "Aye."

"Thank Christ," he growled and then rolled her onto her back and settled heavily between her legs.

She let out a surprised gasp and moaned at the weight and pressure of him right where she needed it. She wrapped her arms around his back, her legs around his hips…engulfed him with her body.

It felt like coming home.

Lowering his head, he took her nipple into his mouth and swirled it with his tongue. Then he stretched his jaw wide and took the soft mound deep inside.

Her eyes rolled back as he sucked on it. Then he cupped her other breast and squeezed the nipple. She cried out and bucked her hips. She couldn't think, only ride the waves of pleasure crashing through her.

He pressed down with his pelvis, rotating his hips in a slow, steady circle. She squirmed against him, panting as the heat and pressure built in her loins. "Kerr! Oh, God. Aye, right there. Doona stop. Whate'er you do, doona stop!"

Fisting her hands in his hair, like he'd done to her, she tried to tug his head upward for another kiss. But after releasing her breast from his mouth, he stopped. She glanced up…and saw that he was staring at her breasts.

A moment of uncertainty squirmed in her belly.

Does he like them?

They were small and teardrop-shaped, with round distended nipples. He'd rejected her once before because of their size—or that's how it felt at the time—was he thinking the same now?

The memories came crashing back, and the lust that had ridden her moments before fled. Her cheeks flushed, but for different reasons this time, and she tried to sit up.

It was impossible, of course; his weight trapped her beneath him, but she kept trying—releasing her legs from around his hips and shoving on his chest.

He glanced up, startled, and a concerned expression quickly replaced his heavy-eyed arousal. He pushed off her immediately, sitting up on his knees.

She scooted to the top of the bed, still facing him, and wrapped the shirt she wore across her chest and over her knees.

"What's wrong?" He grasped her foot in his hand as if to anchor her in place, to keep her close to him. "Did I frighten you?"

"Nay, I'm not afraid." She tilted her chin up and knew she was giving him her haughty look, but it was an instinctive movement.

"Then what is it? You're upset about something. Talk to me, Isobel."

"I'm not upset." *Liar.*

"Then why are you giving me that look?" he asked. "You do that when…" He trailed off, and a line appeared between his eyes.

She didn't want to know what he was thinking…except she did. Desperately. "When what?" she asked, shrinking a little inside at the scorn she heard in her voice.

He crawled closer to her on his knees, a determined look on his face, and trailed his fingers down her face. "When you feel vulnerable."

"That's ridiculous."

"Nay, you do it with me often. You use it to rule too, to remind people of your authority when you're displeased about something, but with me…"

"With you what?" This time her voice cracked a little, and tears pricked behind her eyes. He'd moved closer again and caged her within his arms, his palms pressed to the wall on either side of her shoulders.

She had no escape. Nowhere to hide.

"You do it when you're scared about something." He said the words slowly, as if he was putting the pieces together. "And when you feel rejected."

She glared at him and pushed against his chest again, but this time he refused to move. "Well, you weren't rejecting me, so your theory is wrong. If I had allowed us to continue, you would ne'er have stopped."

He didn't answer at first—he just stared at her. She forced herself to remain still, her eyes focused somewhere over his shoulder.

"That's not true, love," he finally said. "No matter how hard it would have been for me—for us—I would have stopped. I want us handfasted before we join our bodies together. There is no escaping that outcome for us." He gently cupped her cheek with one hand and turned her head slightly so she looked at him. "But you're right, I hadn't rejected you...so why did you think I had?"

Everything inside her froze. And then her heart began to race. She *had* thought that—felt it in her heart, her body.

She dropped her gaze to her knees, which were pulled tightly against her chest. Her fingers squeezed around the material of his shirt. "You were looking at my breasts," she said softly.

"I remember." His voice had roughened a little, and she glanced up again. Desire was etched in every line of his face, and those dark, hooded eyes seemed even darker, more intense.

"Did you like them?"

His brows raised, and an overwhelming desire to escape welled within her. *Why did I ask that?*

"I'm skinny, Laird MacAlister," she blurted out angrily. "My legs, my hips, my chest. 'Tis naught I can do about my breasts being small."

"Is that what this is about, Izzy?" He sounded incredulous, and she squirmed in her skin.

She tried to duck beneath his arm but he refused to let her go, and when she continued to fight him, he slid forward to sit on her feet. Slipping his hands into her hair like he had when they were kissing, he held her still and forced her chin up so he could see the truth in her expression.

And she could see the truth in his.

He shook his head in wonder. "The most beautiful lass in all the Highlands, Isobel MacKinnon—*my* Izzy—afraid I'll see her naked and find her wanting." He brushed his thumbs across her cheeks. "Ye wee idiot, that couldnae be further from the truth. I find everything about you, everything you do, appealing, even when you're trying to dunk me in manure. You're not individual bits and pieces, Isobel, you're a whole woman, and I want you in your entirety."

Those damn tears pricked the backs of her eyes again. "You didn't always think that."

"What do you mean?"

"When I was younger. You said cruel things."

A stricken look crossed his face. "Tell me. I knew something was wedged between us. This is it, aye? What foolish, addlepated thing did I say?"

She sighed and dropped her head forward until her brow rested on his chest. He loosened his hands around the strands and used his fingers to stroke her scalp. It soothed her.

"It doesn't matter. I was fifteen. I'm sure my perspective now would be different."

"'Tis true, but the feelings are still there between us. Is this when you tried to kiss me at Gavin's wedding to Cristel? I'm sorry if I was cruel. I doona remember much of it. I was deep in my cups with the lads. Gavin was the first of us to marry, and we all felt he was making a mistake."

She snorted. "It was a mistake, but if he hadn't made it, we wouldnae have Ewan. Or Deirdre."

"Aye, 'tis also true, and well worth Gavin's years of torment. But I still want to know what I did, lass. Please."

She forced her mouth to open and her tongue to work. It would be good to say the words, to exorcise the memory from her mind. "You laughed at me. Pushed me away. You told me to come find you when I'd grown a bosom—which I never did—and then you went off with a very well-endowed widow."

He groaned. "I'm sorry. I should have handled it better. In fairness, I was a grown man, and you were still a lass. If I had been receptive to your advances, that would have made me the kind of man my brothers and I have put down." His muscles tensed beneath her forehead. "A man like my father."

She looked up at him. Those dark eyes had hardened, and his jaw had clenched.

"I may have overreacted because of that," he continued. "I'm sorry I hurt you, Isobel. I can only imagine I must have been... discomfited."

She nodded, sympathy for him welling in her breast. "I can see that now. I know you aren't a cruel man, Kerr, and you love bairns of all ages."

"Including you at that age."

"Aye. And I adored you. But I didn't feel like a child at fifteen. Most of the lasses I knew were already flirting with the lads, some were kissing them, some were doing more than that. One girl in the village had even married at that age."

"And probably had a bairn six months later."

She shrugged. "Maybe. I canna remember. The point is..." She struggled to put her thoughts into words, to describe the strength of her feelings back then—and the gaping wound that had ripped through her young body when he'd turned and walked down that hall with another woman. "I had such certainty, back then, and..."

"And you knew that I was meant to be yours, as surely as I know now that you are meant to be mine. Me pushing you away—laughing at you—was the greatest of betrayals."

She closed her eyes and nodded. "It hurt me."

He pulled her into his embrace. "I'm sorry, love."

She rested her cheek against his chest, feeling spent...yet also lighter, somehow, at the same time. Maybe she would say "yes" the next time Kerr asked her to marry him. Or maybe she would ask him.

Aye, that sounds like me.

"Izzy?"

"Mmmm hmmm?" she murmured, feeling like she could stay exactly where she was forever.

"Can we speak about your breasts now?"

Her eyes popped open, and she yanked back her head so she could see his face. "What?"

"Well, you asked me a question, and then you ne'er let me answer."

"What question?"

"If I liked them."

"Liked what?" But she knew what he meant, and heat scorched her cheeks. Now would be a good time for a horde of Englishmen to attack.

"Your breasts. I do like them. Verra much. I can describe them to you from memory, if you like—the velvet feel of them, the sweet honey taste, the hard round nubs at the end that almost made me lose my seed like a lad—but I'd do a better job if I could see them again."

She pushed on his chest—hard—and he laughed as he tipped back all the way. He gripped her waist and pulled her with him so she sat with her legs splayed over his waist, staring down at him.

The shirt she wore gaped open. His eyes drifted down to her breasts, and his laughter turned into a sigh. She fought the urge to cover up…but at the same time, she wanted him to look at her— to feast his eyes on her body.

It filled her with nervous excitement, like a lass about to ride a horse for the first time.

She was exposed to him, open to him. And he was right— she felt so vulnerable. But she also felt like she'd mounted that horse and was galloping across an open field, screaming with exhilaration.

She searched his face for clues as to what he was thinking, feeling. His cheeks and lips were tinged red, and his eyes were dark and intent—the lids at half-mast and his pupils slightly dilated.

A vein pulsed quickly in his neck, and she slid her hand up his chest and laid her finger on it. Closing her eyes, she concentrated on the feel of his blood pounding through his veins—for her.

When he released her waist and brushed over her nipple, she

sucked in a startled breath—more a moan, really—and opened her eyes to watch his thumb circle the nub in a steady, intoxicating rhythm. The rough calluses scraped across her sensitive skin and sent little forks of lightning down between her legs and to her swollen lips.

"In case you had any doubt," he said huskily, "the sight of your breasts, so small yet still so soft and plump, with those hard round nipples pointing out at me, makes me want to throw away all my good intentions and bury myself here." He gripped her hip and pushed up with his pelvis, his cock rubbing against her, causing her breath to escape on a shuddering sigh. "You make me lose myself, Isobel."

He grasped her hands, entwining their fingers so they were palm to palm, and brought them down to rest on his chest.

His gaze was aroused yet determined, and she had a moment of disquiet. She let her eyelids drift shut, knowing where he was going next and wanting to delay it. This was Kerr, after all.

"Isobel, look at me."

She shook her head. The blissful fog she'd been floating in was almost gone.

"Look at me."

He'd commanded her, but beneath the words was an entreaty that spoke to a neediness within her. She opened her eyes...and found herself lost in the dark intensity of his gaze.

He really had such a powerful, striking face. She could stare at it for hours.

"We canna do *this*..." He pushed up with his hips again, and her lips parted on a groan. "...until we do *this*." He squeezed her hands. "Do you understand what I'm saying?"

"Aye...I understand, Laird MacAlister. And I'm not happy about it."

His eyes jumped to hers. "Why not?"

"Last night, I asked you to stop pressuring me about marriage, but you ne'er listened—again. You do what you want, and to hell with what I want. You're moving too fast. I feel like you're trying to trap me."

Not only him; she felt trapped by her own needs as well.

His brow rose incredulously. "I woke up, Isobel, and you were kissing me. More than that. I was practically inside you."

"Did you want me to stop?"

He chuffed out a frustrated breath. "Of course not."

"Then if I wake up beside you again, I'll do it again—if I want."

He squeezed her hands. "Only if you say the words, sweetling. Not before. Tell me you intend to marry me, Isobel. Commit to me. Please."

It felt like an ultimatum, and her jaw clenched. "You're not listening. Besides, I havenae heard you commit to me yet."

Surprise flashed in his eyes. "You're right."

He sat up quickly, and she let out a startled squeak. He pressed her hands tightly between their bodies, causing her breath to catch in her chest. She did not want this now, but God's blood, a part of her wanted to hear the words.

What will he say? How will he commit to me?

He lifted her hand and kissed her palm, the softness of his lips against her skin making her shiver. "I want to marry you, Isobel MacKinnon. I want to join our lives and our clans together." He kissed her other palm. "I want to have children together, to lead our people together. Isobel, I want you. I commit my life to you." He released her and slid his hands into her hair. "Please, dearling...say you'll marry me."

She hesitated, that softer side of her wanting so badly to do as he asked, to be his...to shelter against him and lead beside him, to finally know how it felt to have that big body inside of hers—God knows she'd wanted that for years.

But another part of her felt backed into a corner, like he was controlling her—again.

And most importantly, not once in all those heartfelt words had he told her he loved her.

A hollow ache formed in her stomach. "Nay," she said quickly and swung her leg over his body. She stood and hastily retied the neck of his shirt over her body.

He stared at her, a baffled, frustrated look on his face. "Isobel—"

She fled to the table and stood behind the chair, her hands resting on the back of it. "I think we should return."

"Return?"

"Aye. I want to go home. Gavin will be worried."

He stared at her, not moving a muscle—in that predatory way that made her feel so uncomfortable. Finally, he scraped his fingers through his beard and placed his feet into the shoes that sat on the floor next to hers.

His plaid was a rumpled mess, and it jutted upward over his loins. She lowered her eyes, feeing awkward, like he was a stranger and not the man she'd known all her life and had happily slept beside the last few nights.

He rose, grasped his sword that leaned against the side of the bed, and walked heavily across the floor. The scrape of the bar sliding across the wood reverberated through the cabin, and the door squeaked open. Bright morning sunlight poured through the opening. She squinted when she looked over.

"Get ready. I'll be back shortly, and I'll take you home." He sounded distant, and her heart sank. Her Kerr was gone, and that other side of him, the dark side that scared the wits out of her with the raging anger buried deep within his eyes, had taken his place.

The door slammed shut behind him, and she slumped against the table.

A sob caught her by surprise, and she clapped her hand over her mouth. She'd been so happy. Why did he have to keep pushing her?

She slumped into her chair and rested her head in her hands.

Had she finally crossed some line? Would Kerr leave her and stay away for good this time? She didn't want that either.

Panic twisted her stomach, and she tried to squash it down. She wasn't ready to say *yes*. Especially not like that.

But what was the alternative?

She rose from the table and paced back and forth in the small room, four steps across, four steps back. Her jaw clenched, and her panic slowly dissipated as a growing anger took hold of her. He'd told her what he wanted—their clans joined as one, to lead together and have children together—but nothing about his feelings for her. Had she been deluding herself all these years? She thought back on the first time he'd asked her to marry him, in the wind, on the top turret at her castle.

He'd shown more emotion then, but she couldn't remember him telling her how he felt then either. She stopped and slipped on her shoes, her anger at a fever pitch.

This felt better. *This* was what they had between them—a storm of thunder and fire.

She would demand he tell her his true feelings. She would demand to know if he loved her.

She would *not* marry someone who didn't think she was the sun, moon, and stars all rolled into one. She would be his only choice—as he would be hers.

Reaching out, she grasped the handle and yanked the door open. It crashed against the inside wall with a loud bang. She didn't bother to cover herself with the extra plaid, and she sure as hell didn't take the time to put on her arisaid.

She crossed the threshold and had taken only a few steps away from the cabin when a strong arm wrapped around her from behind and a hand clamped over her mouth, muffling her scream.

Not for a second did she think it was Kerr, and terror exploded in her stomach. The man wasn't quite tall enough or broad enough or muscled enough—although he was certainly powerful enough to contain her struggles, as she thrashed her body and kicked her feet, rendering her helpless.

This was what Kerr had meant. A big, strong man could easily overwhelm and restrain her. She'd have but one chance to surprise him, and then she'd run for Kerr like the hounds of hell were on her heels.

But what could she do? Kerr had said to inflict pain, but she couldn't reach around to twist his stones, and he held her head so tightly, she couldn't jerk back with it and smash his nose.

She darted her eyes in every direction, looking for some way to escape. She couldn't see the man, but she noticed something was wrong with his arm—it was twisted and scarred—and his hand and fingers were misshapen. The wounds, healed but still pink, crisscrossed his skin like the gashes on a chopping block.

She'd seen scars like these before—on the town miller. His hand had been crushed in a terrible accident years ago. These wounds looked relatively recent.

"Well, well. Who do we have here?" the man said into her ear, his tone triumphant. "As I looked upon thee, I saw a great Highland beauty. It seems I've caught not just a lass, but a lady. Tell me, dearest, where is your laird?"

Isobel dug her nails into the man's pink scars, tearing and scraping at the still-tender flesh.

He cried out in pain, and his arms loosened. Without hesitation, she smashed the back of her head into his face and heard a sickening crunching sound. He stumbled and she leapt ahead, racing across the clearing toward the trail she'd taken yesterday with Kerr.

"Bloody whore! I'm going to kill you," the man screamed behind her. "Get her!"

"Kerr!" she yelled. "Kerr!"

Men appeared from out of the woods—three of them—and converged on her. She shrieked and darted toward the lean-to. She was as fast or faster than most of the men she knew; she could outrun the warriors in the forest...and hopefully find Kerr.

She was almost there, passing the lean-to that stood at the edge of the clearing, when someone grabbed her arm and yanked her back.

Eighteen

KERR SHOVED ISOBEL BEHIND HIM, HIS CLAYMORE HELD IN AN upright position in front of him, and stepped back into the lean-to, squeezing her against the pile of wood inside. Her body heaved and shook against his spine, and when she wrapped her arms around him, he quickly removed them.

"Wait," he ordered, his tone sharp. He returned both hands to his sword hilt and balanced his weight on the balls of his feet.

He was fully in warrior mode now and had men to slay—three of them coming from the woods, possibly more, plus the man at the cabin who'd put his hands on Isobel. The timing of the first kill was critical to sustain the least amount of damage to himself, keep his lass safe, and take them all out.

Let them come to him.

Three, two, one…he stepped forward, thrusting his sword through the first man who tore around the corner of the lean-to. A killing blow. When he pulled back his sword, blood splattered across his bare chest and arms. He lunged forward onto his left foot and arced his blade sideways, almost taking off the second warrior's head. He died instantly, blood spurting up from the wound.

The third warrior was upon him almost before Kerr had time to react, and he dropped to the ground and rolled as the man swung his sword. Kerr rose fluidly and struck back, the blades clashing as the men fought—once, twice, three times. His enemy was fast and skilled with his weapon, but he wasn't strong enough against a warrior as powerful as Kerr, and on the fourth blow, Kerr knocked him off balance, and he fell into the lean-to beside Isobel. She screeched and climbed the pile as Kerr stabbed the man through the stomach and dragged his blade sideways. His intestines spilled out in a bloody mess.

"Behind you!" Isobel yelled.

Kerr darted sideways and heard the whistle of the other blade as it swung past his ear. Close. Too close. These were elite warriors, not huntsmen or simple travelers.

He rose as a log flew past his shoulder from behind and hit the fourth warrior in the face. The man stumbled back, and Kerr shot forward and speared him through the heart. The last warrior fell to his knees and clutched his chest, his mouth open, his eyes wide with shock and horror.

Kerr shoved him back with his boot, clearing the space in case more men came at him. When none appeared, he moved cautiously to the edge.

Releasing one hand from his huge sword, he smashed his elbow into the wall beside him, creating a jagged crack in the board just big enough to see through. He scanned the cabin and surrounding trees—the glade appeared empty.

But if a sniper were in the branches, he wouldn't show himself until it was too late.

His gaze fell on a bushy tree on the other side of the clearing. The angle was perfect for the glen and the cabin, but not good for the lean-to where Kerr and Isobel were hunkered down.

If Kerr were the sniper, and his focus was the cabin, that's where he would hide. They hadn't expected Isobel to escape.

He turned and scanned the bodies before choosing the smallest warrior, who lay crumpled on the ground by the wood pile. Kerr tucked up the man's plaid to cover the blood stains on his shirt, and then rolled him onto his side.

"Doona look," he said to Isobel as he straightened.

"Why? What are you going to—"

Lowering his sword, he carefully pierced the tip through the dead man's neck, so it entered and exited below the ears.

Isobel gasped and slapped her hand over her mouth.

With a grunt, Kerr hefted the body until the warrior appeared to be standing upright. Muscles straining, he moved carefully to the front of the lean-to again, and then looked through the jagged hole. Slowly, he pushed the body out of the lean-to until the sniper, if there was one, could see it but not the blade.

Either the archer would shoot thinking the body was an enemy and reveal his position, or he would climb down from the tree, believing his friends had won.

Or he wouldn't react at all, and Kerr would have failed to protect Isobel.

Not an option.

Every second seemed like an hour, and eventually Kerr's arms began to shake. He whistled, a little desperate now, as if calling for the other man. Finally, he saw the leaves tremble, and he stared intently, looking for an arrow tip—anything to pinpoint the sniper's exact position. He'd only get one shot with his dagger, but at that distance he wouldn't be able to hit his enemy, anyway.

How can I draw him out?

When no one appeared, he brought the body back in, carefully swinging his sword around, so it looked like the man turned and entered the lean-to. He couldn't keep propping the dead man up and depleting his strength—he may have to fight again.

When the puppet was out of sight, Kerr tilted his broadsword, and the body slid off the point and hit the ground with a thud.

Behind him he heard Isobel gag. "'Twas necessary," he said curtly, still eyeing the tree through the hole he'd made.

"Why did you do that? Is someone else out there?" she asked.

"Aye."

"Who? I hate it when you get like this, Kerr. Tell me what's—"

"I want you to scream," he said as curtly as before, his focus on the tree. "Loudly, like you're being assaulted." When she didn't respond, he pointed his sword behind him in her direction, and said, "If you want to stay alive, Isobel, do as I say. Now!"

She screamed. And cried. And screamed again. "No. Get off me! Please!"

Movement in the trees. A man stepped into the clearing with his bow raised in their direction. He walked toward the lean-to cautiously.

"Keep it up," he said to Isobel, and then after she screamed and pleaded some more, he forced a loud laugh like he was Isobel's assailant, having fun with her. It turned his stomach.

The archer lowered his bow slightly. *Good lad. A little farther.*

Kerr had just unsheathed his dagger, when another archer stepped from the tree line, his bow raised.

"Bloody hell," Kerr cursed under his breath.

"What is it?" Isobel whispered from close behind him.

"More men. Keep doing what you're doing, it's drawing them out."

She continued to cry and beg, and he laughed a few more times and whistled.

The second archer almost ran across the clearing toward them. It didn't take long for him to overtake the first archer and drop his bow completely.

Kerr wasn't worried about him; he could take him out easily. But the original archer was another story.

The man looked angry and frustrated, and he spoke sharply to the second archer, who ignored him. He knew they could be walking into a trap.

Pausing, he raised his bow a few more inches then began walking in a sideways arc, so he could see into the lean-to while he was still far enough away to kill someone from a distance.

Kerr needed a shield—fast! The man could probably release two shots in the time it took Kerr to reach him...after he'd killed the other archer.

And he was out of time. He put the dagger between his teeth again, pointed his claymore straight ahead, and braced his feet.

"Stay low and keep back," he whispered around the blade to Isobel.

"Be careful," she whispered back, and laid her hand lightly along his spine.

Moments later, the careless archer hurried around the corner with an excited leer on his face that Kerr was more than happy to wipe off. He thrust hard into the man's chest, so his claymore went all the way through, before lifting the body off the ground—one hand on his sword hilt, the other fisted around the man's neck to keep him upright…and then, shielded by the body, ran straight at the other archer.

Arrows thudded into the dead man's back in quick succession—one, two, and then a third one flew by, grazing his scalp. But Kerr was close enough now, and with a loud grunt, he heaved the body forward, sword still protruding from the man's back. The body hit the archer hard and knocked him backward, the tip of the claymore embedding in his thigh.

The second archer screamed, but Kerr was on him in seconds, his dagger in hand…and he drew it across the man's throat, from ear to ear. Warm blood gushed from the wound and over his hand.

Standing, he yanked his sword from both bodies and glanced around the clearing, his breath sawing through his lungs. No one emerged to continue the battle. In his bones, Kerr knew the fight was done.

But for how long?

Six highly trained warriors had attacked them. They were here for a reason—and it wasn't a good one.

"Kerr!" Isobel cried out. He looked over his shoulder. She was as white as the linen of his shirt she still wore, but she was safe.

"Are you hurt?" she asked.

"Nay. All is well, lass."

He scanned the clearing again to make sure, and then walked toward the lean-to, a little wobbly as usual in the aftermath of battle. His boots squished with each step and when he looked down, he saw blood covering every inch of his body.

None of it was his.

Isobel had never seen him fight before, never been so close to the gore of battle before. Would she see him differently now? For the better…or for the worse?

She was standing in front of the wood pile, her head lowered and her hand tugging on something at her side. "I canna get it out," she said, sounding on the verge of tears.

It was a miracle she wasn't a sobbing heap on the ground. She'd kept it together admirably and had been an asset during their fight. Memory rose of how she'd thrown that log into the fourth warrior's face, and pride surged in his chest.

That was *his lass*. And she would soon be *his wife*; he'd make sure of it.

No one will take her away from me.

"Kerr, I canna get it out, and I doona want to tear your shirt." Her eyes kept jumping around her to the dead bodies on the ground before darting back to her side.

"Get what out?" He slowly drew near, finding it harder to put one foot in front of the other, his legs as heavy as boulders. "What are you pulling on?"

"The arrow. It went through the material, and it's stuck in the wood."

He came to a halt, his eyes widening in shock as horror smashed through him. She pulled her hands away, and he saw the feather end of the arrow poking out right next to her waist, so close to her body, it had pierced the linen of his shirt. A single drop of blood, a scratch at most, marred the white material.

That arrow, meant for him, had almost killed her.

His knees buckled beneath him, and he crashed to the ground.

Her head jerked up. "Kerr!"

She yanked frantically at the material, trying to get to him. Finally, it ripped, and she raced to his side and onto her knees. Grabbing his shoulders, she rubbed her hands over them and then down his chest. Blood smeared all over her as well. "Where are you hurt? Oh dear God, Kerr. Where are you hurt?"

He grasped her arms and tried to reassure her, but he couldn't catch his breath to speak. His heart raced so fast, it pounded in his temples and caused flashes of black in his vision.

In trying to save her, I almost killed her.

"Get up, Kerr! Get up!" she yelled, slipping her arm around him and trying to lift him. "I'll take you back to the cabin. You can tell me what to do there. You must have some special herbs in your pack."

"Nay, I canna rise," he puffed out. "I doona think I'll e'er rise again. Not after that."

He meant it facetiously, and was referring to the arrow hitting so close to her side, but she burst into tears and threw her arms around him, sobbing.

"What can I do? Tell me what to do! You canna die on me, not yet. We have our whole lives ahead of us."

"You mean that?" he asked, cupping her head and pulling it back so he could see her face. "You want to be with me?"

"Yes! Of course I do."

"Then say the words." He grasped her hands and held them between their bodies. "There is nothing I want more than to hear you commit to me right now. Say the words, Izzy. Please. Especially since…"

"Since what? You are not dying, do you hear me, Kerr MacAlister? I will not let you die." She glared at him so hard, her face turned pink.

"You canna stop it, dearling. No one can. But when I do die, I want to know that you're my wife."

She nodded fiercely, tears streaming down her face and her chest heaving. He knew that he was tricking her, even though he hadn't said anything untrue. But at this point, after the way things had ended between them at the cabin earlier, he felt like he had no choice.

He was a desperate man, and desperate men did desperate things.

She squeezed his hands. "I am yours, Kerr MacAlister. For now and forever. I commit my life to you, my body and heart to you. There will never be anyone but you. We are one before God. Husband and wife."

"Husband and wife," he repeated, and then dug his hands into her hair and kissed her—soft, excited presses of his lips to hers, and then deeper and harder—more carnal—as he slanted his mouth across hers and took control.

His strength came back tenfold, and he dragged her across his lap.

She gasped, her sobs turning into pants as the heat flared between them. He scooped her up in his arms—one arm behind her back, the other under her knees—rose with her, and then strode purposefully toward the cabin.

Finally!

All he could think about was her pledge to be with him—and only him—always and forever. He'd done as Gavin had wanted, as he wanted, and now Isobel was his—and he was driven by his need to join their bodies and consummate their marriage.

"What are you doing?" she gasped.

"I'm taking you to bed, Isobel."

She struggled to get down, and he tightened his hold. "Have you lost your bloody mind? We were just attacked." She stabbed him in the chest with her finger. "And how can you suddenly walk?"

"Inspiration, dear wife. Your kisses revived me. Your pledge of devotion invigorated me."

"So you lied to me? You weren't dying?"

"I ne'er said I was dying. I said I couldnae stand after seeing where that arrow had landed. My words were all true. Six men couldnae take me down, but one arrow too close to your heart cuts my knees out from under me like a swing of Eirik's giant axe."

Her eyes bore into him. "You will ne'er get me into the marriage bed if you doona put me down this instant."

He knew that tone, and he knew that Isobel could hold a grudge better than anyone. His steps faltered, and he came to a stop in front of the porch. Slowly, he put her down, keeping his arms around her waist.

"We are handfasted, Isobel. You said the words."

"I thought you were dying."

"You said you wanted us to spend our lives together, that there would be no one else for you *but* me."

"I thought you were dying!"

"So it was all lies?"

"What? No, I didnae say that."

"Then what are you saying, wife?"

She grasped his hands, pulled them away from her, and then stepped back. "You're covered in blood, we've been attacked, and Diabhla is nowhere to be found…and you want to tup me?"

"I would ne'er just tup you… well, mayhap sometimes, but you would like it."

"Kerr, this is serious!"

He squeezed her hands. "Aye, love, I know. But you doona have to worry. Diabhla is exactly where I left him—in the woods—and our enemy is defeated."

She shook her head, a pinched line forming between her eyes. "You're not thinking straight. Are you sure you didn't take a blow to the head?"

"I'm sure. More than sure." He stepped closer to her and dropped his voice coaxingly. "Make love with me, Isobel."

She stepped closer to him too, but it was to jab her finger in his chest again. "That man who attacked me called me a great Highland beauty, and he quoted part of the song Gregor's minstrel wrote about me—*As I looked upon thee, I saw a Great Highland Beauty*. But the lyrics were wrong. It's not a *Great Highland Beauty*, it's the *Beauty of the Highlands*."

"'Tis a good thing I killed him, then. We wouldnae want him singing the wrong words. It may have caught on."

"It did catch on. The last person who sang those lyrics to me— the wrong lyrics—was Branon Campbell...right before you came storming up to us at the stables."

The hair rose along the back of Kerr's spine, and he couldn't help looking around the clearing again. Every instinct he had told him they were alone, but what if he was missing something? He squeezed the back of his neck, and pain shot up into his skull.

Maybe he *had* taken a blow to the head.

She was right. 'Twas insanity to stay here a second longer than they had to. He grasped her arm and pulled her toward the cabin—for different reasons this time. He wanted her under cover.

"That wasn't Branon Campbell. I would have recognized him," he said.

"I know it wasn't. The man who grabbed me had horrible scars all along his arm and the back of his hand, and his fingers were deformed. It looked like his arm had recently been crushed."

"I don't remember that, but he's dead now, so he's not a threat. You threw the log in his face, and I finished him off. They're all dead." They'd entered the cabin, and Kerr moved directly to the bowl of water on the table. He rinsed the blood off his hands and splashed it on his face and chest. Then he returned to the porch, tossed it out, and retrieved fresh water from the rain barrel for Isobel. She did the same, scrubbing hard to get it off her hands. He squeezed her shoulder and kissed the top of her head. "You did well. That man may have killed me, otherwise."

'Twas untrue, but he wanted her to believe it—to ease any conflict she might have about helping him kill the man. She nodded and buried her face in his chest. Her body shook, and he squeezed his arms around her. "You're safe now. They're dead."

*Nay. T*he word whispered in his head. *Move.*

His instinct was always right. He'd missed something.

He kissed the top of her head. "We have to go." Her dress lay spread out on a chair in front of the fire, and he handed it to her. "Get dressed," he said, gathered up his plaid and bag, and made sure the fire was cold.

He paused at the door and scanned the clearing while he waited for Isobel. When she was ready, he whistled for Diabhla. The stallion appeared, and Kerr quickly attached the pack to the back of the saddle. Isobel reached up to mount him, but he shook his head and grasped her hand. "Not yet. I want to keep him between us and the trees, just in case."

"And we need to check the bodies," she said.

His desire to get Isobel to safety warred with his need to look for clues to identify the assailants. He wanted to see those scars on the fourth man as well. It was possible the man had been in the cathedral last spring when Deirdre had brought the roof down on their enemy. One man had escaped the cave-in—the man in charge.

Maybe it was the same man.

He clicked his tongue to get Diabhla moving and pulled Isobel along beside him. When they reached the lean-to, he directed her into the sheltered area and then positioned Diabhla in front of him, so he could search the bodies of the archers from a relatively protected position.

He dumped out their sporrans first and found nothing of interest, but when he checked the seams and hem of the first archer, he felt coins inside—plenty of coins. The amount of which would buy someone's loyalty…or pay them for betrayal.

He ripped the seam and dumped the coins into his own sporran.

"Did you find something?" Isobel asked.

"Gold coins, too many to count. If we needed more proof that these men were not simple brigands, this is it."

"I haven't found anything yet," she said.

He looked over and saw Isobel crouched on the ground, her face grim, searching the first man who had attacked them. Her hands were bloody again, and her newly clean arisaid had red smears on it.

"Sweetling, you doona have to do that," he protested. "I can do it."

"So can I. I tore out the lining of his sporran, turned his boots inside out, and checked his plaid. Is there anything I'm missing?"

"If his hair is tied back, make sure nothing is hidden in it. It's an old trick I've used before when my hair was longer." As soon as he said it, he realized his mistake and groaned. The first attacker's hair was short, but the second attacker, the one he'd almost decapitated, had bushy red hair bound by a thong. She moved toward his head after the slightest of hesitations.

"Leave it, Isobel. I'll do it."

She didn't bother to answer him this time. Instead, she released the dead man's hair tie and sifted her hands through the strands.

He sighed and returned to the two men he was checking. Neither of them had their hair tied back, but when he checked the first archer's boots, a piece of parchment fell out.

"I found something," he said as he unfolded the page. Writing scrawled across it—brief and to the point—but it was enough to make his heart pound. He breathed in deeply and then cracked his jaw, his anger simmering below the surface.

So they think they can take my land, my clan, my home away from me.

He read it twice more to make sure he hadn't missed anything and then refolded it and put it in his sporran.

"What does it say?" Isobel asked, standing now by the bodies she'd been checking. She held her hands, smeared with red, away from her clothes.

"It says I've been betrayed."

"Truly?"

"Nay. It says: Clan MacAlister, September first, and a man's name."

She gasped. "That's only three days hence."

He ground his teeth before responding. "I know."

"And who's the man?"

"My steward, Fearchar MacAlister. He was my father's man. After I killed my da and uncles, I kept him on to help with the transition. Obviously, that was a mistake."

"You couldnae have known. You needed someone. You were barely grown, Kerr, only eighteen."

"Nay, seventeen—I'd had my birthday with Gregor and my brothers before coming home. But it doesn't matter, I should have known. The man's a coward, and he's greedy. And he should have…"

"He should have what?"

"He could have done more to help my mother. But I forgave him, I forgave them all, because my father was a monster, and to go against him didn't only mean your death, it meant the torture and humiliation of you and everyone you loved."

He grabbed Diabhla's reins and tugged him toward Isobel, intent on the other two bodies inside the lean-to, especially the one she said was badly scarred. Was he the head of the snake, the lone man Gavin had seen riding away from the cathedral—the only one still alive?

The body closest to him was the man he'd held up with his sword like a puppet, and he dropped the reins and checked him first. His hair was a light reddish color, and when he turned him over to check his arms, no fresh scars marred the skin, as expected.

He turned his sporran inside out and tore out the lining, then checked his shoes and plaid. Nothing useful.

"Kerr," Isobel said.

He looked up to see her crouched over the last man's body. His hair was dark, and Kerr stepped forward expectantly. She raised wide eyes to his. "He doesn't have any scars either."

His brow furrowed in confusion as his eyes dropped to the dead warrior's unblemished skin. "But you said the man who attacked you…"

"…had horrible scars on his arm." She finished his sentence for him. "I dug my nails into them, tore the pink skin and yanked on his mangled fingers. 'Tis how I got away."

Kerr took a steady breath, and then slowly turned his head toward the cabin. He stepped to the hole he'd made in the board earlier and peered into the clearing.

Movement caught his attention on the other side of the glen—a shaking bush and falling leaves. He listened and realized the birds had fallen silent.

And then warriors stepped out of the trees.

Nineteen

KERR GRABBED DIABHLA'S REINS, DARTED TOWARD ISOBEL, AND grabbed her hand. "Run!" he whispered, his tone urgent.

The lean-to was right beside the tree line—the entrance facing away from the cabin and the approaching warriors. They dashed into the woods, and Kerr hoped like Hades the enemy hadn't seen them.

But that would only buy them a small lead. The other men would find the bodies soon, and if they had a good tracker, they would be on their trail in minutes.

"What did you see?" Isobel asked, her breath heavy as she raced beside him through the trees.

"More soldiers. The man who attacked you must have run back for reinforcements. I should have checked the bodies immediately."

Inside, he raged at himself, furious that he'd delayed and put Isobel at risk. If she hadn't forced him to listen to her, or if she'd been agreeable to his advances, they'd be caught in the cabin right now.

"How many men?" Isobel asked.

"I doona know. I think 'tis an army heading toward my clan. Scattered, most likely, to avoid detection. We're right in the thick of it."

He slowed and then leapt into the saddle and pulled Isobel up in front of him. His first instinct was to get to the creek and try to lose the men tracking them. After that, if they followed in the direction of the current, they'd end up at the beach where Eirik said he'd stashed his longship—hopefully.

"Where are we going? Do you have a plan?" she asked, her voice tight and worried.

He squeezed his arm around her waist. "We need to get back across the loch. Then I need to get home."

"Not without your allies. Kerr, you canna attack them on your own."

"I need to be with my clan, Isobel, to defend against these invaders. I need to lead my people. We have spies inside. Betrayers. I canna wait."

"And me?" she asked.

He hadn't thought that far ahead. He only knew one thing. "Safe."

"I am safe. With *you*."

"As long as there's breath in my body, aye."

A shrill whistle sounded behind them, and men yelled in the distance—from different directions.

Kerr cursed and guided Diabhla onto the trail they'd walked along yesterday. He let the stallion gallop full out, and they arrived at the creek within minutes. Diabhla leapt into the water, and Kerr directed him against the current—in the opposite direction of the loch—and looked for a way up the other bank that would track the horse's prints.

A muddy path appeared, and they climbed it before emerging onto a grassy trail heading north. He scanned the ground as they rode. They needed a place they could veer off the trail again without the warriors in pursuit noticing. When they came across a rocky section, he slowed.

In the distance, men yelled to one another, and he fought the urge to rush.

"What are you doing?" Isobel asked, panic in her voice. "Shouldnae we be heading back to our boat? 'Tis the other way!"

"Aye, we will, but first I want them to think we're heading this way. The fewer men on our heels the better." He brought Diabhla to a halt near the edge of the trail. A tall, sturdy oak with long branches hung over it.

He slid from the saddle and dug into his saddlebag, pulling out four small bags with drawstrings.

"What are those for?" Isobel asked.

"To wrap over Diabhla's hooves. The material will obscure his tracks." He crouched and quickly moved around the horse, securing the covers.

When he was done, he laid a few stones back in place that his own feet had dislodged, and then mounted again. This time, however, he rose, stood on the horse's back, and pointed to the branch above. "If I lift you, can you climb up, move to the trunk, and make your way down? Follow one of the lower branches as far into the woods as possible."

She nodded, and he helped her up. Diabhla stood steady as she bent over to tie her skirt up between her legs.

He'd just lifted her when he heard horses splashing in the water down the trail behind them. Isobel wrapped her legs around the trunk. "Go," she said as she pulled herself up. "I can manage."

A shout filled the air, and he glanced over his shoulder. "They've found our trail."

When he looked back, Isobel had already crawled halfway to the trunk of the tree. He wanted to shout instructions to her, tell her to hide, but she was an intelligent, resourceful woman. She didn't need his guidance.

He sat and urged Diabhla forward, breaking into a gallop. Ahead, the trail veered to the right. Kerr leaned forward over the stallion's neck and held on, his knees pressing tightly to the horse's sides.

"*Gearr leum!*" he commanded, directing the stallion to the left rather than following the trail. The horse jumped a good twenty paces into a small, grassy clearing, and then raced into the woods.

Kerr found the densest foliage to hide behind and watched, breath held, as fifteen enemy warriors passed by. He couldn't tell if the man with the scars was among them.

After they disappeared, he removed the bags from Diabhla's feet and circled back through the woods to find Isobel. She was still up in the tree, but on a branch, thick with leaves, that extended far into the woods.

"Do you think that's all of them?" she asked, as she lowered herself onto the saddle and settled in front of him. She sounded anxious, and for a moment, Kerr considered lying to her. But she deserved to know. And if anyone could handle the truth, it was her.

"Nay, lass," he said, as he directed Diabhla toward the loch and spurred him into a trot. "I think we'll come across small pockets of them throughout the forest. Some will know we're here and will be looking for us. Some won't. They're heading in secret toward my clan. I had hoped more would follow our false trail."

"How can we possibly make it back to our boat with so many of them out there?"

"We willna have to. Eirik told me he left *his* boat on a beach not far from here. I'm hoping he hasn't moved it. We should be able to make it there without too much trouble."

Now he *was* lying to her. "Whate'er happens, I'll keep you safe, Isobel."

They moved as swiftly and quietly as possible, staying off the game trails. Oftentimes, Kerr relied on Diabhla to let him know when someone was approaching. His stallion would tense, turn his head, or swivel his ears. Several times they had to hide as enemy warriors rode past.

One of the groups had upwards of fifty men. They hid behind a thick prickly bush to avoid being seen. Kerr had his sword in hand and his dagger clenched between his teeth, ready to fight. One young soldier stopped to pick some berries and almost lost his life because of it.

When it was safe, they continued on, always keeping the creek on their left but staying away from the bank.

"Are they heading toward the loch too?" she whispered. "Will they have a boat there?"

"Nay, I doona think so. They'd need several big ships to get them across, and that would draw too much attention. They'll ride to the end of the loch, and from there, head straight toward Clan MacAlister."

"How will they get through your borders?"

"They'll have a way. Same as they snuck through Callum's borders last year and through your borders in the spring."

"And they were defeated both times. And before that, against Darach and Lachlan. We'll defeat them this time too, Kerr."

"Aye, lass. I promised you a clan to lead by my side. I willna be losing it now. And I willna leave *our* people at risk."

She squeezed the hand he rested on her waist. "Nay, *we* will not."

———————

Isobel could smell the loch and knew they were close to the beach.

Thank God!

As deathly afraid of the water as she was, she couldn't wait to get on the boat and away from their enemy. She would worry about drowning once they were out of range of any arrows or daggers like the one Kerr currently held in his fist. She knew they'd be vulnerable once they reached the beach, and she prayed they'd be able to find the boat easily.

A fine tremor ran through Diabhla, and she leaned forward and stroked her hand along his neck, trying to calm him. She understood how he felt. Behind her, Kerr stiffened, and he tugged on the reins so the stallion veered into a copse of birch trees.

"Shhhhhh," he whispered to her.

Not again!

She closed her eyes and swallowed. Never again would she

bemoan the fact that she hadn't been trained to fight. Swords and knives flying at her head in real life wasn't nearly as exciting as it was when she imagined it happening on some great adventure.

She heard horses approaching and then a twig snap. Lifting her lids, she squinted through her lashes toward the trail. Kerr had warned her that if he was forced to fight, she would have to dismount. As much as she wanted to hide away, she needed to see what was happening in case she had to get down in a hurry.

Four burly warriors on sturdy horses were passing their copse about fifteen paces away, and she squeezed her lips together to stop a fearful squeak from escaping. If any of them were to glance in their direction, surely they would be seen. The cluster of birch had small gaps between the trees, and while the huge stallion blended into the shadows, it was now midday and the sun was bright.

One of the other horses swiveled its ears and then turned its head toward them. It let out a nicker. Unlike Kerr, its rider ignored the warning.

Happily, Diabhla did not respond.

Kerr had been focused and abrupt since they'd been on the run, and while his attitude and demeanor—his intensity—had irked and even scared her in the past, in the face of real danger she found it comforting.

She knew that this man, her almost-husband—although she planned to argue that fact when the time was right—would keep her alive. The fact that he'd tricked her into handfasting him under questionable circumstances could be sorted out when they were safe.

The last rider was almost past them when a bird trilled above their heads. Kerr tensed even further when the grim-looking warrior glanced up at the sound. After a moment, he dropped his gaze down again, but then realization hit, and he spun his head back toward them, eyes wide. Kerr's dagger quickly lodged itself into his forehead, knocking the man backward.

Before he even hit the ground, another dagger pierced the rider in front of him in the side of the neck. That man let out a strangled yelp as he fell, blood squirting out from the wound and alerting the two men ahead of him to the danger. Kerr's third dagger missed by inches as his next target spun around.

Isobel found herself dislodged from Diabhla without even a warning. She landed on her feet and took several unsteady steps back as the stallion leapt past her through the trees. Kerr was leaning forward, his claymore raised in one hand and his body poised for battle.

His huge sword was a perfect fit for such a massive warrior.

He charged toward the two remaining soldiers. One of the horses reared back and almost dislodged its rider. When the horse came back down, Kerr thrust upward with his sword and pierced through the man's body before he had a chance to regain his balance.

The last warrior turned and spurred his horse away from the fight. Kerr leaned over and pulled his still-vibrating dagger from the tree it had landed in moments ago and flung it at the retreating soldier. The blade hit the man squarely in the back, and the last of their enemy fell.

The sudden silence was deafening, and Isobel stared at the scene of blood and carnage in shock. Like before, once the conflict had started, the men had died at Kerr's hand in moments—all four of them.

She took a deep breath, and then another, wanting to stay strong for him, to show the same kind of clarity and resolve as he had shown. He knew what had to be done to keep her safe, and he was doing it.

And she wanted to be...worthy of him.

Aye, this man, this laird and warrior, had only one thing in mind—to protect her, to protect his clan, and to protect his friends and family. And he succeeded...every...single...time.

He was deadly…yet magnificent.

How did I not see this before?

"Isobel, come," he said curtly, his sword hilt already poking up from behind his shoulder. "We have to keep moving."

He retrieved his daggers from the first two men who had died, wiped them on a patch of grass, and then re-sheathed them along each arm. She tried to step forward, but her knees had weakened, and she didn't think she could walk. Her chin wobbled at her helplessness, and she hugged the tree for support.

God's blood, she was back to feeling useless, when yesterday she'd felt invincible!

He didn't say a word as he rode back to her, lifted her into place, and then cantered Diabhla to the last man killed, so he could draw his dagger and sheath it at his waist.

"'Twas necessary to kill him," he said gruffly, as if forcing out the words. "He would have brought more men down upon us, aye?"

She nodded, and then had to swallow before speaking. "Is that the end of it?"

He directed Diabhla off the trail again and kept going before answering. "I doona know. I suspect there will be men on the beach waiting for us. We'll need to lay low and watch for a while, try to spot where Eirik might have hidden the boat and then…"

"And then what?" she croaked, but she knew what he was going to say.

"Kill as many men as I can so we can get to the boat unencumbered. Once I decide 'tis time to go, we'll need to move quickly."

She nodded, feeling a heaviness come over her. Or maybe she just stopped trying to fight it. She slumped against him, and his arm tightened around her waist. "You willna be harmed, Isobel. Ever." He said it fiercely, like a savage warrior of old…and she knew it to be true.

But if something happened, and he did die here today, she would rather die with him than go with the men responsible.

"Kerr." She said his name softly, not wanting to alert the enemy, but also because she felt vulnerable—physically and emotionally. But this time she allowed herself to stay with the feelings instead of pushing them down.

"Aye?"

"You ne'er doubted me."

"Of course not…about what?"

Her heart squeezed. He didn't even need to think about it. Or know what exactly they were talking about. His actions had shown his true estimation of her.

And revealed his true estimation *to* her.

"That the man had scars on his arm and hand. You ne'er doubted I'd seen them even though he wasn't one of the dead men at the lean-to. Or that I could get down from that tree without being seen. You left me to crawl out of sight in time and stay out of sight without falling, believing I could do it."

"Aye."

He sounded a little confused, as if he didn't understand why she was even bringing it up, and that made her heart squeeze a little more.

"It means a great deal to me. Thank you." This time her voice was even softer.

"Always, Isobel."

He stopped and slipped off Diabhla. Then he gave her his hand to help her down. She could see the loch through the break in the trees ahead, and she followed his lead, creeping forward carefully.

At the edge of the bluff, he lay on his belly. She did, too, and peered through the foliage. The creek they'd been following flowed out into the loch about twenty paces to their left. To her surprise, she couldn't see any men on the beach, and relief flowed through her.

Now they just had to find the boat!

She turned to him, a wide, excited smile on her face, but he was peering at the sandy beach with a pensive expression. Her smile dipped, and she looked back, trying to understand what he was seeing—or wasn't seeing.

"Did you expect to find men here?" she whispered.

He half shrugged. "Not exactly. The smart thing for them to do would be to stay hidden and draw us out. And if the man who grabbed you is who I think he is, he has proven himself more than smart over the last few years—also shrewd and careful. We canna underestimate him."

He curled his fingers into circles, and then stacked his hands together like a telescope. With one eye closed, he looked through the tunnel at the beach. "I doona see him, but he's there. It's where I would be if I were him. He will have assumed we have a boat, and he's sent men out to look for it." He pointed to the side of the beach that stretched out on the other side of the creek from them. "My guess is he started searching at the opposite end from where we are. He thinks we came from the south—which we would have done if we'd landed here instead of where we did. Luck may be on our side this time."

"Which means...we're going over there?" She pointed her thumb in the opposite direction.

He nodded. "Eirik and Siv were coming from the north. I think he will have stashed the boat at the end of the beach on this side for a quicker escape. 'Tis more strategic."

"And what you would have done."

"Aye."

He crawled backward, and then rose to a crouch and continued searching the trees, returning periodically to peek over the edge at the beach. Isobel searched too, but other than seeing the actual boat, she didn't know what she was looking for. She wasn't sure she was helping at all.

Diabhla followed them sedately, content to munch on whatever patch of grass he found. Isobel suspected he didn't feel at all useless—not like she did.

When they reached the end of the beach and there was nowhere else to look, Kerr rubbed the back of his neck in frustration. "It must be on the other side of the creek."

She looked deeper into the woods. "Why couldn't he have hidden it farther in?"

"It's a small longship, Izzy. Made for crossing the North Sea. It will be heavy. He wouldnae have pulled it farther than he had to."

"How far would you have pulled it?" she asked.

His brow puckered a little, but he looked to the beach and then walked a few paces inland from where they were standing. And then a few more. "Up to about here, I guess."

"Eirik is bigger than you. Stronger than you too, I'd wager." He winced a little, and she rushed ahead, reassuring him. "Only a wee bit. But how much farther than you do you think he could have pulled the boat?"

His eyes grew thoughtful, and he nodded. He stepped farther into the woods, and then kept going. When he stopped, he stood about twenty paces away.

"Izzy," he called her name softly.

She hurried forward. He was staring at a fallen tree and a clump of branches. He reached down and pulled away an armful of twigs and leaves. Underneath, a flat, carved piece of wood stuck out.

"What is that?" she asked.

He rubbed his palm over the wood, and then traced the sanded edges with his fingers. A small, satisfied smile curved his lips. "A rudder." Then he turned to her and kissed her—brief and hard on the lips. "And I wouldnae have found it without you."

Twenty

"HOW ARE WE GOING TO GET IT BACK TO HIM?" ISOBEL ASKED as she dragged a huge branch off the longship.

Kerr looked up from the dragon head he'd been studying at the bow of the ship and found himself hard-pressed not to smile. For a moment, he forgot the danger they were in and just stared at her. She had dirt smeared on her face, a tear in her arisaid, and dead leaves caught in her hair, which was a tangled mess.

She'd never looked more beautiful to him.

If only the lasses who'd been vying for his attention all these years had known the way to his heart wasn't through fine clothes, coquettish looks, and pretty curled locks. Nay, he'd trade those any day for a lass with a keen wit, an impertinent tongue, and a desire to see him covered in manure.

"I'm not sure," he responded, and then rubbed his chest to ease a twinge of guilt that had lodged there. "I'll have someone return it once we're back. Hopefully Eirik won't have come looking for it in the meantime and found it stolen."

He grabbed the gunwale, heaved the vessel onto its keel with a grunt, and then let out a soft whistle as he admired its craftsmanship. The man was an explorer, a warrior, and a master ship builder.

A mast with a sail wrapped around it was secured down the center of the hull. Four oars were tucked down beside it. He pulled two loose and fitted them through the oar ports for later.

He inspected the heavy mast, which was on a hinge and could be easily mounted upright again if needed. He wondered about detaching it entirely to lighten the boat, but it looked like he would need special tools. Besides, it was one thing to steal a man's ship, another to take it apart.

Eirik might never forgive him.

"Can you leave him some money for it?" Isobel asked as she removed some debris that had fallen into the boat.

He'd been pondering that very question. He had more than enough money and jewels on him to cover the cost, but he suspected if Eirik were here, the Norseman would refuse to take it.

Good thing he wasn't here.

"Aye, love, I will. A lot of it. And I'll leave a note too." He reached into his sporran and pulled out a sack of gold—a goodly price for the boat. He didn't know if Eirik could read, so instead he took out something else and added it to the purse—a curled lock of white-blond hair secured with a blue ribbon. If his brothers had known he carried a part of Isobel with him, he would never have heard the end of it.

He dropped the coin purse to the ground and laid a few twigs over it. Eirik would find it.

"How are we going to move it?" Isobel asked, and he looked up to see her eyeing the boat worriedly.

And no wonder. The longship was about three times the size of the skiff they'd rowed across, and solidly built—it would have to be to make it safely across the North Sea.

He lowered it back to the forest floor, moved to Diabhla, and fished a long rope out of his pack. "Diabhla is going to pull, I will push, and you will guide it as best you can. There's a path, of sorts, from when Eirik first pulled the ship up. Rocks have been cleared and stumps removed. The hardest part will be getting it over the lip at the edge and onto the beach, but once we're there, the sand will make it easier."

If we aren't under attack.

He was sure that as soon as they appeared on the beach, a cry would go up. They would need speed to get to the water as quickly as possible. That was their only escape. Two of the enemy's archers were down. He hoped they didn't have more.

He turned the rope into a harness and secured it around Diabhla's chest and back. Isobel watched him closely. Her fingers moved unconsciously as he looped and pulled the heavy cord. Then he ran the length of it back to the boat and attached it to a metal ring on the prow.

They were ready, and his gut felt as knotted as the rope he'd just tied.

"Which side do you want me on?" Isobel asked as she tucked her skirts up between her legs again.

He couldn't answer. His jaws felt soldered together. What if he was making a mistake? Maybe he should hide here with her for a few days until the soldiers had passed.

It would be too late for his clan by then, but he would know for sure that Isobel was safe.

She looked at him closely. "You're worried."

"Aye. If something should happen to you…"

"It willna. You said I wouldnae be harmed. I believe you."

He groaned and shoved his hands through his hair. "But what if I'm wrong?"

She stepped toward him and leaned against his body, toes to toes, chest to chest, and wrapped her arms around his back. Turning her head, she rested her cheek above his heart. He sighed and wrapped his arms around her too.

"It's a chance we have to take. If I am to lead your people, you canna sacrifice them for me. 'Tis the other way around. You either leave me here to fend for myself and go save them, or we go together. I'll not have it any other way." She raised her head and held his gaze. "I will be worthy of them, Kerr."

His throat was so tight he couldn't speak. If the enemy didn't know she was with him, he might consider leaving her. But they did know, and they would search until they found her.

He nodded and then leaned down and kissed her. She pressed her hand on the nape of his neck and cleaved to him.

A shout sounded in the distance, and he braced himself. It was now or never.

Kerr broke off the kiss and hurried to the stern. He raised the ship with a great heave and placed his hands on either side of the dragon's tail that rose at the back. "Keep the ship level, if you can. I'll stop Diabhla at the edge of the woods and then push the boat over the bluff. I need to control the descent to the beach so I doona damage the hull."

"I'll do my best," she said, gripping the gunwale and bracing her feet.

He whistled, and Diabhla leaned into the harness. Kerr pushed with all his might, and the boat shifted forward. He dug his feet in, taking one step, then another, until he was practically running. Ahead of him, Diabhla pulled, encouraged by Kerr's whistles to keep moving. Isobel ran beside the boat, hands on the gunwale as she maneuvered their path as best she could, a look of concentration on her face.

When Diabhla neared the tree line, Kerr whistled sharply for him to stop. He did, his sides heaving and his haunches quivering. Kerr kept pushing, using the momentum to turn the boat slightly and shove it up beside his horse.

"Hold it steady," he said to Isobel, and then crawled forward to the edge of the bluff. He looked out and spotted three warriors crossing the creek. They'd be on them in minutes. He considered going on the offensive and killing them first, but then two more men crossed behind them, heading in their direction. He cursed under his breath and looked back to the beach.

The water was about sixty paces away, and the drop down to the sand wasn't that far. Isobel could easily jump down on Diabhla.

He crawled back and rose beside her, letting the boat rest against his thigh. "I want you on Diabhla while I lower the boat. When I give the signal, jump down with him and run straight to the water. The rope will pull taut, and he'll slow, but I'll be pushing from behind like before. You'll have to lead him into the loch, but don't expose yourself by sitting up high. Stay as low as possible on his neck."

"*You'll* be exposed," she croaked.

"Aye, but I'll be moving too fast to hit." It was a lie, and he could see in her eyes that she knew it. He squeezed her hands. "Isobel, whate'er you do, doona shy away from the water. He'll sense your hesitancy and slow down. If he slows, the boat may tip, and we'll ne'er get moving again in time. Keep going straight out to sea. He can swim with you in the saddle. Doona turn around. Doona even look back. I can get to you once we're far enough out."

"And if you canna?"

"Then close your eyes, dearling, and hold onto his mane. Diabhla is a strong, fast swimmer. I have no doubt he'll get you to the other side safely."

Tears swam in her eyes and trickled down her cheeks. He wiped them with his thumbs, kissed her, and then whispered against her lips, "We'll live to share our marriage bed, Izzy. I promise you."

———

Isobel sat high up on Diabhla's shoulders, in front of the harness, and held the rope so it didn't get tangled. Her breath rushed in and out of her lungs, and her heart pounded. She couldn't stop the tears from streaming down her face.

Beside her, Kerr had nudged Eirik's boat as close to the edge of the bluff as possible and stood with his hands on either side of the dragon tail. His concentration was fierce, and every muscle clenched as he prepared to lower the ship to the beach and get them to safety. His sword poked up behind his head, and a breeze from the water blew his thick, dark hair around his face and shoulders. He looked like a magnificent warrior of old.

This was how she would picture him. Always.

"Remember," he said, his voice rough, "stay low, ride as fast as you can into the loch, and keep going. Aim for the other side, Izzy, and doona look back."

She turned forward, closed her eyes briefly, and nodded. Then she stared at the land across the loch. That was where Kerr wanted her to go. That was her destination.

With a grunt, he shifted the boat forward, breaking through the tree line. She looked down at him, she couldn't help herself, and stared at the massive warrior—her warrior. In a few beats of her heart, he pushed the boat halfway over the bluff and then lowered the prow smoothly to the sand. The muscles in his shoulders, chest, and arms bulged, and his strong face was etched into a strained grimace.

He took a breath and pushed forward again, cutting a line in the sand with the keel. When he reached the edge of the bluff, he shoved the boat forward as far as he could, heaved it up into the air, and then jumped down onto the sand below and caught it against his shoulder. With another grunt, he lowered it all the way down.

A yell sounded from across the beach as they were seen, followed by more yelling and sharp whistles. Then men began appearing from different places in the woods, running toward them, their plaids flapping behind them and their weapons raised.

"Go, Izzy! Go!" Kerr shouted. He began pushing the boat toward the water, letting out his own sharp whistle that pierced her ears and sent Diabhla leaping into motion.

She held on tight as the stallion arced over the bluff and landed on the beach beside his master. The boat glided easier this time, and Kerr was already practically running with it through the sand.

Hope burst through her heart. *We're going to make it!*

Diabhla raced past, and she let go of the rope. It stretched out behind them and then tightened. The jolt almost knocked her off his back, and she had to re-seat herself. Behind her, Kerr whistled at Diabhla to keep pulling. The stallion heaved forward in the harness, and they picked up speed again.

"Get low, Izzy," Kerr yelled at her, and she leaned forward on the horse's neck, keeping pressure on the reins so he stayed on the shortest route to the water.

They were about halfway there when she looked back...and gasped. Men had streamed onto the beach behind them, all the way along—too many to fight, maybe thirty of them—some on horses, some on foot. And they were closing in fast.

But what scared her the most were five men on foot directly behind Kerr with their swords out and murderous expressions on their faces. And they were gaining on him.

"Behind you!" she screamed, but he didn't stop or turn around...he kept pushing the boat and whistling at Diabhla to keep going. The enemy drew closer to him with every step.

Just when she thought it was too late, he lunged forward, shoved the boat as far ahead as he could, and dropped to the sand and rolled.

He came up with his daggers in both hands, slicing through the stomach of the man who had tried to jump on top of him and stabbing his other dagger into the next man's throat. Both warriors fell, and Kerr hurled the dagger he'd used to kill the first man into another man's chest, stopping him in his tracks.

The two men following slowed, and Kerr turned and chased after the boat. She wanted to wait for him, but he yelled, "Faster!"

She looked back to the loch and urged Diabhla to keep going— they were almost there. His hooves pounded into wet sand— finally!—and she rejoiced inside. Kerr would catch up; they would make it!

Then something flew past Diabhla's head, and he shied away from it, breaking his rhythm and darting sideways. She almost fell off a second time. The only thing that saved her was that she'd been hanging on so tightly around his neck and one of her legs had gotten caught in the harness.

"Arrows!" Kerr yelled behind her. "Stay down!"

Terror for him welled within her. She glanced back again. He was pushing on the boat's stern and completely exposed.

His feet had just hit the wet sand when another arrow flew through Diabhla's tail. The stallion screamed and reared on his hind legs, and this time she couldn't hold on. She fell back and hung upside-down for a moment before her leg wrenched free and she tumbled to the wet sand.

Kerr was there immediately, pulling her clear of Diabhla's hooves. He dragged her behind the boat, which had tipped onto its side, facing them. More arrows landed near them on the beach, making the sand spit. One hit the dragon head with a loud thunk.

"Don't move!" he roared at her as he drew his sword.

Diabhla was rearing and kicking, still attached to the boat and jerking it around in his panic. Kerr brought his sword down on the rope and the stallion leapt free, racing away from them along the water's edge.

"I think he's hit!" Isobel cried. She crouched at the water's edge behind the gunwale. Gentle waves lapped at her skirt.

They were so close!

Kerr looked over the edge and then ducked down again as another arrow flew through the air where his head had been. He came up immediately with his dagger in his hand and flung it on the same path back toward the archer with a mighty grunt.

Isobel peeked up and saw the dagger fly. It passed men with swords, on foot and on horses, until it hit the archer in the shoulder. The man staggered back, his dark hair hanging down on one side of his head, the other side bare. He grabbed the knife hilt with both hands and pulled it out, before dropping the knife and pressing his hand to the wound. Even from this distance, Isobel could see his arm didn't look right.

Is that the man who grabbed me at the cabin?

She couldn't be sure as Kerr shoved her down again and then jumped over the boat. She heard swords clashing and men groaning, before Kerr appeared at the boat's prow and yelled, "Move!"

He grabbed the dragon by the neck and heaved the vessel toward the water. She scrambled back, her skirts getting soaked as the water rose, and he disappeared again—swords ringing in the air as the battle continued.

She heard sobbing and realized it was coming from her. She tried to stop, but it felt like her heart was breaking and her stomach was trying to force itself into her throat.

Kerr was on the other side, roaring and grunting—she knew it was him. *She knew it.*

She looked over again and saw men scattered around the boat, dead and dying. Kerr, his shirt ripped up the back and hanging from him in rags, was pulling a sword out of another man who had fallen.

But more warriors were closing in.

There's too many of them!

He was cut and bleeding, battered and bruised. When he raised a hand to push his hair out of his face, she saw a tremor run through his muscles along his spine. And he was favoring one side.

How many battles had he fought today? How far had he pushed that bloody boat?

He tore his shirt off with a loud *rip* and dropped it to the sand. The same shirt she'd worn yesterday and last night, loving the smell of it, the feel of it—of him—against her skin.

It couldn't end like this.

She crawled to the pointed bow, wedged her shoulder under the gunwale and pushed with all her might toward the water. The boat barely shifted…until a wave lapped underneath and lifted it. The vessel glided forward and stopped. Then the next wave came, and the next, and before she knew it, she was kneeling in water up to her waist.

The boat was partially submerged. She would have to flip it onto its keel.

She pushed to her feet, grabbed the gunwale, and tried to force it up, but it was too heavy with the water that was already inside.

Lifting her head, she searched for Kerr. And froze.

He had both hands on his huge double-edged sword, swinging in an arc at the enemy, keeping them back for only a moment before they surged forward again, getting closer every time and pushing him another step toward the water. He roared and put on a burst of speed, slicing and stabbing into bodies. The mob fell back.

But some of them had crept to the side and were edging around him. He stepped back, trying to stop them, but then the ones in front pressed forward.

He towered over them all—his arms longer, his legs longer, his back and shoulders massive…but even he couldn't defeat so many men.

She desperately wanted to cry out to him, but she feared she would distract him. She wanted to run to him, to help him, but she knew he would protect her and not himself.

She tried again to right the ship but ended up slipping and crashing into the gunwale. Pain thudded through her arm and chin, but it was dulled, muffled through heartache and sorrow, through fear that this mighty Highlander was going to die because of her.

If she hadn't left the castle, if she hadn't insisted on staying once they were here, if she had married him two years ago, when she knew he wanted her to…

A big man darted past Kerr and tried to get to her. Kerr released his sword with one hand and flung his last dagger, hitting him in the back, but now three more men were right on top of him. He kicked and punched, knocking two of them back, but the third man landed a heavy blow to his stomach, and Kerr staggered, tripped over the body of the man he'd just killed and went down. The attacker lifted his sword and brought it down triumphantly, but Kerr rolled, grabbed the dagger from the other man's back, and stabbed it into his stomach.

He rolled again, onto his knees, but a sword arced down toward his neck.

She screamed...and saw a flash of white. A blur of teeth.

The man with the sword fell back as Siv launched herself at his throat with a ferocious snarl. Blood jetted up, drenching the huge, savage wolf—and the men at the front of the attack yelled in terror. Some tried to run, others stabbed at her with their swords, but she was fast and deadly, and tore through the enemy.

Then Isobel heard pounding hooves and a thundering voice yelling in another tongue—a war cry. She looked over and saw Eirik—his long dark hair streaming out behind him and that giant axe held aloft in his hand—riding Diabhla toward them along the wet sand like Lucifer after a sinner.

"Kerr!" she sobbed. "It's Eirik!"

Kerr had pulled himself up again and resumed the battle, both hands on his sword, carving into the enemy with renewed vigor. Their attackers fell back under the new assault, some scattering like rats as Eirik on Diabhla dove into the fray, hacking and slicing with speed and accuracy.

The last few men turned and raced toward the trees, Siv snapping at their hamstrings.

Isobel watched them run, her chest heaving as she sobbed. On the bluff, she saw the archer Kerr had hit with his dagger sitting slumped over on a great white charger. And there were more men on the bluff. What were they waiting for?

"Is it over?" she cried. "Are they leaving?"

Kerr turned and ran through the water toward her, his eyes never leaving hers, a shattered expression on his face. He was covered in blood, and this time she knew some of it was his.

He scooped her up into his arms, her feet dangling, and squeezed her so tight she could barely breathe. He dropped his head into the crook of her neck and shuddered, his breath sawing in and out of his lungs in strangled gasps. She hugged him back as hard as he hugged her, her arms crushing his shoulders and the nape of his neck, and she cried like her world was ending.

Which it almost had.

He fell to his knees, still holding her, the water swirling around their waists. Slowly, his breathing eased. "Never again, Isobel," he croaked. "Do you hear me? You will never be in danger like that again!"

Something hit the back of Kerr's head and jingled. She glanced down and saw the bag of gold he'd left in the woods for Eirik sinking through the water to the sand below. Kerr scooped it up and peered back at Eirik.

"You steal my boat and leave me gold?" the huge Norseman asked from the water's edge, hands on his hips and a disgusted look on his face. Diabhla stood behind him and Siv sat on her haunches at his side—her head reached his waist. "*Minn askr* cannot be bought. She is priceless!"

He held up what looked like long, curled blond hair—her hair?—tied in a blue ribbon. "For this, however, I will give you a ride across the loch." And then he laughed heartily.

Siv bounded toward them into the water and dunked under the surface. She jumped up with a splash and an excited bark. Darting close, she nipped at Isobel's sleeve, nuzzled her ear, and then licked Kerr's face. Kerr dug his hand into her scruff and playfully shook her head before he yanked her close and kissed the side of her nose.

The wolf jumped away, swimming deeper into the loch. When she returned, she rose to her feet and shook her fur, getting water everywhere. Isobel laughed and hugged Kerr, but the laughter soon turned into another sob, and she pressed her hand to her mouth.

Enough, Isobel.

Kerr gave her one last tight squeeze before standing with her and setting her back a step. He quickly splashed water over his face, chest, and arms until the blood was rinsed away. She could see the actual cuts on him—and there were many, although most were not deep.

When he saw the concerned expression on her face, he kissed her briefly and said, "Doona worry, love. I've had worse."

He turned to the boat and pulled it upright, the water sloshing around inside.

Eirik splashed into the loch and grabbed the gunwale. "Never before has there been so much water in *minn askr*. Not even when I crossed the sea from Normandy."

"Let's dump it before they regroup," Kerr said. "They must be waiting for reinforcements. There are bands of them scattered throughout the woods."

"*Ja,* we saw them. We would have been here sooner, but they were in our way."

Kerr cleared his throat. "Thank God you came when you did."

"I thanked them all," Eirik said. "Freya in particular. She urged us on."

They lifted the boat and turned it over so the water dumped out. One of the oars fell, and Isobel pulled it toward her before they righted the vessel.

Shouting sounded from the bluff, and when she saw the white charger jump onto the sand, she gripped Kerr's arm. But only a few men followed the horse away from the bluff, and the man reined in his mount.

Eirik glanced over his shoulder. "They are afraid of Siv, *ja*? And they should be. She is a fierce warrior. But it will not last forever."

Siv charged to the edge of the wet sand and spread her feet in an aggressive stance, her tail pointed stiffly behind her and her head slightly lowered. She growled ferociously. Isobel hoped the sound would carry.

"Can we go now?" she asked nervously.

"Aye." Kerr lifted her by the waist, and she let out a surprised yelp. He put her in the boat, and then whistled sharply for Diabhla. The stallion's ears pricked up, and he sloshed forward through the water. He still wore his harness, and the extra rope was folded on his back. Kerr fastened it to the dragon's tail.

Then he pressed his cheek to Diabhla's and murmured soft, soothing words. The stallion blew out a sigh and leaned into him. The sight made Isobel tear up again.

After a moment, Kerr climbed into the boat with his saddlebag, followed by Siv who curled up in the stern. Isobel handed him a set of oars which he quickly slid into the ports, before doing the same for a second set that she assumed Eirik would use.

Another whistle sounded behind them, and this time more men appeared and started running down the beach toward them, their weapons raised. "Move to this end with Siv, *kaerr dottir*," Eirik said to Isobel, sounding as calm as he had when he was cooking rabbits.

She clambered over the benches, three in total, her sodden skirts slowing her down as Eirik pushed the ship into the water and then jumped over the gunwale from the side. Her stomach clenched as the boat rocked, and she closed her eyes.

By the time she had settled down in the aft with Siv, Eirik and Kerr had found a quick, steady rhythm. They rowed so fast that the wind blew against her wet hair and clothes, and she shivered from the cold.

When she felt brave enough to look behind them, she was afraid she'd see arrows flying through the air, but they were out of range, and the enemy had stopped their pursuit about halfway to the water and stood staggered on the beach, dwindling in size with every pull of the oars.

Finally, she breathed a sigh of relief.

They were safe, and soon they'd be back at her castle and Kerr could ride out with the force of his allies at his side. After what they'd been through, he would realize he couldn't fight this enemy alone.

He would never want to leave her side again.

Twenty-One

"HOW DID YOU FIND THE SACK OF GOLD I LEFT YOU?" KERR asked Eirik quietly from the bench behind him. They were about halfway across the loch, angling southwest with no other boats in sight. Isobel had settled against Siv, and while she wasn't sleeping, she looked done in—and he didn't want to rouse her.

Putting down his oars, Eirik turned in his seat and faced him. Kerr continued to paddle slowly, so they stayed ahead of Diabhla who swam strongly behind the boat.

He, on the other hand, was tired; he needed to conserve his strength for the long, hard days ahead of him.

"Siv found it and brought it to me," Eirik said, rolling his shoulders and then stretching his arms to the sky.

Kerr shot him a quizzical look. "But you weren't coming from that direction."

"After that. She chased some of the men into the woods when you were busy with Isobel. She must have smelled it—you put an actual piece of her in with the gold. Do you want it back?" He reached into his pocket for the lock of Izzy's hair.

"Nay, you keep it—and anything else that is mine. Anything. If you hadnae arrived when you did, I would be dead and they would have her." A shudder ran through him as he said it.

Eirik leaned forward and squeezed his arm, and then said solemnly, "I would ask for your first born, but with my luck, the child would end up looking like you rather than Isobel."

"Aye, 'tis true," Kerr said with a snort, and Eirik sat back, laughing.

Isobel glanced over at them, looking lovely despite her

bedraggled appearance. She was covered in one of Eirik's furs, which would keep the cold out, but lying against a wet wolf, in wet clothes, couldn't be comfortable.

He needed to speak to her, and when he thought about what he had to do—how he had to let her go—a heaviness fell upon him.

He sighed, put down the oars, and opened his sporran. "I have my mother's jewels with me—passed down from her grandmother. I had intended to give them to Isobel when the time was right, but—"

Eirik squeezed Kerr's hand shut over the opening. "Thor's stones, close your bloody bag." Then he picked up his oars and continued to paddle forward.

"You willna take anything?" Kerr asked.

"*Nei*."

"You're certain?"

Eirik shot him a dark look, and Kerr finally closed his sporran. He let it drop between his legs and raised his hand to scrub through his beard. "I need one more thing from you."

Eirik raised his brow. "If this one more thing is what I think it is, she will not be happy. And if *she* is unhappy, Siv will be unhappy. And I love my wolf."

Kerr couldn't help smiling. "But you'll do it."

"*Ja*, of course. I would ask the same for my wife."

Kerr let out a sigh of relief, and then reached across and clasped the Norseman's arm. "Thank you. I canna stand to see her in any more danger. Do you know where her castle is?"

"*Ja*."

"My foster brothers and foster father should still be there. I'll write a note for you to give to them."

He pulled his saddlebag toward him and opened it. After searching through it, he found a piece of parchment, and in a separate case, a small quill with a stoppered bottle of ink. He laid the ink on the bench beside him, dipped his quill, and started writing.

After a few minutes, Eirik asked, "How will you stop Isobel from getting off the boat when we land? She is a determined woman. She will not listen to you when you tell her to stay with me."

Kerr signed the letter, laid it aside, and repacked his quill. "I'll swim."

On Eirik's quizzical look, he lowered his voice and continued. "She's afraid of the water. If I jump in and swim to shore with Diabhla, she canna follow me."

His friend raised his brow. "Your wife will not be happy. And from what I hear, she is vengeful. She will make you pay for this choice." He said it with such relish that Kerr couldn't help smiling.

"She isna my wife. Not really. I tricked her into handfasting me, and the marriage wasnae consummated. But you're right, she will take it upon herself to show me my folly."

"*Ja*, as I said…your wife."

Kerr huffed out a breath, halfway between a laugh and a sigh. He didn't know exactly what Isobel would do, but he had no doubt about what *he* had to do.

Pointing toward a distant spot on the opposite shore, he said, "Do you see the point where the land juts into the loch? Row in that direction. There's a beach before the promontory with a trail that will lead to Clan MacAlister. I'll jump out as you row past. It willna be too far a swim."

"Everything will get wet," Eirik said.

"I'm already wet. And everything will dry."

"All right. But you should tell her first, *ja*? I do not want her angry with me for the rest of the trip."

Kerr looked over and saw that she was alert and watching them—and she had a suspicious frown on her face, which was better than the blank, almost stunned expression she'd worn before. Still, he groaned silently. "I'll tell her now."

"What are you two whispering about o'er there?" she asked.

Kerr folded the parchment and handed it to Eirik. Then he crawled past him toward Isobel. The Norseman moved to Kerr's empty seat and picked up the oars.

Isobel's eyes widened as the boat rocked, and she gripped the gunwale above her—as if that would stop the movement. When he sat down and the boat stilled, she released a pent-up breath.

"You look pensive," she said.

He hesitated, and then slid off the bench and squeezed in beside her, nudging them over. Siv grunted and gave him an annoyed look. With a flick of her tail in his face, she hopped over the benches in the other direction.

The boat rocked again as Kerr repositioned himself. Isobel closed her eyes this time, and a white line formed around her pinched mouth. When Kerr grasped her hand, she squeezed it so hard he thought he might be bruised.

So worth it.

"I know this longship is well-built and sturdier than the smaller one we rowed across on the way there," she said, sounding a little breathless, "but it moves so smoothly through the water I almost feel as if I'm…in the water…if that makes sense."

"It does," he said. "Especially as you're sitting on the hull, so you're actually below the surface."

"'Tis verra disconcerting."

"Aye. Do you want to sit on the bench?" he asked.

She shook her head. "I think it would be worse to see the water all around me. And I doona want the boat to rock anymore."

"Then come here, love. Lean against me. I'll be your anchor." He put his arm around her, and she snuggled into his chest. He sighed heavily and closed his eyes. "We are fortunate to be alive, Isobel. When I think how close—"

"Shhhh, Kerr. We're safe…and together."

"But we shouldnae be. This whole thing is my fault."

"Nay, 'tis my fault. I'm the one who set out to trick you, to get you on that boat. And then once we were on the other side, I refused to go back. I caused this. Me."

"Nay, sweetling. You were only reacting to all the things I've done to you o'er the years. You were right. About everything. I didn't see it at first, but…I was no different than my father."

She gasped and fisted her hand in his damp shirt. "Doona say that. You are nothing like your father."

"Perhaps I didn't kill anyone, but I manipulated situations to keep suitors away from you, like you said. And I controlled and intimidated people with my physical presence and my words. I was happy other men were afraid of me."

Isobel sighed. "If we're telling truths then…so was I."

His brow rose. "Truly?"

"Aye. It allowed me a certain amount of freedom—I didn't have a steady stream of suitors vying for my attention, and I didn't have any pressure to make a decision. Everyone left us to sort it out ourselves—which meant I had a lot of time to do whate'er I wanted."

He grasped her hands. "But doona you see? That's where everyone went wrong. They shouldnae have assumed anything about you, and you shouldnae have felt any pressure—by me or anyone else. You're a strong, intelligent woman and you have the right to control your own destiny. Exactly as your mother wanted. I tried to take that away from you—and look where we ended up."

"On a rickety boat with a bloodthirsty wolf and a mad outlander."

"I heard that," Eirik said.

Kerr huffed out a laugh. Isobel too. But then he sobered. "If another woman had done to me what I did to you, I would have been upset, to say the least. If they had rowed me across a lake against my will, and then tricked me into handfasting them, I would have hated them."

"Even if it had been me?"

"Nay. Never." He raised his hands and trailed his fingers down her face. "Isobel…everything I've done, I did thinking it was the best for us. But I understand now how misguided that was, how controlling. And I'm so sorry, love. There is no 'us.' There ne'er was."

She inhaled sharply and pulled away from him, a confused and hurt frown forming on her brow. He scrubbed a hand over his face. "I'm messing this up. I'm sorry—again. What I'm trying to say is… I willna hold you to the handfasting. No one needs to know about it. Ever. You are free."

A sick feeling twisted inside Isobel. She didn't feel happy or free—or in charge of her own destiny. Instead, she felt a rising sense of panic. And her mind was spinning so fast and out of control, she could barely concentrate on anything Kerr was saying.

Something cold pressed into her palm, breaking through to her, and she looked down to see a gold ring.

"'Twas my mother's," he said. "Not from my father, but from her grandmother, whom she adored." He turned the ring over, and she gasped at the beauty of the large amethyst—a rich purple color, perfectly shaped, and unblemished. Surrounding it were tiny crystals and fresh-water pearls. "I want you to have it, not as a promise, but…so that when next I see you, if you're wearing this ring, I'll know that you welcome my attention. If you're not wearing it, you needn't say anything to me at all. I'll leave, I promise you, and I'll ne'er speak of it again."

He closed her fingers over the ring. "You're free, Isobel. *You* decide what's best for you. You doona owe me or anyone else anything."

She looked up at him, feeling gutted. He was letting her go? Just like that? When all she wanted was for him to hold her?

And what did he mean? *When next I see you…*

He gently cupped her cheeks, his gaze roaming her face as if to remember this exact moment. Then he lowered his head and kissed her. A simple press of their lips together. He didn't push, he didn't increase the heat between them or slide his tongue inside her mouth. Nay, it wasn't that kind of kiss.

This kiss cherished her, revered her. But it was also a kiss of partings, and when she realized that, she pulled back from his embrace...not in rejection but in fear. He was *not* leaving her.

"Nay!"

He slid his palm to the nape of her neck and held her still. "I love you, Isobel MacKinnon. I always have and I always will. And if you choose to wear my ring, I swear I'll be a better man than I have been—and a better husband to you in the future." Then he kissed her one last time.

She closed her eyes, stunned and unable to make her tongue work. Her heart pounded in her chest, and her throat had thickened with emotion.

He loves me.

But then he released her. Moving quickly, he leaned over the edge and unfastened Diabhla's lead from around the dragon's tail.

"Kerr," she croaked, reaching out to him as he stepped away. He held onto the lead and directed Diabhla to the front of the boat.

Eirik lifted the oars as he went by and let the boat drift. Then he nudged Siv with his foot, who bounded over the seats to plop down beside Isobel and nuzzle her with her nose. The boat still rocked, but this time Isobel kept her eyes open—and on Kerr.

She slid forward onto her knees, her hands gripping the seat in front of her. She tried not to look at the empty expanse of water around them. "What are you doing?"

If they were anywhere but on a boat surrounded by water, she would grab his arm and demand he tell her what was going on. They were still hours away from her land and their allies.

"Please, come here." She'd intended it to be an order, but it came out pleading.

When he picked up his saddlebag and threw it over his shoulders, panic beat in her chest and propelled her forward. She crawled over the benches toward him, desperately trying to *not* see the water all around them.

Eirik steadied her as she went by and then moved to the opposite end of the ship next to Siv.

"Kerr!" she said again, straddling the last bench and clenching his shirt. He wasn't wearing his boots or socks and was busy stuffing his plaid into his saddlebag. Her panic increased.

What is he planning? But deep down she knew, and her hand trembled.

The ring fell from her fingers and landed with a clang on the bottom of the boat. She leaned down for it—it was his mother's—but it rolled away, and she had to let go of him to reach it.

When she grabbed it, she shoved it onto her thumb—a tight fit—so she wouldn't drop it again. She wanted him to see it there and know that she had made a decision. She was choosing him.

And where he went, she went.

The boat dipped suddenly, and she let out a startled yelp. She tried to grab onto him again, but he'd stepped onto the keel and was lowering himself into the water.

She grasped his arm, still wrapped over the gunwale, her fingers stiff as talons. "No!" she squeaked. "You're not going without me, especially without your brothers and Gregor by your side. You'll be killed!"

"My allies will come, Isobel. You and Eirik will tell Gavin what has happened. They'll arrive only a day or two behind me."

"But that might be too late!"

"Leaving my people without their laird for even one more day *will* be too late. I need to protect them, Isobel."

"I need to protect them too. I'm their lady. 'Tis my right!"

"Not after what happened. Isobel, I let you put my clan—"

"Our clan."

"—first because I was selfish enough to want you as my lady, leading beside me no matter what. I put them before you, and you almost died. Do you know what those men might have done to you? How you might have been treated? I couldnae save you. I was as good as dead. Eirik saved you, not me. Siv saved you."

"Eirik is not my husband. You are."

"Nay, I'm not. I tricked you."

"I doona care."

"I do." He grasped her hand in his, as gently as he could, and kissed it. "Tell your brother and the others what has happened. And tell them to hurry."

He released her hand and pushed away from the side of the boat. She stretched out her arm, tried to grab him back, but he was out of reach.

"Kerr!" she screamed. "Come back!" But he turned away from her and started swimming toward the shore, Diabhla's lead gripped in his teeth.

"Come, Lady Isobel," Eirik said behind her, his voice gentle. "Please, sit down."

But she ignored him, edging closer to the gunwale, the lapping of the water against the hull sounding to her ears like the loudest hammer in the smithy. He couldn't leave her. He was her husband. Her place was at his side, and with their clan.

And he loves me!

Finally…he'd said the words.

"Kerr Anghos Finnian MacAlister!" she yelled, letting go of the gunwale and rising near the edge. Her words were loud and strong, and her fear and panic faded. He turned his head and looked at her, his stroke faltering when he saw her on the gunwale, her chin raised, her shoulders back. "You forget yourself, husband. *You* do not decide what is best for me. I decide."

Then she jumped off the boat.

Kerr launched himself toward Isobel before she even hit the water, the blood surging in his veins and pushing him faster, harder, than ever before.

But the distance between them was too great, and she plunged beneath the black waves.

Fear squeezed his chest and shoved upward into his throat, choking him. Where was she?

He should have known she would jump, known she would go with him no matter what. Isobel always went after what she wanted.

But how could he have anticipated *this*? She was deathly afraid of deep water.

She broke the surface and dragged in a great gulp of air. "Kerr!" she screamed, her arms flailing and her breath sputtering.

"I'm coming, Isobel. Hold on!"

But she dipped under again—she always did, no matter how hard she tried to stay afloat.

He dove down and saw her sinking, her arisaid tangled around her and stopping her from kicking her legs. He grasped her hand and tugged her up, wrapping an arm around her waist and swimming for the surface.

They broke through together, and Isobel heaved air into her lungs, then coughed and spewed out water. She clung tightly to Kerr's neck, her head on his shoulder, her legs around his waist.

Siv had jumped in too, but she stayed back. Eirik drew the boat closer. He reached an oar out to them. "Hold onto this," he said, keeping the blade steady.

Kerr hooked his elbow over the paddle and rested there, working to get his heart rate under control. He caught Eirik's eye, who shrugged. "It is as I said. She is not happy to be left behind. Do you want me to take her back and tie her down?"

"Nay!" Isobel protested and then started coughing again. "I'm going...with you."

Kerr ground his teeth together. She would jump in again if he tried to leave her. But what would happen to the Norseman if he arrived at MacKinnon land with Isobel trussed up? They would have his head.

He couldn't ask his friend to do that.

He shoved his wet hair back and looked over his shoulder. Diabhla was still swimming for shore, but the stallion could easily veer off course. Or the rope could get caught between his legs. He couldn't wait much longer; he had to decide now.

"God's blood, Isobel. You could have drowned!"

"Aye."

"Aye? That's all you have to say about it? I had to let go of Diabhla's lead. He isna safe out there on his own." He released the oar, and they sank back into the water. She let out a fearful gasp.

"Do you plan to swim to shore?" he asked, as he stroked through the water with one arm until he reached the boat's prow.

It was a rhetorical question, and she didn't respond other than to look guilty.

Good.

He grasped onto the ring at the front and called out to Eirik. "Can you row ahead of the stallion, so I can secure him?"

"*Ja.* But wait, Siv has your pack." The Norseman hauled the wolf back into the boat with Kerr's saddlebag in her jaws. Eirik tossed the bag to the bow and it caught on the gunwale. Kerr reached up and slipped it over his shoulder. He hadn't even realized it had floated away.

Sitting back down, Eirik picked up the oars and headed toward Diabhla.

Isobel squeezed Kerr tighter when they moved, and something cold and hard pressed into the side of his neck. He looked down, but all he could see was her fist.

He lifted his hand to investigate, and when he felt his mother's ring on her thumb—his ring—happiness burst though him... which was opposite to how he wanted to feel right now. She'd put herself in danger—again. He wanted to nurse that anger.

He tried to tamp the joy down, but it still smoldered like an ember in his gut. Maybe she put the ring on so it wouldn't fall off. Maybe she planned to remove it once they landed.

Or maybe she would keep it on for the rest of her life—which could have ended a few minutes ago and might still end any time between now and when he killed the men who were trying to kill them.

His anger returned full force. Good.

Maybe he should consider Eirik's offer to tie her up and return her to Gavin...

They passed the stallion, and he spoke gentle words to the horse so as not to spook him. When they were a little ahead of him, Kerr let go, and Eirik backed off with the boat.

"Do you see the lead?" Kerr asked him.

"*Ja*, it is trailing behind him on the far side."

Kerr moved over, and then grasped Isobel's arm and tried to move her around him, but she hung on tight. "Get behind me, Izzy. Hold onto my shoulders, not my neck."

She shifted reluctantly. He could feel the vein in her wrist thrumming under his thumb when he held her arm, hear her panicked gasps, and feel the quick puffs against his wet neck when she tucked in close to him. He spoke soft, slow words to calm her, like he had to Diabhla.

"No sudden moves," he said, as Diabhla approached them. He grasped the lead near the stallion's head and then gathered it up. The horse blew out a breath when he neared, and Kerr gently rubbed his cheek.

"I want you to move over into the saddle," he said. "You're going to ride him like you would on land but hold onto his mane, not the reins, so you doona pull his head. If you feel like you're going to float away, squeeze your legs against his sides. We'll be ashore in no time."

"I willna be too heavy?" she asked, and he noticed her teeth had started to chatter.

"Nay, the water will take much of your weight. Pull your skirts up so they doona trap your legs."

He floated next to the stallion, kicking to stay abreast with him, and rested a comforting hand on his withers.

"I'm ready," Isobel said, and then slid her leg and arm over Diabhla's back, grasped his mane, and let go of Kerr.

Kerr drifted away, wanting to give the stallion more space. Isobel had a moment of panic, and he calmly said, "Hold his mane and grip with your legs. If something happens, I will dive under and drag you up again."

She nodded jerkily.

He raised his gaze and met Eirik's. The Norseman was standing in his boat, watching them, Siv on the bench beside him. He inclined his head in farewell. "You are a good man, Kerr MacAlister. I will tell your brothers and Gregor MacLeod what has happened here and give them your note."

"I canna thank you enough, friend. Godspeed."

"*Ja*. Until we meet again." He raised his hand in farewell, and Kerr did the same.

Eirik sat down and grabbed the oars. He turned the ship and began rowing away, picking up speed. Siv moved to the stern and watched them. Then she tilted back her head and howled. Diabhla's ears twitched, and he jerked his head at the sound. Isobel squeaked and gripped his mane harder.

"You're all right," Kerr said. "Both of you." Then he put the lead in his mouth and struck out for shore.

Twenty-Two

Isobel shook out Kerr's almost-dry plaid and carefully laid it on top of another plaid that she'd spread on the floor of the cave. She kneeled down, pleased with the softness of the makeshift bed, and then flattened out any ripples in the material.

She wanted everything to be as close to perfect as possible for Kerr's return.

A small fire, encased in a ring of rocks, burned in the center of the cave, and she glanced around the enclosure, looking for something else to do. She'd already cleaned up the area as best she could and laid out her arisaid beside the fire to finish drying, as well as Kerr's saddlebag, his sporran, and everything that had been inside them—including a hairbrush, which she would take advantage of later.

Outside, a horse nickered in greeting, and she rushed to the cave's entrance. Fortunately, the sky was clear and the moon bright, and she easily made out Diabhla a few feet away, loosely tied to a tree outside the cave. Kerr's large figure approached, carrying an impossibly big load of wood. The sight made her shiver, and that soft place between her legs swelled and tightened with need.

She couldn't wait for him to come inside.

During their swim to shore, she'd been too frightened to think about anything except drowning, but after that had come long hours riding Diabhla, in which all she could think about was seducing her husband, especially when his big body had been pressed tightly behind her in the saddle. Although the sight of him jogging through the forest beside the stallion in his thin white shirt that fell midway down his thighs had been just as arousing... and inspiring.

She'd had so many ideas, she didn't know where to start.

She quickly loosened the tie of her white linen shift so the neck fell open, and then fluffed out her tangled hair, hoping that the light from the fire would shine through the thin material and reveal a sight too tempting for him to resist.

She intended to become Lady MacAlister in more than name tonight.

He glanced up, and when he stumbled upon seeing her, she dipped her head to hide her smile. "Are you well?" she asked.

"Aye," he said huskily. "I tripped on a rock. It's been a long day."

She stepped back as he drew near, dropping her lashes enough to be seductive. "Come in then. I've made our bed. You can lie down, and I'll rub your brow."

He stopped abruptly and turned to her, one eyebrow rising. "I've known you since you were two months old, Isobel MacKinnon, and I've ne'er heard such a tone from you. Or ever imagined you'd utter such words."

She pouted, trying to make it look pretty.

His other eyebrow rose. "Or make a face like that!"

Her eyes narrowed, and her hands flew to her hips. He grinned. "That's more like it." Then he dumped the extra wood by the fire.

"Should I just take my shift off, then?" she asked, pleased to see his head jerk up and his grin disappear. She started to gather the material in her hands, raising the hem inch by inch, biting her lip to stop her satisfied smirk when his shirt quickly tented out in front of him.

"Nay!"

"Are you sure, husband dear?" She raised it over her knees and kept pulling.

His skin had flushed, and his eyes, fixed on her bare flesh, glittered in the firelight. "Isobel, wait…please."

She pulled the material up another few inches, her thighs almost fully revealed now, and teased him with the darker depths hidden beneath. Just when it seemed as if she would pull the shift all the way up, she turned to their bed, put an extra swing in her hips as she walked toward it, and sat on the plaid. "I'll wait, but only if you bring me the hairbrush and come sit with me."

Kerr exhaled a long, pent-up breath and rubbed his hands over his face. "I doona think that's a good idea. We're both tired, and we canna wash before bed."

"We were swimming earlier today."

"And since then I've run through the forest, gathered up two loads of firewood, and been on a horse—you have too."

Her eyes fell on the full flask hanging from his belt. They'd finished the ale on the trail when they'd eaten their meal of cheese and apples, and since then, he'd found water and filled it up. She'd wager he'd washed himself too. 'Twas in his nature.

She rose to her knees, lifted her hem again, and then ripped off a piece of linen from the bottom. She held out her arm toward him. "I'll wash for you then, dearling. Please, pass me the water."

His Adam's apple bobbed. He tried to speak, but his voice cracked. He cleared it and then said, "You doona have to do that."

"I want to. And then I can wash you."

"Isobel," he said, sounding pained. He lifted his gaze to the ceiling and muttered something beneath his breath before saying, "I'm hungry; we havenae had much to eat today."

She barely held back her grin. "You can eat me."

His gaze came crashing down, and he seemed to grow bigger, more intense, if that were possible. She used to be afraid of him when he got like this, but now she liked it. All that intensity and attention turned on her. And when he'd been fighting for their lives, she'd welcomed the extra fierceness.

"I doona think you know what that means," he growled.

"I doona think you want me to know what that means," she countered.

"Have you done it before?"

She laid the cloth down and sat back on her hip. "Come over here and I'll tell you. I promise to stay on my side of the bed…for now." He took a predatory step toward her, and she shivered, the muscles clenching down low in her belly.

Aye, she liked him like this a lot.

"And doona forget to bring me the brush."

He picked it up and then trudged toward her. It wasn't that he didn't want her, that much was obvious—temptingly so—but he was fighting something within himself—a conflict he hadn't had this morning when they'd almost tupped back at the cottage.

What has changed?

No doubt it had something to do with her almost getting killed. Or maybe her near-drowning. Or the danger they were riding into at his clan.

But none of that mattered. She would always win this battle because she had a secret weapon.

He loved her—he'd said the words, and he couldn't take them back.

"What are you smiling like that for?" he asked as he released his belt and pulled his sword and scabbard over his head. He laid them beside the plaid, and then sat on the farthest edge before tossing her the brush.

"Like what?" she asked as she caught it, curious to know what she'd been projecting.

"You looked smug."

"Smug?" She didn't like the sound of that.

"Aye, but also excited and happy."

That was better. She started working the bristles through her tangles. "I am excited. And happy. And perhaps also a wee bit smug." She dropped her gaze to his cock, making such a large, long bulge under his shirt. She was tempted to crawl over there, lift up his shirt, and put her lips over it, but when she raised her gaze to his, he looked even more determined to keep his distance.

He drew up his feet and locked his arms around his knees. "Isobel, I doona think we should do this tonight."

He'd said it firmly, a steel in his voice he rarely used with her, and it gave her pause. "Why not?" she asked, truly wanting to know. "You wanted to this morning."

He sighed again. "Aye, but things have changed since then. Things have happened that have made me doubt—"

"Is this because you think you didn't save me at the beach? Because you did. First, you doona know if you would have been killed or what would have happened before Siv and Eirik arrived. Second, the only reason Siv and Eirik came for us was because of the bond you created with Eirik. You did that by knowing whom to trust and being someone Eirik could trust. He respects you, Kerr. I heard what he said before he left. He thinks you're a good man. As do I. I couldnae be more proud to call you my husband."

He stared at her, unblinking, and when a tiny tremor moved through his lower lip, he firmed his mouth. "Thank you," he said, sounding hoarse. "I hadnae looked at it like that, but…that wasn't what I was going to say."

"Oh. Well, what do you doubt, then? Is it me?" A sick feeling invaded her stomach, and she dropped her hands from her hair. "Is it because I'm impetuous at times? Do you no longer love me?"

"Nay, Izzy, it's not that. It's…" He pressed his lips together and then inhaled, as if he was trying to figure out what to say and how to say it. "Your life almost changed today—irrevocably. At the very least, you would have been taken prisoner, held captive, and then returned to Gavin. At the very worst… God's blood, I doona even want to think about the worst that could have befallen you."

"But it didn't." She reached out and squeezed his hand. "I'm here, Kerr, right beside you. Safe."

"Aye, by the grace of God."

"Doona you want to celebrate our aliveness?" She yearned to close the distance between them, but she knew this was important to him. He had to get the words out or they'd continue to eat away at him.

"Of course I do. Desperately." He hesitated, and then moved closer toward her on the plaid. "I had two thoughts running through my head this morning when we were fighting for our lives. How much I love you, and how you've barely stepped into the woman I know you're meant to be. I couldnae allow you to be taken from the world so young."

Her throat tightened. "I couldnae be taken from *you* so young."

"Nay, you're bigger than me, Izzy. You light up the world. My family—"

"I doona care about your family."

"You should." He released her hand to shove his fingers through his hair, tugging sharply on the ends. "When we leave here tomorrow, we'll ride all day, and arrive at the farm of a woman named Una MacAlister. Una lives on the edge of MacAlister land with her twin lads…who are my brothers."

Her eyes widened. "How old are they?"

"Fourteen."

"And their names?"

"Andrew—Andy for short—and Aulay." He smiled, and the moroseness that had befallen him eased a little. "You'll love them."

She smiled back. "I'm sure I will. I canna wait to meet them." But then her happiness faded as the darkness within him came back.

"Una was taken by my father—who was her laird and was supposed to protect her—as payment against her father's debts. Her father had been injured before she was born, and they were verra poor."

Isobel's throat tightened, and she pressed her hand against it. "What do you mean he took her?"

"He sent his men to their home, dragged her from her parents, and brought her to the castle—where he hurt her and abused her in every way…for months."

"Nay!" she cried. "How old was she?"

"Seventeen. A lass I'd known, played with my entire life. A lass my ma tried to protect—until she couldnae even protect herself."

"But surely your people—"

"They did naught, Izzy. Naught when he took Una. Naught when he murdered my mother. Naught when he stole from them and abused them. They were frightened and beaten down."

He huffed out a breath before continuing. "I know you've heard some of the stories, but you should know everything. I killed my father, Isobel. I killed my uncles and my cousins. I spared only one family member—my father's youngest brother, Dùghlas. He had a gentle soul, and I couldnae bring myself to go after him. He'd already been torn to shreds by his family."

She cupped his cheek and drew his head down until their foreheads touched, keeping connected to him, close to him. "You wouldnae have done those things if it hadn't been necessary—to save your people, to save Una."

"I saved her life, aye, but not her spirit. Her laddies did that. The things my father did to her damaged her body but also her soul. By the time I freed her, she was heavily pregnant and had a fresh scar running down one side of her face. He'd tortured her."

He said the last angrily, his hands fisting. Isobel squeezed one of them. "What happened to her?"

"She refused to return to the village. By then, her parents were dead by my father's hand, so the boys were born at the castle. When she was ready, she chose to isolate herself from the world at the farm. It was my mother's farm, and now it belongs to her."

Tears welled in her eyes. "And you still take care of her."

"I help out as much as I can, and I do my best with Andy and Aulay, but it will ne'er be enough to make up for what my father, my family, did."

"Do the lads know?"

"They know I'm their brother and their laird. And they know

that someone cut their mother and I killed him for it. Soon, I'm sure, they'll know that the man was my father—and theirs."

Isobel sighed heavily, understanding how that knowledge would affect the lads. How angry they would be—maybe at their father, maybe at the world in general. She hoped they wouldn't be angry at Kerr, and they would accept his help as they worked through their feelings—and directed their anger appropriately.

"This is the man who bore me, Isobel. This is the blood that runs through my veins. My father liked to break people. He chose his victims carefully. I canna believe he took Una to hurt her father—that poor soul wasn't relevant to Madadh MacAlister in any way. And she was a pretty lass, but there were many pretty lasses in the village. Nay, he took her to hurt someone else. My mother, maybe. Or me."

"Because she was a friend?"

"Aye. And because my ma often helped her family." His voice thickened, and he cleared his throat. "The point I'm trying to make is…"

She waited, but when he didn't continue, she put the brush down, cupped his other check, and kneeled right in front of him. "The point is that your father was a terrible man who did terrible things, and so somehow that means deep down you must be as terrible and not good enough to be my husband. Is that about right?"

He gripped her hands. "Think about it, Isobel. If someone told me my father was a demon made flesh, I would believe them. He lived to ruin people, to shred their bodies and their souls. And many in his family were the same. What if…"

"What if you're the same?"

"Aye. Or my blood. What if I ruin our bairns, pollute their bodies with my bad blood? Why would you want to take that chance, take on the dark legacy of my family by becoming my wife when you are worth so much more? Isobel, you could be a queen. You could rule this country!"

"I doona want to rule this country. I want to rule our people beside you. I love you, Kerr MacAlister. As much as you love me. You're no more polluted by your father's blood than Andy and Aulay are."

He dropped his head, shaking it in denial, but she held on tight. "They didn't grow up with him," he said. "They ne'er had to return to that castle year after year, not knowing if this would be the year he would stab me through the gut, or kill my horse, or hurt one of my friends. If this would be the year I couldnae protect my ma from him—only to have him kill her when I wasn't even there."

He sucked in a heavy, strangled breath that broke her heart, and she wrapped her arms around him, tears streaming down her face. His shoulders heaved, and she tightened her grip, desperate to take all that pain away, to mend the heart that surely must have shattered upon finding his mother dead. How could she piece it all back together?

If Madadh MacAlister were alive today, she would not rest until she'd killed him.

"Our bairns will be as good and kind and loud and annoying as you are, dearling. They will ne'er experience any of the things you described because your mother taught you how to love and be loved, and how to care for people and protect people. How to help others no matter how hard your own life. Their blood willna be tainted because yours hasn't been tainted."

They stayed like that for a while, and when she sensed the storm had passed, she brushed her fingers through his hair and nuzzled the side of his neck. "If it makes you feel any better, you must know that I willna be dissuaded tonight. Verily, my love, you doona have a choice. I hold all the weapons, and I will only accept your surrender. 'Tis no point in fighting against it."

He huffed out a laugh, and then raised his arms and squeezed them around her body. "The bairns will be loud, but with you as their mother, they'll also be crafty and cunning. I'll ne'er have a moment's peace, avoiding their traps and tricks. Not to mention the unwitting suitors our daughters will bamboozle. I'll die in my grave an old man at forty."

She snorted. "Our daughters will be too young for suitors when you're forty." Then she leaned back and picked up the hairbrush. "Turn around."

He raised a brow quizzically but did as she asked, sitting with his back toward her. She moved closer, still on her knees, and spread her legs so his spine rested against her. Then she raised the brush and gently pulled it through his hair, running her hand down the locks after the brush.

Neither of them spoke as she moved around his head, brushing from his brow to the tips of his hair that hung to his shoulders. The rhythm of the movement and the softness of the strands under her hands lulled her and helped ease the need she had to comfort him. Especially when he leaned more heavily against her.

She thought he might have fallen asleep, but then he said, "My mother used to brush my hair. No one has done it for me since she died."

"I will do it for you every night before we go to bed."

"Every night?"

"Aye."

"And what if I want to do other things?"

She smiled and pressed more closely behind him, her lips soft against his ear. "Then you'll have to wait."

"All right. But doona tell my brothers. I wouldnae hear the end of it."

She snorted. "I wager they'd tell their wives, and then find themselves at the end of a brush in no time…and asking for it."

She put the hairbrush down and moved backward on her knees. "Lie down."

He did, slowly, those dark eyes looking up at her, glued to her face. She leaned down and kissed him, a simple, soft press of their mouths, and then she rose, walked to the fire, and put another log on top.

The wood started to crackle, and the flames whooshed. Turning to him, she grasped her long shift, raised it over her body, and tossed it onto the plaid beside his knees.

A loud exhale blew through his lips, and his gaze drifted over her naked body and back up to her face. "You look like an angel, Isobel. My angel." He grasped his cock through the material. "What you do to me, love. I'm afraid I'll lose my seed just by looking at you." His voice had deepened, sounding more like a growl, and she shivered.

She walked toward him slowly, feeling as powerful and womanly as she'd ever felt. His hips rolled upward as she neared, and a groan rumbled from his chest. Reaching down, he grasped his shirt at the backs of his thighs, lifted his arse, and pulled it up.

"Nay," she said, and he hesitated. "I want to do it."

He lowered back down, that huge muscled body still covered at the front—a present she wanted to unwrap. In this moment, he was so beautiful to her—the dark intensity of his eyes, and the thick almost-black silkiness of his hair, the strong planes of his face, and full lips.

"Anything for you, Izzy. I am yours."

Her heart stuttered, and she stretched her hand out to him. He raised his arm and they linked their fingers together, palm to palm. Then she stepped over his thighs, her legs spreading wide, and she stayed that way, her very center exposed and open to him.

It made her heart race and wetness gather between her legs.

She wanted him to look at her, to be aroused by her.

He dropped his gaze, and she watched, fascinated, as his body changed—a pulse fluttered in his throat, his eyes darkened, a tinge of red spread up his chest and over his neck and cheeks, his lips parted and flushed, looking fuller than before, wetter. His breathing had increased, too, and his chest rose and fell quickly, sometimes jerkily, as the muscles in his belly clenched.

A forbidden, wicked desire infused every inch of her, and she moved her hand to the front of her stomach and rested it below her breasts. Then she slid her palm down her body. He groaned when her fingers pushed through the curls below, the hair slick from her own arousal, and stroked over the hidden nub, sending a pleasurable jolt through her body that made her gasp and her hips jerk forward.

Kerr gripped her thigh in support. His other hand, still holding hers, squeezed tight. "God's blood, Isobel," he said hoarsely. "Come down so I can taste you."

She smiled and shook her head, loving this powerful feeling that flared within her. It turned her body languid, yet burned her up from the inside at the same time. She kept pushing downward, her fingers spreading her swollen flesh. Closing her eyes, she sighed, feeling intoxicated as she hovered over her entrance. It pulsed with an ache that begged to be filled.

When she opened her eyes, the look on his face as he watched her was pure torture…and she loved it.

"I told you I was hungry, Isobel," he growled, and then he tugged her off balance. She fell forward into his hands with a surprised cry. He held her up by the hips, his gaze glued to hers, and that wicked smile she'd shown him moments ago transferred to his face. "You said that I could eat you."

She balanced her hands on his chest, shocked but excited too. *So excited*.

Lowering her down until her knees rested beside his ears, those big hands slipped behind her arse and guided her forward. When his mouth opened wide over all that swollen, aching flesh, every thought in her head shattered.

"Ooooh!" she groaned as he devoured her.

His tongue, heavy and soft, drew up through her folds to the nub at the top, and when he touched it, rubbed against it, the breath shuddered from her lungs in a desperate squeak, only to have him slide back down and start again.

Before long, she'd picked up his rhythm and rocked her hips against him in time with the strokes of his tongue, sliding back as he swept forward, and thrusting forward as he slid back, harder and faster until she felt ready to burst.

"Oh, dear God, dear God!" she chanted, her mind spinning out of control, her body completely at his mercy. He was relentless, holding her in place, using the flat of his tongue up the center and the tip around the nub.

When he actually pushed within her, she lost her mind and began to shake, her pelvis jutting against him as a whimper broke from her throat.

Then she screamed, long and hard, as she reached that pinnacle and fractured into a thousand pieces, jerking and thrashing against him. His fingers dug into the flesh of her hips and thighs as he held her tight, not letting her come down from the peak, driving her upward again.

She fisted her hands in his hair, sobbing from the pleasure, from the intensity that was almost too much.

She tugged on the strands. "Kerr! Please!"

Suddenly, he sat up and raised his knees so she was wedged between his thighs and abdomen.

"Lift my shirt, Izzy."

Her mind was in a fog, and it took everything she had to comprehend what he was asking. Her body still shook, and that ache—the one he'd driven her up to a second time—had not yet been assuaged.

"My shirt!" he ordered again, hoarsely, almost desperately, and this time she released his hair and dragged her hands down his body to his waist, grasped the material and pulled it up.

He groaned as he shifted his hips and lowered her down. The blunt, round head of his cock pushed through her folds, and she easily slid over the tip. It felt incredible, the growing pressure exactly where she needed it, the feeling of being stretched and filled making her moan.

"Support yourself, Izzy," he groaned. "On your knees and go slowly, dearling. I doona want you hurt."

She didn't listen and rocked her hips roughly until she felt a sudden pinching pain as she slid over him. "Oh," she gasped, and tried to pull away.

"Nay, Izzy. Doona retreat." His hand on her waist kept her in place. "Please. I'm barely inside you."

He released his hand and gently brushed the hair back from her face, his eyes, dark and wild, intent on hers. "Your body will accommodate mine."

Then he released his other hand from beneath her and palmed her breast, squeezing her turgid nipple between his thumb and finger. She gasped and slipped down a little farther, her flesh giving way. It did hurt, and she sucked in a breath, but it also felt… satisfying, and like she wanted to be connected at the very root of him, joined as closely to him as possible.

She wanted to envelope him all the way inside her body.

Her head dropped back and she closed her eyes, circling her pelvis over him until she was all the way down. "I'm all right, now. My God, Kerr, it feels so good!" Her voice came out deeper and rougher as the carnality of the moment intensified.

He gripped his shirt and lifted it over his head, using it to wipe his face at the same time. Then he tossed it to the side. She stroked her hands up his chest, driving her fingers through the crisp hair and then over his shoulders.

Cupping the back of her head, he nuzzled her neck. "Ne'er in my life have I had so much pleasure or been so happy as I am right now."

"'Twill only get better. Kiss me, Kerr."

He pulled her forward slowly and fused their mouths together. Closing her eyes, she breathed out, licked her tongue between his lips, and then gently rocked her hips, allowing her body to soften as she took the weight off her knees.

The fit was tight as she settled around him, but it no longer pinched, and when he was fully lodged inside her body, she nipped his lip and undulated against him, rubbing the tips of her breasts through all that crisp hair.

He responded with a groan and deepened the kiss, his head angling, his tongue hot in her mouth.

She couldn't get close enough, and when she lifted her arms around his neck and pulled him tightly against her, he wrapped his arms around her back. They held each other, skin to skin, their bodies thrusting synchronously, their lips melded together.

He broke off the kiss and heaved in a gasp of air, one hand dropping to her arse and squeezing. "Izzy, I canna last much longer."

Lowering his knees a little, he laid her back along his thighs, one hand on her breast, the other squeezing between their bodies. "Does that feel good?" he asked as he circled his thumb over her nub.

She almost laughed at the question, but instead a deep moan came unbidden from her throat. "Aye," she finally breathed out, the single word all that she could manage. The tension in her body had built so quickly that she couldn't keep a thought in her head.

His thrusts increased, and he sucked her other breast into the hot cavern of his mouth. First one, then the other, the rhythmic pull against his tongue matching the rhythm of their bodies down below.

Her legs wrapped around his arse, and she dug her heels into him as that rhythm roughened, hardened. She threw her head back, and he grabbed her hips to control her movements.

A keening broke from her throat, rending the air, and then she came apart, her body shaking as powerful waves of pleasure washed over her, stealing her breath.

Right on her heels, Kerr roared and jerked against her. "Isobel!"

She wrapped herself around him, loving this man more than she'd ever thought possible. He held her so tightly she could barely breathe, but she didn't care, as he continued to whisper her name, his body rigid, his muscles contracted—before he collapsed backward onto the plaid—like a puppet whose strings had been cut.

He loosened his hold with a heavy exhale and cupped the back of her head against his chest, still sucking in air, his heart pounding beneath her ear.

Finally, he puffed out a slower breath that ruffled her hair. He let his arm at her waist fall to the side, while his fingers gently massaged her scalp.

"Lady MacAlister," he huffed. "'Tis possible you woke the whole of the Highlands with your screaming." And now he was the one who sounded smug. And she loved it.

When she didn't respond, he asked, "Naught to say, my love?"

She inhaled a few more times until she had enough air to speak. Still, she had to do so in bursts. "If I had known what I was missing all these years, Laird MacAlister, I would ne'er have tried to dump you in manure."

Twenty-Three

"You ne'er told me if you'd done it before," Kerr said to Isobel quietly as they crouched at the edge of the tree line, observing the farm. They'd been watching for signs of Una and the lads—or anyone else, for that matter—for the last ten minutes. The sun had already dipped over the horizon, but he couldn't hear any noise coming from the cottage, which was unusual for his brothers.

"Done what?" Isobel asked, matching his whisper.

"What were your words, exactly? *You can eat me.*"

She turned her head to him and then huffed out a soft laugh. "Have you been sitting here the whole time stewing about whether I've been intimate in that way with someone besides you, husband?"

"Nay…not the *whole* time." He sighed. "I'm sorry, Izzy. You doona have to explain yourself to me."

I just want you to.

She grinned and made a motion with her hand for him to continue.

"Unless you want to," he added, aloud this time.

She clamped her hands over her mouth to muffle her laughter. When she had her mirth under control, she sighed and whispered, "You did surprise me. I ne'er imagined doing what we did last night. I thought it would be more along the lines of what we did this morning."

He grunted as the sight of her spread before him on his plaid floated through his mind. The sky had started to lighten, and he'd wanted to continue on their journey, but he couldn't resist loving her in that way first. Or touching her intimately as she sat in front of him on Diabhla. Or taking the extra time to tup her properly when they'd stopped to eat. The patch of grass they'd found had been soft and the ground beneath it smooth.

"You still havenae answered my question," he said.

"Dearest, I am well-informed about carnal intimacy. Most of which I want to try with you...for the first time."

"And how have you come to be so informed?"

She shrugged. "People talk when they think no one is listening."

"And you're always listening?"

"Aye."

Feeling settled now on that issue at least, and interested in exploring later what else she'd heard, he returned his attention to the cottage.

Where are Una, Andy, and Aulay?

Smoke came from the chimney, and the windows were open, but he couldn't hear any voices or laughter. Unease began to bubble through his gut.

"You're worried," Isobel whispered.

"A little."

"Is it possible the man from the beach beat us here?"

"Anything is possible, but 'tis unlikely. Why come here and not go to the castle or to the village first? We know he's placed spies and traitors there."

"To get to your brothers and Una, maybe?"

"Aye, but...this is not the place to take power. 'Tis not strategic for him to come here."

"Then why did we come? Other than to see your family, of course."

"I need people I can trust, and the lads are excellent marksmen, as good as any of my foster brothers. They've been trying to best each other for years." He rubbed a hand over his jaw, wondering how to bring up the next reason. "And there's one more thing..."

She swiveled her head toward him, obviously having heard something in his voice she didn't like. He glanced over and saw her eyes had narrowed on him.

"Nay," she said. "I willna stay here."

"Isobel, 'tis too dangerous for you to go with me. You could—"

"Nay. If there is a battle, I will do as you say, but until then I will strategize with you and help unite *our* clan. My presence is a boon to you, husband. A reminder of the alliance between Clan MacAlister, Clan MacKinnon, and the others. As well as a reminder that you are a powerful laird worthy of a lass like me."

She said the last in a queenly fashion, and he had to agree. It heartened him that Isobel knew her worth, but better than that, she knew how other people perceived her worth, and she was smart enough to make it work for her—and for them.

She had evolved from a trickster lass into a formidable woman. A queen among queens. And his wife.

Still…

"We doona know yet who is behind this conspiracy. It could be anyone. Gregor and the rest of us have been wracking our brains trying to figure it out, but we have few leads. Is the man on the beach the same man who planned the attack at the cathedral and rode away after Deirdre brought the roof down on them? My gut is telling me *yes*, but does it end there? Or is someone else holding the reins?"

"You mean like the Campbells. Did you speak to Branon Campbell after he threatened me at the stable? Could he be part of it?"

"We did. And yes, I think he is part of it, especially now that we can tie him to the man on the beach—thanks to you. We brought an artist in to record his face, and we'll be tracing his steps in Edinburgh last winter, but that will take time. He says he didn't return to the Highlands until last month. If that's true, then he canna be the man who led the attack on your clan last spring."

"Why was he in Edinburgh?" she asked, and then she gasped in horror. "Do you think the crown's involved?"

He weighed her question. "Nay, I doona think so. These attacks, the drive behind them to keep going after so many failures, feels personal to me."

"Against you and Clan MacAlister?"

"Aye. Or maybe against Gregor."

"Why you or Gregor? Why not Gavin or one of your other brothers?"

"Because they've all been attacked, the attacks failed, and the conspirator moved on to attack someone else. If it was personal toward one of them, why not attack them again? And why leave Gregor and me until the end? Nay, this has to do with the attack on Gregor led by my father all those years ago that ended up with me and my brothers fostered to him."

She looked back to the farm, and he could almost see her brilliant mind working behind all that soft, silky blond hair. After a moment, she said, "Well, it canna be your father."

"Not unless he's come back from the dead. I stabbed him through the heart and then burned his body."

"Could it be anyone else in your family? We know of at least one traitor in the clan."

He pressed his lips together, the shame he felt over killing his family mixed with the grim knowledge that he'd had to do it and intense relief that Isobel had still wanted him, *loved* him, despite knowing that truth.

He picked up her hand and squeezed it. Thank God he hadn't had to give her up.

"No one is left alive except my uncle Dùghlas, Andy, and Aulay—that I know of. The others attacked in waves over several days—my uncles, my cousins, several high-ranking warriors in the clan, and the men they commanded."

"How did you survive?"

"Gregor had trained me well. He knew my father would try to kill me, and he'd prepared me for it. He'd also placed several key people within the castle to help me when the time came." Kerr recalled the sudden onslaught of violence that day…and the relief when he discovered he wasn't alone—but also the grief upon finding his mother, gutted, in the middle of the Great Hall, left there for the dogs to gnaw upon while the warriors supped around her.

He cleared his throat. "My mother was a huge help too."

Her brow rose. "Your mother? I thought your father killed her before you came home?"

"He did. Hours before. What I meant was her kindness to the clan over the years—a clan she was not born into—rallied them to my side. Warriors, farmers, villagers. She'd made an impact on people, and while they'd been too afraid to fight for her when she was alive, her death at my father's hands, and then his death at my hands, propelled them into action and they stood with me shoulder to shoulder against the others. We razed the devils to the ground and pledged peace, aid, and prosperity."

Tears welled in her eyes, and she cupped his cheek with her hand. "That's what we'll remind them of—and this usurper, whoever he or they are, will not be able to get his hands around their throats."

He turned his head and kissed her palm. "Tell me again."

"Tell you what?" she asked, but she was smiling, and he knew that she knew what he wanted.

"Tell me you love me, wife. I want to hear it at least five times a day for all the hardships you've put me through the last four years."

Her eyes dropped to his mouth, and she leaned toward him. "I love you," she said just before their lips touched.

A snicker—a double snicker—broke out behind them, and Kerr sprang up and twisted around at the same time as he pushed Isobel against his back and drew his sword.

Then two balls of fury streaked through the trees toward them, yelling Highland war cries. Kerr raced to meet them, noting how they broke rank and attacked him separately rather than together. The wee idiots.

He growled with dissatisfaction. Their greatest advantage was to act as a team, and instead they were trying to beat each other to him.

No time like the present to show them their mistake.

He chose the attacker in the lead, hitting his blade with such force it spun the assailant around, and then Kerr booted him in the arse. The lad fell forward into his brother, and his blade flew from his hand. Kerr caught it—a weapon he'd bestowed upon Andy for his thirteenth birthday—as the lads tumbled to the ground together.

Behind him, he heard a door slam. Looking over his shoulder, he saw Una standing on the cabin's porch. "Andy! Aulay!" she cried.

"They're here, Una!" Kerr yelled back.

"Ma! Kerr's brought a lass with him!" Aulay said from beneath his brother.

"And he was kissing her!" Andy added, mashing his brother's face into the ground as he stood.

"Kerr's here?"

"Aye!" the lads said together.

"Well, come in, all of you, before it's dark."

Kerr heard the door shut again, and he assumed Una had reentered the cottage. Right now he had to keep his eyes on his brothers. They were still likely to attack.

He sheathed his sword and forced a scowl. "You broke rank. Again. Your greatest strength against an enemy is your togetherness. If you had attacked at the same time, using the positions I showed you, I would have had a difficult time choosing whom to fight. Use that hesitancy against your enemy and attack together. Always."

"We were going to trick you," Aulay said, rising now too, "but Andy was supposed to fall back and let me dart in."

"Nay! 'Twas me who was supposed to dart in," Andy said.

"Then it wouldnae have been a trick!"

Kerr couldn't help grinning. The boys' argument brought back memories of arguments he and his foster brothers had all had with Callum when they were lads, especially Lachlan.

Now, Kerr would stick to any plan Callum made, even if it killed him. His brother had a mind like one of Isobel's brilliant traps.

Suddenly, the lads stopped arguing, their words petering out as if they'd lost their breath. Their gazes shifted from him to a point on his right, and Kerr didn't need to look to know that Isobel had moved out from behind him and stood there.

He took advantage of their distraction, and this time he attacked first, tossing Andy's sword aside and using his long reach and greater height and weight to tackle the lads to the forest floor.

They yelled and fought back. When they both got their feet up on Kerr's chest and shoved, he let them topple him over backward. Another good lesson in working as a team. They jumped on top, and he wrestled with them, letting them win—which was getting harder to do every time. He reckoned they would be as big as him when they were fully grown.

Looking up past their young, fierce, identical faces, he saw both Isobel and Diabhla had moved closer and were staring down at them. The sight made him laugh. The twins easily pinned him after that and cheered triumphantly. They jumped up and broke into a victory dance that resembled a cross between a Highland Fling, a Sword Dance, and a headless chicken running around the farmyard.

Kerr rose, too, and grabbed Isobel around the waist. He spun her in a circle, making her laugh, and then he leaned in and claimed the kiss he'd been denied. When he pulled back, he looked over and saw his brothers watching them, their faces screwed up into identical masks of disgust and fascination.

"Lads, this is Isobel, my wife—and now your sister. She is Gavin's sister too—by blood, of course—and I've been pining for her for four long years, but finally last night..." Isobel elbowed him in the gut, and he laughed, but also winced. His wife had sharp elbows and she knew how to use them. "Izzy, this is Aulay and Andy."

"Good day to you, Andy and Aulay," she said. "I think we're going to be great friends. Do you want to know why?"

"Why?" they asked in unison, looking skeptical.

"Because I like to build traps, traps to catch people in, like your brother." Their faces brightened with interest, and she stepped toward them, linked her arms through theirs, and led them to the cottage. "The last one was a hole I dug in the ground that I filled with manure. He almost fell in. I was originally building it for Gavin, but Kerr can be annoying, doona you think? He deserved it more. Also, I am friends with a giant wolf named Siv, and I know an even bigger and fiercer warrior than Kerr. Maybe one day I'll introduce you to him."

Kerr sighed, knowing he deserved it.

They'd completely forgotten about him and left him to pick up the mess. Both lads had abandoned their specially made swords on the ground, and he had to hunt around for their scabbards. When he came back, it was to see his wife and his brothers almost at the cottage door with Diabhla at their heels.

Now *that* hurt. "Diabhla!" he yelled. "Not you too!"

———

Isobel scooped up the lamb stew from her bowl, trying not to eat like one of Farmer Busby's hogs but hunger gnawed at her, and the meal was delicious. Using her spoon, she plopped a chunk of meat and onion on her bread and took a big bite.

"Mmmmm," she moaned, closing her eyes as she savored her

food. When she finished, she took another bite, and then glanced across at Una, who sat on the other side of the table beside Kerr. They couldn't have looked more different, Una being slight and fair-skinned with freckles, red hair, and pale blue eyes, and Kerr resembling a dark avenging angel.

My angel.

And of course Una's scar, which Kerr had warned her about. The white, jagged line ran down the left side of her face from the corner of her eye to her chin. The sight brought tears to Isobel's eyes—not for how it looked but because she couldn't imagine how frightened, and in how much pain, Una must have been when Madadh MacAlister had carved it there.

Taking another bite, she deliberately redirected her thoughts to Aulay and Andy, who sat on either side of her, crowding in because they had no sense of personal space...perhaps because they were twins and always together. They looked nothing like their mother. Instead, they resembled Kerr but with chestnut-brown hair and hazel eyes.

She wondered if her children with Kerr would look similar, but maybe with her blue-green eyes.

She swallowed and took a sip of her ale. "Una, this may be the best stew I've e'er tasted."

"Thank you," the woman said a little shyly. She'd barely touched her meal and had an air of nervousness about her that made Isobel even more determined to win her over. She'd also glanced several times at the door, as if she wanted to escape.

"Kerr taught me how to make rabbit stew. It was good, too, but this..." She took another bite. "Mmmmm."

"Mine was as good," Kerr protested as he shoveled another spoonful into his mouth.

"I didn't say it wasn't good, but we've had two full days of eating apples, berries, and cheese. Verily, roasted squirrel would have tasted divine at this point." She laughed, and Una gave her a strange smile.

"Ma makes the best roast squirrel," Aulay said.

"Aye, she roasts it in a pan with honey," Andy added.

Isobel's cheeks heated as she glanced across at Una. "Oh…that sounds…delicious. I doona think I've e'er had squirrel."

"'Twas my mother's recipe," Una said softly. "She used to make it for me before…when I lived at home. I had a knack for catching squirrels, and sometimes 'twas all we had."

Regret and shame swirled through Isobel like a growing storm. Her appetite disappeared, and she laid down her spoon, feeling like an overprivileged fool—she'd grown up eating whatever she wanted, not to mention she called a castle her home. And until yesterday, she'd never known any real danger.

Compared to many Highland women, she'd led a charmed life.

Now she was married to a powerful laird who made her squeal and sigh in the dark, while Una had suffered at the hands of a devil and raised her sons alone, away from her clan—afraid and ashamed.

Una leaned across the table and squeezed her hand. "Please eat, my lady. I am not offended. I have been more than blessed these past fourteen years. Your husband has made sure of that."

Isobel nodded and picked up her spoon, but she'd lost her enjoyment of the meal. "I will eat, Una, as long as you call me Isobel. Or Izzy, if you prefer. 'Tis what Kerr often calls me. We are family now. I wouldnae have it any other way."

Dimples appeared in Una's cheeks as she smiled. "I would be honored, Izzy."

Kerr winked at her approvingly, and she felt as if she'd redeemed herself somewhat.

"Would anyone like more to drink?" Una picked up the pitcher and refilled Kerr's cup. She glanced at the door again as she did it. Had Kerr noticed?

"Aye, please." She held up her cup, trying to quell an uneasiness that began to simmer in her stomach.

"I've met your brother several times," Una said as she poured the ale. "I look forward to meeting him again at the wedding."

Everything had happened so quickly that Isobel hadn't even thought about having a priest marry them. "We'll have it when the danger is passed and my family and Kerr's family are both here."

"Danger?" the boys exclaimed together, their heads whipping up.

Isobel glanced at Kerr, wondering if she'd revealed too much. He'd said he wanted to enlist the boys' help, but maybe he'd wanted to speak to Una about it first.

"Does this have to do with the assaults on your foster brothers?" Una asked, worry etched onto her face.

Kerr nodded and pushed his food to the side. "Izzy and I were attacked and almost killed yesterday by an enemy force. Fortunately, we intercepted a note and gold coins intended for a spy at Clan MacAlister. The note indicated another assault is planned in two days' time at the castle."

Una gasped, and the twins shouted out in protest.

"But that may have changed," Isobel added reassuringly. "Perhaps he called it off, now that he knows we know."

"Or he pushed up the timeline," Kerr said. "The man is getting more desperate with every loss."

Una palmed her forehead and groaned. "That explains it."

Kerr's gaze swung to her sharply. "Explains what?"

She peered up at him, a distressed look on her face. "Your uncle Dùghlas…"

"What about him? Tell me, Una."

"We've been corresponding for years. Mostly him to me—writing isna as easy for me as it is for the lads, but I've enjoyed receiving his letters o'er the years. Dùghlas and I were friends before he left for Edinburgh."

Kerr's brow rose. "*Close* friends?"

"Not like that," she answered. "But I was sad when he left, even though I understood. He asked me to go with him, but I couldnae leave my family—not with my da being so ill. Did you know that your mother gave Dùghlas money and helped him escape your father?"

"Nay, but I suspected. I'm glad she helped him. What has you worried now?"

Isobel glanced at the door, that uneasy feeling still with her, and suddenly things fell into place. A coldness swept through her as she realized why Una's gaze kept returning there. She hadn't felt trapped; she'd been expecting someone. "He's coming here tonight. Isn't he?"

Una and Kerr looked at her, and then understanding dawned on Kerr's face. He jumped up and strode to the door, drawing his sword.

When Diabhla whinnied outside, she jumped up from the bench. "It's too late!"

A knock sounded—three short raps and two long. Kerr halted, and then he picked up the twins' swords in their scabbards and tossed them to Aulay and Andy. "Guard your ma and Izzy, and remember what I taught you."

Aulay tipped the table over, and the dishes and food crashed to the floor. He pushed his mother down behind it. Grabbing Isobel's arm, Andy pulled her back too, but she fought him and stayed where she was.

"Kerr! Branon Campbell said he'd been in Edinburgh. And your uncle—"

"I know, Izzy."

The door burst open, and a slight, redheaded man surged in, his sword out. His gaze landed on Kerr, and something passed between them. Then another man, almost as big and dark as Kerr, shoved past him. "Una!" he yelled.

Kerr pressed the point of his sword to the man's chest, stopping him. He froze and raised his gaze to Kerr's. His eyes widened fearfully, and his cheeks blanched.

"Uncle Dùghlas," Kerr said evenly as the redheaded man shut and barred the door behind him. "Why are you here?"

Dùghlas blinked and slowly let out his breath. "Kerr, 'tis you. For a moment I thought you were Madadh back from the dead. I wasn't expecting you. It has been many years." He glanced around the room. His eyes landed on Isobel and the twins, on the overturned table, the broken dishes and spilled food and drink on the floor. "I heard a thump and dishes breaking. I was worried…"

"Worried about what, Uncle?"

"About Una and her boys. That I'd brought danger to her door…again."

"What do you mean *again*?" Kerr asked.

"When I left last time…your father must have known that I'd asked her to go with me. That I cared for her."

Understanding surged within Isobel. "'Twas because of you!" she gasped. "He took her to hurt you, not Kerr or his mother."

Grief etched into Dùghlas's face. "Aye," he croaked. "I should have known he would do it."

His gaze returned to the overturned table. "Una, if you're there, please know again how sorry I am."

Isobel waited, and then a moment later Una straightened from her hiding spot.

"Ma, no!" Aulay exclaimed.

"'Tis all right, son," she said. "Dùghlas was a good friend of mine before I birthed you and your brother. He's a good man."

The tears streamed down Dùghlas's face now, and he dashed them away. "Not so good. I should ne'er have left. I should have killed him." He looked at Kerr. "Like you did. Still a lad, and you did what I could not."

Then he bowed his head and kneeled. "Laird MacAlister, I pledge fealty to you and Clan MacAlister. I am your servant, to be used as you wish, forever more. I have come to tell you of a plot against you."

"And your men outside?" Kerr asked.

Isobel's brow rose. How did he know there were men outside? She double-checked the windows—aye, they were shuttered to keep out the cool night air. Had the other man somehow conveyed the information to Kerr?

Dùghlas lifted his head. "They're my friends, my guild-mates. Not my men. Ten of us, all loyal to one another—a group I fell in with when I first arrived in Edinburgh. We've been active every year in performing the folk plays during the feast of Corpus Christi."

"And you brought them with you when your clan is on the brink of war—and you're in the middle of it?" Kerr asked.

"Nay, I couldnae stop them. They came of their own accord when they saw I was leaving. They knew something was wrong and that I was in danger."

Kerr lowered his sword, grasped his elbow, and helped him stand. "Tell me everything, Uncle."

"I've been approached by a man who wants me to take o'er Clan MacAlister. I pretended to agree because I knew if I didn't, he—they—would kill me. The plan is to get rid of you and put me in your place. In a year or so, I would be next, and they would take over." He grasped Kerr's arm. "We need to act together. I am supposed to meet the man in the village tomorrow night. I had hoped to find you at the castle beforehand and decide what to do. This is even better."

Behind Dùghlas, the redheaded man moved his fingers. Isobel watched, fascinated, as Kerr nodded almost imperceptibly. Was it some kind of code between them? And who was this man?

"When did he approach you?" Kerr asked.

"In the spring. He came into my workshop in Edinburgh. At first I thought he looked familiar, with dark hair and light eyes, but I couldnae place him. I knew better than to contradict him. He was dangerous despite his easygoing facade."

"His name?"

"He wouldnae tell me, but at one point, I heard someone refer to him as Bran or Breandan or something similar."

"Branon," she said, and Kerr nodded.

"Aye, that could be it. He…he reminded me of your father, playing games with words, testing me, friendly one moment and then deadly the next. I went along with him, but I sent you a letter as soon as I could." He turned to the man behind him. "Malcolm, tell him what you know."

Malcolm stepped forward. He bowed his head to Kerr. "Laird. Everything Dùghlas has said is true. I sent the missives two days before we left Edinburgh. Not only to Clan MacAlister but to all the lairds in your alliance."

Dùghlas looked surprised. "Good thinking, Malcolm. He did that on his own. He's the smartest apprentice I've e'er had."

Kerr nodded. "I'm sure he is. 'Tis good my brothers know. They will proceed with caution, and Callum in particular will be thinking five steps ahead." He sheathed his sword in the scabbard that hung down his back. "Aulay, Andy, help clean up the mess. We need to plan."

"Do your mates want some ale?" Isobel asked. "You must be parched after your journey."

"Aye, thank you, lass."

"Maybe some food too." She looked at Una. "I can help."

Una nodded and picked up the pitcher from the floor. "Of course." She hurried to the counter and started preparing.

Dùghlas stepped closer and bowed his head to her. "My lady, I am Dùghlas MacAlister." He looked from her to Kerr and then back again. "Are you…?"

"Aye," Kerr said, laying a hand on the small of her back. "Dùghlas, this is my wife, Isobel."

Dùghlas beamed. "Of course! And as lovely in person as they claim in the song." He gently picked up Isobel's hand and turned it to look at the amethyst ring on her thumb. His eyes filled with tears again. Truly, he was a gentle soul with an overflowing heart. "Your mother's ring. She tried to give it to me when I left, but I told her to save it for you. That one day you would give it to a woman you loved as much as you loved her."

Kerr swallowed and nodded. "And I did."

Then Dùghlas broke into song with a deep, lush tenor—the song penned about her, the one she usually hated. But this time, she lost herself in the wonderful richness of his voice, and when he came to those all-important lyrics, she listened carefully, wanting so desperately for him to sing them correctly.

"*As I looked upon thee, I saw the Beauty of the Highlands.*"

She relaxed and smiled up at Kerr. Glad for him, and for Una—for all of them—that Dùghlas could be trusted.

———————

"There's another way in," Dùghlas said, waving Kerr over to sit on the log beside him. They'd built a fire in the yard, and Dùghlas and his men were eating and drinking the food and ale that Una, Isobel, and the lads had handed out.

Dùghlas's mates were a friendly bunch, witty and entertaining. When he introduced Kerr and Isobel to them, they broke out into a theatrical version of Izzy's song. Kerr wagered that if she hadn't been laughing so hard, she would have pummeled them for it.

From what he could gather, they were artists and craftsmen and even actors and bards in their spare time; some sang, others played instruments and wrote song lyrics—a perfect fit for the artistry in Dùghlas's soul that his brother had tried to destroy.

Kerr grinned at the antics, happy and relieved that his uncle had found happiness.

He sat on the log and leaned toward Dùghlas. "You mean...a

place to climb over the castle wall? I resealed the mortar years ago, so it's smooth and difficult to climb."

"Nay. I'm not talking about the wall, I'm talking about the tunnels in the castle and under the wall. They were my sanctuary when I was a lad. 'Tis how I escaped so much of Madadh's brutality."

Kerr found himself speechless. *What tunnels?*

Isobel came up behind him and wrapped her arms around his neck. "What are you two talking about?"

"The bloody tunnels in my castle," he roared. "That I knew naught about."

"Oh, aye," she said, nodding her head.

"Oh, aye? That's all you have to say?"

"Well, 'tis a castle. We have them at Castle MacKinnon."

Kerr shook his head. "Unbelievable. Who showed them to you?" he asked Dùghlas. "Obviously not my father."

"Nay, I found them myself. I spent much of my childhood alone, hiding in the library. I started searching for them after I found a letter written by my great-great-grandfather that referenced one of them." His brow furrowed in the firelight. "I hid in there for four days once when Madadh first became laird and was on a tear." He looked across at Una, still pouring ale. "If I'd stayed, maybe I could have saved her."

"You canna think that way," Isobel said, stepping around Kerr to sit on his lap. He liked how she snuggled into him, free with her affection. "If Una had been saved early on, she wouldnae have had Andy and Aulay, and she would ne'er wish for that."

Dùghlas sighed. "I had no idea my brother knew I cared for her. She was my first real friend—her heart so open and accepting. I ne'er felt like a misfit around her."

Isobel leaned forward and patted his uncle's knee, but Kerr's mind was spinning with all the new possibilities. "Where does the tunnel under the wall come out?" he asked. "Do we need to sneak in at night, or—"

"We are *not* sneaking in," Isobel said firmly. "You are the clan's laird. The people are fortunate to have you. And I am their lady. We will ride through the village with our heads up high and smiles on our faces. You will introduce me as your wife, remind them of our alliance, and that they are safe and prosperous because of you. And then we will invite them to our home for a celebratory feast!"

The others' laughter had died down, and when Isobel stopped talking, the crackling fire was the only sound breaking the silence.

"We will remind them what it was like to live under the yoke of your father," she continued. "The injustice and cruelty they faced on a daily basis. Open communication will win their hearts and minds and bring to light what is hidden in the dark."

"And if we're attacked, Izzy?" Kerr asked. "What then?"

"Then you will fight, and you will win. Kerr Anghos Finnian MacAlister, you are the greatest Highland warrior this land has e'er seen!"

A cheer went up from Dùghlas and his friends. "Make an entrance!" they exclaimed. "The MacAlister laird and his lady. The Beauty of the Highlands and the Greatest Highland Warrior! And we will be your guard."

Andy and Aulay raced over.

"Can we come with you, Kerr?" Andy asked. "We can fight too. We'll do everything exactly as you taught us."

"Aye, we can hide in the trees and shoot them with arrows!" Aulay exclaimed.

Kerr wanted to say no and lock the boys up. If he didn't, he knew they would follow him. He wanted to lock Isobel up, too, and keep her safe with Una until he returned.

Neither was the right choice, though. He needed them.

All of them.

He looked at his wife, lowering his voice so only she could hear. "Where will we place the sharpshooters?" He knew the answer, but he wanted her to know it too.

She stared at him for a moment, the firelight glancing off her hair and throwing highlights and shadows across her face. She looked like a goddess of old, and inside he grunted with approval.

Finally, she was his lady—and ruler by his side.

She raised her chin ever so slightly and straightened her shoulders in that queenly fashion he loved. And then she spoke with authority.

"At our castle."

"Aye, Lady MacAlister. We'll sneak them in and put them in the rafters of our home."

━━━━━━

Isobel wrapped her arm around Una's shaking shoulders. The slight, redheaded woman had tears streaming down her face and her hands clamped over her mouth, undoubtedly holding in an anguished howl.

How could she not? Her lads were going to war.

They rode on either side of Dùghlas, their swords on their hips, a bow across their shoulders and a quiver of arrows across their backs. Kerr had given a note to Dùghlas for Father Lundie, the only other person at the castle he knew he could trust. He'd also told Dùghlas that the steward, Fearchar MacAlister, was a spy. His uncle needed to incapacitate the traitor before Kerr and Isobel arrived.

Dùghlas frowned darkly upon hearing that news and muttered under his breath. Isobel sensed he already had a history with the steward—and not a happy one.

Standing beside Malcolm, whom she now knew was a spy placed with Dùghlas years ago, Kerr watched them go, a troubled look on his face. The Merry Men—the name they'd given to Dùghlas's band of friends—gathered around them, shouting their goodbyes and wishing them good fortune.

Kerr had spoken to Una first about the plan to send the lads to the castle through the secret tunnel in order to set them up as snipers. They were to spot any other archers on the wall or in the crowd and take them out before they could hurt him or Isobel.

As much as it pained her, Una had agreed. She knew that the twins would follow them no matter what, and at least at the castle they would be hidden and kept out of the fray if a battle broke out.

But the mission was still dangerous, and Isobel wished that Kerr had sent Malcolm along with them.

Slowly, the three of them faded from sight as the night swallowed them up. A moan broke from Una's mouth, and she turned and fled into the cottage.

"Una!" Isobel cried out, and then hurried after her.

She hovered at the door, not wanting to intrude but also desperate to give comfort to this brave, resilient woman who had collapsed, sobbing, on a bed in the corner.

Her need to comfort her won out, and she rushed to the woman's side and sat with her, rubbing her back as her own tears fell. The last person she'd comforted in this way had been Deirdre, when Gavin had left to battle the MacIntyres and the MacColls—his allies at his side.

This battle was different. They were alone, and they didn't know whom to trust. They had to march boldly into the castle with their clan and claim their rightful home, routing out the spies and traitors who would let the enemy in and try to kill their laird and lady.

And they would need Una's help.

When the sobs died down, Una sat up, wiping her face. "I'm sorry, but the lads are all I have. I canna bear to see them ride into danger."

"I understand. They're still so young, but I suspect it would be hard at any age."

"Aye."

Isobel grasped Una's hands, her eyes tracing the woman's scar. It cut through her cheek, but it hadn't left her eye disfigured or her mouth twisted. Still, Isobel suspected that in Una's mind it looked worse than it actually did. She'd noticed how she turned the scarred side of her face away from people, and Kerr had told her that she ne'er left the farm.

That needed to change for all their sakes.

"Una, come with us tomorrow," she said. "We need your support."

The woman gasped. "Nay, I couldnae."

"Why not?"

"Because…because I canna, Lady MacAlister. I've ne'er been back to the village."

Isobel held her gaze, her heart filled with sympathy for the woman. "I know you were hurt in your past, and that those scars, both inside and out, have never fully healed, but now is your time to embrace the woman you are—a survivor, a mother, a woman capable of owning her own land and running her own life—scars and all. Show everyone what that man did to you, and show them the strength and resilience that enabled you to overcome it. You have accomplished so much. You've raised two wonderful young men, you run your own farm. Stand with us. Help us. Please."

Una sighed and looked down at her hands. They trembled within Isobel's grasp. "I promise to think about it." Then she leaned forward and hugged Isobel. "You're a kind woman, Lady MacAlister, like Kerr's ma. I'm glad he has you." And then she wiped her cheeks and stood. "But you doona look like a lady in that stained dress, dirt on your brow, and your hair a tangled mess." She moved toward the kettle, filled it, and put it over the fire. Then she opened her wardrobe. "We doona have much time. Kerr will be in soon. I heard him tell the others he wants to leave before dawn. I'll sleep in the barn. I have a pallet set up in there."

Isobel stood up in protest. "You canna give us your bed."

"I already have, and he's agreed." She pulled a beautiful plaid out from a box in her wardrobe. "Now come and look at this. 'Twas a gift from Kerr many years ago. I've ne'er worn it. It will be perfect for you. A plaid fit for a queen."

===

Kerr sat on the bed as gently as he could, but still it dipped under his weight and Isobel rolled toward him. Her eyelids fluttered open sleepily, and he silently cursed himself. He'd washed up with the leftover bath water, as quietly as a mouse, and now he'd woken her anyway.

"I'm sorry, love. I didn't mean to wake you," he whispered as he lifted the blanket to slip under the covers. He paused when he saw her, as naked as she'd been last night, and he huffed out a breath, his already hardened body turning to granite.

"Doona be sorry," she said. "I meant to stay awake."

She shifted over to make room for him and opened her arms. He crawled in beside her, so they lay facing each other, chest to chest. The bed was too short for him and his feet hung over the end, but it ceased to matter when she lifted her top leg, wrapped it over his hip, and then kissed him.

Nothing mattered but the feel of her in his arms and the taste of her in his mouth.

"Are you sure, Izzy?" he asked. "I know you're tired. It's been a long few days, and tomorrow will be just as long, with as little sleep."

"I'm sure. If aught goes wrong tomorrow and we forgo this intimacy tonight, I would regret it for the rest of my life."

He wrapped his arms all the way around her and pulled her close. His instinct was to tell her nothing would go wrong, but he couldn't lie to her—and if he did, she would know it for a lie.

"I feel the same. As quiet as I was washing up, I kept hoping you'd wake."

She smiled against his mouth, and they kissed again. Then she urged him closer, and he rolled over on top of her. She wrapped her other leg around his hip and welcomed him into the cradle of her thighs.

"If I could freeze time, this is where I would want to spend eternity," he sighed.

She giggled and rocked her hips against him—an invitation. "Doona you think you'd be happier if we were a little farther along? Eternity is a long time."

As much as he wanted to press inside her, he slid his shaft up through her wet folds instead, and then let his weight bear down on her nub. He thrust slowly and methodically against her.

She sighed. "God in heaven, that feels good." Wrapping her arms around his back, she massaged the muscles along his spine, and then dug her nails in as her body shuddered.

The carnality of her response made his blood surge, and he fought to maintain his steady rhythm. Cupping her face at the same time as she pulled his head down, their lips melded together—kissing, stroking, sucking.

He palmed her breasts, squeezed her nipples. She moaned into his mouth and slid her own hands down to his arse, digging her nails in there too.

"Come inside me. Now, Kerr. Please."

"Aye, love."

He wrapped his big hand under her arse and tilted up her hips before nudging into her body and sliding all the way inside her.

The heat of her, the soft slickness of her surrounding him, almost made him lose his seed, and he ground his teeth as he concentrated on slowing down. He didn't want to reach the pinnacle without her.

But then she broke off their kiss with a whimper and pressed her head back against the bed. "More, Kerr. Please!"

His stones tightened and pulled taut against his body at the need and want in her voice—at the demand.

She was close too.

He held her in place, pulled out almost all the way and then surged back in, letting his weight bear her down, his body rub against hers. She groaned and he did it again and again until her heels dug into the small of his back and her pelvis pressed upward—completely open to him.

His control began to shatter—body jerking, muscles clenching, his breath exploding from his chest in hard gusts.

He stroked harder, faster, as short breathy moans broke from her lips—rising to a squeal—before her body clamped down on his in waves.

"Oh, God! Kerr!"

He thrust one last time, shuddering and shouting her name.

Always her name.

After the last contraction eased, he collapsed against her, both of them gasping for air. After a few moments, he rolled onto his back and pulled her into the crook of his arm so she rested against his chest.

"Correction," he said, his breath still coming in short gusts. "This right here is where I would freeze time."

She wrapped her arm around his waist and slid her leg over the top of his. "Aye, this is as near perfection as we could e'er find."

He squeezed her tight, fighting that ever-present, nagging fear for her.

How can I ride into danger with her again?

"Una is going to come with us on the morrow," she said drowsily.

He looked down at her. "Truly?"

"'Tis not certain, but I think she'll surprise us, surprise herself too. She will remind our people of who your father was and what could happen again if they give in to terror and darkness."

He sighed and kissed the top of her head. "I've been encouraging her to leave the farm for years, but she's ne'er been willing.

People know she's here, of course—I have warriors watching her, and farm hands have come to help her, especially during harvest, but most of the clan havenae seen her in years. 'Twill be good for her to face that fear."

Kerr idly stroked his fingers along her arm, hoping she would fall back asleep. For him, it was an impossibility—it always was before battle.

"I canna imagine how she managed on her own with two bairns," Isobel said, breaking into a yawn at the end. "Were you here often in the early days?"

"Some, but I also had much work to do at the castle and with the clan. 'Twas a time of turmoil after I killed my father." He stroked her hair behind her ear. "She wouldnae take any help from the women either. I offered her the aid of my old Nan, a good woman, but she refused. She raised those boys entirely on her own."

She shook her head, a tiny movement against his chest. "Do twins run in her family?"

"I doona know. But they run in my family."

She pushed onto her elbow and stared down at him, looking and sounding wide awake now. "Your family?"

He nodded. "I was a twin. Maybe I should have told you that before we consummated our marriage."

"What happened to the other bairn?"

"Stillborn. A wee lad, much smaller than me, my ma said. 'Twas probably for the best. My father would have turned us against each other. Look what he did to my uncle Dùghlas."

"Did she actually see the bairn? Was she certain he died? And who was born first? You or your brother?"

"I doona know, Izzy, and it doesn't matter now. 'Twas thirty years ago. I've ne'er heard a whisper to contradict what my ma told me."

She sighed and settled back down against him. "You're right. I thought...maybe..."

"Nay, there's naught more to the story."

She nodded and moved her hand over her belly. "Other than the possibility that I may have not one but two giants growing in my belly soon."

He groaned. "Doona remind me. The idea of you birthing just one bairn gives me nightmares." He pulled her close again and whispered in her ear. "I canna stand the thought of losing you, Isobel… Are you sure you willna take pity on me and stay here in the morning?"

She kissed him and then whispered back, "Not this time, dearling."

A knock sounded on the door—loud and sudden in the silence.

Kerr rolled from the bed and reached for his sword. "Who's there?"

"Malcolm, Laird," the voice came through the door. "A man has arrived with a message."

He grabbed his shirt from the back of a chair and tugged it over his head.

"Who, other than your uncle and foster brothers, knows that we're here?" Isobel asked, her voice rising in alarm. She slid her shift over her head as well.

"I doona know." He picked up his plaid and tossed it to her.

At the door, he knocked, two short and three long raps. When Malcolm rapped back, using the proper sequence, Kerr unbarred and opened the door. Isobel crossed the room to stand beside him.

Malcolm entered, followed by a man bundled up in a plaid. "Laird MacAlister!" the man said. "By God's grace, I've found you!"

"Father Lundie?" Isobel asked.

The priest turned his gaze to her, and his eyes widened in shock. "Lady MacKinnon, does your brother know you're here?"

Kerr wrapped his arm around her shoulder. "Isobel and I are married, Father. We handfasted one another several days ago. 'Tis Lady MacAlister now—and aye, Gavin knows our whereabouts."

The priest let out a happy-sounding gasp and squeezed their hands in each of his. "My most heartfelt congratulations. When order is restored, I would be honored to marry the two of you in the church—as I did Gavin and the other lairds."

"Aye, Father," Isobel said. "That would be wonderful. But tell me, how did you know where to find us?"

The priest's face fell, and when he swayed on his feet, Isobel grasped his arm and led him to a chair at the table. He collapsed onto it. She quickly poured him some water and handed him the cup.

He drank deeply and then put the cup down. "I was running from the castle, hoping to find someone—anyone—in time, and I ran into your brothers Andy and Auley and your uncle Dùghlas. They told me you were here."

"What's happened?" Kerr asked, crouching beside his chair.

"Father Grant has been murdered, and traitors are within your castle." His voice broke, but he took a breath and continued. "I hid inside the priest hole earlier today and saw a devil of a man with terrible injuries on one side of his body suffocate a priest—after your steward put drops of poison in his drink."

Isobel gasped and crossed herself. "Why would they do that? Are you sure it was poison?"

"Aye. The man said *'Tis too late for any more poison, Fearchar. He has to die tonight.*" A sob broke from the priest. "Father Grant couldnae move, he was too sick. He wrote to me not long ago and asked me to come. He thought evil had taken hold of the castle." The priest looked up at Kerr and grasped his hand. "An army is coming, Laird MacAlister. This demon of a man plans to take over your clan."

Twenty-Four

"SMILE, DEARLING!" ISOBEL CALLED OUT TO KERR FROM THE saddle of her horse as they rode toward the village. She twitched those perfect lips at him and flashed her sparkling smile, causing his inner warrior to roar back at her ferociously—*Danger!*

A trap awaited, and he was headed straight toward it—a deranged grinning woman, a grief-stricken priest, and a past trauma victim who looked ready to bolt into the woods at any moment by his side. He'd placed Malcolm—a capable warrior—on point, but covering his rear and to the sides were craftsmen and theatre folk. One of the Merry Men had given up all pretense of being a guard and had started playing his pipe as he rode, while another was juggling.

But Kerr knew the plan...excite and engage the villagers so they came up to the castle with them for a celebratory wedding feast.

The traitors canna keep all of Clan MacAlister out of my castle!

He cracked his jaw and forced his lips back over his teeth in what he thought would pass for a grin. Then showed it to Isobel.

"Oh, dear God!" she groaned. "You look like every bairn's, and their parents', worst nightmare."

"If anyone hurts any of the bairns or their parents in my clan, I will be a nightmare! These are my people, Isobel. And this man... this murderer—whatever his name is—thinks he can kill me, kill my family, kill my priest and get away with it?"

He roared at the end, and Una let out a frightened squeak while Father Lundie dabbed tears away with his handkerchief.

"Control yourselves," he said to them firmly. "Una, you chose to come with us. Do your part or you put your sons in danger. And Father Lundie, hold it together, man, so we can see justice done for your friend and brother."

He whipped his head around, intent on blasting the Merry Men, but two bairns, a lad and a lass around eight years old, Eilidh and Hamish, were following them, giggling quietly as they watched the juggler, who was playing the fool for them.

He turned back and caught Isobel's eye. "Was this your plan all along?"

She shrugged. "Well, we doona want the people running to the castle in fear, now, do we? The traitors may close and lock the gates on us. And no one will really believe they're our guards." She looked back at the musician and the bairns dancing behind the Merry Men. "Who better to entice the people than the Pied Piper?"

"Their laird, perhaps. Or their lady."

She reached across the distance between them and squeezed his raised hand.

He squeezed back and released a heavy, frustrated sigh. "Who is this man, Isobel? What does he want of me? This is personal. It must be because of my father."

"The reasons doona matter, Kerr. All that matters is gathering our people safely within the castle walls. We doona want them harmed when a frustrated army comes through, expecting to occupy our home."

He peered into the woods as if the army would suddenly appear. They were exposed and vulnerable, and he had too little information. How many spies were in the castle? How many of his people had been compromised? When was the enemy expected to arrive today? And how many warriors?

Hopefully, his brothers would be able to cut them off. Or if they couldn't, they could squeeze the enemy between them and the castle walls—with Kerr's forces raining arrows down upon them from the battlements.

A woman appeared ahead of them with a lass about Aulay and Andy's age, pushing a cart full of freshly baked bread. They gazed up at the riders, eyes wide with astonishment.

The lass, in particular, stared at Isobel, who looked resplendent in the midmorning sun despite not having slept more than a few hours last night. They'd been on the road well before dawn, trying to beat the approaching army, and Una had come in early to help with Isobel's new dress and hair.

She looked as beautiful as he'd ever seen her.

Not only a lady...a queen.

"Laird MacAlister!" the woman cried, her smile creasing her face. "Good day to you, sir."

"And a good day to you too, Ailsa." This time, the smile on Kerr's face was genuine. "Ailsa and Donaldina, may I introduce you to Lady Isobel MacAlister, my wife and your new lady."

"Oh!" Ailsa exclaimed. "Welcome, my lady! And my heartfelt congratulations on your nuptials."

The young girl beamed when Isobel smiled at her. "Thank you. Will you come with us to the castle to celebrate? The whole clan will be there."

"Now?" Ailsa asked, looking astonished.

"Aye, now!" Isobel laughed. She grasped Kerr's hand again. "'Tis a gathering to celebrate our union and that of our two clans— allies and family." She waved behind her at Una and the Merry Men. "We have entertainment—the best from Edinburgh—and old friends here to celebrate with us."

Ailsa looked at Una, and then she gasped. "Una?"

Una nodded, her smile tremulous. An errant tear slid down her face, and she quickly dashed it away. The woman cried out and rushed forward, her face crumpling with emotion. Una slid from her horse, and the two merged into a tight embrace, laughing and crying.

"It's been so long!" Ailsa said, pulling back and cupping her face. "I canna believe you're here and looking so well." Her fingers traced the scar down her cheek. "I'm so sorry I've ne'er been out to your farm. It was so awful what happened to you, and then afterward you didn't want to see anyone."

"I'm sorry. I couldnae, I just… I couldnae."

"Nay, doona apologize. And you doona need to explain. You were so hurt by that devil of a man." Her gaze darted to Kerr, a worried look on her face as if she feared she'd said too much.

He hated that his people had been so beaten down by his father that they were still afraid even after fifteen years. "A devil if ever there was one," he agreed. "I miss my ma dearly."

The fear in her face changed to sympathy, and she reached her hand out to him. "As do I, Laird. She was a good woman. She ne'er deserved such a fate."

"I swear to you, and to all the clan, Ailsa, that while there is still breath in my body, I'll fight for you and for all our people."

"I know you will. Just like your ma. Thank you, Laird MacAlister." And then her face lit up with excitement. "And we would be honored to come to your wedding feast."

Isobel laughed again. "We want everyone to come. And we'll take all of your bread if you have enough. Please tell your friends, your family, that today is a day of celebration!"

"I will," she said. She dropped a curtsy to Isobel, and the shy Donaldina copied her. Isobel dipped her head in acknowledgment and winked at the lass.

"Will you come with us?" Ailsa asked Una. "My ma would love to see you…and my brother too."

Una looked at Kerr. He nodded. "We'll make our way to the square, and then leave for the castle after that. Encourage everyone to come!"

"Aye, Laird," they said, and then hurried off, Donaldina between them.

Isobel released a heavy sigh when they were out of earshot. "It's begun."

Kerr nodded. "I doona know how much time we'll have before the enemy arrives in force." He signaled to the Merry Men. "Go and do as my wife instructed you to do when I wasn't there. Be amusing and entertaining. Tell everyone about the feast."

"Aye, Laird."

"And you too, Father Lundie. Convince everyone you can to join us on the walk up to the castle." He looked up at the sky, gauging the time. "I want to leave by noon."

Kerr's cheeks hurt from smiling, even though every step Diabhla took across the open bluff, from the village to the castle that loomed at the end, felt like a death knell. At the same time, he couldn't help checking over his shoulder to make sure the enemy army wasn't coming up behind them.

He closed his eyes and said a quick prayer for all of their safety, especially the bairns who were darting excitedly through the crowd, scaring their parents who kept yelling at them to *stay away from the cliff!*

And no wonder. The drop down to the beach below was not one a child—or anyone—could survive.

The entire village, plus people from outlying farms, had joined them, some riding, some walking, and some traveling in wagons because of injury or age. Several people pushed carts full of food and drink for the feast. Isobel had assured him the kitchens would need it for such a big impromptu celebration.

He just hoped they made it to the celebration part of the day alive.

A few men had been quietly taken captive at the village and restrained in the church—MacAlister warriors who'd appeared alarmed at his presence and had tried to run. They had pleaded with him for mercy and then confirmed what he'd already known—other traitors were at the castle and in the village. Warriors, but also regular folk who had been bribed or blackmailed.

A similar method to the one his father had used all those years ago when he'd convinced the other clans, including Isobel's father, to attack Gregor MacLeod.

Good had come out of those desperate times, and he prayed good would prevail here too.

"I've heard about your castle, of course," Isobel said from atop her horse, looking up at the soaring stone fortress on the cliff. "But until you see it in person, you canna imagine the true beauty and majesty of it."

Kerr reached over and grasped her hand. "It's piles of rocks, Izzy. That's all. Not until you step inside will it be my home."

She smiled, a real one this time, and then lifted their clasped hands and kissed his knuckles. "The gates are open. That's good, aye?"

"Aye. It means the warriors manning the gates—or most of them—are still loyal. The man from the beach, the one who suffocated Father Gregory, doesn't have enough influence yet, to have taken over all the key positions. They weren't expecting us."

"And the ones who aren't loyal didn't expect their families and friends to ride up with us," Isobel added.

"True."

He studied the battlements and saw warriors lining it. Some of them shouted and waved at them, curious and excited to see all the people heading toward them. Others had started to gather at the gates, and a few were riding or walking toward them.

"Laird MacAlister," a young woman called up to him from the ground beside Diabhla. She carried a swaddled bairn in her arms, and worry had painted dark shadows and etched lines around her eyes. A tall, lanky lad tugged on her sleeve as if to pull her away.

Kerr leaned down toward her. "Breanag, lass, what's troubling you?"

"The babe needs medicine, but the steward, Fearchar, would-nae allow the healer to help us anymore unless Billy agreed to put something in the ale at the castle. He works in the kitchens, Laird, and he's afraid if he doesn't do it, our sweet Ollie will die. Please, help us. Ollie is starting to weaken again."

Kerr's mouth tightened, and his face heated with fury—not at the young parents but at the depravity of the men who had put such a wee life at risk.

He inhaled deeply and slowly before he spoke. "Billy, you willna add anything to the ale, do you understand? And if anyone approaches you to do such a thing, you will tell me." Billy nodded jerkily, his eyes wide and a pulse drumming in his neck. "I have already taken care of Fearchar, but you both must stay quiet about it until I say so. Agreed?"

"Aye, Laird," they said together.

He peered over his shoulder. "Where's the healer? I doona recall seeing her."

"She's at the castle," Billy said.

"Is someone ill?"

"I-I doona know."

Kerr blew out a breath. Another person for him to worry about. He reached toward Breanag. "Please, may I hold Ollie?"

"Of course," she said, smiling shyly.

Warmth filled his chest as he cuddled the tiny bairn close to his heart. Isobel leaned over, peeked at the babe, and then gasped quietly. The lad looked unwell.

"Kerr," she said urgently, brushing the tips of her fingers over the bairn's forehead.

"I know." He kissed the babe's brow, and then handed him back to his mother. "My foster brother's wife, Amber MacKay, is the finest healer I've e'er met. I'll speak to Lachlan when he arrives and arrange for you to take Ollie to see her."

"Laird MacKay is coming?" Billy asked.

"Aye."

"And the other lairds?"

When Kerr nodded, Billy's eyes brightened with relief.

"I've heard stories of what it was like before you led the clan, Laird MacAlister. Stories I can barely believe, let alone understand. But these last few months, I've seen how quickly fear has shaped our lives. How we're…susceptible to it. I doona want my little lad to grow up feeling that way. I doona want him afraid."

Kerr clamped his hand on Billy's shoulder. "Neither do I. And I promise I'll fight so he doesn't have to."

"And please know that you can always come to us," Isobel added. "Let the others know too."

Billy straightened his shoulders and put a protective arm around his wife. "Aye, Laird," he said, and then disappeared into the throng.

Kerr whistled for Malcolm, who was guarding their rear, and he rode up beside him. He looked like Kerr felt—grim, worried, like they were heading into a trap.

"Riders approaching," Kerr said. "Watch their faces. Read their eyes. They should be excited and happy for us, not worried or fearful. If they're loyal, they'll want to help us set up the feast, to invite everyone in. If they're not, they'll try to dissuade us from coming inside and give excuses as to why we canna have our feast today."

"And watch whom they look to," Isobel said. "They'll want support from their fellow conspirators and will make eye contact."

"Aye, Izzy. Good point. Their eyes and actions will lead us to the others. Doona kill them unless they attack. It may be they're like Billy and being forced to make an unbearable choice."

"We can lock them in the guard house by the gate," Malcolm said. "We doona want them to our rear."

Kerr looked behind him and spotted Father Lundie, deep in conversation with a woman who looked upset. Another member of his clan put into an impossible situation?

"I want the portcullis jammed once everyone is in. Under no circumstances do I want it raised for anyone but our allies. I'll ask Father Lundie to do it."

"Father Lundie?" Malcolm asked.

"Aye, he's done it before at Castle MacKinnon."

"Laird MacAlister!" a rider called out, the voice happy and excited, and one Kerr recognized. He whipped his head around to confirm, and relief flowed through him upon seeing the young blond-headed MacKinnon warrior—a favorite of all the lairds.

"Finnian! What are you doing here?" Finn would protect Isobel if he could not.

"I escorted Father Lundie on his journey. We arrived yester—" His eyes widened. "My lady! Is our laird here too? Are the other lairds?" His brow creased, and he sought Kerr's gaze.

"They will be. Quickly, Finn. What do you know about the castle? Is anything happening that shouldnae be happening?"

Finn's brow smoothed out in understanding, and he nodded. "I dropped off the Father at the church and made my way to the castle barracks yesterday evening, but my reception was cool. The commander in charge, an older warrior named Craigh, said I couldnae stay, but then Gillis heard and stepped in. He was irate."

"Gillis is in charge while I'm gone," Kerr said. "I appointed him two years ago. He's not part of my father's old guard. 'Tis good to know he's loyal."

"What's happening? Is there a plan to overthrow you? Our allies would ne'er stand for it."

"'Tis why our enemies have tried so hard the past few years to get rid of them. The man in charge is dangerous and desperate. I'm glad to know you're safe."

"Only because I didn't sleep in the barracks last night."

"Where did you sleep?" Isobel asked. Finn's cheeks flushed, and Isobel raised her brow. "Oh! Well…how fortunate you have a lass here."

Finn shifted his attention back to Kerr. "Laird, I doona think Gillis can help you. I looked for him today when I couldnae find Father Lundie. No one has seen him since last night."

Kerr sighed, knowing more good men would be compromised before the day was out.

They were almost at the portcullis when two other riders approached them. Only one looked happy to see them, and he'd called out to a lass who was walking with the group of villagers. The other rider kept peering back through the gate as if seeking guidance.

Traitor number one.

His laird was right in front of him. That's who he should be looking to for guidance.

"Follow my lead, Finn. We need to move the villagers in first and then start taking out the conspirators. Oh, and one more thing…"

"Aye, Laird?"

"Isobel isn't your lady any longer. She's my wife."

"Laird MacAlister! What's happening?" a short, sturdy middle-aged warrior asked as Kerr entered underneath the raised portcullis with Malcolm by his side. Isobel rode behind him, guarded by Finn.

"He's the one who wouldnae let me stay in the barracks," Finn whispered as they dismounted.

Kerr nodded and turned to the man. "We're having a feast, Craigh. A celebration of my marriage to Isobel MacKinnon, now MacAlister." Kerr watched the warriors' faces who had gathered around him. To his relief, most of them broke out into cheers and excitedly welcomed Isobel—the same as the villagers.

She stayed on her horse—he'd insisted—and waved and smiled from the saddle.

One man's expression was pure panic, however, and when he darted toward the guard room, Kerr signaled Malcolm to follow him without drawing any attention.

"But, Laird," the first warrior said. "'Tis not enough time to plan a feast. I'm sure Mistress Cook would agree. Perhaps if we planned it for tomorrow, that would give us all time to prepare."

"Hmmm, perhaps you're right," Kerr said. "Let's look at the scheduled rotations. I want as many men as possible at the feast. We can thin out the guard a little for one day, aye?" He ushered Craigh in front of him and followed the same path Malcolm had taken. When they approached the closed door, he said loudly, "The feast will raise everyone's spirits!"

Upon entering the guard house, Craigh came to an abrupt halt, but Kerr pressed him forward, his dagger out, and kicked the door shut.

Malcolm crouched over the other warrior, tying a gag around his mouth. The traitor whirled and gasped, but Kerr gave him no time to yell or draw his weapon before he pressed his dagger to the man's throat. "How many others?"

"Laird! Surely, I doona know—"

Kerr pressed the blade deeper and a trickle of blood ran down his skin. "Gillis MacAlister is dead. A good man and a good warrior, sworn to keep the clan safe in my absence. Unless you can give me something useful, I will slit your throat as easily as you and the others slit his." Kerr was guessing as to Gillis's fate, but the look on Craigh's face confirmed it.

Fury and regret tore through Kerr. Gillis had two lads, nine and ten, and a five-year-old lass. His wife had died in childbirth. "I want names. Who's in charge?"

"I doona know all of them. Fearchar was the one with the money. I did as he told me to do."

"And who paid Fearchar?"

The traitor whimpered. "I've only seen him a few times, and I ne'er learned his name, I swear. But Fearchar said once that he was our true laird—the one our old laird wanted to rule after him."

"So, he's a MacAlister?"

"I doona know. His hair is as dark as yours, but his eyes are light. The last time I saw him, I barely recognized him—he'd been injured."

"In the collapse of the MacKinnon cathedral."

"'Tis what I heard. I doona know any more. Please…Fearchar is in charge."

Kerr loosed that deep, dark part of him, let the fury rise into his eyes. "Nay, Craigh," he snarled. "That's what you doona understand. I am laird here, and *I* am in charge."

Then he hit the man hard enough that he crumpled to the ground. "Restrain him."

Isobel sat astride her mare and welcomed everyone who came through the gate—led, of course, by her entertaining band of Merry Men. Dùghlas's friends crossed to the far end of the bailey, near the keep, and continued with their juggling, music, and other hilarious acts.

The castle folk came out, too, and shouted enquiries to the villagers—*What's going on? What's happening?*

She heard hers and Kerr's names bandied about several times, as well as that song—*that bloody song she hated*—being recited by different groups until the Merry Men picked it up and performed a similar version to the one they sang for her last night.

At least their version was amusing.

When the last person came through the gate—a young man pushing a cart with a frail elderly woman in it—Isobel knew that despite the existence of several traitors in the clan, and people willing to hurt newborn bairns, the majority of the MacAlisters were good people.

Now it was up to her and Kerr to dig out the rot.

"That's the last one, my lady," Finn said.

Father Lundie stepped out from a shed beside the gate, holding a long sword in his arms. "Do you want me to disable the portcullis now? 'Tis the same mechanism as Castle MacKinnon. I'll jam the sword into the chain just before the grill hits the ground. It took a day and a half for them to raise it last time."

"I remember. I was covered in mud from a trap I'd been building, and I couldnae get in. Kerr teased me about it afterward for days. Hmmm. Suddenly I'm feeling the urge to forgo our wedding feast and build another trap."

"Is that a *yes*, my lady?" the priest asked with a smile.

"Aye. For all we know, the army could be making their way around the castle as we speak."

Consternation crossed Father Lundie's face, and he hurried back into the shed.

Kerr and Malcolm had disappeared again, and when a large warrior appeared and strode toward them, a twinge of unease knotted her belly. His smile didn't reach his eyes.

"Finnian," she warned.

"Aye, my lady. Stay behind me." He urged his horse in front of hers as the warrior, much older and heavier than Finn, drew his sword and darted forward.

Isobel gasped, her heart in her throat, but before the two warriors clashed, the man dropped to his knees and fell forward. Finn's horse reared, and he backed up, blocking her. "Arrows!"

She peeked around him and saw the shaft and feathers penetrating from the warrior's back. "'Tis all right. That's from our side."

Finn's brow raised. "We have snipers in place? Of course we do. Who are they?"

"Kerr's half brothers, Andy and Aulay. And his uncle is here too." She stared at the body, feeling a little sick as a pool of blood formed under him. She knew what he'd intended for them, and for Father Lundie and Kerr as well, but she couldn't help thinking that only moments ago he'd been alive.

"We need to move the body." She slid off her horse before he could stop her. She didn't want one of the twins to shoot Finn by mistake.

"Isobel!" Kerr said firmly, striding toward them. "Stay there."

Behind him, she saw Dùghlas, and relief swept through her. "You're well?" she asked.

"Aye, my lady." He had blood on his plaid and a bruise on his chin.

Kerr saw the body with the arrow sticking out, and his gaze flew to Isobel.

"I'm uninjured," she said. "One of your brothers took him out before he reached us."

He nodded. "That would be Aulay. They've taken down several others as well. Did anyone else see it happen?"

She scanned the crowd in the bailey, but they'd moved away from the portcullis, following the Merry Men. "None of the villagers, but whomever we're fighting must have. They'll know by now about Andy and Aulay."

"Doona worry about them, their positions are safe. I designed the hides for the snipers myself."

Suddenly, a loud rattle and then a crash sounded behind them. She jumped and turned to see the portcullis lowered almost all the way to the ground. No one could get in or out. Unfortunately, Isobel's mare darted forward into the bailey, startled. She called her back, but the mare kept going.

"She's all right. She'll head to the stables." Kerr crouched in front of the dead man and raised his head. "I doona recognize him. Finn, drag the body to the guardhouse, and then tell Malcolm to use the key I gave him and lock the door."

Father Lundie came out of the shed beside the gate, cleaning his hands on a cloth. He had a smudge of oil on his nose. Isobel took the cloth from him and wiped it off.

"Good work, Father," Kerr said.

"Thank you. I pulled the chain, and it's well and truly stuck. No one will be able to get in or out."

"Well, then," Kerr said. "We've successfully completed the first part of Isobel's plan."

"My plan?" she asked, a smile tilting her lips.

"Aye. And it was a great one. The villagers are safe, the army is locked out, and several traitors are already dead or disarmed. Now what?" he asked her.

Isobel stared at Kerr, eyes wide in surprise. She hadn't thought this far ahead. She tried to put herself in the minds of the clan. *What do they need? Beyond safety, shelter, and food, what are they missing?*

She closed her eyes and waited for an answer. Finally it appeared, crystal clear in her head, and she nodded. "Now we tell them the truth…and ask them to choose."

"And what are they choosing?"

"Their future."

―――――――――

Kerr grasped Isobel's hand and climbed the stairs that led to the MacAlister keep. He didn't like being so exposed—or exposing Isobel—but he had to reach out to his people, to talk to them, as Isobel had said, about their future. And in order to do that, he had to be vulnerable, which meant trusting his brothers, his uncle, and the many men and women who were loyal to him, to keep them safe.

They stopped on the fifth step and faced their people. A cheer burst forth from the crowd. The bailey was half full, and the soldiers on the battlements looked inward, also cheering. He had a moment of annoyance, but he knew no one could get into the castle—or as importantly—get out.

He may not know the name of the man leading this attack, but he would wager his life he was still within the walls.

And I will find him.

"He's out there," Isobel said, her thoughts attuned to his.

The sun beat down on them, and most of the clan had rolled back their sleeves and loosened the ties of their shifts. No one wore a cloak or had their hood pulled up. The traitor would be easy to spot.

"And if he does escape, where will he go?" she continued. "He's a marked man with those injuries, and your castle—your beautiful, majestic, impenetrable castle—is built on a cliff. We'll either run him down, or he'll jump and die from the fall. From what I could see, the coastline is craggy and dangerous."

"Aye, 'tis even worse on the other side—several gorges run deep into the bluff. Defensively, the castle is perfectly positioned."

"So he needs someone to let his army in."

Kerr nodded.

"Well, then, his plan is ruined, isna it? He'll be desperate and furious by now. He'll show himself soon, he willna be able to stop himself."

Kerr lifted their clasped hands and kissed the back of hers. "I love you, Izzy, and I love the way you think. Promise me you willna go on any nighttime jaunts like you did at Clan MacKinnon. 'Tis easy to misstep here and fall to your death."

She grinned. "I promise. And I love you too."

The crowd whistled and called for their laird and lady to speak.

"You first," Kerr said.

Isobel lifted her chin slightly in that way he loved, and straightened her shoulders. Now she looked like a queen. She raised her voice. "I'll only speak as long as every one of you promises ne'er to sing that awful song again!" She said it with a grin, and the clan erupted into laughter. "And if you do, be warned that I am a master trickster, and you will find yourself on the receiving end of one of my pranks. In a few months' time, you'll be less inclined to call me the Beauty of the Highlands and instead will be moaning to your neighbor that I am, in fact, the Devil of the Highlands!"

More cackles as well as a few more rounds of the song. She shook her finger at them and then raised her hand for silence.

"But remember this…I am yours—always—devil or angel. And I am your laird's—always—devil or angel."

"Devil!" Kerr interjected to more hilarity.

"And I promise to do whate'er I can to help every single one of you—when I'm not plotting a new trick!" She tilted her head back, laughing, and Kerr couldn't help bestowing a kiss on her lips. His people cheered again.

"Our alliance, ever strong, is now even stronger!" she continued. "You have seen dark times, and your laird, my husband, fought for you when he was barely a man. He avenged the harm done to his clan."

She reached out for Una, who climbed up to the fourth step and took her hand, facing the crowd.

"He avenged his uncle—not much older than himself—also abused and beaten down."

She nodded to Dùghlas, who climbed the stairs to stand below Una.

"And he avenged his ma…"

She raised her eyes to the heavens.

When she looked back again, the crowd had quieted, sensing the change in her tone of voice and her demeanor. "And he still fights for you. Clan MacAlister… You heard the portcullis fall. What you didn't hear was the jamming of that gate. Danger approaches from outside these walls. But danger also lurks within—within the walls of your castle and the walls of your hearts. We will beat the physical dangers among us, but in order to truly win, the clan must beat the fear ingrained within them from so many years of tyranny. We have a chance to start again—all of us together. Please, let go of that fear, trust your laird and your neighbors, and let's take that chance together."

Frightened murmurs rippled through the crowd. Kerr raised his hand, and they quieted. "An army approaches—the army of a man who believes he has the right to lead this clan, the right to see to the well-being of the land, of you and your friends. For now, we are safe inside our walls, and our allies—the MacLeods, MacKinnons, MacLeans, MacKays, and MacKenzies—are on their way.

"We have jammed the gate because there are men inside these walls, women too, who would open it and let the invaders enter."

Shouts of dismay erupted from the crowd.

"'Tis true," Kerr said. "Some would do it because they feel trapped, others for gold. A few because they want things to return to how it was under my father's rule. We have captured many of them." He placed his hand over his heart. "But so many others have been turned against you out of fear—for themselves and for their loved ones.

"Please, come to us. Tell us what you know, what has been demanded of you. Only by shedding light on the atrocities that are happening can we come together as a clan and support one another."

He looked out and saw Billy and Breanag, holding Ollie, in the crowd. "And doona judge others too harshly. Some have had to choose between the lives of their children and doing a deed that helps the enemy. Or perhaps the exposure of a soul-destroying secret."

He gritted his teeth, thinking about all the ways his clan could have been compromised.

"It is something my father would have done, and it has no place in our society. Please come forward so we can catch the blackmailers and banish them from our midst. But mostly so we can help you. And if you've already done what they asked, come forward anyway. We need to know the extent of what has been done or more people will be hurt."

He patted his fingers over his heart. "Darkness canna thrive in the light. Hate canna continue in the face of love, and fear canna spread when we practice acceptance. Share your troubles, share your burdens, support one another."

The door to the keep opened above him, and he glanced up to see Malcolm and Finn appear with Fearchar restrained between them. They walked down the stairs. The clan gasped as they recognized the prisoner.

Kerr turned back to them. "Fearchar MacAlister has been charged with treason, with bribery, and with the murder of Father Gregory, among others. He's not the only perpetrator, but he is one of the worst, and he'll be sentenced for these heinous crimes. If he has hurt or threatened you, speak to me or Isobel about it. Or reacquaint yourself with Dùghlas and talk to him. Or take spiritual counsel with Father Lundie."

"Or with me," Una blurted out. "You can come to me."

"Aye," Isobel said. "Una is a wonderful listener."

"Lastly," Kerr said, "know that there is a man among us—a dangerous man—whom we need to find. But please, if you see him, doona try to apprehend him. Let the warriors of Clan MacAlister, most of them honorable men, do their duty. They want to help."

"What does he look like?" someone shouted from the crowd.

"On a day like today, with the sun warming our skin, he will be covered in his cloak. He led the attack last spring against Clan MacKinnon and was caught under the crush of rock that fell from the cathedral. He is badly scarred and disfigured down the left side of his face and body. He will be driven to cover up those scars."

"And he is in the castle with us? Hiding?" someone asked.

"I believe so."

A scuffle broke out at the back and someone yelled, "He's here! I see him."

Kerr could see two warriors dragging a hooded figure through the crowd toward the keep. He released Isobel's hand and hurried to the bottom of the stairs. The crowd backed up and cleared a path between them.

He was so focused on the man being restrained by the warriors, he ne'er noticed the flash of steel in one of the warriors hands until it was almost too late. He jumped backward like a cat, landing on the stairs, and the man barely missed slicing through his belly. The man kept coming, his reach long and his dagger sharp, but he collapsed suddenly, and when he fell forward, an arrow stuck out from the back of his neck.

Kerr drew his sword, berating himself for not having done so earlier. He stepped quickly to block the stairs so the black-hearts couldn't reach Isobel. But the other two had also fallen. The remaining guard had Malcolm's dagger protruding from his throat, and the cloaked man in the middle, the man who'd planned the attacks on Kerr, Gregor, and his foster brothers, had fallen to his knees. Dùghlas's sword, his hand still wrapped around the pommel, was pushed through his stomach.

His hood had fallen back, and Kerr saw his nemesis clearly for the first time. His dark hair was shoulder length on one side of his head and his eye blue. On the other side, his scalp was bare and scarred and the skin on his face looked like it had been scraped off and healed over. His eye on that side was closed, the eyebrow gone, his nose destroyed, and his mouth twisted.

If this had been any other man, Kerr would have had great sympathy for him. Blood had started to bubble from his mouth, and his eyes grew dull. He was not long for this world.

Grasping the sword hilt over Dùghlas's hand, he pulled it out. His uncle looked at Kerr, stunned, the color blanched from his skin and his eyes glassy. Kerr doubted he'd ever killed anyone before.

"Sit on the stairs, Uncle," Kerr said. "Catch your breath."

"Nay. 'Tis all right. I just need a moment."

He nodded and then looked over as the scarred man fell backward. Kerr cursed. He'd hoped to get some answers, but his enemy had breathed his last breath. His head slumped to the side, the scarred half of it exposed.

What was his name?

His clan had pushed forward for a better look, and Kerr cupped his hands over his mouth. "Back up! 'Tis a grisly scene and not suitable for bairns! Be assured that the man we sought has been killed by Dùghlas MacAlister."

His clan cheered—bloodthirsty lot—and then did as he asked. He stepped around the bodies, looking at the guards first, but he didn't recognize them.

Malcolm hovered behind him. He pointed to the second man, whom he'd killed with his dagger. "He was in Edinburgh. I saw him twice."

"And the other?" Kerr asked.

"I havenae seen him before."

They crouched over the body of the scarred man. "'Tis a terrible injury," Malcolm said.

"Aye. And a just punishment." Kerr turned the man's head so the uninjured side of his face looked upward, his blue eye still open. With the disfigurement on the other side of his face hidden, it was easier to focus on the man's features.

Suddenly Kerr's breath caught, and a band squeezed around his chest.

"'Tis Branon Campbell!" Malcolm exclaimed.

"Nay, it's not possible. I saw Branon Campbell at Castle MacKinnon less than a week ago. I spoke to him. These scars are months old."

"Well, maybe there's two of them, then. I ne'er forget a face," Malcolm said.

Kerr closed his eyes, his heart pounding in his chest. "Twins. They run in the family."

"Whose family?" Malcolm asked.

Dùghlas stepped closer. "Ours. Open your eyes, lad. I doona know why I didn't see it before, but this is how the child in me remembers Madadh MacAlister—cold, lifeless eyes and a dead face."

Kerr stared at the body. *His brother. Nay, brothers! Twins like he'd been, like Andy and Aulay.*

How might they have turned out if they'd had his mother's love, Gregor for guidance, and his foster brothers' support? Or would they always have turned out this way, wanting what was his?

As if the steward had read his mind, Fearchar shouted out, "'Tis Brian Campbell you're staring at! Your father's rightful heir."

Kerr straightened and glanced over at Fearchar, who stood at the bottom of the stairs still in restraints and held by Finn. He signaled the MacKinnon warrior to bring him closer.

"If he's the rightful heir, why is he named Campbell and not MacAlister? He's a bastard, aye? And I would have thought Branon Campbell was younger than me when we met."

"Our laird planned to marry their mother—a Campbell lass, cousin to Laird Campbell—as soon as he'd rid the clan of you. He wanted Brian to rule…with Branon by his side."

Kerr huffed out a humorless laugh and shook his head. "My father would have pitted the two of them against each other at the first opportunity. What's the real reason, Fearchar? To join the clans? To build an alliance between Clan MacAlister and Clan Campbell?"

Fearchar's eyes narrowed, and he didn't respond.

"Aye, that's it right there. My father wanted a bigger army to go after Gregor MacLeod." He spun toward Isobel, feeling gutted to know that his father had ruined two more lives, and for what? A second chance to defeat the man who had defended himself on his own land? The man who had taken in a lad Madadh MacAlister had never cared about and taught him how to be a warrior, a laird, and a good man?

He searched the stairs, looking for Isobel. He needed her warmth and light right now…but his wife wasn't there. "Where's Isobel?" he asked, striding forward. He spun in a circle, searching for her tall, willowy figure, her crown of white-gold hair.

"Where's Isobel?" he asked again, yelling this time.

Everyone was turning around looking for her, but she never came forward. She never slipped her hand into his. Blackness descended upon him.

"Isobel!" he roared.

Twenty-Five

"I HAVE THE LAD. IF YOU SHOUT OUT, HE'LL DIE. AND THEN you'll die. Do you want your husband to see your blood running onto the grass, Lady MacAlister?"

Isobel froze where she stood at the bottom of the stairs. Kerr and the others had all rushed down in front of her to see the man in the cloak they were dragging through the crowd. Una stood beside her, but her attention was rapt on what was happening—same as everyone else.

A sharp, pinching pain poked into her back on the left side. She closed her eyes and tried to quell her fear.

How could he have Andy or Aulay? Kerr had said he'd designed the hides so no one could see them. One on each side of the bailey.

The knife pushed in farther, and she gasped at the pain. "Please, stop," she whispered.

"Then back up slowly."

She took a hesitant step to the side of the stairs before doing as he asked. Where were they going? She didn't know the castle's layout; she'd never even stepped inside her new home.

Her gaze rose high to the other side of the bailey, wondering if one of the lads—Andy, she thought—would see her.

Please shoot. Please shoot!

But maybe Andy was the one he'd taken. Or maybe he hadn't taken either of them.

"Tell me the lad's name," she whispered.

"Why?"

"I want to know!"

Suddenly people were yelling, and the crowd surged away from her. She could hear Kerr cursing, and the sound of his great sword being drawn.

She tensed, struggling to go to him, and a hand clamped over her mouth. She tried to remember what Kerr had told her to hit—nose and stones—but her assailant wrapped his arm around her neck, increasing the pressure, and she grew weaker until blackness swooped down upon her.

The jostling woke Isobel—her face and chest slapping against a rough plaid, her arms hanging down toward the ground. She couldn't focus properly, couldn't formulate any thoughts. Maybe because her head was pounding and each new jostle shoved something hard into her stomach, making her want to vomit.

And then it came back to her.

Kerr!

Her first instinct was to move, to yell out for him, but something stronger urged her to stay still. She couldn't scream even if she wanted to, because a rough piece of plaid filled her mouth and was tied around her head.

In front of her was the back of a man's plaid, and below that, his feet slapped against a stone floor. She realized he carried her. The object jabbing into her stomach must be his shoulder.

He didn't have Andy or Aulay. He'd tricked her and was trying to escape!

Suddenly she heard Kerr roar out her name in the distance. "Isobel!"

The man cursed and picked up speed.

A fury exploded within her, and her muscles surged with strength. This man thought he could steal her from her husband? Take her right out from under his nose?

Then he shouldn't have left her arms and legs loose.

Grasping the edge of his plaid, she yanked it up, grabbed his stones with her other hand, and then twisted as hard as she could.

The man screamed and tumbled forward onto the stone floor, taking her with him. Her elbow hit the hard surface as she fell backward, and pain splintered up into her shoulder. She cried out, but the gag in her mouth muffled the sound.

Pushing herself up with a groan, she tried to squirm out from under him, but his body lay heavily over her legs, writhing in agony and trapping her in place.

He lifted his head, and surprise shot though her—Branon Campbell!

"I'm going to carve out your eyes for that," he grunted, reaching down for his dirk hanging from his waist. He'd just drawn it from the leather sheath when she pulled her leg free and smashed her heel into his nose, shoving him over backward.

Isobel turned and ran.

───

A man's scream sounded from inside the keep, and Kerr raced up the stairs and through the heavy wooden doors, Malcolm and Finn at his heels.

Where is she?

"Isobel!" he yelled again as he tore across the great hall toward the stairs that led to the upper levels and the open-air courtyard. The scream sounded like it had come from up there.

He heard another outburst—softer this time—and a thump. Somewhere above him his wife was fighting for her life. He ran as fast as he could, taking the stairs four at a time.

"Aulay!" he yelled.

His brother was on the third level in a hide-out. He might find her sooner.

"I'm here…" And then a moment later Aulay continued, "I

see her, Kerr! But I canna get to her, she's on the other side of the courtyard! Run, Izzy! He's behind you."

"Shoot him!" Kerr screamed. "Shoot him!"

And then he heard Isobel yell, "It's a dead end!" and his blood ran cold.

He knew exactly where she was, and he couldn't get to her in time.

———————

Isobel ran down the endless hallways—Branon Campbell not far behind her with murder in his eyes. She'd glanced back at the last corner, and his face and shirt had been covered in blood that dripped from his nose. His arms pumped ferociously as he ran to catch her, his knife gripped in his fist.

She tried to rip the gag from her mouth, but yanking it only tightened the knot, and she couldn't untie it without stopping—so she kept tugging on it, hoping to stretch the material and pull it loose.

When she heard Kerr calling for her and Aulay, and then Aulay calling back, she slowed, trying to figure out how to get to them.

The hallway she was in turned into an open-air courtyard, and she sped up. Surely there must be a way down from here. She turned onto the longer side of the courtyard, still running, and looked to the paving stones below, guessing she was about three stories up.

Then a flash on the other side caught her eye, and she screamed Aulay's name behind the gag.

"I see her, Kerr!" Aulay called out. "But I canna get to her, she's on the other side of the courtyard! Run, Izzy! He's behind you."

Terror filled her, and she put on a burst of speed.

"Shoot him!" she heard Kerr scream. "Shoot him!"

Desperately, she yanked on the gag and ripped it over her lip.

Elation filled her, but only for a second as the open hallway ended in a stone wall. "It's a dead end!"

"Nay, Isobel," Aulay yelled, running along with her on the other side. "There's a hidden door past the pillar. 'Tis the one I came through with Andy and Dùghlas."

"Izzy! I'm coming!" Kerr yelled, but he sounded too far away.

From behind her came a roaring laugh. "You're too late, Brother. I'm going to slice her open and throw her down for the dogs to eat like our da did to your mother."

She reached the end and passed the pillar, but she didn't see a door or a handle. "Aulay!" she cried. "How do I get in?"

"I doona know. Keep trying. I'll hold him off."

The twang of an arrow sounded from across the courtyard, and then Branon cursed behind her. She tried to ignore the sounds of conflict and squash down her worry—for herself and for Aulay—and kept pushing on the stone wall and pulling and turning every protrusion.

She heard another twang of an arrow, and then a dull thud and a groan. But the groan didn't come from behind her this time.

She dropped her forehead against the wall, knowing it was too late.

Aulay had been hit, and she was still trapped...until the stones shifted. Isobel gasped and shoved on the rock. It scraped open into darkness. Crouching down, she stepped through and then swung the heavy door into place behind her.

It clicked shut, and she turned into the darkness and fled.

———

Kerr came barreling around the corner and ran straight down the long side of the courtyard, but Isobel wasn't there—neither was Branon Campbell. He stopped and peered over the edge, his chest tight and throat aching, but she wasn't dead on the ground below either.

Where is she?

"Kerr," a voice groaned.

He looked up and saw Aulay on the opposite side, lying near the edge. A dagger was lodged in his thigh.

"I'm sorry," his brother said. "I missed. She went through the secret passageway. He followed her moments before you arrived."

The sound of feet pounding behind him filled the air, and he saw Malcolm and Finn tearing around the corner. "Malcolm! Go down the other side. Aulay needs help. Finn, come with me."

He ran to the end and saw the pillar. "Is this it?"

"Aye," Aulay said. "But 'tis not easy to open."

Kerr waved Finn over. "There's a passageway behind this pillar. Isobel went through first and Branon Campbell followed her. Twist, pull, and push every stone and knob until you get it open. Then go after her!"

"Aye, laird."

"Aulay," Kerr called out, racing to the wall at the end. "Where does the tunnel come out?"

"Directly below us. It's a staircase that switches back and forth."

Kerr pushed on the wall—another hidden door, but this one was well used. He stepped through to the battlements outside. "I'm going this way."

The midafternoon sun shone brightly after the shadows of the castle. Squinting, he grabbed a rope coiled in the corner and tossed it over the crenellated edge. It unfolded in a graceful fall. He couldn't see either Isobel or Branon and tried to quell the sick roiling of his stomach. Just because he couldn't see them didn't mean Branon had caught her.

He gripped the rope, stepped up onto a merlon, and lowered himself over the edge. He'd just wrapped his feet around the rope and begun to slide downward when he heard a grating sound and a startled yelp. Looking down, he saw Isobel tumble out of an opening in the stone wall below. She looked back inside and then grabbed her skirts in her hands and ran.

"Isobel!" he called, but she must not have heard him and kept running. Moments later, Branon appeared, sword in hand, and took after her.

"God's blood!" Kerr yelled. He narrowed his stance on the rope and slid down as fast as he could, jumping off before he even hit the bottom.

He was as close to Branon as Branon was to her…which meant he wasn't close enough. "Branon!" he yelled, hoping the man would turn around and face him.

Both Branon and Isobel glanced over their shoulders, and he saw the stark terror on Isobel's face—and the mad glee in Branon's face. He didn't care if he died as long as he killed Isobel first, and she knew it.

Her frightened sobs floated on the wind back to him, and he tried to pick up the pace. How could he slow Branon down?

"Brother!" he yelled. "Doona do this. Take me instead."

"Nay, Kerr!" Isobel screamed. "He'll kill you and then still kill me!"

He had only one dagger left on him. If he threw it, and he missed, he could hit Izzy—kill her himself.

But in the distance, another danger loomed.

The gorge.

Panic ate away at him. The fall would kill her for sure.

He was running out of time! He drew his great sword and tossed it ahead of him like a spear. It landed just short of Branon, and Kerr let out a heart-rending roar.

Branon laughed delightedly.

But Kerr was lighter now, and the lift allowed him to run faster.

"I'm almost there, Izzy. You have to stop! Do you remember what I said about nighttime jaunts?"

She didn't answer, and when he was about to repeat himself, she yelled back, "And if I were to keep going?"

"You'd ne'er make it. Doona do this. Please! There has to be another way. Promise me you'll do what I say, when I say it."

She didn't answer, and his stomach clenched as the edge of the gorge drew closer.

"Izzy!"

———————

Isobel's heart was breaking. If she did as he asked and stopped before she hit the gorge, Branon would kill her, and then Kerr would kill Branon, possibly killing himself. If she jumped, she would most likely die, and then Kerr would kill Branon, possibly killing himself.

She should jump. Maybe she could make it.

But…Kerr had trusted her today when she'd wanted to gather up the villagers and enter the castle with their people rather than sneak in. That had been her plan, and he'd trusted her that it was a good one.

He trusted *her*.

If this was their last moment alive together, she wanted him to know that she trusted him too.

"I promise!" she shouted.

He yelled back, "Get down!"

She didn't slow, just let herself drop. She landed hard, scraping and dragging on the earth, limbs twisting and her sore elbow jamming. And then she rolled.

Too fast. She was going too fast. She tried to dig her fingers in, to slow herself down.

At the same time, she expected to feel Branon's sword slice through her body at any moment.

But instead, he landed on top of her, skidding over and in front of her. They slid to the edge together, and when they reached it, Branon tipped over, almost slowly, his eyes closed, and tumbled, end over end, into the gorge.

Sticking out of his back was Kerr's dagger.

She teetered, half on the bluff, half off, afraid to move. Afraid to breathe.

And then Kerr's arms were dragging her back. Tucking her into his shaking body and crawling to safety.

When they were a good ten paces back from the edge, he finally stopped and squeezed her so tightly she could barely breathe.

It was worth it. Who needed air when she could wallow in the scent of the man she loved? Both of them...alive.

Finally, her husband stopped shaking, and he let out a long, slow breath. "Can I take you back to my castle now and lock you in the highest tower?"

She huffed out a laugh. "Is there a bed in there? And will you be staying with me?"

"I think that can be arranged."

"Good, but doona get your hopes up. I may not be able to move for several weeks."

He pulled away from her slightly so he could look down at her. "Now you look more like my Izzy. Bruised, scraped, and dirty— the true Beauty of the Highlands."

She patted her head. "Is my lovely hair ruined? And Una's beautiful plaid?"

"Completely. I should throw it into the gorge."

"Better it than me."

He closed his eyes and squeezed her again. "Thank you for trusting me."

She turned her face into his skin and kissed the pulse still pounding at the base of his throat. "Thank *you* for trusting *me*."

In retrospect, he was doing better than she would have expected. If she had seen him barreling toward the edge of a cliff and out of control, it would have taken her weeks to recover.

"I think we should start my self-defense lessons again, and this time we can start with you teaching me how to take a fall."

He groaned. "Good idea. And maybe some sword fighting and dagger lessons as well."

"Sword fighting and daggers?" she exclaimed, leaning away from him so she could see his face. "I thought you didn't want to teach me how to use weapons?"

"That was before someone tried to take you away from me—again."

"You would have been proud of me. I lifted the back of his kilt, grabbed his stones, and twisted. He screeched like a newborn bairn."

He didn't say anything at first. Then his shoulders started to shake, and he snorted. Air wheezed up from his lungs, and before long he fell over onto his back, laughing uncontrollably.

And she was right there with him.

When they finally stopped, she stretched out on top of his body, her ear over his heart. "I love you, Laird MacAlister."

He kissed the top of her head. "I love you too, Lady MacAlister."

"How much?" she asked.

"More than life itself. If you had gone over that edge, I would have been right behind you."

A sob pushed up from her throat, catching her by surprise, and she turned her face into his chest. "Do you think you can carry me home now, husband?"

He sat up and pulled her into his arms. "Aye, Izzy. I'll always carry you home."

Epilogue

KERR STARED INTO GAVIN'S FURIOUS EYES AND KNEW THAT he wouldn't come out of this unscathed. His foster brother, now his brother-in-law, looked ready to kill him rather than welcome him into the family.

Gregor, Darach, Lachlan, and Callum gathered around them in the library, ready to step in if things got out of hand, but Kerr could see that they were enjoying themselves—and that they agreed with Gavin. They wouldn't intervene until one or both of them was bloody.

Which didn't suit him, as he was getting married—again—in an hour.

No doubt they'd have money on the encounter. The bastards.

Gavin leaned forward until they were almost nose-to-nose and jabbed his finger into Kerr's chest. "Of all the irresponsible, reckless, addlepated things to do… Isobel could have been killed!"

Kerr closed his eyes, breathing deeply to keep himself calm. Then he heard Lachlan whisper, "The 'chest poke.' I should have doubled my wager."

"Even I couldnae have predicted that," Callum whispered back.

"She wasn't killed. I protected her," Kerr said, opening his eyes and restraining himself from breaking that damn finger.

Barely.

"You wouldnae have had to protect her if you hadn't run off with her!"

"I tried to get her to go back, Gavin, I swear. She wouldnae leave. You know Isobel."

His foster brothers grunted in agreement.

"Which is why you shouldnae have left with her in the first place!"

They grunted in agreement again.

"Even I could have told you that, Son," Gregor added.

Kerr ignored him—and the others too. Squaring his shoulders, he met Gavin's gaze. "Perhaps so, but I doona regret it. We're together now because of it." Then he poked his finger back into Gavin's chest. "But you shouldnae have taken Deirdre, my cousin, off of MacKinnon land last spring. At least I ne'er intended to hand her over to someone else and tear her away from her son!"

"Oooooh, a low blow," Darach whispered, and the others nodded.

Gavin's face contorted with guilt. "I brought her back, which you ne'er did. And I gave you one free punch for it."

"It wasn't free." He raised his fingers to the bridge of his nose. "You damn well broke it in retaliation!"

"And I'll do it again!"

A door slammed shut behind them, making them all jump. The sound of six swords being drawn filled the room.

Too late.

Isobel stood there, her shoulders back and her head held high in a regal fashion. She looked like an avenging queen, and he smirked.

"You're in trouble now," he whispered, and then raised his voice so Isobel could hear. "Dearling, they ambushed me! All five of them. And Gavin is threatening me!"

Behind him, Callum snorted and Gregor muttered something beneath his breath.

"Izzy," Gavin said, stepping toward her. "You doona have to marry this donkey."

"She's already married!" Kerr protested.

Gavin raised his fist to him. "And I can make her a widow easily enough."

"Oh, for the love of God," Isobel said and then marched toward them. "Everyone put your swords away."

The sound of six swords being resheathed filled the room.

She glared at Gregor, who shrank back a little, and then eyed his other foster bothers one by one. Kerr barely stopped himself from hooting. They were afraid of his wife! He could lord it over them all now and threaten them with Isobel every time they stepped out of line.

"What were you thinking?" she asked them.

"They were thinking they could make a little gold," Kerr said from behind her, grinning widely. "They wagered on me and Gavin fighting."

She turned to him, her hands on her hips. "And what were you thinking?"

His smile dropped. He tried to look wide-eyed and innocent. "Well, I wasn't thinking so much as praying that Gavin wouldnae hit me in the face and break my nose—again—when you and I are getting married in under an hour. So, really, I was thinking of you."

He swept his eyes over her, her face glowing and her eyes sparkling, her long hair curling down her back. Her dress was made of the finest MacAlister wool and colored in beautiful reds and greens with a stripe of blue. "You look lovely, by the way." He lifted her hand and kissed her fingers. "My angel."

Her eyes softened as she smiled at him. Then she turned back to the others and held out her palm. "Give me the money."

Lachlan didn't protest, he just opened his sporran and gave her everything they'd wagered.

She wrapped her fist around it, and when she realized she had no pockets in her wedding finery, she stuffed it into Kerr's sporran. "My husband will hold this for me. Consider it a wedding gift."

Gavin sighed, but Kerr could tell his anger had faded. "Izzy, are you sure?" he asked. "The choice is yours—always. But is this who you truly want?"

"Aye, Kerr is who I truly want. I wouldnae have it any other way." She reached out and squeezed his hand.

He swore he saw his brothers and Gregor melt at the sentiment like a gaggle of young lasses.

"He's not on your bad side for what he did?" Gavin asked.

"Nay, Brother. And according to Kerr, I doona have a bad side. Or a good side. Just me. Which is one of the reasons I love him."

"But…he took you across the loch, knowing you couldnae swim. He stole you."

She leaned into Kerr, a smile on her lips. "Aye, my Highland thief. 'Twas exactly as I'd planned."

His head whipped toward her. "You planned?" he asked.

She shrugged, smiled mysteriously, and then tugged him toward the door. "Come on. We have a wedding to attend. And no talking about the Campbells tonight. Any of you. You can discuss your plans against them another time."

"Speaking of the Campbells," Gregor said, and his foster brothers snorted. When Isobel shot him an exasperated look, he said, "Well, you said tonight. I was only going to mention that I know Campbell's wife, Tara. She is…was…my Kellie's cousin. It broke our hearts when we heard she was to be married off to him. She was only seventeen and Campbell was already an old man." He sighed. "She had a lot of spirit. I haven't seen her since Kellie's funeral. I hope he didn't break her. I should have kept track of her over the years. I should have followed up."

"'Twould make things easier if that crafty old badger up and died on his own," Darach said.

"Aye, 'twill not be an easy assault," Lachlan added.

"Maybe we could turn Tara against him," Callum said.

Gregor shook his head. "Nay. I willna put her in such a position. She has her children to think about."

"Gregor," Isobel protested. "That's verra sad, but…you promised. I doona want any talk about war during my wedding."

He kissed her cheek and then stepped with her through the door. "Aye, dearling. Let's go get you married to my son—again—and make me a happy father."

He stopped and looked back over his shoulder at Kerr and his brothers. Then nodded with satisfaction. "If Kellie were alive, she would be so proud. Such good men—all of you—and married to even better women."

Keep reading for an excerpt from

HIGHLAND
PROMISE

available now from Sourcebooks Casablanca

Prologue

MacLeod Castle—The Isle of Skye, Scotland
1432

GREGOR MACLEOD STARED DOWN THE LONG WOODEN TABLE at the five Highland lairds seated in front of him and resisted the urge to smash his fists through the wood. Blackhearts, every one of them.

Drawing a vicious-looking dirk from within his linen sleeve, he leaned back in his chair. His legs stretched out in front of him and his plaid fell open to reveal brawny thighs. Firelight from the hearth danced along the dagger's blade as he slowly played with it.

The lairds watched…waited, revealing little in their expressions. They expected to die.

The thought pleased Gregor and he smiled. "'Tis my right, and the right of every member of this clan, to cleave your heads from your necks, to feed your bodies to my hounds. Though in truth, I doona think they'd have you—treachery and cowardice sours the meat." He flipped the blade in the air, caught it, and dug the tip into the wooden table. "So I'll take your sons instead."

Stunned and outraged faces stared back at him. His smile widened. He would foster a boy from each laird and make their sons his sons—bond them to him and to each other so they became broth-ers, united their clans, and kept the people safe.

It had been his dear Kellie's wish to her dying day.

"You mule-loving devil. I'll not give you my son!"

Gregor glanced to his left, at the red-faced man who had spoken: Laird MacLean, father of Callum MacLean. A terri-ble laird, he had brought disorder and hardship to his clan. Still, Gregor suspected the man loved his son. For that, and only that, he commended him.

The lad, seven years old, was the youngest of the five Gregor wanted and already showed signs of reason and intelligence—the opposite of his undisciplined father. Callum would make a good laird if his skills could be paired with honor and loyalty, traits Gregor intended to instill in all the lads.

"I'm afraid, Laird MacLean, no is not an option. This isna a debate. You have lost and I am reaping the spoils—your sons. One from each clan who came together and dared attack me. That is the cost of your treachery."

MacLean swore loudly and grumbled under his breath but didn't offer any further resistance.

Gregor waited for the next laird to speak.

"And if we doona comply?"

The question, soft and measured, came from Gregor's right. He stared at the man two seats down from him: Laird MacKenzie, father of Darach MacKenzie. A tall man, strong of mind and body, the laird was resolute and disciplined—traits Gregor had seen in Darach, the second-youngest of the lads, at eight years old.

"If you doona comply, Laird MacKenzie, you will be hanged, and I will still foster your boy."

"He'd revenge me."

"He could try."

The laird nodded, still calm, but his cheek twitched before he raised a hand to cover it.

At the end of the table, Laird MacKay roused himself. His voice was low, the words halting. He took a labored breath. "I willna give you Donald, but you can have my Lachlan. Donald will be laird by Christmas. He is needed to unite my clan. Lachlan is close to his brother, looks up to him. 'Twill be a good alliance."

Gregor met the laird's eyes. They were tired, troubled. The eyes of a dying man.

Having met both lads, Gregor suspected Donald would make a good laird, but Lachlan would be great. At nine years old, he already recognized his mother's manipulations and duplicity, and refused to play her games.

"Aye," Gregor said. "I'd be happy to take Lachlan and support Donald as laird."

The MacKay laird closed his eyes and nodded. When he opened them, they were wet. Gregor found himself pleased to ease the man's burden, despite being his enemy.

He switched his gaze to Laird MacKinnon, who sat in the first seat on his right. The big, tough, blond man had crossed his arms over his chest and glowered straight ahead. Another man who loved his son.

"You ask too much," he said when he noticed Gregor watching him. "I canna do it."

Gregor waited.

"Would I e'er see him again?" the laird asked, his voice breaking.

"Aye. You may have the lad back at harvest, but if he's not returned, I'll consider it a grievous breach and act accordingly."

MacKinnon grunted and still scowled, but his arms relaxed. Gregor knew him to be a man with a big heart, loyal and fair. All good qualities in a laird, but he lacked the necessary discernment to use them wisely. His son, Gavin, ten years old, mirrored his father in many ways. He could be taught to look beyond the obvious and see people's hearts, judge with his head as well as his emotions.

"I agree," MacKinnon said and leaned toward Gregor. "But if I e'er discover you are abusing my lad, MacLeod, I swear on my life, I will kill you."

Gregor nodded. "As I would you if you harmed my own." He held out his hand to the laird. "I will teach your son well, MacKinnon." The big man hesitated before taking Gregor's hand. MacKinnon would consider it an oath between them until his dying day. Gregor was well pleased.

Last, he turned to Laird MacAlister, seated two down on the left, father of Kerr MacAlister, who was the oldest boy and also ten. He suspected Kerr might be his most difficult charge, but the most rewarding if all went well. He'd never met the lad, but Gregor had heard he stood up to his father, who was a mean, controlling bastard.

MacAlister had instigated the attack against Gregor's clan, persuading or threatening the other lairds to go along with it. Gregor had known in advance they were coming and had trapped his enemies. 'Twas a gamble that had paid off.

"Naught to say, MacAlister?" he asked the last laird.

"You've no sons of your own. Will you be choosing one of the lads to succeed you when you die?"

Gregor was not surprised by the question. "You've already tried to kill me and failed. Doona think you'd be any more successful a second time."

MacAlister shrugged, his greasy, dark hair sliding forward to hide his eyes. "You misunderstand me—"

"I understand you, all right." Gregor pulled his dirk from the table and flung it past MacAlister's ear. A lock of hair drifted down as the knife embedded in a wooden shield mounted on the opposite wall. "As always, you want my land. MacLeod land. You canna have it. Maybe one day your boy will have it, maybe not. I give no promises to anyone here."

He looked around the table at each laird, his gaze hard, unblinking. Finally, he came back to MacAlister. "You will give me your son, or you will give me your life. Choose."

MacAlister's nostrils flared before he nodded.

Gregor placed his hand palm down on the middle of the table, and the lairds followed suit one by one until five palms lay over his. MacAlister was last.

The ache in Gregor's heart eased just a wee bit. His Kellie would have been proud.

One

DARACH MACKENZIE WANTED TO KILL THE FRASERS. SLOWLY.

Lying on the forest floor, he peered through the leaves as his enemy rode single file along the trail at the bottom of the ravine. Midway down the line, a woman, tied belly down over a sway-backed horse, appeared to be unconscious. Rope secured her wrists, and a gag filled her mouth. The tips of her long, brown hair dragged on the muddy ground.

In front of her, Laird Fraser rode a white stallion that tossed its head and rubbed against the trees in an attempt to unseat him. The laird flailed his whip, cutting the stallion's flanks in retaliation.

To the front and behind them rode ten more men, heavily armed.

The King had ordered the MacKenzies and Frasers to cease hostilities two years before, and much trouble would come of helping the lass, let alone killing the laird. Still, the idea of doing nothing made Darach's bile rise.

"You canna rescue her without being seen."

The whispered words caused Darach's jaw to set in a stubborn line. He refused to look at his foster brother Lachlan, who'd spoken. "Maybe 'tis not the lass I want to rescue. Did you not see the fine mount under the Fraser filth?" Yet his gaze never left the swing of the lass's hair, her wee hands tied together.

"Fraser would no more appreciate you taking his horse than his woman."

"Bah! She's not his woman—not by choice, I'll wager."

They'd been reaving—a time-honored tradition the King had not mentioned in his command for peace—and could easily escape into the forest unseen with their goods. They'd perfected the procedure to a fine art, sneaking on and off Fraser land for years with bags of wheat, barrels of mead, sheep, and horses.

Never before had they stolen a woman.

He glanced at Lachlan, seeing the same anger and disgust he felt reflected in his foster brother's eyes. "You take the stallion. The laird willna recognize you. I'll get the lass."

Lachlan nodded and moved into position while Darach signaled his men with the distinctive trill of the dipper—three short bursts, high and loud pitched. The MacKenzies spread out through the heavy growth, a nearby creek muffling any sound.

The odds for a successful attack were in their favor. Ten Fraser warriors against Darach, the laird of Clan MacKenzie; his foster brother Lachlan, the laird of Clan MacKay; and three of Darach's men: Oslow, Brodie, and Gare. Only two to one, and they'd have the element of surprise.

As his enemy entered the trap, Darach mounted his huge, dark-gray stallion named Loki, drew his sword, and let out a second, sharp trill. The men burst through the trees, their horses' hooves pounding.

Two Frasers rode near the lass. Big, dirty men. Men who might have touched her. He plunged his sword into the arm of one, almost taking it off. The man fell to the ground with a howl. The second was a better fighter but not good enough, and Darach sliced open the man's side. Blood and guts spilled out. He keeled over, clutching his body.

Farther ahead, Lachlan struggled to control the wild-eyed stallion. The Fraser laird lay on the ground in front of Darach, and Darach resisted the urge to stomp the devil. He would leave the laird alive, even though he burned to run his sword through the man's black heart. Fraser's sister's too, if she were but alive.

In front of Darach, the mare carrying the lass thrashed around, looking for a means of escape. The ropes that secured the girl loosened, and she began sliding down the beast's side.

Just as her fingers touched the ground, he leaned over and pulled her to safety. Dark, silky hair tumbled over his linen lèine. When the mare jostled them, he slapped it on the rump. The animal sprang forward, missing Fraser by inches.

Damnation.

Placing her limp body across his thighs, Darach used his knees to guide Loki out of the waning melee.

Not one Fraser was left standing.

———

They rode hard to put as much distance as possible between them and the Frasers, and along game trails and creek beds to conceal their tracks as best they could. When Darach felt they were safe, he slowed Loki and shifted the unconscious woman so she sat across his lap. Her head tipped back into the crook of his arm, and he stilled when he saw her sleeping face, bruised but still lovely—like a wee dove.

Dark lashes fanned out against fair cheeks, and a dusting of freckles crossed her nose.

She looked soft, pure.

God knows that meant nothing. He knew better than most a bonny face could hide a black heart.

Slicing through the dirty gag, he hurled it to the ground. Welts had formed at the corners of her mouth, and her lips, red and plump, had cracked. After cutting her hands free, he sheathed his dagger and massaged her wrists. Her cheek was chafed from rubbing against the side of the mare, and a large bruise marred her temple.

His gut tightened with the same fury he'd felt earlier.

Lachlan rode up beside him, the skittish stallion tethered behind his mount. "If you continue to stare at her, I'll wager she'll ne'er wake. Women are contrary creatures, doona you know?"

Darach drew to a stop. "She sleeps too deeply, Brother. 'Tis unnatural. Do you think she'll be all right?" Oslow, Brodie, and Gare gathered 'round. It was the first time they'd seen the lass.

"Is she dead, do you think?" Gare asked, voice scarcely above a whisper. He was a tall, young warrior of seventeen, with the scrawny arms and legs of a lad still building up his muscle.

Oslow, Darach's older, gnarly lieutenant, cuffed Gare on the back of the head. "She's breathing, isna she? Look at the rise and fall of her chest, lad."

"I'll do no such thing. 'Tis not proper. She's a lady, I'll wager. Look at her fine clothes."

Lachlan snorted in amusement and picked up her hand, turning it over to run his fingers across her smooth palm. "I reckon you might be right, Gare. The lass hasn't seen hard labor. 'Tis smooth as a bairn's bottom."

Darach's chest tightened at the sight of her wee hand in Lachlan's. He fought the urge to snatch it back.

"She has stirred some, cried out in her sleep. I pray to God the damage isna permanent." Physically, at least. Emotionally, she could be scarred for life. His arm tightened around her, and she moaned.

"Pass me some water." Someone placed a leather flagon in his hand, and Darach wedged the opening between her lips. When he tilted the container, the water seeped down her cheek. He waited a moment and tried again. This time she swallowed, showing straight, white teeth. Her hand came up and closed over his, helping to steady the flask.

A peculiar feeling fluttered in Darach's chest.

When she made a choking sound, he pulled the flask away. Her body convulsed as she coughed, and he sat her up to thump her on the back. Upon settling, he laid her back down in the crook of his arm.

"Christ, we doona want to drown her, Darach—or knock the lungs right out of her. Maybe you should give her to one of us to hold for a while?" Lachlan's laughing eyes told Darach his foster brother deliberately provoked him. Another time-honored tradition.

Gare jumped in. "Oh, aye. I'll hold the lass."

"You?" Brodie asked. "You canna even hold your own sword. Do you think those skinny arms will keep her safe? I'll hold the lass." Brodie was a few years older than Gare and had already filled out into a fine-looking man. He was a rogue with the lasses, and they all loved him for it. No way in hell would he be holding her.

"Cease. Both of you," said Oslow. "If anyone other than our laird holds the lass, it will be Laird MacKay. If she be a lady, she'll not want to be held by the likes of you."

Darach glowered at Lachlan, who grinned.

Then she stirred, drawing everyone's attention. They waited as her eyelids quivered before opening. A collective gasp went up from the men, Darach included.

He couldn't help it, for the lass staring up at him had the eyes of an angel.

They dominated her sweet face—big, round, innocent. And the color—Darach couldn't get over the color. A piercing, light blue surrounded by a rim of dark blue.

A shiver of desire, followed by unease, coursed through him. He tamped down the unwelcome feeling.

"Sweet Mary," Gare whispered. "She's a faery, aye?"

All except Lachlan looked at Darach for confirmation. He cleared his throat before speaking, trying to break the spell she'd cast over him. Not a faery, but maybe a witch.

"Nay, lad," he replied, voice rough. "She's naught but a bonny maid."

"A verra bonny maid," Lachlan agreed.

Her throat moved again, and Darach lifted the flask. Opening her mouth, she drank slowly, hand atop his, eyes never leaving his face. He couldn't look away.

When she'd had enough, she pressed his hand. He removed it, and she stared up at him, blinking slowly and licking her lips. Her pink tongue tempted him, and he quelled the urge to capture it in his mouth.

Then she raised her hand and traced her fingers over his lips and along his nose, caressed his forehead to the scar that sliced through his brow, gently scraped her nails through the whiskers on his jaw.

A more sensual act he'd never experienced, and shivers raced over his skin.

Finally, she spoke. "*Par l'amour de Dieu, etes-vous un ange?*"

Acknowledgments

Well, we're here…finally. Officially, Kerr is the last foster brother to find love and get his Happily Ever After, the conspiracy has been revealed, and peace has been restored to the Highlands. The series is over. Unofficially…we'll see!

(I'm looking at you, Gregor MacLeod.)

I'd like to thank my editor, Christa Désir, for her insight into this particular story and her help in honing the various characters and story lines and bringing the manuscript together so perfectly. Much appreciation, Christa, for helping to make *Highland Thief* the best book possible. And to the design team, led by Dawn Adams, who have once again hit this cover out of the park. Big kisses to you all—I love it!

I also want to thank my previous editor, Cat Clyne, who discovered The Sons Of Gregor MacLeod in the Wattpad "slush pile" five years ago and offered me a contract for all five books. Thank you, Cat, for believing in me and in these stories, and for putting this series into the hands of readers. I'm sure my fans thank you, too!

As usual, much love and appreciation go out to my writing tribe, most importantly my fellow Mermaids—in particular Carol, Elizabeth, Jaycee, Kari, Layla, and Melonie. Thank you, ladies, for the chats, shared knowledge, and support. You da best!

And of course, to my family. It's been a tough one. You all are rock stars, and I'm so glad that you're the ones I get to isolate with—my happy little bubble.

Lastly, I want to thank my readers who so joyously embraced Gregor MacLeod, his foster sons, and the amazing women who brought these Highland lairds to their knees. Your enthusiasm and love for their stories fill my heart. I'd hug you all if I could.

It's been a blast.

About the Author

Alyson McLayne is an award-winning writer of contemporary, historical, and paranormal romance. After earning her degree in theater at the University of Alberta, she moved to the west coast of Canada and worked in film for several years before buckling down and finishing her first published book.

She lives in Vancouver with her prop master husband, twin nine-year-olds, and a sweet but troublesome chocolate lab named Jasper. Soon to join the family are a couple of crazy kittens named Shadow and Topaz.

Alyson loves coffee, listening to podcasts, and watching Harry Potter with her kids. In case of emergencies, she keeps a stash of dark chocolate in the cupboard, which she savors late at night when she's writing…and everyone else is asleep.

———

Want more of Kerr and Isobel? Sign up for Alyson's newsletter at alysonmclayne.com to read a bonus epilogue that takes place on Kerr's and Isobel's wedding night!

You can also check out Alyson's Facebook page at facebook.com/alysonmclayne for all her latest news or follow her on BookBub at bookbub.com/profile/alyson-mclayne to be notified whenever she has a new book coming out.

Thanks for reading!